ALSO BY KARIN HARLOW

Enemy Lover

Available from Pocket Star Books

KARIN HARLOW
ENEMY MINE

POCKET STAR BOOKS

New York London Toronto Sydney New Delhi

Pocket Star Books
A Division of Simon & Schuster, Inc.
1230 Avenue of the Americas
New York, NY 10020

This book is a work of fiction. Names, characters, places, and incidents either are products of the author's imagination or are used fictitiously. Any resemblance to actual events or locales or persons, living or dead, is entirely coincidental.

First Pocket Star Books paperback edition September 2011

POCKET STAR BOOKS and colophon are registered trademarks of Simon & Schuster, Inc.

For information about special discounts for bulk purchases, please contact Simon & Schuster Special Sales at 1-866-506-1949 or business@simonandschuster.com.

The Simon & Schuster Speakers Bureau can bring authors to your live event. For more information or to book an event contact the Simon & Schuster Speakers Bureau at 1-866-248-3049 or visit our website at www.simonspeakers.com.

Cover illustration by Gene Mollica

Manufactured in the United States of America

10 9 8 7 6 5 4 3 2 1

ISBN 978-1-4391-7787-7
ISBN 978-1-4391-7797-6 (ebook)

To Dad, I miss you

ENEMY MINE

HER DECEPTION KEPT HER ALIVE.
AND SHE LIVED TO KILL.

New Year's Eve
Whitechapel, London

Selena strode down the dark, slippery alleyway. Her warm breath curled in robust swirls around her head as she exhaled. Her four-inch heels clicked on the cobblestones smoothed by thousands of feet over hundreds of years, defiantly echoing the distant beat of a nearby nightclub's entertainment. Her quick, confident stride dared any man, woman, or beast to challenge her. It was fitting, she supposed, that her quarry had picked such an infamous area to ring in the New Year.

It would be his last celebration.

Abruptly, she stopped to pinpoint his exact location.

Her arms hung loosely at her sides and her fingertips tapped an anxious staccato on her smooth leather pants. A brisk wind shoved her black leather duster away from her before it settled loosely back around her body, cocooning her against the elements and whatever else might attempt to provoke her this night.

On a nice day, London was damp and cold; now, in the dead of winter, it was frigid. But she'd dressed for the occasion. She'd forsaken her normal Miami-heat wear for head-to-toe leather.

She raised her chin and stared up at the gray moon.

Clouds traced across it as the damp air began to mist. She detested London weather.

The muffled night sounds of straggling merrymakers drifted along the alley to her ears. She lifted her nose, closed her eyes, and inhaled. To a human, the air reeked of rotted food, urine, and misery. To her, half-daemon, the air could not have smelled sweeter.

Her quarry was near. His sulfurous scent overrode every other scent for miles.

The three platinum-set stones in her necklace warmed. She smiled and absently stroked them. Nanorians. Her talismans. More precious than any gem, the daemon hearts held power beyond what any mortal could wield.

Only a few beings knew how to harvest them, and fewer still possessed the power and cunning to extract one from its protected spot: a Hellkeeper's chest.

She, however, would have no problem separating the rare stone from her quarry.

Her body twitched with anticipation as raucous laughter mixed with the driving beat of the nightclub. She leapt onto the edge of an overflowing Dumpster, using the stench to mask her own scent. Her human mother's people called her *cazadora,* huntress. Because she divested daemon-possessed humans of their ill-gotten gains and dispersed them to the less fortunate, they believed she was a modern-day Robin Hood. The image veiled what she really was, an outlaw *asesina,* an assassin, with only one prey: Hellkeepers. Seven of the most powerful daemons in Hell, and the only ones who possessed the treasured nanorians.

A group of four drunken revelers stumbled into the

slick alley. She knew immediately all four were human. However, the largest male, the one she had been tracking for almost a week, the one who stank like Hell, was the one she focused on. And God help the poor human who played unwitting host to the Hellkeeper lurking inside him.

After Selena harvested the nanorian, the human might survive. If he didn't, she'd feel a fleeting sense of regret, but would look beyond to the bigger picture. One less Hellkeeper on this earth not only served a personal vendetta, but it was in the best interest of mortals as a race.

The scent of alcohol wafted around her head. Good. She liked the unsuspecting to be drunk. That made it much easier to fill their heads with terror to distract them.

Ah, yes, the human mind, it was such a lovely thing to waste.

Turning her attention to the three who were clueless about the treacherous company they kept, Selena noiselessly pulled a long sword from the sheath strapped to her back. With both hands grasping the worn leather grip, she bent her head over the blade and pointed it at the three. Silently, she tapped into their thoughts, then began her incantation, conjuring up each one's deepest, darkest fears. Immediately, they stopped moving while the one possessed continued to walk toward her.

Terrified screams shredded the still air. One human placed his hands over his eyes and stumbled backward. Another covered her ears and fell to her knees on the stone. The third turned and fled, falling twice before clearing the entrance to the alley.

The possessed human stopped short, but not out of fear. His human form expertly surveyed the area. When he caught sight of her, power twined with malevolence pulsed off him in waves, slamming against her chest. Selena held steady.

"Would you dare challenge me, human?" he demanded, his daemon voice thick and thunderous. The woman and man behind him fled. Now it was just the two of them. Selena smiled at his erroneous assumption. Not only wasn't she human, but, no thanks to her father, she was one of the most powerful daemons he'd ever encounter.

He was in for a surprise.

Keeping her sword at the ready, she hopped from the edge of the Dumpster to the ground, disturbing the thick waves of his power.

His throaty growl would have sent a lesser being running for the hills, but Selena had trained for years for moments like this. To make sure she had every advantage tonight, she had also fortified herself with more than her sword, her training, her hatred, and the power of her nanorian necklace. Tonight, she'd taken a healthy shot of Rev—the forbidden blood of the most powerful Otherworld beings. It coursed through her veins, making what was already powerful, virtually undefeatable.

She was more than prepared for a brutal and sustained battle.

"Indeed, Baphomet, I not only challenge you, but I intend to rip that daemon heart of yours right out of your chest."

He threw his head back and laughed. Selena took the opening. She leapt into the air, lengthening her body behind the sword so that she resembled a sleek, leather-clad dagger. She would do her best to spare the human's life, but there would be damage. There always was; it was part of the hunt.

The daemon responded more swiftly than she expected. He grabbed the razor-sharp tip of her sword and yanked it hard, sending her flying against the brick wall of the building behind her. She hit with a harsh thud, knocking the wind out of her.

Damn!

She leapt into the air and collided with his human body just as he lunged toward her with her sword in his hand. He sliced at her, catching her right shoulder. Pain seared through her flesh. As she tumbled back against the wall again, the daemon taunted, "You know who I am, what I am, and how to fight me. I am unimpressed if *you* are the rogue hunter the Order has put a bounty on." He laughed low, demonically. "I don't see why others fear you, but I look forward to collecting my reward."

"You'll take the Order's gold even as you break every law it forged in the blood of the Five?" Selena's statement wasn't a question, but it *was* a tad hypocritical. The Order, ruled by the Five—leaders of each immortal order: vampire, daemon, lycan, the fallen, and those prissy fey—had been created to prevent immortals from killing each other and, in so doing, destroying the one thing they all needed to survive: humans. The rules were simple and strictly enforced. Possessing humans for pleasure was forbidden—but so was hunting immortals, especially your own kind. She mentally shrugged. She'd never been one for following rules.

A malicious sneer twisted Baphomet's words. "In a matter of months, the Order of Five will be no more. Taking its place will be the Order of One, with Apollyon as supreme leader."

Selena snorted in contempt. The Order was indestructible, even *if* the daemons broke off. At the Order's helm was Rurik, an ancient and powerful vampire. "Even Hell is not powerful enough to vanquish Rurik and the Others."

The Hellkeeper threw his head back and laughed. "Mademoiselle Death Dealer, you do your kind a grave disservice. There will be no war between the Others. We have found a simple way to break Rurik and his hold on us by removing the one thing his kind requires to survive. Human blood."

The Hellkeeper's laughter was so deep and so potent the percussion of it lifted her long braid off her back. It whipped around, slapping her in the face. She flung it away, narrowing her eyes at the arrogant creature. "When Hell freezes over."

Selena somersaulted up into the air; flinging her hand out, she kicked Baphomet's arm with her right foot and caught her sword with her left. As she twisted and came down, he snatched the sword from her hand as if she held no power. For the first time in months—no, years— indecision made her falter.

His demonic laughter shook the stone alley beneath her feet. "My strength is superior to yours, even with the hearts of my brothers you so insolently wear around your neck."

He was strong. Stronger maybe than the ones before him.

Raising her chin, she said, "I possess the power of your brothers and it is fueled by my hatred for your kind. When I have your heart, I'll savor the power you so arrogantly dangle before me."

"I'd say you harbor a bit of arrogance yourself. But then, you've always been daddy's little girl, like it or not, eh?" He tsked when Selena softly cursed him. "Come now." He beckoned. "Come die by your own sword."

Selena shook her head, then withdrew her second sword from the crisscrossed sheath on her back. "Not tonight, Bap ol' boy. Not until you leave that body and show your true self."

"I am no fool, outlaw. I know, ridiculous as it is, that you value this human's life. I don't, so what do I have to lose?"

With a quick jab, Selena ran the human through.

The poor guy screamed as Baphomet hissed and bellowed his outrage.

If he did not exit the dying host, he would die with it.

She grabbed her other sword when it clattered to the cobblestones. "Hmmm," she murmured. "I guess you were wrong." Selena stood above him, swords at the ready. "It will be your last mistake."

Anxiously, she waited for the daemon to purge itself from the human body. She'd have only seconds to catch him before he fully materialized into his most powerful daemon form.

Baphomet began to emerge from the human's mouth and nostrils as a vapor that quickly solidified. When he was half-cast, Selena cut him in half.

Wicked screams rent the air. She stepped on the daemon's head, grinding it into the ground. She needed all of him in his daemon form to harvest the heart. She skewered his throat with her sword. "Come to me quietly, Baphomet, come to me quietly and I will make your end as painless as possible."

"Release me," he begged as his cloven hands scraped at her legs. This daemon's natural form was a brimstone-breathing goat. He was powerful and agile; his hind leg dug into her side, piercing her skin.

"Your release will serve only to make you a permanent resident of all seven Hells!"

She grabbed his horn and pulled it away from her side as he jerked to gouge her. Then she hacked at the tendons of his back legs, grounding him. Fire from his screams singed her skin, but he kept his hold on her.

"Release me, daughter of Paymon, release me and I will share my king's secret. If you kill me, the fate of humanity is at stake."

"The fate of humanity is at stake as long as you bastards keep possessing them." She sliced off his right hindquarter.

"Would you sacrifice your daughter and the world's daughters for my heart?"

Every cell in her body froze. "I have no daughter!"

His laughter mocked her. "So you say. . . ."

Selena saw red. Her hand shook. How did he know about Marisol? Only the nuns and the priest who cared for the girl knew of her child's existence. Did Paymon, that miserable excuse for a sperm donor she had spent years avoiding, suspect her daughter lived even though Selena had so convincingly staged her death? Fear and uncertainty infused her. Her father, a cunning Prince of Hell, would never divulge such a suspicion to a Hellkeeper. The knowledge was powerful in itself, and to admit anything would be daemon suicide. There was no honor among any of them, only continual jostling for power. If Paymon knew Marisol lived and where she was, he would have acted. Bap was blowing smoke up her ass. Marisol was safe amongst the nuns of the sacred order of St. Michael's.

Selena swept the worry away and focused on grinding the arrogant daemon into a goat burger. Thrusting her sword deep into Baphomet's chest, she could feel the vibration of his heartbeat against her steel. She hesitated to finish him off. There was a sadistic part of her nature that only reared its head when she came face-to-face with her father's kind. Their momentary suffering for all the pain they inflicted was a small price for them to pay.

Baphomet had fully solidified; his body parts lay in pieces on the ground around them. It looked like a butcher shop. Though she had him at a gross disadvantage, his vital parts still worked. With methodical precision, she began to cut around his heart.

"The daemons have united," he screeched. "They weary of being cast aside by the Others. In two months' time, the legions will possess every mortal soul that walks the earth."

Selena turned her blades, digging deeper, loosening the stone.

"*Spare me* and I will tell you how!"

She dared not look at his red, glowing eyes. A Hellkeeper of his level could easily hypnotize her into a trance, one she would never recover from.

"Tell me first, you damn goat, and if I believe you, I will spare half your heart."

"Every immortal order with the exception of the daemon needs humans in one capacity or another to survive. Without humans, they would all perish."

"Tell me something I don't know."

"Whoever controls the humans controls the Others."

"No one order can completely control the humans."

"But one can annihilate them. My king, *your* king, Apollyon, will destroy humanity if the Order refuses to relinquish power."

Selena stifled a gasp. Daemons were cruel, they were corrupt, they were lying, thieving bastards, but would they destroy humanity to spite the Order? Yes, *yes,* they would!

Baphomet capitalized on her shocked silence and sank his razor-sharp teeth into her hand holding the sword lodged against his heart. For the briefest of seconds, Selena's grip loosened. The daemon took full advantage of it. His dismembered front leg grabbed the sword and turned it back on her, running her through. Selena gasped and grabbed at her chest. Warm blood seeped through her fingers. Baphomet laughed tauntingly and with his other severed limb snatched the sword from her hand; this time he speared her abdomen.

Liquid pain scorched through her as her vision clouded. Doubling over, Selena dropped to her knees, fighting to remain conscious.

It would pass. It always did when she was fortified with the Rev. She would not die. She couldn't! Not when she was so close.

He hacked at her back and her shoulders, forcing her

facedown onto the cobblestones. Her strength ebbed with each heartbeat. Vaguely, Selena wondered if she was wrong. Had Baphomet accomplished what no one else ever had? Had he mortally wounded her?

No! She would not die by daemon! She had not completed her quest. Her quest to collect all seven nanorians and, with them, possess the power to destroy the being who'd repeatedly raped her mother, driven her to madness, and ultimately killed her: Prince of the Seven Hells, her daemon father, Paymon. He answered to few. But he would answer to her. And once he was dead, she would be reunited with her daughter, her sweet little Marisol. That part of her she'd had to give up, after giving up so much already, because of the danger Paymon posed to everyone she loved.

For the briefest moment, Selena pictured her daughter laughing and playing, but Marisol wasn't alone. Instead, she was accompanied by the only man Selena had ever loved. Johnny. Marisol's father and Selena's biggest regret. Because she had loved him, she'd had no choice but to destroy him. Otherwise, Paymon would have. She gritted her teeth, hating her father more at that moment than at any other time in her life. Because of him, who he was, what he'd made her, her life was what it was. With his death, she would be free.

He'd tried to kill her. He'd failed. She'd be damned if she'd let this Hellkeeper get the bragging rights.

Focusing, Selena moved her left hand into her duster pocket and felt for the syringe there. Deftly she popped the cap and jabbed it into her belly, using the weight of her body to push the plunger.

Power infused every cell in her body. Her wounds closed.

Without turning over, Selena acted as if she were indeed dying. "Tell me before I surrender your brothers' hearts. What does Apollyon plan?" she breathlessly asked.

Baphomet rolled her over with his dismembered back leg. His hairy goat face was distorted and ugly. His limbs were struggling to reattach themselves, but the damage was extreme.

"Apollyon has created chaos and instability in much of Asia Minor. And with that instability comes opportunity."

"Opportunity for what?"

"The acquisition of fissile products."

The hair on the back of Selena's neck stood. "What kind?"

"A refueled core from a nuke sub."

"He would not dare!" she gasped, trying hard to appear as if she were dying.

"Apollyon dares what no other immortal would."

"He's out of his daemon mind!"

"Do you know how many millions of humans a dirty bomb of this magnitude can destroy?"

"Apollyon plans to threaten the Order with a dirty bomb?" she asked, unable to keep the shock from her voice.

The daemon knelt on his front legs next to Selena, his goat body now nearly intact. He leaned in close, his rancid breath assaulting her nostrils. "Yes," he breathed. Heat singed her cheeks, burning her eyelashes off. She held steady. "In less than a month, a lead cask full of enriched uranium will be on its way to a human contractor who will construct the bomb. If Rurik refuses Apollyon's demand for control?" Baphomet threw his head back and laughed. "Boom!"

It was incredible—it was terrifying—it was brilliant and could work! While she had no great love for the Order and had never met Rurik, his iron fist kept all of the Others from destroying each other.

Baphomet lowered his head, aiming a razor-sharp horn at her throat, intending to rip the necklace from her as he gouged her to death.

"Fuck you, Baphomet—" Selena grasped the sword lying next to her; in a wide, powerful stroke, she separated the daemon's head from his shoulders. She leapt up and kicked back his writhing body and pierced his chest with the other sword. In the precise pattern of a pentagram, she cut into his flesh and around his beating nanorian, severing the arteries, and freed it. What was left of his body dropped to the ground, where it would turn to ash. Selena pressed her prize into one of the empty settings in her necklace and turned to the human. She knelt beside him and felt for a pulse.

She found the barest hint of one. She pulled the syringe from her pocket and injected him with what little was left of the Rev.

She did not wait to see whether it revived him. She had no idea how it would work on a human, but it didn't matter. It was his only chance. If it worked, it would do more than revive him. She supposed it was a fair trade.

It wasn't called Revive for nothing.

As she ran, Selena made plans. Baphomet's news wasn't information she could keep to herself. She was going to need a little help if she was going to stop the annihilation of humanity.

CHAPTER ONE

One month later
Southern base of Tian Shan mountain range,
Kyrgyzstan

Nikko had a bad feeling about this op.

Flurries salted the frigid February landscape. For as far as the eye could see, it was hard, gray, and uninviting. Lying on the edge of a ragged mountain ledge, Nikko cursed the sudden Siberian cold front that had come in the night before. This part of the Tian Shan was frigid under normal winter conditions; now it was arctic. He should have prepared for changeable weather. Because he hadn't, he'd spent the last eleven hours in twenty-below temps with nothing more than standard cold gear to keep him warm. He had only himself to blame for the needles prickling in his fingers and the lack of feeling in his toes. Even so, he'd spend the next eleven hours in exactly the same position if that's what it took.

Ironically, his moniker was Ice, and he lived up to the chill factor. He was cold, calculating. He had disconnected from his conscience the day he killed the only woman he'd ever loved. Not even the guilt he'd buried so deep inside got to him now. He had sunk to the lowest of lows; nothing was too dirty for him to do. Nothing and no one thawed him. It was what kept him alive and made him the perfect L.O.S.T. operative, one uniquely qualified to handle the rigors of his current mission.

He was a machine.

Hardwired to withstand pain, be it torture, the elements, or emotional strikes. It was what he did and who he was. Like the Terminator, programmed to carry out his duty.

Shoot him, burn him, rip his heart out and toss it to the vultures. He'd survive and revive.

Just as he'd survived the worst kind of betrayal a man could endure.

It had made him stronger.

Vigilant.

Alone.

He gritted his teeth and raised his high-powered binoculars to focus on the empty road below. Close by, a highly trained CIA extraction team and a dozen Kyrgyzstan commandos stood at the ready. Miles beyond, a Chinook 47 lay in wait with his L.O.S.T. team.

It was do or die. Since word of a hijacked cask of enriched uranium from the Mayak Processing Plant in Ozersk, Russia, had hit the president's desk three weeks ago, every federal agency had gone on high alert.

But it was the Last Option Special Team the president had called to locate the lead cask, take possession of it, and escort it to US soil, where it would safely be stored.

Nikko was point man on this mission, and he would die before he let the cask make it to Osh, Kyrgyzstan, where the Russian underground had their own plans for it.

Once Nikko's team secured the cask, the Chinook would come and haul the almost six-ton payload to the American Transfer Center outside Bishkek, the capital of Kyrgyzstan, and see that it was whisked back to the United States. Failure was not an option.

Nikko shuddered to think what could happen if the uranium fell into the wrong hands. The solid-lead cask made the enriched uranium handleable without taking precautions. Tons heavy, it would require special equipment to move it around—but all a terrorist had to do was pick a site, dig a hole, drop the cask in, toss in a few hundred pounds of TNT, then *boom*. A dirty bomb of that magnitude would not only leave a chunk of the world contaminated for centuries, but it could be death to hundreds of thousands of people.

Nikko's internal alarm beeped. For a mission of such urgency and worldwide implications, it had been a cakewalk.

Too smooth.

So smooth Nikko suspected they were going to pay for it.

He checked his satphone's GPS tracker again. Their target was five minutes out. Turning, he studied the men who, like him, were willing to risk their lives to protect the world from greedy warmongers with no regard for any life unless it came with a hefty bank deposit.

The four CIA agents were typical government-issue spies. Aloof. Capable. Deadly when they had to be. Once the semi was secured, they'd inspect the cask for leaks; given the green light, they would transfer it onto the Chinook. But first, the commandos would do their part. And God help the Russians. The Kyrg commandos were out for blood. They were tired of the Russian dogs who held them powerless.

They reminded Nikko of his *real* team. The Last Option Special Team operatives were the only people on earth Nikko trusted with his life. He had not been keen on the idea of splitting up, but it made sense. If something happened out here, only one L.O.S.T. operative would be lost. Not three. They were too valuable to risk losing en masse. Not that he planned to fail. L.O.S.T. never failed. In the seven years he had been part of the covert agency, they had lost only one operative. And that was last year to a— Nikko shook his head, still unable to believe Shane had been killed by a vampire. Crazy shit that was.

All ego aside, L.O.S.T. operatives were the best of the best. Maybe because they'd all been pushed at some point to be their worst.

He turned his attention back to the road and focused through his lenses. Lowering his binoculars, he signaled his crew. It was time.

As one, CIA, Kyrg commando, and L.O.S.T. swarmed down from the ledge and into a concealing crevice, then straight toward the blind side of a steep-graded hairpin turn. As the semi approached, they knew the driver would have to reduce his speed to a snail's crawl to round the tight angle of the turn. After all, his cargo had the potential to be the most virulent mass murderer in the world.

As it slowed and began to pass, they hit the ground running, staying low, approaching from the rear. Nikko hopped on the back of the trailer as it downshifted to make the turn, then hauled himself up to the roof. He moved to the front of the trailer and sprawled flat. Taking a small, battery-powered handsaw from his backpack, he began to cut a hole in the trailer top. Within moments, the air brakes hissed, and the trailer shimmied and shook as it came to a slow-rolling stop to inch around the sharp curve.

As planned, the commandos swarmed the back of the trailer while two of them broke off, charging toward the cab on either side. Nikko watched from his vantage point as he kept cutting. The Kyrg running along the driver's side began to signal the driver, who watched the activity intently in the side mirror. Not part of the plan. Nikko rolled over and dropped behind the commando and snapped his neck as the other commando came around the front, yelling to the driver to duck. Nikko pulled his pistol and shot the traitor right between the eyes. They'd been set up, damn it!

Hoisting himself back up to the trailer roof, he leashed his fury. "Abort!" he roughly whispered into his mic.

"Roger that," one of the spooks said.

"Sir," one of the commandos said, "we cannot abort!"

Without warning, the back doors of the trailer crashed open. Armed men swarmed out. At the same time, rounds tore through the rooftop of the trailer, spraying Nikko in his thigh and forearm.

"Fuck!" he cursed, and rolled off the roof, hitting the rough road below, before taking cover behind one of the huge tires. Swiftly, he scanned the area. Three of the four spooks and half of the commandos were down. Unsure if the remaining commandos were friend or foe, Nikko was not taking any chances. One by one, he picked them off until they all lay motionless on the cold mountain roadside.

Massive chaos ensued among the armed mercs. Gunfire rose above their frantic voices yelling to each other in Russian and, oddly, Spanish as they frantically searched for him.

Nikko kept his cool, methodically picking off one merc, then another, as he moved beneath the trailer. An RPG blasted from somewhere above him, smashing into the hillside. Clumps of earth and rock slammed against the trailer.

"I'm hit! I'm hit!" the last spook standing screamed.

Nikko watched from behind one of the massive tires as three mercs descended on the spook's writhing body on the hillside. Nikko knew what they would do to him, and once they had the information they wanted, they'd kill him piece by piece. Nikko aimed for his counterpart's head and pulled the trigger. The man's body jerked, then slumped to the ground.

Pulling a GPS device from his right thigh pocket, Nikko removed the protective cover on the double-sided tape and stuck the GPS to the undercarriage of the truck. He pulled out his satphone to alert his team it was all going to shit.

Voices shouted back and forth. The mercs were looking for him. Nikko stuffed the phone into the thigh sleeve of his cargo pants, then crawled along the opposite roadside using the trailer as cover and worked his way toward the sheer edge of the road. He would drop if he had to.

Pulling a grenade from his belt, Nikko crawled

around the trailer and positioned himself. He noticed for the first time he was losing blood. A warm, damp stream from his forearm dripped onto the road. Heavy boot-steps rounded the trailer from either end. He ducked back under the trailer and changed direction. If he could get to the crevice, it would offer enough cover for him to hold them off until the cavalry arrived.

Blinking against the fog that blurred his vision, Nikko tossed the grenade ahead of him and to the right, dispersing the soldiers who hadn't, unbelievably, bothered to look under the trailer for him. When it exploded, heavy boots ran from the exact place he needed to go. Quickly, Nikko hoisted himself up on a hot axle and maneuvered his way toward the cab.

"*KpoBb!*" a merc shouted, his voice closing in.

They had spotted his blood.

Nikko was outmanned ten to one. If he stayed where he was, he'd be captured. Then he'd be dead, but not before he was treated to a bout of From Russia with Love torture. The Russians were the best at it. He had the scars to prove it. Capture was not an option.

He rolled out from under the trailer and tossed another grenade behind him, then another and another until he was wedged into the crevice he'd exited less than fifteen minutes earlier, with the steep incline of the mountain behind him. He had meager cover, but it was enough. He slung his M16 around from his back by its strap and opened fire. He was answered with blinding pain as the percussion of an RPG blew him ten feet into the air and slammed him against the mountainside. Slowly his lacerated body slid down the gravelly surface to the bottom of the crevice. His chest was shredded; his head ached like the morning after a three-day drunk. His extremities twitched as shock claimed him.

Heavy boots stormed toward him. A barrage of argument in Russian over whether he was worth torturing.

"Is dead," a voice said.

A strange sensation of cool heat swirled within his chest cavity as his life oozed out and death rushed in. But oddly, his hands and feet weren't cold anymore, they were warm. He blinked away the blood in his eyes. Suddenly the sky was blue. The gray had been absorbed by white, puffy clouds. The sun shone brightly, causing him to squint, and the salt of the nearby ocean toyed with his senses. Overhead, gulls called. A cottage shimmered like a mirage under the sunshine.

He was home.

Nikko tried to smile but couldn't. That little summer cottage on St. Michael's Island had been a happy place once; it was the place he'd fallen in love. The place where his life had shattered into a million tiny pieces, killing the most vital part of him long before today.

Now fate was determined to finish what little life Selena had left him. *Selena.* He choked on the thought of her. There hadn't been a colder-hearted murdering bitch on the planet. But he'd taken care of her. She couldn't hurt him again. He still loved her. Guilt dragged down by regret washed through him in waves. He'd killed her. The only woman he would ever love.

His chest burned. His throat constricted.

The sunshine began to fade.

He was dying.

The harsh voices around him trailed off, followed by the slamming of doors, the release of air brakes. He'd been left for dead. At least they hadn't hacked off his limbs to drag them behind the trailer, a warning of what they were capable of. He had no ID that could link him to the US. Neither did the dead spooks.

He heard the loud beep of the trailer as it backed up, then the deafening rev of the diesel; the sounds shook him to his foundation. This was it. He was going to die here, on a road to nowhere in a Podunk country like a possum on the side of the road.

At least the trailer was trackable, he thought before he closed his eyes. With extreme effort, Nikko moved a hand to his chest, flinching when his fingertips sank into warm, pulpy tissue. He could feel the slow beat of his heart against his fingertips. Blood washed warm and thick across his palm.

Who knew it wouldn't hurt? At least not physically. It was the memories he'd pushed so far down into his soul that threatened to swamp him, punishing him in a way his numbed flesh could not.

He told himself not to think of the family he had abandoned as a teenager.

Or the child who had been taken from him before he could meet her.

Longing raged inside him anyway. Fury spiraled in harsh thrusts against his damaged heart. If he could, he'd kill all over again the woman who'd taken that tiny life from him.

He cursed. *If* he was heavenbound, he would see his baby girl, but her mother had taken away even that possibility. Because of what he'd done to her, and for every damn thing he'd done afterward, he wasn't bound for the pearly gates. No, he was bound where babies did not dare to go.

Darkness descended over him.

He was tired of the rage, of the anguish, of the longing.

He let go of his anger and gave himself up to whatever was coming to take him.

"Johnny. . . ," the soft, feminine voice called. It was his given name. From a different time. A different life.

Despite his blood loss, his pulse spiked. "Selena—" How could it be? She was dead. He had killed her, with his own hands.

"*Sí, corazón,*" she whispered.

His eyes fluttered open. He must be in Hell. She was exactly as he'd last seen her. The most beautiful creature on earth. Dark and deadly, with the face of a siren, the voice of an angel. All disguising that she was a heartless, betraying, murderous bitch. She had pushed him to commit an unspeakable act. He hated himself for being like her.

"I told you the next time I saw you it would be in Hell," he said, barely able to enunciate the words. "And here we are."

She threw her head back and laughed. That laugh had brought him to his knees more than once. Now she was the one who knelt and touched his cheek with her fingertips. He set his jaw, not wanting to enjoy her touch but relishing it anyway.

"You're bleeding, Johnny," she softly said.

He grasped her hand and squeezed it with what

strength he had left. He wanted to hurt her as she had hurt him. She'd destroyed the one beautiful thing in his life. "Are you behind this? Is this *your* dirty work?"

"Always suspicious, aren't you?"

She smiled. While he could not feel the hole in his chest or any of his other wounds, her smile was like a hot knife twisting in his heart.

"Go to Hell, Selena."

She smiled again, the magnitude of it blinding him. She lifted her clasped hands over her head. The glint of metal caught a sliver of the sun's straining ray.

"No, Johnny Boy." She brought her arms down in a hard motion, stabbing him directly in his broken, beaten heart. "*You* go to Hell."

Selena stood in shocked silence. The last person she'd expected to see here or anywhere for that matter was the only man she would ever love. Because of her, he had been sentenced to death. She had been aware of his escape during transport from jail to prison. It had taken every ounce of will she possessed not to go in search of him. But that would have defeated her original purpose. She was dead to him. For his safety, she must remain so.

She stared down at the man whom she had caused irreparable emotional damage.

Johnny.

He had not moved since she'd injected him. From where she stood beside him, Selena felt his life force, faint as it was, battling the damage to his body. Watching over him wasn't going to speed things along. She needed to leave. If she did not, her entire mission would be compromised. She was here to hijack that semi, and its deadly cargo.

Only she couldn't leave. Not—quite—yet.

From the moment she'd seen Johnny magically appear on this lonely stretch of road in Kyrgyzstan, long-suppressed feelings had rushed to the surface: regret, fear, anger, and a longing so deep her heart ached. Memories of their two years together swept through her. It had been eight years since she'd last seen him, but it seemed as if an entire lifetime had passed. She could still see the horrific pain and anger in his eyes when in a fit of rage he had tried to kill her. As far as he and the law knew, he had.

Now, on her quest for the cask Baphomet had spoken of, she had had a bird's-eye view when the ambush played out, led by none other than Johnny Cicone.

Before she could recover from the shock of seeing him, he'd gone down, and she'd had to wait for the trailer to start moving before she could get to him. When she saw the carnage that was his body, she had not given her actions a second thought. She had given him her reserve shot of Revive, a combination of blood serums extracted from donors not of the human world. Then, for safe measure, she had injected him with the individual vampire serums she had just collected in Siberia and St. Petersburg.

It was his only chance to survive, and she owed him that.

Revive was illegal. If she was caught with even a

drop of it on her person, she would be executed on the spot. Nonetheless, she transported the drug and the serums needed to make it for an important man, one who wouldn't be pleased when she returned empty-handed.

Joran Cadiz was not a man you failed. She shrugged off his impending wrath. She could always hunt again. It wasn't the vampire she feared disappointing, it was Señor Balderama, *el patrón*.

The head of Los Cuatro, a man with a mission—a mission Selena shared, one Cadiz knew nothing about.

Joran was her connection to the immortal world she shunned. Los Cuatro was her human connection, in a world she fought to fit into and a cause she believed in.

It was funny how fate intervened. While she was hell-bent on hijacking the cask Apollyon was after, so was Los Cuatro, but for different reasons. Humanitarian reasons. As a Los Cuatro agent, Selena had come to Kyrgyzstan to locate it and hijack it. But now, because of Johnny, she'd been waylaid.

She must go. With her powers, she would easily be able to pick up the trailer's location and do what she had come to do.

She looked up at the afternoon sun, then back to Johnny. She could do nothing more for him. He'd either live and thrive thanks to the Rev, or he'd die. . . . She'd given him a chance. She owed him more—but not in this lifetime.

Off in the distance, the faint but unmistakable sound of a helicopter disturbed the silence. Johnny's backup? Selena knelt beside her beloved and touched his cheek.

It was cold. Her heart stutter-stepped. She prayed to his God that he survived, then brushed her lips across his cold ones. "Good-bye, Johnny," she softly said, then stood and turned west.

She sprinted down the opposite crevice to a sleek, black motocross bike, then roared off after the trailer.

CHAPTER TWO

Nikko woke to the sting of frigid air slapping his face and full memory of the ambush and his failure. His body felt light, and—tentatively—he touched his chest. Beneath the ravaged body armor and shredded fatigues, smooth skin. *What the hell?*

He bolted upright, realizing he was in no pain. Scrambling to the top of the crevice, he surveyed the carnage and destruction that was the roadside. The bodies of the fallen agents, mercs, and commandos littered the scene. Their bodies were still mangled, bloody messes, while his . . .

His body-armor vest. It was in pieces, his jacket blown to shreds. Blood covered his cargo pants and his skin. He poked his finger through the hole in the fabric covering his thigh, then examined the one in his sleeve.

"What the hell?" He hurried to the nearest CIA agent and touched his chest. His body was still warm. How much time had passed?

The distant *twap-twap-twap* of a chopper caught his attention. Should be his extraction team. But he wasn't taking any chances. Nikko grabbed the M16 from the fallen spook and another from the agent lying next to him. He dug for his satphone, but it was in pieces on the side of the road. He took cover in the crevice and waited.

Friend or foe would be determined in less than ten, and he was preparing for foe.

The sudden vision he had imagined as he lay dying lingered on the fringes of his brain. Selena Guerrero.

No fucking way.

He'd been shot up and bleeding, so out of it he'd started hallucinating. He'd killed her with his own two hands! Had been convicted and sentenced to die for her murder! Yet even with his dying breath, she would not leave him alone.

He looked out over the horizon. He could see for miles with a newfound clarity. Rocks. Struggling flora. The gray, barren colors and textures of the terrain.

The chopper was getting closer, his hearing so acute he knew it was an American-made Chinook 47. His L.O.S.T. team. They were coming for him. A sudden gust of wind brought the blood scents of the dead with it— the smell so intense, he covered his mouth and gagged.

Nikko ran, unable to stomach it. His legs carried him swiftly across the hard earth. He easily jumped over a ten-foot-wide ditch, only realizing what he had done when he landed on the other side. Then he cleared the next one, which was even wider.

What had happened to him? He felt like Superman.

The chopper came into view. Nikko waved his arms until it set down fifty yards from him. He grinned when he saw fellow L.O.S.T. operatives Gage Stone and Dominic "Satch" Satriano hop out and come running toward him. His grin faded as they approached.

He could smell their excitement and their relief. Hear the hot rush of their blood pumping through their hearts. *Shit.*

"What the hell happened, Cruz? We lost you on the satellite."

Nikko clasped hands with each man, frowning when each winced in turn.

"Jesus, Cruz, I'm happy to see you, too, but lighten up," Stone said, withdrawing his hand and shaking it.

Satriano shook out the pain in his own hand. For a second, Nikko stared at his hand, wondering whether his near-death experience was fucking with his system, the adrenaline in his veins giving him a high he'd never before experienced.

"Cruz," Stone yelled, jerking Nikko's head up.

"The Kyrgs set us up," Nikko said. "The trailer was loaded with Russian mercs. They came out fighting, caught us completely off guard."

"You think the Kyrg government had a side deal with the underground?" Satch asked, shaking his head.

"I don't know what the hell to think."

"Did you tag the trailer?" Stone finally asked.

Nikko nodded. "Yeah, let's get a lock on it."

They started toward the chopper. "You look pretty fucked-up, bro," Satch said, tugging at Nikko's torn vest.

"Nothing but superficial stuff, I'm fine. They're messed up," Nikko said as he slowed, pointing to the downed men. Grim lines etched Stone's and Satch's faces. "We can't leave them here," Nikko added.

Satch nodded. "We'll call Godfather from the helo and get our boys home. The Kyrgs can bury their own."

"Let's get out of here and track that cask," Nikko said, jogging back to the chopper.

As the chopper lifted into the air, Satch slid a laptop out from a backpack and booted it up. In seconds, they had the trailer Nikko had tagged on the grid. "Heading due west."

Nikko nodded. "There's only one person with the means, motive, and firepower to maneuver a double cross like this. Vladimir Noslov in Osh. His underground stronghold."

"Due west of here," Stone grimly said.

"Damn it!" Satch roared. "We lost the signal!"

"They must have found it and disengaged it," Nikko said. He grabbed a pair of binoculars hanging from an overhead hook and moved up into the empty copilot seat.

Fully aware that his vision was superenhanced just like the rest of him, Nikko put the binoculars to his eyes and locked in on the tractor-trailer tracks. He still did not understand the enhancement, but he didn't question it. All he knew was that it was damn amazing and could help them now.

He pointed to a sharp turn of the tracks. "They've changed direction. Take the compass point due north," Nikko said to the pilot.

"How the hell can you see those tracks even with the lenses?" Stone asked, coming up behind him.

"I just can." Nikko pointed to the tracks again. "Turn forty-five degrees west. We're back on track to Osh."

Nikko tracked each new turn the trailer made. They kept low, but the farther they traveled, the more aware Nikko was that their airspace was running out. Even though an American base was in the northern part of the country, this area was run by criminal cartels. A low-flying American military chopper was a prime target.

"Target dead ahead three hundred meters," Nikko warned.

"I have a visual," the pilot said. "One desert-cammie tractor-trailer, coming up hard at twelve o'clock. One hundred meters and closing."

"Slow down and bank," Nikko warned. "They have RPGs." But even as Nikko said the words, he saw that the back doors to the trailer had been left open. Empty.

"Son of a bitch!"

The chopper set down and they hurried to the empty hull. Several sets of tire tracks led away from the abandoned trailer. All of them deep. Any one of the six sets could be carrying the cask.

"Damn it!" Stone cursed.

"Call in our location, Satch, and have the satellite do a perimeter search for the trailers. They couldn't have gotten too far. We'll get locks on them, then track them via satellite."

Satriano nodded and sprinted to the chopper to call in the orders.

"It's too dangerous for us to split up, Cruz," Stone said. "We're going to have to pick one and stay with it while the other five are tracked until we can get more teams assembled."

Satch whistled from the chopper, motioning them to hurry the hell up.

As they boarded, he said, "Satellite images show six trailers, all six headed west."

"If we go deeper, we're begging for trouble," Stone said. "We're going to have to back off."

"We can't!" Nikko said. They had come too far. Too many lives had been lost to turn tail.

"Looks like they've got company," Satch said, watching the screen. "A motorcycle following a mile behind, closing in fast."

As the chopper whirled upward and turned west, Nikko's skin chilled. There was no way. . . . "Can you go back and see which direction the bike came from?"

"Stand by."

Nikko's heart pounded in his chest. He refused to believe what his gut screamed was true.

"From the ambush coordinates."

Jesus.

"We're entering restricted air," the pilot warned.

Satch and Stone looked to Nikko. Unless he wanted to create an international incident, he had no choice.

"Abort," he angrily said.

"We'll keep tabs on the trailers via satellite. I'm calling it in," Satch said.

Nikko yanked his headphones off and threw them so hard they shattered into pieces on the steel floor. His fellow operatives looked as troubled as he felt. Once those trailers hit Osh, even with the satellite tracking, locating the cask would be like looking for a needle in ten haystacks. Running his hands through his hair and then over his face, Nikko shouted, "Fuck!"

Stone and Satch looked in shock at the damage his temper had caused, then glanced at one another. Stone jerked his chin at Nikko. "You on something?"

"Something." Nikko shook his head and looked out the open door toward the mountains. His body still thrummed with a strength and power he had never before experienced a power he knew wasn't just the result of stress-induced adrenaline. Had Selena been a hallucination after all? And if she hadn't been a hallucination, neither had whatever she'd injected into his chest.

He turned back to Stone. "Something happened to me out there. Something weird. If I didn't know better, I'd swear I died and came back to life, but only after someone shot me up with something first. And even worse—"

"What the hell can be worse than that?" Satch hissed.

"Being brought back to life by a dead woman."

CHAPTER THREE

Lost Souls Night Club, South Beach, Miami

Agitated with her "guest," Selena paced the small space in her office. "I don't have it," she said for the fifth time.

Miguel Ramos, muscleman and messenger for Joran Cadiz, the half-Dutch, half-Cuban reigning lord of the Miami underworld, grinned like the arrogant man he was. Ramos wielded his machismo like a sword. He liked to draw blood and often did; but while his tactics as Cadiz's enforcer worked on most souls, they didn't work on her. In a throwdown, she'd win and they both knew it.

"What do you expect me to tell Joran? That you lost the serums on the way home?"

His disdainful sneer made her bristle, but she simply shrugged. "Tell him whatever you want."

Narrowing his eyes, he grabbed for her. Hissing like a cat, Selena turned on him, tossing her long, black hair behind her squared shoulders. "Mind your manners, *señor*. You forget I do more than bite."

He stayed in her space, but dropped his burly hands, his gaze wary.

Good. He wasn't as stupid as he looked.

"You've been paid," he pointed out.

Selena moved around her desk, yanked the top

drawer open, and withdrew a corporate checkbook. She scribbled a check, tore it out, and handed it to him. "Consider Joran reimbursed."

"Cash isn't the only way you've been paid." Ramos shook his head and tore the check in half, letting the pieces fall to the floor. "The serums, *señorita,* or I am afraid I will have to damage you."

Selena studied him. He was built to fight. Barely six feet tall, broad-shouldered, thick-necked, with bulging muscles, and mean as hell. She had seen him in action. Although she knew she could best him, she wasn't in a mood for a fight at the moment. Since her return from Kyrgyzstan, she felt off center. Confused. Anxious.

Seeing Johnny after all this time had thrown her for a triple loop. Then she had done the ultimate in stupidity—given him the very thing she had been prepaid to deliver to Joran. But what was she supposed to do? Let him die?

Sure, he'd left her for dead once, and as much as she'd wanted to return the favor, something had stopped her. Something she didn't want to analyze too closely and certainly not right now.

She looked sideways at Ramos. With a weary sigh, she said, "Do you really want to do this, Miguel?"

He peered back at her, then shrugged. "I would rather fight you than return to Joran empty-handed."

She nodded in understanding. Joran was not a man you said no to, even when the no came from another. Still, she could not give him what she did not have. "Joran is no fool. He needs me. Besides, how do you think he'd feel if you told him his fast track to the serums had dried up because of you?"

Ramos stood silent and contemplative for a long moment, then strode toward her office door. When he opened it, the cacophony of the club downstairs burst into the room, disturbing the quiet like a Category 5 hurricane.

She welcomed it, the sense of familiarity and contentment it brought. Good or bad, this was home. She was tired of Miguel Ramos and tired of running from one end of the globe to the other, extracting the specialized serums from their specialized hosts so that Joran could produce mere drops of the coveted and outlawed Rev. But she would not be serving Joran unless it also served her own agenda.

Theirs was a simple arrangement. In exchange for vital information on her father's movements and his demonic world, she extracted the ingredients for the life-restoring Revive. The perk was, she had her own personal stash and was not above using it. The Rev kept her in top fighting form, and outlaw that she was, fighting kept her alive.

Joran's intel had been crucial to her. He'd never steered her wrong, moving her ever closer to her goal: the collection of all seven Hellkeeper hearts. Once she possessed them, there would be no need for the Rev. The combined energy of the heart stones would create the ultimate power source. She would be invincible, and she needed to be that if she was to have any hope of destroying dear ol' Dad and finally living a normal life with her daughter.

She'd sleep with the devil if it meant one more heart.

Selena threw her head back and laughed, causing Ramos's brows to furrow.

How ironic.

"You have failed. Now Joran will listen to me," Ramos said over his shoulder. "Despite your lineage, you're as useless as the pathetic humans who gather here. You're more like your mother than we thought."

Selena stiffened. Ramos's big mouth was his undoing. Nobody talked trash about her mother. *No one.*

Selena sauntered toward him. The four stones in the necklace she never removed warmed. Like thousands of tiny pinpricks, the power surged into her body. Slowly, she inhaled, drawing it deep into every cell.

Realizing he had awakened a sleeping tiger, Ramos turned fully toward her, his eyes wide. Being the macho asshole he was, he didn't run. Instead, he lunged toward her.

Perfect.

Selena thrust out her hand and shoved the air. Ramos's chest compressed, forcing the air in his lungs outward with a loud whooshing sound. He stopped dead in his tracks as if he had hit a wall.

Selena closed her fingers inward one by one until she made a fist. Ramos gasped, tearing at his throat.

Selena tightened her fist and lowered her arm. As she did, Ramos dropped to his knees. His eyes bugged out of his red face; saliva ran from his rubbery lips.

She savored the power. Felt it threatening to overtake her.

As quickly as she'd made the fist, Selena opened her hand, and Ramos fell to the floor, gulping for breath. Holding her own breath, she almost closed her eyes, swamped with relief.

She had to be careful; a daemon had the power to

move air, but only because of the stones she'd taken from the daemons did she have the power. If she allowed it to control her, she would be no better than those she hunted.

Standing over Ramos, she nudged him with the toe of her gold Gucci sandal. "Get up. Tell Joran if he wants to talk, he knows where to find me." She nudged him harder and he rolled out of her office. With an imperceptible flick of her wrist, the door slammed shut behind him.

Selena let out a long breath.

The embedded stones in her necklace continued to warm her skin. Absently, she stroked the jagged orbs as well as the necklace's empty settings. Once they were filled, she would have the power to see into the next world and beyond. Right now, though, she felt dirty, the way she always did when she came back from one of her serum runs. The feeling didn't go away simply because she'd come back empty-handed. In fact, it seemed to have amplified.

While Joran Cadiz was a means to one end, her work for Los Cuatro was a means to another. But more pressing was the daemon king's desire for nukes. How on earth was she going to stay ahead of that? Was she supposed to ring up Rurik and tell him what was up? If she did, he'd know who she was, what she had done. She was an outlaw among immortals.

She'd killed four Hellkeepers and more than a few low-level daemons.

There were no gray areas. It was forbidden, under any circumstances, to hunt your own kind or Other kind. There was no opportunity to defend one's actions. Punishment was immediate death.

Restlessness broke through her fatigue. She strode out to her balcony. It was an unseasonably balmy night. Warm air brushed across her cheeks, tender as a lover. Her nipples tightened as a sizzle of electricity rippled through her. She set her jaw and closed her eyes, not wanting to think of the only man who had touched her so intimately.

The man who'd tried to kill her and nearly succeeded.

Her kryptonite.

Johnny Cicone had been as hot-blooded and as hot-tempered as they came. Their passion had been unquenchable, their arguments epic, and their end a Shakespearean tragedy.

She pictured him lying on the side of that mountain road, his chest ripped open, his heart bleeding out. As strong as he'd always been, she couldn't have imagined him surviving those wounds. Even as he lay dying, he'd scorned her.

He had hardened. Hardened to impenetrable. And she knew she was the cause.

From the moment she'd met Johnny, she'd known how it would end. But she couldn't help herself. She'd fallen hard. Toward the end, she'd tried to fool herself that maybe it could work, but when she'd gotten pregnant, she'd had no choice but to face reality.

Her father's rage that she would not join him in Hell knew no bounds. After he drove her mother to suicide, he'd gone after Johnny. When her father discovered she was pregnant, he'd vowed to take her child. The only way to save the man she loved and her child was to make a preemptive strike. So she'd made it impossible for Johnny to forgive her and, in so doing, ended their relationship, so that Paymon would no longer use her love for him against her. Then she'd hidden her child in a place where even her father would not dare go. But that didn't mean she hadn't loved Johnny. She would always love him. Her actions didn't mean she didn't miss him. Or that seeing him lying on the ground, his blood draining from his body, hadn't almost destroyed her.

Maybe it had. By shooting him up with the Rev, she'd risked not only Joran's wrath, but Johnny's as well. He would know she was alive, and if she knew Johnny, she knew he would turn the world inside out until he found her. Then her father would think they had reunited. She could only hope Johnny believed he'd hallucinated her. And why wouldn't he? He'd killed her. Or at least thought he had.

Selena rubbed her hands up and down her bare arms, gazing out at the marina and the softly bobbing sailboats and luxury yachts, including her own, *Black Widow,* illuminated beneath the silvery moonlight. The spicy scents of the night combined with the crisp salt of the ocean to create a familiar perfume, one she greedily inhaled. The vibrations from Lost Souls reverberated through her body. Thick, hot, urgent. It reminded her of who she was and how things had to be.

She shook the thoughts of Johnny and their daughter from her head. It didn't matter who he was or had become. She could not turn back time. She could not stop what she had set into motion.

She was like a wounded shark, and the minute she stopped moving, she'd drown.

So she would continue to swim. And destroy anything in her path that tried to keep her from her goal.

That included Johnny then and it included Johnny now.
It had to.

Turning, Selena sauntered back into her office. With
an imperceptible flick of her hand, the carved paneling
behind her sleek black desk opened, revealing a bird's-
eye view of the manic bodies gyrating below to the
Latin salsa beat. As far as clubs went, hers was *el punto
caliente*. Sleek, dark, with subtle jewel tones embedded
throughout the place. The glass-and-ebony bars glowed
from soft underlighting, highlighting bottles of upscale
liquor behind them. Private rooms circled the second
level much like luxury boxes at a stadium. They opened
to a full view below; for more private affairs, the smoky-
glass doors could be closed. Soundproof.

Lost Souls was known as a safe haven to those of less
than impeccable reputation. Just like her. The cacophony
of the music's percussion combined with the seductive
scent of sex, lust, and power was as potent as the Rev.
She inhaled deeply, the energy giving her strength. The
club amused her, kept her in comfort, and fed her in a
way neither the Rev nor the stones at her throat could.
The effect of the Rev was like steroids, temporary and
intense and always edged with the threat of addiction.
The stones gave her power when she needed it, but
they, too, were a threat. The club, however, and those it
attracted, fed her true self in a way she could relish, without fear of losing control. For her kind, the more sexual
energy that thrummed around her, the more her natural
power surged. She closed her eyes, tilted her head back,
and listened. "Yes," she whispered. "Drink, dance, make
love." Her lips tilted up into a smile. "Open your lonely
souls. Let me in, tell me your secrets." She smiled and

then laughed. "And I will tell you lies." How could she not? Everything about her was a lie.

Gather lost souls. Lure the daemons. Hunt them, kill them, and take their power.

It was amazing how much effort it took to get an audience with Daddy.

Her eyes flashed open. "Soon, Father, I will reveal myself," she said softly. When she did, he would pay for raping her mother and holding her hostage. For letting her go only to repeatedly come back until she was finally driven to take her own life. He would pay for the threats against Selena's daughter and the attempts on Johnny's life. He would pay for what he'd forced Selena to become and what he'd forced her to give up.

He would pay for it all.

Even as she held the thought, a dull throbbing began in her temples caused by the pounding pulse of the music. Then the air in her office chilled exponentially, almost as if the doors to Hell had been opened. She froze, barely stopping from whirling around.

Few things on earth caused Selena concern, but one of them was standing behind her now, framed by the French doors that led to her balcony. Slowly, as if she hadn't a care in the world, she turned to face him, walked around her desk, then made a show of leaning back against it. She pressed a button on the underside of her desk and the window to the club closed softly behind her. Imperceptibly, she nodded, acknowledging the supreme ruler of Miami's notorious underworld: Joran.

"Your lapdog just left," Selena drawled as her gaze swept lazily over the vampire. He was, she supposed, a dead ringer for the Spanish-born actor Antonio

Banderas, but bigger, broader, and certainly more deadly. His thick, black, shoulder-length hair framed an intense face with deep espresso-brown eyes etched with green striations. Sensuality poured off him in waves. While most of it bounced off her, some of it didn't. The daemon in her stirred. *Damn it.*

Selena laughed off the disconcerting feeling. "Are you attempting to seduce me, vampire?"

He grinned slowly. "I would—never . . ."

Selena pushed off the edge of her desk and turned her back to him, then looked coyly over her shoulder. Joran had made his willingness to bed her plain from their first meeting years ago. "I may be half-daemon, a fact I curse every day of my life, but my human will is stronger than any daemon urge. Don't waste your glamour on me, Joran. Save it for someone who cares."

He laughed deeply and entered her office. She cursed under her breath. He didn't stop by often, but when he did, she couldn't keep him out unless she wanted a good ass-kicking. She was strong, but he was stronger. "Still regret that you invited me in so long ago?"

Selena shook her head, moved around to the chair behind her desk, and sat down. "I'm going to assume you spoke with your pit bull?"

He nodded and lifted his hand. With a slow sweep of his fingers, he moved the only other chair in the room from the corner to behind him. He sat down and adjusted his black-silk tailored suit. "I did."

"And?" She sat back in her chair.

"I'm disappointed, Selena."

A vision of Johnny's bloody body lying still in the dirt flashed before her eyes. He would be even more disappointed if she told him what had happened to the serums. "It couldn't be helped. I'll go back next week and round up twice the amount for half the cost."

"I think not. I think you'll go earlier and I think you'll do it at no charge."

Selena lifted her chin and stared straight into his eyes, which were beginning to redden just around the edges. Slowly, she sat up straight and inhaled, giving the stones around her neck the cue to pay attention.

Standing, she planted her hands palm down on her desk, leaned forward, and spoke slowly. "I think, Joran, you have somehow gotten the impression that you call the shots." She exhaled. The stones warmed. "I'm an independent contractor. I decide who, what, where, when, and how much. Not the other way around."

He smiled lazily and purred, "Yes, I know. But I also know, if it involves a nanorian, you will do exactly what I want. On my terms. Isn't that right?"

She looked sideways at him and fingered the four around her neck. "Perhaps."

"I happen to know there is one right here in Miami."

"If there is one in Miami, I'll find it, without your help."

"Even when the daemon has possessed a human body as insidious as half of Hell?"

"That's none of your business." She could, it was just harder. Black-hearted humans had the uncanny ability to hide the scent of a daemon. Maybe because they were so much alike.

"Ah, a trade secret. Okay, I'll give you that one, but only because I have my own." He stood so fast that even with her enhanced vision she didn't see the movement as anything but a shimmer in the air, like a ripple on a glassy pond.

He stood inches from her now. "A Hellkeeper is running roughshod over some of my assets in Hialeah. That's bad enough, but the daemon is hiding inside the body of one Armadeo Vegas."

She started at the name. Madeo Vegas was a one-man death squad for *cubano* mafioso Luis Fernandez and a frequent patron of Lost Souls.

"What do you want me to do that you can't do yourself? Just go bite the prick and drain him. The daemon will have to vaporize or die with the body."

"I can't. He has knowledge of something I need."

"And this something you need?"

"You know I don't discuss my business."

"Oh, come now, Joran, I think we have gone a little past your being shy. Tell me what you want. Specifically."

"I will tell you this much: My protection, some of which offers you the same blind eye, is proving to be less than protective. In the last two months, many of my—associates have been incarcerated with alarming regularity. It seems those with whom I have financial agreements—and who happen to be the same persons with the power to look the other way—no longer choose to. Vegas has a hand in their newfound sense of justice. I want to know how Vegas is getting to them."

"How do you know it's Vegas?"

"I have eyes and ears everywhere, Selena. You know that." Joran smiled tightly. "I want the information. You'll get it after you expel the Hellkeeper from Vegas's body and take possession of it yourself."

Her? Possess a human body? And even worse, human

scum? Selena laughed. Shaking her head, she walked over to her balcony door and opened it. "You're a funny guy, Joran. Real funny. Now leave."

He was all over her in the blink of her tired eyes. The door slammed shut and she found herself sprawled on her back across her desk. Joran's heavy body pinned her to the desktop.

He stared hotly into her eyes, his blazing red. His nostrils flared, his lips twitched, and just beneath, she saw a hint of fang. "You will do it or I will lead Paymon to your doorstep."

He would not dare! "Then who will you get to do your dirty work?" she sneered.

"Do you think you are the only half-breed out there who can do what you do?"

"I'm the only willing one with the skills to do it and not get caught by the Order. How do you think Rurik will react once he knows his old buddy from across the pond is hijacking immortal blood to create a banned substance?"

Joran picked her up and flung her across the room. She slowed the velocity of her body to keep from slamming against the wall, then hovered just above the smooth granite tile for a moment before lowering to it.

Joran grinned. "We need each other, Selena. Why not make the best of it?" He slipped his hand into his breast pocket and withdrew a small syringe. He wagged it in front of her. "It's fresh."

Rev.

When she reached out to take the syringe, Joran held on to it. "Take this now, and it's understood you get me the information I want tomorrow night."

Selena nodded. Joran's fingers loosened. She'd have done the job regardless. She was too close to her goal to turn away such a perfect opportunity. A Hellkeeper walking into her lair? She smiled. The perfect storm, and one giant step closer to living a normal life with her daughter. For that, she would do just about anything.

Joran walked to the balcony. Over his shoulder he said, "Vegas is coming here tomorrow night for some action. Make sure he doesn't leave until you have the information." Then Joran jumped into the night.

CHAPTER FOUR

L.O.S.T. compound, location classified

Nikko did not walk into the war room, he glided. Every sense he possessed was open full throttle. His vision was as sharp as a hawk's. His hearing that of a bat. His sense of smell as acute as a wolf's. It was amazing and terrifying, and damn if he didn't like it.

He blinked back the brightness of the fluorescent lights above. The darkened flat screens that surrounded the room hummed. Natural body scents mingled with subtle soaps and deodorants. And . . .

He sniffed the air and looked toward Jax Cassidy. The only female L.O.S.T. operative and the only female in the room. She'd had sex recently. Her lover's scent still clung to her. He grinned knowingly at her. She shot him a glare. Did she know he was different now?

"How's Cross?" Nikko asked as he strode past her to his seat on the opposite side of the table.

"He's fine," she slowly said. "How are *you*?"

He sat back and folded his arms behind his head and looked at everyone in the room. "On top of the fucking world."

Godfather scowled. Stone, Satch, and Dante shook their heads.

Cassidy slowly stood, her gaze riveted on him. As

she approached, her nostrils twitched. He knew she had enhanced senses and strength. That happened when you sucked vampire blood regularly. Nikko harbored no hard feelings toward her boyfriend. In fact, while vampire Marcus Cross wasn't officially L.O.S.T., he was a huge asset to the team. Even more important, Cassidy wasn't as grumpy since she and Cross had hooked up. Apparently, vampire sex had its benefits. Images of the last time he and Selena had made love sprang into his mind's eye. He squashed them. No. He wasn't going there. She'd been a hallucination. She was dead. His powers, however, were very real.

Nikko knew how Cassidy had gotten her superhuman strength, but he was still floored by his own. How the hell had he gotten so sensitive? And strong? This morning, when opening his car door, he'd yanked it off its hinges. He'd had to ride his Harley in. Carefully.

"Who'd you bite?" Cassidy asked, her question quieting the room to dead silence.

She knew! Could she smell it? The way he could smell her? His skin frosted. Christ, had he been juiced with vampire blood? A year ago the thought would have repulsed him. Now? His body vibrated with power. It intrigued him on every level.

"Cruz," Godfather began, coming around to stand in his place at the large, round table, "what the hell happened to you out there?"

Nikko shook his head and looked straight into his commander's irritated scowl. "I was blown to hell. I woke up healed and superhuman."

"I read your report. Tell me again about the woman."

Nikko looked around at his team. Only a few of them

were there, the others being off on missions. He let out a long breath. As soon as he said her name, Godfather would have him pulled from the field and thrown into the psych ward. With the exception of Cassidy, each person in the room knew how broken he had been when they dragged him through the very same doors he had just walked through. Beaten, angry, and wanting to destroy himself. It had taken almost a year before Godfather was sure Cruz could function in the field as a L.O.S.T. operative. His first mission was to slip inside an Iranian compound and extract the kidnapped daughter of a prominent American political family. In some ways, he felt as if he'd saved his own daughter. It was the exact mission he needed. He'd never looked back. Now he felt as if his emotional seams were about to rupture. He gritted his teeth, frustrated that after all these years, despite how much he fought it, she could still hurt him. He sat up straight. She could go back to Hell where she belonged! He'd be damned if he'd let a ghost screw up his life now.

"Who was the woman?" Godfather asked again.

Nikko looked straight at his commander. "Selena Guerrero."

A collective round of gasps shivered through the room.

"Impossible," Godfather said.

Nikko shook his head and swiped his hand across his face. "I know she's dead. I *killed* her!" He shook his head again, doubting his own instincts, which screamed it was she. "Maybe it was my mind playing tricks on me. Whoever it was, was the spitting image of Selena." Grinding his jaw, Nikko could not ignore one vital fact.

"Whoever it was saved my life. She injected me with something, directly into my heart. I want to know what and why."

Godfather pressed a button and a state-of-the-art touch screen popped up before them. He tapped several apps; then a phone chirped. "Fulton County Coroner," a brisk female voice answered.

"I'd like to speak to Dr. Meade," Godfather said.

"Who may I say is calling?"

"Mr. Black."

"One moment please."

Several seconds ticked by. "Mr. Black," a deep, authoritative voice said.

"Doctor, I need a report for one Selena Guerrero, DOD June first, '03. I'll wait while you pull it up."

"One moment."

Godfather looked down at Nikko, who suddenly felt warm and not so sure of anything. A heavy sense of dread coursed through him as he waited for the coroner. *Had* he imagined her? Believing he'd seen her had pumped him up almost as much as whatever had rejuvenated him. If she was alive, she'd saved him—why? Did it matter? She had killed more than their daughter the day she aborted her. She'd killed the fire in his heart, and he in turn had extinguished hers. Or had he? He felt as if he were going to puke. His daughter, she was almost seven months! Viable! What Selena had done was morally and legally wrong. She had murdered her! He squeezed his eyes shut, unable to bear the images his mind conjured.

The ME came back on the line. "Guerrero, Selena Honorea, twenty-five-and-a-half-year-old Latina female,

DOA, cause of death, asphyxia due to strangulation. Do you want the autopsy details?"

"Who performed the autopsy?"

"Dr. Elena Mira."

"Who identified the body? And who was the body released to?"

"Roberto Montoya-Balderama on both counts."

Who the hell was that? Nikko wondered. Selena had never mentioned him. In fact, with the exception of himself, she'd shied away from the opposite sex.

"I'd like to speak with Dr. Mira," Godfather said.

"That's not possible. She passed away, almost eight years ago."

"How?"

"She seized on the way to work, lost control of her car, and crashed."

"Was an autopsy performed?"

"I performed it myself. She hadn't been taking her seizure meds."

"Don't you find that unusual for a doctor?"

"Yes. So much so I listed her death as suspicious."

"Was there an investigation?"

"Yes. It was closed and her death was listed accidental."

"Thank you, Dr. Meade." Godfather hung up before the doctor could respond. He looked at Nikko. "Do you know who Roberto Balderama is?"

"No. And Selena never mentioned him."

Godfather looked past Nikko and around the room. "Do any of you know who he is?"

There was collective head-shaking.

Godfather tapped the screen several times and typed in a few words; all around them the flat screens lit up.

A handsome Latino man flashed up. "Roberto Estefan Montoya-Balderama, head of Los Cuatro, a consortium of four heads of Latino states who in the name of preserving the Latino culture as a whole fight those who would destroy it, i.e., drug cartels and unfriendly non-Latino big business."

"Never heard of it," Cassidy said.

"That's because they don't want you to know. In their own way, they are as covert as L.O.S.T."

"What means do they employ?" Nikko asked.

"On the surface, humanitarian. Their intentions seem noble. But there has been recent evidence that they have a little terrorist in them." Godfather pressed another icon and more pictures of Balderama flashed up on the screen. Shaking hands with various heads of state, including the last three US presidents. "Too noble," Godfather mused aloud.

"How ironic then," Nikko said, trying to tamp down his anger that Selena might still be alive, "that among the Russian voices, I heard Spanish voices. And how coincidental that Selena is there in the middle of a uranium heist."

"It's not coincidence. Somehow she survived your attack, Cruz, and Balderama paid a lot of people to make it look like she had died, then killed to cover it up. I'll bet my retirement she's alive and well, and working for Balderama."

"I'll lay odds it was her trailing the convoy," Gage said.

"Damn her!" Nikko whispered. Then more loudly: "Damn her for everything!" He shot out of his chair. "I went crazy when Selena killed our daughter. For God's sake, I strangled her!" He looked around the room at the silent faces of his team. "She died, right there, by my hands." He looked down at his hands as if her blood still stained them. "There were witnesses. I was tried, found guilty, and sentenced to death. *She's dead.*"

"Look at it this way, Cruz," Godfather said. "Had you gone to jury trial, maybe the cover-up would have come out, and instead of being convicted of first-degree murder, you would have pled guilty to attempted murder."

"Because you refused a trial by jury, no one questioned any of it," Stone calmly said.

Nikko stared at the screen, then at his team. He'd killed her. Murdered the woman he loved, the one who'd destroyed a life he so wanted to be a part of. She had made it impossible for him to forgive her.

"With the kind of money Balderama has, and the pull he has in the Cuban community, he could have pulled it off, especially with there being no trial." Godfather stared at the screen and Balderama's smiling face as he kissed a chubby baby as if he were the damn pope. "But why?"

"What value would your ex have to a man like Balderama?" Cassidy asked.

Nikko shook his head, a sudden migraine erupting behind his eyes. He wanted Selena to stay dead. He could live with what he'd done, but he couldn't live with her alive after what she'd done. He inhaled a deep breath and slowly exhaled, then said, "She's half-Cuban. Her mother committed suicide the year before we met. She never spoke of her father."

"Do you know where she was born?" Godfather asked.

"Havana."

Godfather worked his magic, and in less than a minute Selena Guerrero's birth certificate sprang up on the screens. Father: Unknown. Mother: Marta Famosa.

"How did she end up with Guerrero as her last name if her mother's was Famosa?" Cassidy asked.

"*Guerrero* means 'war' in Spanish," Nikko said. "Selena was a fighter. Pissed off at the world. She was probably born with an AK in her hands."

"Could that be what drew Balderama to her?" Satriano asked.

"Maybe she's his daughter. Maybe the mother tried to keep her daughter's paternity a secret so she wouldn't have to share her with Balderama," Godfather said.

It made sense. No, it didn't. Nothing made sense.

"Balderama is half-Cuban and half-Venezuelan," Godfather said, pulling up an article about the young Latino immigrant who was touted by his peers as the César Chávez of the East Coast. "According to his bio, his mother, Alda Balderama, was a Cuban revolutionary. She died in Gitmo in the late seventies."

"And so the plot thickens," Stone said, looking up at the screens.

Godfather looked hard at Nikko. "Let's go on the assumption Guerrero is still alive. For a man of Balderama's status, there had to be a vital reason he would stick his neck out to make these arrangements. That she was in the same hunting grounds as we were in Kyrgyzstan, and assuming she was in the employ of Balderama, then I'd say she is a person of extreme interest. Most especially if she was the one trailing the cask. The bigger question is, did she get it?"

Nikko shook his head, refusing to acknowledge she might be alive. Because if she was, he was not done with her.

"What did she do to you out there?" Godfather demanded.

Nikko struggled with his answer. Not that he would not be honest with his team, but he was afraid he would sound like one of those crazies who insisted they had been abducted by aliens.

"Cruz," Cassidy softly said, "I felt like a complete idiot when I suspected Marcus was a vampire. I did not want to believe my own eyes, or my gut, because it was crazy. And you know how you all reacted. Just tell us what happened. And let us decide what to do with it."

"I was dying, for Christ's sake. Out of fucking nowhere, a woman who looked and sounded like Selena showed up. She called me Johnny. My given name. She talked as if she knew me. Jesus, I was dying! I was hallucinating. She said she'd see me in Hell, and then she stabbed me in the chest with a needle. I woke up and felt like Superman. I still do."

"Superman how?" Cassidy asked.

"I can run faster than a cheetah. My smell is so acute I can tell that you and Cross were at it hot and heavy a few hours ago." He snorted as Cassidy's cheeks pinkened.

"Fuck you, Cruz."

"I can tell each one of you has had at least one cup of coffee." He stood and grabbed his chair. "I can turn this into a perfect pretzel if I want to."

Godfather turned to Cassidy. "What's the soonest you can get Cross in here?"

"Fivish."

"I want to pick his brain on this. If this is something vampire we're dealing with, I want him in on it." Godfather turned to Nikko. "I want you to head down to medical and have the doc draw blood." He looked at the group at large. "I've got some work to do on Guerrero. We'll reconvene here and figure out how the hell we're going to locate and retrieve that cask."

"Are you insinuating Selena is a vampire?" Nikko cautiously asked, knowing she was anything but. "It was daylight when she showed up." He turned to Cassidy. "Wouldn't she have fried if she were a vampire?"

Cassidy smiled grimly. "You've seen what happens to a vampire in the sunlight."

"Exactly. She's not a vampire. I'd know, and there is no way I would have fu—" He cut the word off before he said it. But he would have known all those years ago if she was—different. Wouldn't he?

"What's your problem with vampires, Cruz?" Cassidy demanded, thrusting herself into his space.

"They're dead, for Christ's sake!"

"Don't knock Marcus for what he had no control over. He's a good man and saved your ass in Cairo less than a month ago." Cassidy stalked off toward the opposite side of the room. "Asshole," she murmured under her breath.

Stone and Dante laughed. Satch shook his head.

Nikko wanted to tell them all to get screwed. Sorry if he wasn't right with the whole having a relationship with a vampire thing.

"Let's take a break, boys and girls," Godfather said. "Cruz, I'll let the doc know you're on your way down.

I want everyone to report back here at sixteen hundred. And leave your attitudes outside."

Nikko wanted to apologize to Cassidy, not for his feelings, but for baiting her, but she exited the room before he had the chance. Damn females. He was glad they only served one purpose to him. Easy come, easy go.

CHAPTER FIVE

Nikko had been sitting in the darkened war room for almost two hours trying to sort fact from fiction.

Fact: He'd been shot in the thigh and arm. Then blown to hell by an RPG. Yet he was still alive.

Fact: He was superhero strong, with heightened senses. Hell, he had just stunned the doctor by making a pretzel out of a pair of stainless steel scissors and reading the bottom of the eye chart from one hundred feet.

Fact: He *believed* he'd seen Selena somewhere in between getting blown to Hell and coming to in Kyrgyzstan.

Only seeing Selena was the fiction part of all this, too. Because Selena was dead. He'd killed her. It haunted him every day.

None of the facts added up, yet he could not quite convince himself of the fiction either. Where the hell did that leave him?

Scared shitless that he might be turning into a vampire. The doc was trying to rule that out right now.

Vials of blood had been drawn. He had pissed in three different cups. At the doctor's insistence, he'd had every inch of his body x-rayed, as well as a full-body MRI. Not a part of him inside or out hadn't been pricked, prodded, tested, or palpated.

But he didn't need the test results to know he was

healthy. He didn't need test results to tell him he was getting stronger by the hour. Or that he felt his ice-cold control slipping. Or—God help him—that he wanted Selena alive. That he wanted to see her again. Feel her. Smell her.

He swiped his hand across his face and cursed. Selena was *dead*. He'd imagined her, that's all. Why he would have imagined her while he lay dying, he didn't want to think about.

But he had no choice but to think about the changes he'd undergone. His money, and his hopes, was on some superhuman serum the Russians had concocted. He'd just been a handy guinea pig.

Well, fuck you very much, it worked. Every part of him including his damn libido was heightened. He was walking around with a hard-on a sixteen-year-old would envy. And damn if every time he thought of Selena, it didn't get more of a rise out of him.

The door opened, and his team, followed by a stoic Godfather, walked in and settled around the table. Nikko sat up. "It appears, Cruz, we have a problem," Godfather softly said as he brought up the storyboard. "You weren't hallucinating, and thankfully you've gotten much better at killing in the last few years. Because your first attempt sucked."

Immediately, the image of Selena Guerrero popped up all around them. She looked just as she had all those years ago. A little older but, if possible, more beautiful.

Soft wolf whistles filled the quiet.

"Holy Hell, Cruz," Stone said, "she's a knockout."

Nikko's stomach dropped to the floor. Emotions he'd

long ago buried surfaced. Good ones, bad ones. Vicious, murderous ones.

"Selena Guerrero is alive and well," Godfather said. "And—" He tapped the touch screen. The zoomed-in satellite image of the motorcyclist trailing the convoy popped up. He tapped the screen again, and Nikko watched in amazement as the pixels resolved into a face.

Those eyes—God help him.

Godfather superimposed the motorcyclist's eyes over a current image of Selena. Stunned, Nikko could not deny the obvious. She *was* alive! He hadn't imagined seeing her. His longing rose up to meet his hatred. He sat forward as emotions he had forced from his heart reared up in a wild, dizzying crescendo. It couldn't be true!

Another picture popped up. This one of her strolling on the beach in a hot-pink bikini the size of a postage stamp with some linebacker-size goon walking beside her. Speechless, Nikko stared at her image. Long, silky black hair he could still feel beneath his fingertips waved in a breeze. Expressive black eyes with just a hint of a feline slant looked straight at him. His gaze dropped to her full, pouty lips.

God, he had loved kissing those lips. For hours, they would lie tangled in each other's limbs on the beach and just kiss.

He scowled hard. But she wasn't the same woman he had loved. The light that had shone in her eyes was gone. Now they were haunted and bitter. Her womanly curves were still prominent, more so since it looked as if she had lost some weight. But she was also leaner, more muscular.

She'd be even more dangerous now. Harder to kill. There was no doubt in his heart, he was going after her. And as Godfather had said, he was a whole lot better at killing now.

Nikko dragged his eyes from the screen and looked up at Godfather. "Where is she?"

"Miami." He tapped the touch pad and another round of photos flashed up on the screens. They were of Miami's Gold Coast. "She owns a club in South Beach called Lost Souls. High-end, frequented by high-end-criminal types."

"What the hell is she doing in Florida? Is she so arrogant to think she can walk around and no one would notice that I was sentenced to death for killing her?" Nikko shook his head, not understanding anything. Why had she saved him?

"She keeps a very low profile and goes by de la Roja now. There isn't much intel on her. What I have I got from running a photo-comparison search of her autopsy photo. The feds have been surveilling several Cuban cartel members in Miami. She's popped up in a few of the surveillance photos. I couldn't find anything on her connection to Balderama. But that doesn't mean I won't. What concerns me is the fact that a man like Balderama went to such lengths to make it look like she was dead, and then she shows up in our hunting grounds halfway across the world. Why was she there? Does she work for Balderama, or is she working for a cartel? But more important, was she there for the same reasons we were?" Godfather looked at Nikko, who had still not digested that his ex-lover was alive. "I find the fact that she was on-site at the same time as you more than coincidental."

Nikko jerked his head back and looked at his commander. "Are you insinuating I had something to do with her presence there?"

"Calm the Hell down, Cruz. Of course not. We were compromised in Kyrgyzstan. Then in an elaborate sleight of hand, we lost our target, and now this connection between you and de la Roja. It just doesn't add up. I want to know why she saved your sorry ass after your attempt to kill her. I want to know her intentions and just how much she knows about you and L.O.S.T. I want to know why she was after the cask of enriched uranium, and if she has it—and for whom."

"I want to know what she injected you with," Cassidy said.

"I want the same answers," Nikko said. L.O.S.T. being compromised aside, it didn't matter to him that Selena had saved his life. She had ripped out his heart and soul when she killed their daughter. He had died as much that day as his daughter had.

He sat back in his chair, his mind racing with conflicting thoughts and emotions. All these years he'd hated himself for what he had done to Selena. He had loved her completely. That she'd ripped his heart out did not change that he had murdered her in cold blood. Or so he'd thought. The grief and the self-loathing had eaten away at him. He had done nothing more than walk through the motions of life these last eight years. He ate, he drank, he slept, he worked. Sex was a release, nothing more. He had not lived. He had existed. Now everything was different. He looked up at the screens, and something deep and dark inside him lit up. Selena's smoldering sensuality reached out from beyond the grave and grabbed him.

The door buzzed. They all looked up at the monitor to the right and saw Dr. Soto standing outside. Godfather buzzed him in.

Dr. Soto glanced at Nikko before he looked at Godfather. He handed a flash drive to Godfather, who said, "Tell us in laymen's terms what's going on with Cruz."

The doctor cleared his throat and looked at Nikko again, then at Cassidy, then back to Godfather. "I don't know. I've never seen blood work come back like his."

"Like what?" Nikko demanded, coming forward in his chair. "Am I infected with something?"

"I don't know. Everything came back normal except your blood. It has compositions that I can't identify. I took draws each hour. The compositions doubled in each subsequent draw, as if building, not dissipating." Dr. Soto looked at Cassidy. "Cassidy has several of the same properties in her blood. But Cruz's has traces of others I can't even begin to guess at. I'm working on it though."

Holy shit.

"Your research will stay here on the compound, Doctor," Godfather directed. "Anything you need that you don't have here can be brought to you."

"But I can't—"

"The samples stay here," Godfather firmly said.

The doctor nodded. "Of course."

The door buzzed again. Cross on the video monitor.

Marcus Cross. Vampire or not, he was one hell of an intimidating bastard. And Cassidy's lover. Nikko swiped his hand across his chin. It was all still so damn surreal. During Cassidy's first mission, she'd told the team Cross was a vampire. They'd laughed her into the next state, then pleaded with Godfather to pull her. He'd refused. And it was a damn good thing. Cross proved to be not only a vampire but a damn good one with a human Special Ops background. The son of a bitch had nearly single-handedly saved the US of A from eternal damnation. As time passed, Nikko's initial apprehension had grown into a grudging respect. That didn't mean he was okay with the vampire thing. Even if Cassidy was. It was her life, and she seemed happy. So who was he to judge?

Godfather buzzed Cross in.

He glided into the room as if he were on a conveyor belt. Just as Nikko had earlier.

Cassidy nonchalantly nodded, but Nikko smelled her excitement. Cross was a little more cordial, grinning at Cassidy and showing sharp incisors. Stone crossed his arms over his chest, while Satch and Dante nodded their hellos. Dr. Soto did not utter a word. Godfather extended his hand. Cross took it.

"Thank you for coming in, Marcus. We seem to be out of our element here and could use your help."

Cross nodded as he proceeded into the room. Nikko caught the vampire's surprised stare. Cross's nostrils flared and his eyes narrowed as their gazes clashed. So, Cross detected Nikko's change. And apparently didn't like it. Nikko sat forward, feeling a sudden rush of power coupled with the insatiable urge to fight. Cross felt it, too. Nikko glanced around the room at his team. They sat silent but expectant, picking up on the tension. Cross strode past Nikko and took the seat next to Cassidy, casually draping his arm along the back of her chair, then looked pointedly at the doctor. Godfather quietly escorted the doc out of the room, saying he would be in touch.

Nikko let out a long, slow breath, wrangling with his potent urge to fight the vampire. Was it because he had the same blood?

Ignoring Nikko, Cross looked up at the images of Selena and narrowed his eyes, but did not say a word.

"Do you know her?" Godfather asked, dispelling some of the tension.

Cross nodded. "I've seen her in the company of one or two vampires."

Nikko's blood ran cold. "Who?"

"She runs with the Miami underworld boss, Joran Cadiz."

"How is that possible?" Cassidy asked. "I thought you guys had a handle on that kind of stuff."

Cross shook his head and said, "As in your world you have those who don't follow protocol, we have ours. Cadiz is one of them. He does just enough to look respectable, but he's got his own game. He's formidable and has the backing of many powerful vampires, as well as a host of human unsavories."

Nikko shook his head. Selena was human, not some damn bloodsucker. Rather, she had *been* human. He'd bet his life on it. Now? Fuck, now she could be anything. Maybe she'd been brought back from the grave by a vampire?

"How unsavory and who are they?" Nikko demanded. His shock aside, the only way he was going to get answers was by finding Selena, and that meant tracking her down. Starting with the undead she hung out with.

"There is proprietary information I am not at liberty to discuss. What Cadiz is and does falls under that umbrella."

Nikko stood and turned to face Cross, who postured in response. Anger washed off Nikko in waves; he struggled for control. "I'm sure your vampire code of ethics doesn't include allowing vampires or whatever the hell he is to threaten national security."

"Sit down, Cruz," Cross said levelly.

"Give us the information," Nikko bit off, stepping closer.

In the blink of an eye, Cross stood. As he did, he shoved his hand, palm open, straight at Nikko, who went flying toward the wall. Just as he was about to smash into one of the flat screens, he slowed to a stop and settled gently on his feet. Incredulous, Nikko looked at everyone in the room. Then to Cross for answers. "How'd I do that?"

Cross smirked and sat down next to Cassidy, who had not flinched. He dropped his arm across the back of her chair again and said, "You thought it. Now, before we proceed on the other matter, tell me what happened so I can identify what got you."

Nikko nodded, not sure if he really wanted to know. He sat down in a chair away from his team, then slowly and precisely explained to Cross what had happened in Kyrgyzstan.

"So she injected you with something that you think caused to you become Superman?"

"Yeah. What the hell was it?"

Cross just scowled. "How long has it been since you were injected?"

"A little more than forty-eight hours."

"And you still feel as potent as you did when you came to?"

"More so. It's like it's time-released."

Cross sniffed the air and stood. Slowly he walked toward Nikko.

Nikko didn't like the look in Cross's reddening eyes and barely stopped himself from taking a step back. "Don't fucking try to bite me," he warned.

Stone, Satch, and Dante stood and closed in. Cassidy stood, too. Godfather didn't move.

"Hold out your arm, Cruz, and man up."

When he refused, Cassidy strode across the room, grabbed Nikko's right arm, and shoved up his shirt-sleeve. "It doesn't hurt, you big baby."

Nikko steeled himself. Cross did his dirty work quickly. His fangs sank into Nikko's wrist; instantly he jerked away, spitting the blood from his mouth.

"Jesus!"

Nikko ignored the throb in his wrist. He looked down at the bite wound and the blood oozing from it. "What is it?" he demanded.

Cross swiped his hand across his lips. "It's vampire blood, but something else with it. I'm not sure. But it's potent as hell and tastes like shit."

"A mixture of substances?" Godfather asked.

Cross nodded and looked at Nikko, then up at the

screen where Selena's face still beckoned. "If she injected you, she'll know what's in it or at the very least where to get that information."

"If you had to hazard a guess, what do you think we're dealing with, Marcus?" Cassidy asked.

"Some illegal controlled substance, not of your kind," he flatly said.

Nikko knew there was more to it. Much more. "Like what, vampire steroids?" he demanded.

Cross's face had hardened to granite, and Nikko felt his seething anger. "In a word, yes."

"*Is* there such a substance?" Cassidy asked.

Cross hissed in a breath, then evenly said, "There have been attempts in the past. But it's strictly forbidden. The penalty is death for producing, distributing, or possession."

"But it's possible?" Godfather asked.

Cross nodded. "Possible, and"—he looked at Nikko—"probable."

"How do I get rid of it?" Nikko demanded.

"A transfusion might dilute it, but like my blood, once it gets into your system, it doesn't leave, it only wanes. Except it appears to be doing the opposite in you." Cross stepped closer to Nikko. "Have you had any visions or nightmares? Since you returned?"

"I haven't slept since I came to on the side of that road in Kyrgyzstan. Why?"

"Curious if you've felt the pull of a stranger. When a human receives vampire blood, regardless of how he or she received it, there is a telepathic bond with the donor."

"What if the donor is dead?" Cassidy asked.

Cross smiled down at her and smoothed away a lock

of hair from her cheek. "A very good question, love. In that case there would be no contact."

"Is it possible that someone or some*thing* is draining vampires, then killing them?"

Cross scowled. "If vampires were being drained and dying for it, there would be an uprising in a world you humans have no idea exists. However"—he strode up to the screen and tapped Selena's face—"this one attracts the type of people who have their finger on the pulse of the underworld. We start with her."

Godfather looked pointedly at Nikko. "Pack your bags, you're going to Miami." He looked at Cross. "I'd consider it a personal favor, one I will be happy to repay, if you tag along. Cassidy goes with you both."

"Of course," Cross said.

Nikko was already headed for the door.

CHAPTER SIX

After Joran's visit, Selena tried to think of anything except Johnny, her father, and the anger Señor would express when she told him of her failure to secure the cask. Always in control, now she was out of sorts, off-balance. Her office felt like a cage, the air stifling. Too much pressure. Too much to do. And save the world while you're at it. The urge to bolt and never look back had never been stronger. Her temple throbbed. She rubbed it and sat down at her desk.

She wanted the quiet sanctity of her house. Rarely did she leave the club before closing, but tonight she would instruct Amy Siedlecki, her GM, to take care of it. Selena wanted the solace of solitude and her big, comfortable bed. And sleep.

In minutes, she was at her private dock, then on her Chris-Craft motorboat motoring toward her sprawling Mediterranean manse on Star Island. The mortgage was hefty but the protection priceless. There, surrounded by water, the chance of her father or any daemon getting into her head was nil. Daemons were terrified of water; even big bad Hellkeepers avoided it at all costs. Luckily, she had not inherited that inconvenient trait from her sperm donor.

She docked and disembarked, thinking how nice it would be to have a regular dockmaster/groundsman greet her when she left for work or returned. But that was not in the cards. The fewer people she interacted with regularly, the better. It greatly reduced the chance of her father possessing someone close to her. It was why no one else knew of Marisol's existence. Paymon could not hold anyone's mind hostage for that information. Not even Selena's. While her mother had failed to keep Paymon out of her thoughts and dreams, Selena was half-daemon and possessed the knowledge and will-power to keep her mind closed to the most determined daemon.

That had kept her alive all these years, that and Paymon's being as convinced as the judge who'd sentenced Johnny to death that she was dead. Or so it had seemed. But it didn't matter if Paymon knew she lived. She was stronger now. Wiser. A seasoned killer.

Laughter bubbled from her chest. "Oh, Daddy, I can't wait to see the look on your daemon face when you realize it is your daughter who is cutting out your black heart."

Selena let herself in via the kitchen, and though she wanted nothing more than to climb into bed, she made a detour to her home office. She expected to meet *el patrón* later that day in Little Havana. He would, as he always did, expect a full report. She sighed and plopped down in her chair and turned on her laptop. He was going to be angry. While she could deal with his anger, disappointing him distressed her more. He was a good man, he trusted her, he gave her great responsibility, and she had failed him.

But she still had a chance to redeem herself by obtaining the location of the cask. She smiled as her fingertips struck the keyboard. She hadn't come home completely empty-handed.

A familiar knock disrupted Selena's focus.

The door to her office slowly opened. Selena smiled up at Jujubee.

Ten years Selena's senior, her distant cousin was the equivalent of Dracula's Renfield. Except Juju wasn't daft, deformed, or delusional. Juju was the polar opposite: smart, beautiful, and a realist who had brought Selena back from her own delusional dreams on more than one occasion. A dozen years ago, her mother's third cousin had taken a chance on a better life in America along with fifty other *cubanos* and braved the ninety-mile stretch of Atlantic between Cuba and Florida. Since her mother had welcomed Juju with open arms, so had Selena.

Juju had told Selena just after her mother's death of her dedication to and involvement with Los Cuatro. Selena had come to respect and love the cause with as much conviction as her mother had.

It was good to trust someone in a world where everyone was a potential enemy. Selena trusted Juju as she had trusted her mother. And Johnny. Once.

Juju cocked her lovely face, her dark-brown hair falling in waves around her shoulders, her milk chocolate–colored eyes snapping in aggravation. "Prepare yourself, Selena." Juju set her hands on her slender hips and looked pointedly at her. "Señor Balderama et al are docking as we speak."

Selena sat up ramrod stiff in her chair. "Here? Now? It's four o'clock in the morning!" She hadn't written her report. She hadn't slept in almost two days! She was not prepared to bear *el patrón*'s disappointment. Selena stood up and smoothed her hands down the soft wrinkles of her slinky Chanel jumpsuit. She was still wearing the same clothes from last night. Selena chanced a glance in the mirrored back of her office door.

She might feel like crap, but, thank goodness, she didn't look like it. As always, she looked pulled together. Expensive. Seductive. She dressed sexily on purpose. As the owner of Lost Souls, she projected sleek, understated elegance wrapped snugly around smoldering sensuality. Like a magnet, it attracted daemons because sex gave them power, just as being sexy fueled her flame. She dressed to thrill so that she could kill.

"Selena!" Juju snapped. "Get your head out of your ass. *El patrón* awaits!"

Selena glared at her friend, but her brain kicked into overdrive. "Send him in."

"You will not go to him?" Juju asked, her brown eyes bugging as wide as hubcaps.

Of course, Juju was right. Selena swallowed hard and walked stiffly toward the door. Obviously, *el patrón* knew of her failure, and because he was so furious, he could not wait for their meeting later that day. Instead, he had come to personally exact punishment. So be it. She would accept whatever measure of wrath he chose to mete out. After what she'd done, she deserved it. But that didn't change that she'd do it again if she had to. That's just the way Johnny affected her. He always had.

The aromatic fragrance of fine tobacco and Napoleon brandy preceded him.

Selena stepped back as she opened the front door. Ignoring the dozen blacked-out bodyguards circled around him, she forced a nervous smile. His dark eyes stared unwaveringly at her.

Roberto Estefan Montoya-Balderama, head of Los Cuatro, was of modest height but was an impressive man. Dressed in an impeccably tailored Italian suit, he carried himself as if he were royalty, his deportment quietly and clearly stating, I am all-powerful, I will not *show* you how powerful, yet if you challenge me, you will pay for it with your life.

"*Patrón*," Selena said, nodding her head in respect. She waited until he extended his hand to her.

"*Cazadora*," he said, his voice deep and reverberating.

Selena smiled easier at the term, and a small amount of tension left her, loosening her shoulders. He called her Huntress. He had saved her life the day Johnny tried to take it. He knew all her secrets but two: what she really was, and that she had a daughter. But despite their close-knit history, and her mother's work with Señor, Selena was always a little in awe of him.

"Come in," she offered, taking his hand. As he stepped across the threshold, Selena was reminded of the power this man held. He carried himself as if he were the king of the world, and as far as the Latino world was concerned, he was God. Although most Latin nations in the New World were unaware of his existence and of Los Cuatro, hundreds of thousands of their citizens lived because of his existence.

Balderama had created Los Cuatro, a quiet but powerful organization that represented the best interests of all Latin countries. It was composed of one representative from the richest country, one from the poorest country, one from the most populated country, and one from the least populated country. The Four was its own Latino UN, one that doggedly challenged the drug trade that had infected all of Latin America, and, by doing so, kept each country accountable to her people. Only because of Los Cuatro had the majority of countries not been completely overrun by the likes of Colombian drug czar Pablo Escobar and his successors.

Los Cuatro had maneuvered Escobar's ultimate surrender, then finally his death.

Los Cuatro had backed the bloody underworld war against the infestation of drug cartels in Mexico.

And Los Cuatro was quietly setting the stage to oust Venezuelan dictator Hugo Chávez.

Fate had intervened. Not only was Selena hell-bent on tracking down and taking possession of the cask, but so was Los Cuatro. Thanks to *el presidente* Chávez's fixation with nuclear weapons, she had been called upon to go to Kyrgyzstan, with a personal side trip to Russia, where she had seen to several serum extractions. Her Los Cuatro mission was clear—follow Chávez's men, who would lead her to the cask, track it to its final destination, then hijack it. But she'd failed. Now it seemed both Chávez and the daemon king still had a chance to get their hands on the goods.

Balderama was not going to like what she had to report. "Let us talk privately in my office."

As the door closed behind them, Selena said, "I'm afraid, *Señor Patrón*, I have bad news."

Balderama moved past her, sat down behind her desk, and steepled his big hands. She knew from experience his hands were firm, yet warm. His appeal didn't come from classic good looks, but more from his demeanor: powerful, yet compassionate. His skin was the lighter side of café au lait. His dark eyes carried a hint of blue, maybe from a distant European ancestor? His spicy cologne wafted around her nose; his dark brows butted together in a fierce frown. "Tell me everything. Do not leave out one detail."

Selena drew in a shallow breath and exhaled. "After nearly a week of shadowing Chávez's men, I was able to get the rendezvous information. On my way, I came across a group of five Americans, CIA I think, backed by a dozen Kyrg commandos, who were waiting for the cask seventeen miles southeast of the rendezvous location.

"I assumed their intention was the same as ours. Why, and for whom, I have no clue, but the takedown didn't happen. The trailer was loaded with armed mercs. With the help of the double-crossing Kyrgs, they took out the American contingent, then headed down the mountain and turned west toward Osh. I followed. The semi met up with a convoy. The cask was moved from the original transport into another. Still heading west, the convoy drove onto an airstrip two hours out, and into a hangar. Thirty minutes later, one trailer exited. I followed it, stopped it several miles out, and cannot tell you how royally pissed I was to find the trailer empty."

El patrón had not said one word or indicated by the slightest facial movement his feelings on the matter. "The driver?"

Selena smiled. "I have him downstairs."

Señor Balderama smiled, showing a row of strong white teeth. "Then, shall we have a chat with him?"

"I've had several since my return. He hasn't been very forthcoming, and he has a rather high pain threshold.

I've been letting him stew. I think he might be about done now." Selena walked to a black-lacquered panel on the wall next to her desk and pressed a recessed button. The panel quietly popped, then slid to the side, exposing a door. Selena opened it and turned on the light, revealing a steep stairway. "Let's go stick a fork in him."

Señor Balderama silently followed as she stepped down the concrete stairway. The door at the bottom opened to reveal a small hallway and several doors. Selena opened the first one to the right and flipped the light switch. Harsh light rained down on the lone figure sitting defiantly in a chair, his mouth covered with duct tape, his hands bound behind his back, and his legs bound at the ankles. His right arm was hooked up to an IV.

"*Patrón,* may I introduce Señor No Name, No Rank, No Serial Number. Which I suppose is irrelevant. Because I do know the important facts. From my own recon, I know this man was part of a group of Venezuelans who were engaged in the procurement of a lead cask housing reprocessed enriched uranium, which if strapped to a ton of TNT and detonated could kill or contaminate millions of innocent people. He seems to have no recollection of his nefarious activities and less of who his superiors are and how to contact them." Selena looked at the uncomfortable man tied to the chair, then to Señor Balderama. "You of all people know I am no fool. He doesn't have amnesia, he's just being stubborn. I, for one, am willing to stop playing nice and"—she tilted her head sideways, hoping her casual conversation with *el patrón* would give Señor Silencio the push he needed to cough up the information she wanted—"use more extreme measures to acquire that information."

Balderama's compassionate gaze swept the man from head to foot before focusing on Selena. She wasn't fooled, even if her guest pleaded silently with Balderama for help. *El patrón* was no fool either. Her guest just didn't know it. Yet.

El patrón looked down at the man and gave him a reassuring smile before he looked sharply over at Selena. "How hard did you work for this information? There isn't a mark on him."

Selena smiled tightly. "I prefer more subtle methods of interrogation, *Patrón*. Fists to face, tooth extraction, pistol whippings, it's all so uncivilized, no?"

Selena not only refused to touch her guests, but she didn't have to. She just had to get into their heads. But this guy had proven to be a challenge. He'd been so brainwashed with fear by Chávez's watchdogs, his mind was closed. But she had other methods.

She reached past Balderama and retrieved a long syringe from a stainless steel tray in the corner. She held it up and pushed slightly on the plunger. An arc of fluid shot up into the air. She smiled down at the gagged man, who strained at his bindings. "*Amigo,* do you know what's in this syringe?"

Vehemently he shook his head.

She bent closer and practically cooed in his face, "It's concentrated *E. coli.* Enough to kill every living organism in Caracas." His dark eyes widened. "Do you have family in Caracas?" He nodded, grunting against the tape. "I hope you said good-bye to them." Selena stuck the needle into the IV and slowly pushed the plunger. The man screamed, the sound nothing but a muffle. "The symptoms of *E. coli* poisoning present quickly." She pressed the plunger farther. "Severe cramping comes first, followed by bloody diarrhea, then vomiting. With a dosage this virulent, death will come quickly but very painfully." She reached over him and grabbed another syringe. "Do you know what I have here?"

He shook his head, beads of his perspiration flinging onto her clothes. "This is the antidote." She pressed the plunger and liquid shot into the air. "If it's administered within minutes of contamination, recovery is immediate."

She locked gazes with his. "Now. Are you ready to answer my questions and go home? Or do you wish to die here, in a foreign land?"

Her guest's body contorted against the duct tape. Selena smiled and ripped the wide strip from his mouth. "Did you say you would answer my questions?"

"*Sí*," he gushed. "Give me the antidote now!"

Selena stepped back and tsked. "No, no, *señor*. You tell me what I want to know first. If I'm satisfied, then I give it to you."

"You will bring my family here?"

When word got out he'd talked, his entire bloodline would be destroyed. "I give you my word." She meant it.

"My name is Eduardo Perez, I work for Capitán Juan Perot, who is *el presidente* Chávez's nuclear man. A deal was brokered with the Russians for the cask, but they double-crossed us!"

"Who else wants it?"

He looked at the syringe in her hand, then up at her. "I don't know."

Selena stepped back.

"I swear on my daughter's life!" he screamed. "But—I

heard talk of an auction. The Russian, Noslov, would have that information."

"Where is the cask now?"

"On its way to Russia via Kazakhstan."

"Impossible," *el patrón* scoffed.

"It's true," Perez insisted. "There are tunnels. Hundreds of miles of tunnels beneath the borders."

Selena tapped the syringe thoughtfully against her open palm. She knew about the tunnels, but the man's willingness to tell her about them meant he was probably being honest about the rest. She looked over to Balderama. "*Patrón*, do you have a question?"

"What is the name of your captain's contact?" he asked the driver.

"I don't know his name."

"How do you know he exists then?"

"I—I—for a little insurance, I followed him several times. I never got close enough to hear anything, but I was close enough that if I saw him again, I would recognize him."

"Who else knows of this?"

"No one. I swear. Only me."

El patrón reached over and took the syringe with the antidote in it from Selena. She stiffened when he pushed the plunger, sending the entire contents spewing onto the floor.

Perez screamed. "I gave you what you wanted!"

Balderama smiled tightly. "You betrayed your country. You cannot be trusted."

The doomed man looked to Selena, his eyes pleading for her intervention. She looked calmly to Balderama and said, "*Patrón*, I injected him with saline solution. It's harmless." She pointed to the empty syringe in his hand. "That was the same thing but with some food coloring."

"That is unfortunate," Balderama softly said, and stepped closer to the driver. "Once a traitor, always a traitor." In a quick, expert move, Balderama snapped Perez's neck. Selena gasped and stepped back. She had not been expecting such a vicious act. Not from this quiet diplomat. But then, had he not once told her he had seen the ugliest of what man could do to man?

"Patrón?" she breathed.

Balderama turned fiery eyes on her. "There is no room in our business to coddle traitors, on either side."

Selena stood back and nodded. He was right, of course. Too much was at stake to give a known traitor a second chance.

Balderama pressed his hand to her chin, raised it, and looked deeply into her soul. "Trust no one, *mija*. No one."

Once more, she thought of Johnny. The man who had trusted her and been sorry for it. Balderama stepped back, releasing her. "Our eyes and ears will track down this Noslov. When we have a location, I want you to approach the Russian and convince him to have his auction here."

"In Miami?"

"*Sí*, in Lost Souls. It is paramount I know who is in the market for such a deadly product. Our world is changing every day, *mija*. To protect our culture, we must broaden not only our horizons but also our borders, so to speak. And now more than ever, we must adopt a strategy American football coaches call prevent offense. We get them before they get us."

Selena nodded. She understood.

CHAPTER SEVEN

The Gold Coast at midnight had come alive. Like a living, breathing rock star high on cocaine, it pulsated with vitality and energy unlike any other.

Nikko stood across the street from Lost Souls. Scents and sounds swirled around him, blending into an indistinguishable blob. But he didn't need to be told Selena was inside. He could smell her. Exotic and sultry, her scent overrode all others. He had thought that learning she was alive, then seeing the proof positive in pictures, had elicited a strong reaction from him at the compound, but the reality of it now created an emotional maelstrom inside him. Longing, hate, and betrayal jockeyed for the top spot in his heart. Worming itself between all of those feelings was the unmitigated desire to hold her again, to make love to her—not the cold-blooded killer she was today, but the innocent girl he'd fallen in love with so long ago, before she— Nikko mentally shook himself. He allowed the hatred and his need for vengeance to take control. That would get him through this mission. Keep him sane as his body, his mind, and his soul continued to evolve into something and someone so foreign to him, he would admit only to himself that it terrified him. He was unpredictable even to himself. He battled impulses he had always had control of. His emotions raged. It was becoming unbearable, this thing inside him. He sneered, wanting to bend her to his will, to—he squeezed his eyes shut, not wanting to acknowledge the visions of his taking her until she screamed for him to stop.

No, his desire wasn't simply to fuck her again. Since his arrival in Miami that morning, a new hunger had taken root. For blood. Anyone's would do, but he craved Selena's blood most of all.

Nikko struggled for composure. He was Ice, damn it. He would not blow this mission apart. Put this team at risk. Or himself.

"You smell her?" Cross asked from Nikko's left.

While Nikko did not have the nuances of a vampire that Cross possessed, he had enough of the primal part to make him dangerous. His senses were honed, his strength impressive, and now his desire for blood was driving the vampire in him. Once he had looked at Cross as a freak, one without feelings or humanity. Now, walking in his shoes, Nikko understood what drove him as a man and a vampire and was impressed at how Cross managed to maintain his iron control. Nikko was having extreme difficulty with that.

"Yeah."

"Marcus and I will go in first and get the lay of the land," Cassidy said from Nikko's right.

He nodded, fighting the craving to get to Selena first. Get her alone. At his mercy. The things he wanted to do to her were inhuman. But hadn't what she'd done to him made *her* a monster? Nikko set his jaw. What he had done to her made him every bit as much a monster.

He had dived headfirst into love with Selena. Given her every part of him. Only to be betrayed in the most heinous way a woman could betray a man. He had reacted viciously. He had paid for it with his soul. Now his only regret was that she was still alive. How long that would continue was up to him, and he wasn't feeling particularly generous at the moment.

"Cruz, I don't like that look," Cassidy said, staring up at him, her face wrinkled in consternation. "Plot your revenge later. *After* we get what we came for."

Nikko set his jaw. His revenge would be slow, methodical—

"Cruz, if you give in to the bloodlust, it will destroy you," Cross quietly said. "It's like a drug. If you don't control it, it will control you."

Nikko closed his eyes and only saw red. "I just want to tear her apart."

Cassidy touched his hand. He looked down into her serious but compassionate eyes. "I know you do, Nikko. I don't blame you. But if you can't get a handle on your emotions, millions of lives could be on the chopping block."

Nikko exhaled. Cassidy was right. This mission was bigger, much bigger than his hatred for the woman who owned Lost Souls.

He calmed himself. "Go ahead," he softly said. Nikko scowled when Cassidy looked up at Cross in a way that would melt a man's heart. A blind man could see they were hot for each other and so in sync nothing could sever the bond. Nikko's scowl deepened as he watched them, hand in hand and dressed to the nines, stride across the busy street, past the triple-deep line that wrapped around the corner of the building, to the two defensive-lineman-size goons at the door. Cross leaned into the closest one and touched him on the shoulder. Magically the bouncer stepped aside and the doors opened. They were in.

"This place is hopping," Cross said, his voice loud and clear in Nikko's earpiece.

"It's crawling with half of the FBI's most wanted," Cassidy added.

"Any sign of Guerrero?"

"Give us a minute, Cruz," Cassidy snapped.

Haltering his urge to get inside, Nikko paced back and forth along the sidewalk as Cross and Cassidy scouted the club and got a lock on Selena. Nikko's gaze never wavered from the club entrance as he paced, trying to restrain his impulse to blow by the bouncers and find Selena himself, and then . . . He wondered if he could do that mind-meld thing Cross had done to the bouncers.

Nikko crossed the street, striding straight toward the studded, double brass doors and the two goons standing sentry. Selena's scent intensified. It hit him so hard, his blood raged through his veins. His heart pounded in his ears. He lifted his nose and inhaled.

She was not alone.

His focus shifted.

A heavy male scent swirled possessively around hers. Testosterone-laden pheromones tangled with her estrogen. Selena Guerrero had come a long way in eight years. Red clouded his vision. The L.O.S.T. operative in him told him he was overreacting, that he was putting his team in peril by going in now. The grieving father and broken lover in him told him the only way to heal was to destroy that which had destroyed him. The arrogant vampire blood that raged within told him he could do whatever the hell he wanted.

Nikko strode toward the door. The goons stepped into his path. Nikko shook his head in warning. When they didn't back off, he shoved them aside as if they were two-year-olds and grabbed the curved brass door handle so hard he felt the screws loosen.

When he stepped across the threshold, Nikko felt as if he had stepped into another realm. One not of the human world. Energy sparked dark and dangerous. Pungent scents swirled around him. Hearts beat at different tempos—some languorous, others quick and jittery, while those of the humans beat a steady, rich cadence. The multistory club was dark, with just enough strategic lighting to cast a sensual glow. The air was thick with sultry body heat, both human and . . . not. The tension in Nikko's body amplified. Selena's scent had intensified to critical mass. She was close. Close enough to touch.

Two goons approached him. Another two came up fast behind them. Nikko stood his ground, refusing to back down but determined not to make a scene.

"Tell Miss de la Roja, Johnny is here to see her," Nikko said as they circled him. Their arrogance wafted around him. He stared down the biggest one of the four. "Now."

The bouncer turned on his heel and strode deep onto the dance floor.

"He's with us," Cross said from behind Nikko.

The remaining three bouncers looked surprised, but nodded and left them alone.

"You okay, Cruz?" Cassidy asked, coming around to stand in front of him.

Nikko shook his head. "I'm having trouble controlling the primal parts of me."

"Your body is accepting the vampire blood injected into you, Cruz," Cross said. "Your human will is weak compared to your vampire will. The vampire in you intensifies the primal human. It can be euphoric when both have a common agenda. It's hell when they polarize. Especially when the blood comes from a dominant donor."

"What's that supposed to mean?"

"I'm going to hazard a guess and say your blood, or most of it, came from an ancient, one who as a human had self-control issues. It's not uncommon for a host body to assume some or all of the donor's characteristics. Good and bad."

Cassidy snorted. "That explains a lot." She looked up at Cross and winked. Despite the tenseness of their situation, he cracked a smile.

"You need to find a way to control your temper, and your impulses, Cruz, or it'll get one of us killed. And I'm not feeling much like dying again."

"Nikko," Cassidy said. "Let me make contact with Guerrero."

Nikko inhaled deep into his lungs, then slowly exhaled. "I can do this. I know Selena and what buttons to push. I'll get what we came for."

"Be careful she doesn't push *your* buttons, Nikko," Cassidy warned.

"She's dead to me," he said, and wondered if they believed him.

"We'll be along the perimeter. Keep us updated with your position and what's going on around you," Cassidy instructed before she walked off hand in hand with Cross.

Nikko closed his eyes and inhaled. Selena was close. Her scent swirled all around him. He turned toward the dance floor and opened his eyes. His heart shuddered to a stop. Stunned, he could only stare, not believing his eyes.

She stood across the dance floor at the rail of the sweeping stairway that rounded three floors up, staring straight at him. She *was* alive. A living, breathing entity. No more than twenty feet from where he stood. And she looked—he swallowed hard, trying to ease the rapid staccato of his heartbeat—fucking amazing. She was all woman; not one vestige of the girl he had fallen in love with remained. Blood coursed through him. Hot, thick, potent.

She wasn't alone. A brawny *cubano* stood behind her, his lips pressed against the curve of her throat. His hands slipped around her waist, his big fingers splayed across the curve of her hips. He pulled her back against him.

Rage flared white-hot in Nikko's belly. Selena's gaze never wavered, even as her lover's lips traveled down her throat. Her eyes closed halfway and her lips parted. Her nostrils flared and her nipples tightened beneath the translucent white sheath dress she wore. It hugged her curves like a second skin.

Nikko's gaze dropped from her tits to her taut belly, then lower to the smooth swell of her pussy. He snarled, his rage intensifying, his vision blurring red. Slowly his gaze rose back to hers. A small smile curved her lips, and if lightning had struck him, Nikko would have felt no more of an electric jolt. He wanted her with an intensity that burned.

As much as he wanted her, he also realized she was playing him. Did she think that, after what she'd done, he had a jealous bone in his body? Her lover's hand cupped her possessively. His reaction to another man's touching her infuriated him. He didn't care who touched her!

"I'm going to fuck you tonight," Nikko mouthed. As

the words escaped, his cock thickened to painful. By all that was holy, he *was* going to fuck her.

Her big, feline eyes widened at his audacious statement. He smiled slowly. Yeah, if anyone was going to fuck Selena Guerrero tonight, it was going to be him. And then he was going to demand she tell him where that cask was, whom she worked for, and what the hell she had injected him with.

Nikko's legs propelled him forward, through the wild mass of slick, undulating bodies. As if he were Moses, the crowd parted. He stopped a foot from her. She stood above him on the catwalk. His gaze swept up from her perfectly manicured toes, peeking out of what he guessed were ridiculously expensive designer stilettos, up her smooth calves to her knees, then higher to her thighs the material did nothing to hide, only accentuated. Yeah, she had changed. The Selena he'd fallen in love with would never have dressed so provocatively. She sure as hell would not have allowed a man to grope her in public as she was allowing the gangster behind her to do now.

Nikko's nostrils flared. He could smell her hot, spicy sex. He watched in fascination as her body lengthened and tightened before his eyes. Emotions he had long ago forgotten surfaced and pounded in his chest. God, how he had loved to touch her soft skin. Feel her small hand in his. Hear her laugh at his corny jokes. She'd brought out the best he had to give. He'd loved her with every part of him. His chest tightened until he could barely breathe. Her eyes deepened to onyx, just as they always did before they made love. . . . Nikko swallowed hard and allowed the anger to surface. It had all been a lie!

How dare she stand before him seducing him as another man touched her! His heart demanded retribution, but his body wanted something else entirely. His cock ached so painfully he knew of only one way to ease it.

"Cruz," Cassidy sharply said in his earpiece. "Don't do it!"

He pulled the button mic from his shirt.

"Damn it!" she yelled. "We need that information!"

He took the small earpiece out and slid it in his trouser pocket. He'd get the information. But he wanted something else first.

He maneuvered his way up the crowded stairway, stepped behind Selena and, subtly to bystanders but anything but to the recipient, nudged her Latin lothario down the stairway. A handful of men emerged from the shadows, ready to take Nikko to task. He stared each one down.

Just as her lover had done, Nikko slid his arm around Selena's waist. All Nikko, he spun her around and pulled her hard against his chest. His arm clamped around her slender waist; she didn't resist. Just the opposite. She moved into him, as if she had some right to him.

"Johnny," she breathed. "You found me." Running her hands up his chest, standing on her toes, Selena pressed intimately against him. He stiffened as warning bells sounded. What the hell was her game? Why all sweet and sexy when they both knew what kind of woman she really was? Her tits drilled into his chest, her hips into his hard-on. He resisted her lure. And the way her curves pressed tormentingly into his skin, lighting him on fire.

"Johnny's dead," he ground out. "You killed him." He felt her heart stutter a beat.

He could hear the fast rush of her blood as it pumped frantically through her body. His own heart thudded wildly in his chest. His hands twitched. Here she was, in his arms, when all this time he'd thought he had killed her. He didn't know how to process any of it—laugh, cry, or tear her apart. The anger was easier to deal with. It kept him from doing something stupid.

Her big eyes stared back at him in an odd sense of wonder. She didn't argue or defend herself, just took his rage as if she knew she had it coming. Of course she did!

She'd murdered his daughter! She had it coming and then some.

Her lover shoved his way back up the stairway toward them. Nikko pushed Selena behind his back and faced the murderous man. *"La señorita no te quieres,"* he said.

The woman does not want you. The man's eyes blazed furiously.

"Armadeo," Selena said, stepping from behind Nikko. "I have a bit of unexpected business to attend to."

"I'm your only business tonight." Armadeo snapped his fingers and pointed to the spot next to him. "You, here, now."

Selena laughed low, the sound seductive. "Oh, Madeo, now you push too far. I choose who I conduct business with and when, not the other way around." Her gaze hardened. "Now, agree to my terms or we are concluded for the evening."

His face contorted in rage, but he said, "Five minutes."

"You will not regret it," Selena said, and strode away from them both.

Nikko went after her. Catching up to Selena, he grabbed her wrist. Once again, the contact was electric. He gritted his teeth, afraid he might not be able to control what he wanted to do to her before he got the answers he'd come for. "Somewhere private," he growled, releasing her. Contact only instigated his bloodlust.

She calmly contemplated his order with hooded eyes, then turned and led him to a door behind the DJ booth. As she closed it behind them, she pressed a hidden button beside the doorjamb. A door slid open on the adjacent wall, leading to a stairway. Selena preceded him. Warily, he followed her to the third floor, not once taking his eyes off the subtle sway of her hips. But it was her scent that drew him like a lovesick teenager.

Jesus. Her fucking scent. A siren's call. It clamped unrelentingly around his head and his cock. As they topped the stairwell, she opened a door to a small vestibule from which another door opened into a large octagonal shaped anteroom.

"My office," she said, extending her hand to a single-panel black door at the other end.

Nikko was stretched as tight as he could go without snapping. His human part and the vampire blood wanted the same thing: primal satisfaction. He followed Selena into the office and slammed the door shut behind them. Startled, Selena whirled around and faced him.

Her stormy dark eyes stared up at him in shock, and something else. She was in as much turmoil as he. But she was not afraid of him. And that pissed him off. She should be. "Why didn't *you* die, damn it!"

"Johnny," she said, her voice clogged with emotion.

"Don't fucking *Johnny* me! You killed my daughter!"

"No," she gasped. "I—"

"*Don't* lie to me." He yanked her to him, wanting to ease

his pain by hurting her. His lips swooped down on hers, gnashing teeth against teeth. And she took it. Her scent intensified with her body heat. "Bitch," he hissed, and bit her bottom lip. The taste of her blood incited his raging libido to terrifying heights. He ripped her dress down to her waist. Her smooth caramel-colored breasts popped out, the dark areolas pebbled, her nipples so hard they looked like little beads. Voraciously, Nikko laved one, then sucked it against the roof of his mouth. Selena gasped. Grasping his shoulders, she arched into him.

Her response only added fuel to his fury. What was her game? Did she think all was forgiven? He growled, pushing her against the edge of her desk. "Why did you let me think I killed you?" he demanded, shaking her. At her failure to respond, he clamped both hands around her neck. "I hated myself for what I did to you. I hated that I killed you!" His thumbs rubbed up and down her throat. "I loved you!" he shouted, tightening his grip. "You destroyed it."

Her eyes glistened with unshed tears. God! He wanted the pain to end! But he would not be like her again and kill the thing he loved above all others. And God help him, he still loved her.

"Johnny," she rasped, placing her hands on his.

"Don't," he roughly said. "Don't try to justify any of it." His hands slid from her neck to her breasts. He cupped them tightly before he slid his hands to her waist. He yanked her against him, so that her legs straddled his thigh. Her dark eyes sparkled and her full, red lips parted expectantly. Her nostrils flared, her instincts dead to rights. He was the predator, she the prey. Her heart beat like a thousand drums against his chest. He did not have to like her to want her. He did not have to forgive her either. His blood scorched his veins. Every cell burned for her.

He could take her, right this moment, and she would not stop him. He slid a hand up the curve of her back to her shoulders and into her scalp. He fisted a hank of her hair and pulled her head back so that her body arched into him, her tantalizing breasts smashed against him, her long, smooth neck fully exposed.

"You have created a monster, Selena," he breathed as he lowered his lips to her jugular. "A monster with an insatiable appetite for you."

He laved his teeth down the thick artery, drawing blood. Selena trembled in his arms, but she did not fight him. Indeed, her skin warmed and her sex scent blossomed. His eyes widened in surprise. The taste of her was like a shot of adrenaline. He pressed his lips to the bite and took more.

Lightning flashed in his head, his heart, his dick. Nikko closed his eyes and experienced a sublimity he could not describe. Her blood infused him with power, energy, and a hunger so ravenous he feared he would lose all control.

"You no longer have control over me, Johnny," Selena breathlessly said.

He laughed softly against her sultry skin. "I have control over your body." He thumbed a hard nipple. Her back arched to breaking. He pressed his thigh more firmly between her thighs and rubbed. She moaned. "You're wet for me."

She dug her nails into his shoulders. Nikko closed his eyes and slowly counted to ten. He wanted her on her back and him buried inside her to the root. But he knew if he went there, he'd be back for more—

He licked the wounds he had inflicted, the vampire wanting more blood, the human fighting hard to resist. She shivered and moaned. He cupped her bare breasts, his dick so damn hard for her he was on the verge of giving them both what they wanted.

"What were you doing in Kyrgyzstan?" he demanded against her throat.

"Visiting relatives," she breathlessly answered.

"Liar." He nipped her neck and squeezed her breasts just short of hurting her.

She moaned, arching against him.

"What did you inject me with?"

"I didn't inject you with anything," she rasped.

Nikko yanked her hard against his erection and stared her straight in the eye. "Tell me what I want to know, or so help me God, Selena, I'm going to fuck the answers out of you."

Her lush lips parted. The tip of her tongue licked her top lip. Every ounce of blood in his body shot straight to his dick. "I dare you to try."

It took every bit of willpower Nikko possessed not to throw her across her desk and take what he wanted from her. With more than a little regret, he released her and stepped back. "I'm not here to play games with you, Selena. I came for answers. I'm not leaving without them."

She pulled the torn fabric of her dress up and hopped off the edge of her desk. "Then make yourself at home— you're going to be here awhile."

He grabbed her arm as she moved past him and pulled her around to face him. "Really, Selena? Is that how it's going to be? You fuck up my life and go on your merry way, I miraculously come back, and you can't give me the fucking time of day?"

She yanked her arm from his grasp. "I've moved on, Johnny. You should try it."

He clenched his jaw. "I have. Now answer me. Why were you in Kyrgyzstan? How are you affiliated with Roberto Balderama, and what the hell did you inject me with?"

Selena let out a long breath. "I was in Kyrgyzstan on business that is none of your business. Señor Balderama was a dear friend of my late mother, we keep in touch. And what I injected you with?" She shrugged. "If I told you, I'd have to kill you, and that would defeat the purpose, wouldn't it?"

"Why were you following the trailer?"

She strode over to the door and opened it. "I've told you all I'm going to tell you. I have work to do, please leave."

Nikko strode to the door and put his hand over hers on the knob. "We're not even close to being done, Selena." Jealousy tore through him when he thought of her with Madeo. "Go fuck your Cuban. Make sure you wash his stench off before you come back downstairs. I'll be waiting for you."

He slammed the door shut behind him.

CHAPTER EIGHT

Selena's knees wavered beneath her. She steadied herself against the closed door. Every inch of her—body, heart, and soul—screamed for succor. Succor only Johnny could give her.

What had just happened? One minute she'd been lulling Armadeo into believing he'd get lucky, and the next minute her past in the form of Johnny Cicone came bursting into her present with a vengeance. Old wounds had been ripped open, and she was bleeding from the inside out. He still had the power to make her knees weak. Cause her heart to ache.

He looked good. Too good. The first time she laid eyes on him ten years ago, it was the sparkle in his crystal blue eyes and his easy smile that had caught her attention. If she had met him for the first time tonight, his dark, dangerous looks would have lured her. His jet-black hair, smoldering blue eyes, and sinful lips aside, it was the way he moved, arrogant, sleek, sure, pantherlike, that turned heads. There was nothing weak or unsure about the man. Everything about him was extreme.

And it was going to be extremely difficult to maintain her composure when he was near. Selena pushed her long hair from her eyes. She'd survived the past eight years because she'd had purpose, but everything was different now. Johnny knew she was alive, knew she was after the cask, and knew she had injected him with something illegal. He wasn't going to go away until he had his answers. If he stayed, they would both be vulnerable not just to each other, but to her father. It was why she had been so cold at the end of their encounter. For her sake, but for Johnny's, too.

Dear God, where had he come from? Whom did he work for? How had he found her? And, *Dios míos*, he had changed. He was not the man she had known. But did she really think he would be? Not only had what seemed like a lifetime passed, but the Rev she'd injected Johnny with had worked, and then some. If she had just met him, she'd swear he was a full-blown vampire, albeit a new one. He was having control issues. Not only had he yet to learn how to manipulate his new abilities, but the shot of Rev didn't seem to have run its course of a few days as it did with her. Was it because her half-daemon metabolism was faster?

Rev was not created for humans. Joran had created it to revive dying vampires. In her case, it was like a prolonged shot of adrenaline with healing properties. Giving it to Johnny had saved his human life, but at what cost?

She rubbed her fingertips against her sore neck. He had broken her skin and tasted her blood while he ravaged her. Her skin warmed. She closed her eyes and recalled his touch. How she was on the verge of begging him for more. No one made her feel so alive, so wanton, so—

Her eyes flashed open. How had she allowed herself to be so vulnerable? And dear God, why?

But she already knew why. It had been the daemon

part of her. Even Madeo drew a certain amount of desire from her with his touch. It was the nature of her beast. But only Johnny inflamed every inch of her. She had not been able to control it all those years ago, and she could not control it now.

It was why she had resorted to such extreme measures to drive him away from her in the first place. She didn't have the strength to stay away from Johnny, so she had forced him to make the break. She'd made him believe she'd killed their child. Made him hate her. The primal vampire in him wanted her now, but his human hatred would keep him away from her.

It was what had saved his life long before she'd saved it in Kyrgyzstan.

She slowly pushed away from the door. If she had to do it all over again, she would. Their daughter was safe. Johnny was safe, and she had the tools and skills to destroy the being who would take it all away in a heartbeat.

Absently, Selena stroked the stones around her neck. No help there. Her response to Johnny had been instantaneous combustion. While she wanted to blame it all on her daemon half, her human female heart had broken a thousand times when she saw him. Had yearned for him. Had reveled in his passion, regardless of what drove it.

Next time she would call upon the power of the nanorians to resist him.

Next time?

She shook her head. There could be no next time. She'd be damned if she'd meet him. His threats to shut her down meant nothing. He had no idea who she was or the power she held over half of Miami's most influential men and women. She knew their dirty little secrets, secrets they would kill to protect. If she had to, she'd use her power to keep Johnny away.

With her resolve firmly in place, Selena pulled the vestiges of her thoughts and her $2,000 Versace sheath up over her tender breasts and hurried into her private rooms to change. She had work to do, and her window of opportunity was quickly closing.

As Nikko strode down the hidden stairway, he reinserted his earpiece and mic.

"I'm wired," he said, stepping into the club.

"Cruz!" Cassidy's voice blared into his eardrum. "You fucking moron! What did you do?"

"Got a little payback." Being with Selena had only whetted his appetite for more. It pissed him off, his inhuman need for her body. So did his human need for the same.

He'd known it would be painful to come face-to-face with her again. What he had not expected was the catastrophic collision of emotions, all of the love, suffering, and longing that came crashing down on his resolve, his confidence, and his heart all over again. She was alive! He still could not believe it.

But his encounter with Selena had proven fruitful by what she refused to tell him. She had vital information. He was hell-bent on getting it. By whatever means necessary.

He scanned the perimeter and caught sight of

Cassidy and Cross standing one floor up. As he turned to approach them, Armadeo stepped in front of him, flanked by four of his soldiers.

Nikko slowed and gauged them. He could take them, wanted to beat the sawed-off runt of a man to a pulp. But he wasn't going to. Regardless of who ran it, Lost Souls served an important role. It was a haven for criminals at the top of the food chain, and it was a hot spot of underground information. Hell, probably enough power and money were in the club to stage a successful coup in most countries around the world. What better place to pick brains, throw around some serious cash, and find out who had an unexpected inventory of enriched uranium?

"You will pay for what you just did with your life," Armadeo hissed as he approached.

"That's Armadeo Vegas, aka *el carnicero,*" Cassidy said in Nikko's earpiece.

The butcher.

"Cuban kingpin Luis Fernandez's captain and numero uno assassin. Known for his penchant for carving his victims—alive—and delivering their body parts in white butcher paper to the victim's friends, family, and business associates."

"Got it," Nikko said.

Vegas's eyes burned a preternatural red. It didn't faze Nikko. After that encounter with Selena, nothing fazed him. He strode straight toward Vegas. "We can take this outside, *señor,* or if you want to ruin the lady's reputation for running a clean club, we can take care of business right here." Nikko stopped less than two feet from him.

Vegas twitched anxiously. He obviously wasn't used to

anyone taking up his personal space. Especially with his goons so close.

Nikko stepped closer.

"Outside," Vegas said, striding past Nikko, slamming into his shoulder.

"We're right behind you," Cassidy said.

As they approached the main front doors, Selena materialized out of thin air, stopping all of them in their tracks. Nikko's body instantly responded to her. His heightened sense of hearing picked up the quickened rush of her blood. She was just as aware of him.

Emotionally, he might despise what she had done, but as a man, he admired everything about her. He'd wreaked enough havoc on her white dress that she'd changed into a black two-piece sarong number. The slinky material was nothing but a thin haze of gossamer. The way it shadowed her curves and valleys played with a man's imagination. One thing he didn't imagine was her nipples puckering under his heated gaze.

"Madeo," she purred, slipping between Nikko and the gangster. Her exotic, spicy scent wafted across Nikko's nostrils. He fisted his hands, forcing the heat in his blood to cool. "My apologies for deserting you, but I had urgent business to attend to. Now," she seductively said, leaning into him, "I am all yours." As she rubbed against the man, Selena deliberately locked gazes with Nikko, the taunt in her eyes clear. She took Madeo's hand and placed it around her waist. "Let's make this a private party."

Madeo yanked her possessively to him. "Don't make me wait again."

"Oh," she huskily purred, "I won't."

Heat spread like wildfire through every cell in Nikko's body. The urge to rip her out of the man's arms was so overwhelming, his muscles hurt.

He shouldn't care that another man touched her. She was dead to him. Yet the sight of Vegas's hand on the small of her back disturbed him viscerally. He took a step toward them.

Selena swept past Nikko and Vegas's goons to a set of brass elevator doors. The same type of brass doors that opened to the anteroom to her office. The doors opened and closed behind Selena and Madeo.

Nikko headed for the hidden stairway leading to Selena's office.

"Nikko?" Cassidy's voice called over the mic. "You okay?"

The compassion in her voice stopped him. "I'm fine. Behind the DJ's booth is a door that leads to a hidden stairway, which leads to the third-floor office. That's where she's headed. Stand by," Nikko said into his mic. "I'm going to play a fly on the wall."

As the elevator door closed behind them, Vegas grabbed Selena and whirled her around. Under any other circumstances, she would break a man's arm for touching her so rudely. She curbed her instinct to put him in his place. The assassin was too valuable to her to allow pride to interfere.

Selena threw her head back and laughed seductively, grabbing his hand and pulling him toward the back of the elevator. "Are you jealous, Madeo?"

He scowled, and her laugh deepened.

"I like my men jealous."

Vegas maneuvered her into the corner of the elevator and braced his hands on the wall on either side of her head. "You push me to my limit, *tentadora*."

Selena was an expert when it came to letting a man think he had control of her. She smiled seductively at his tense face, running her hands up his chest. His body stiffened. The elevator doors opened. "*Vamos, señor.*"

She slid her hand into his and led him into the anteroom outside her office and private rooms. The large, octagonal room was soundproof, the smooth granite floors easy to clean. Tucked safely in a hidden sheath in the wall to her right were her swords. Tonight would not be the first time she had used the anteroom as her kill room. It would be the first time she extracted a nanorian here.

Armadeo's heart rate had climbed with his excitement. With it, she got her first whiff of Hellkeeper. She turned and smiled alluringly as she backed toward her swords. "What would you like me to do to you?"

The Hellkeeper stench intensified. She could feel sorry for Madeo, being possessed and not knowing it, if he were not as twisted as the daemon who drove him. "The question is not what you can do to me, Selena," Vegas purred as he slowly stalked her, "but what do I plan to do to you."

Ah, another sadistic bastard. Why wasn't she surprised? Vegas was among the worst of the worst. His kind fed on the pain he inflicted on others. It was why she had not initially been able to detect the stench of the Hellkeeper reigning supreme inside him. The two were so much alike their odors blended, but tonight the

Hellkeeper was in full control and his stench now permeated the room.

Selena reached behind to the small of her back and withdrew a black-pearl-handled switchblade from its satin sheath. "Let me guess . . . ?" she said, showing him what she held. She pressed the small switch, and the six-inch blade flicked open with a warning click.

"Yesssss," Vegas said, slowing his approach. His excitement was evident in the glassy shine of his eyes, and the sheen of sweat that broke out across his upper lip. His burgeoning erection was hard to miss. He slid his hand behind him and slowly withdrew an impressive butcher's knife.

Selena's blood warmed. "Ah, just like the Boy Scouts, you're always prepared." She flipped the blade in her hand over and caught it by its razor-sharp tip. "I was a stellar Girl Scout."

Nikko watched, fascinated, from his vantage point behind the door he'd cracked open at the top of the stairway. What the hell was Selena doing? Playing a deadly game of chicken? He watched her move around Vegas with the grace of a ninja. He ignored his initial instinct to protect her when Vegas pulled his blade. Something in the way Selena held herself, the way she handled the switchblade, held him back. Lightning quick, she stabbed the thug in the thigh.

Nikko flinched, her strike surprising him.

Vegas grunted, taking a swipe at her but missing by a foot. She was already on the other side of the room.

Circling . . . With panther grace, she stepped around Vegas, taunting him with words. She stuck him again. Vegas swiped at her in a wide arc. Selena jumped back as his blade barely missed slicing her belly open.

"Close, *señor,* but not"—she lunged, jabbing him in the arm that held the knife, and withdrew—"close enough." Vegas's eyes turned murderous red. He was bleeding from three different wounds.

Transfixed by what was playing out before him, Nikko realized his jaw hung open. Cassidy and Cross needed in on this, but he knew if he uttered a single word, Selena would know she had an audience. It would throw her off-balance—potentially get her hurt. Nikko shook his head in silent awe. Vegas was in big trouble.

"*Punta!* I'm bleeding to death!" Enraged, Vegas lunged at Selena, his blade finding flesh this time. He got her on the waist. She turned with a roundhouse kick, sending him sprawling on his back. She jabbed him in the thigh. Higher this time and deeper than the first strike.

The assassin bellowed in pain.

"Cruz," Cassidy's voice called in his earpiece, "what the hell was that?"

Nikko couldn't respond, so gingerly he tapped out in Morse code on his mic to stand by and listen to what was going down.

"Copy," Cassidy whispered.

"Oh, c'mon, Madeo, I just nicked your femoral artery." Selena tossed the bloody knife in her hand, expertly catching it by the handle. "I could have severed it."

Vegas dropped his knife and grabbed at his thigh, frantically trying to stem the steady blood flow.

"Relaaax," she crooned, "you have some time. Instead of five minutes to bleed out, I'd say you have a good ten or fifteen."

"*Punta!*" he hissed.

"I can save you, Madeo. But it will cost you."

He glared at her. "What do you want?" His voice had deepened.

The hair on the back of Nikko's neck stood straight up. *What the hell was that?*

Selena continued to walk slowly around Vegas, taking her time, making him squirm. "Actually, I don't want anything from you, I just want that dirty Hellkeeper hiding inside of you to come out and play."

Madeo's skin blanched white. He dropped to his knees, slipping in the pooling blood at his feet. "*What?*" he gasped.

"You're possessed, Madeo," she explained matter-of-factly. "The only way to unpossess you is for the daemon who is too cowardly to show himself to leave your human body. Because if you bleed out, your imminent death will force his hand. You die, he dies. Unless—"

"You would challenge Hell!" a voice blasted from Vegas, the force of the breath so harsh Selena's hair flew backward and the door Nikko hid behind slammed shut.

What the Hell is that? What is a Hellkeeper? Can Selena handle it? Confused and a little intimidated by what he did not understand, Nikko carefully opened the door. The scent of sulfur permeated the air. Nikko covered his nose, it was so repulsive. His eyes, though, were riveted on Selena.

The woman had balls. She didn't appear fazed in the least by this new threat. She moved behind Vegas, grabbed a hank of his hair, pulled his head back, and stuck him in the neck.

He screamed, trying to twist out of her grip. She dropped him as if he were on fire and nimbly stepped back. The screams morphed into deep demonic growls.

"I challenge Hell, Malphas. Now, I challenge you to show yourself," Selena said as she continued to move around Vegas.

Nikko's heart beat like a drum in his chest. What the hell was going on here? Daemons, Hellkeepers. Selena challenging one to a fight? *What the fuck?* Nikko tapped on his mic.

"Welcome to my world, Cruz," Cross softly said in Nikko's earpiece. "Hellkeepers are powerful daemons who possess potent magic. From what I've just heard, I suspect your Selena is the rogue daemon hunter the Order has put a sizable bounty on."

Fuck, Nikko silently mouthed, not fully comprehending what Cross's words meant.

Vegas collapsed onto the floor, the pool of blood widening around him.

"You would take a human life to draw me out?!" the daemon voice blasted.

Selena shrugged. "It won't be the first time. Besides, it's not much of a human life."

Her calm demeanor amazed Nikko. He suspected when that thing came out, it was going to be nasty and she'd need help.

"Selena!" Vegas cried, dragging himself toward her.

His hands reached toward her, his bloody fingers scraping her toes. "Save me! I will give you anything!"

She contemplated him for a long moment, and with each heartbeat more blood pooled on the floor. "You have nothing worth saving, Vegas."

"You will burn in the fifth Hell for this!" the Hellkeeper roared.

"I doubt it," Selena calmly said. "Show yourself, Malphas. You have something I want."

"Your girl has some balls, Cruz, and she's going to need them," Cross whispered in his earpiece. "Malphas is the Keeper of the Fifth Hell."

Keeper of Hell? Daemon hunter? How could Selena, a mere mortal woman, possibly have the power to kill something so powerful?

"No mortal can match a Hellkeeper without some serious assistance," Cross said.

Selena turned and reached into a hidden sheath on the wall behind her and withdrew two silver swords. The serious assistance?

She stood above Vegas, who had stilled as the blood around him grew in diameter. "Show yourself, Malphas!" she commanded. "Or die forever locked inside a mortal!"

Deep, demonic laughter shook the room. Selena smiled triumphantly as vapor snaked out of Vegas's gaping mouth. Nikko watched, too stunned to move as the tip of the vapor began to take shape.

"The daemon will emerge as a vapor," Cross said, "then materialize into its natural form, probably some type of animal."

The vapor formed a large beak, then the head of a bird.

"A bird," Nikko whispered.

"A raven," Cross clarified. "To destroy it, she'll need to remove its heart."

Selena stood close, her swords at the ready. When the head was fully formed, she hacked it off the body that began to take shape beneath it. The daemon roared. A minute later, hacked-up bird parts littered the marble floor.

"Where is the uranium cask?" she demanded.

Nikko's head snapped back. If his heart rate had not been elevated before, it was now. He heard Cassidy's sharp gasp.

The yellow beak opened and hissed vapor at Selena. She covered her eyes and stepped back. The wings reattached to the body. "Ask Vegas!" Malphas taunted.

Selena dragged Vegas's body away from the raven. She pulled off her slinky top and quickly wrapped it above his thigh where she had stuck his vital artery and formed a tourniquet.

Nikko swallowed hard. She was bare-chested and—damn, she turned with those swords in her hands, her hips swaying, her back straight, her breasts sitting up so firm and high—

The bird's torso flew at her. She hacked it in half, then dug the black eyes out of the head. "You are so not worthy, Malphas," she gritted as she twirled her swords like batons; then with the precision of a surgeon, she cut the shape of a pentagram in the center of the feathered chest. The daemon screamed. "You are a discredit to all daemons!"

"We need that information," Cassidy hissed.

Selena set a sword aside and reached into the daemon's chest. As she did, one of the clawed feet rose from the floor and grabbed her sword, rising above her head with it.

"Behind you!" Nikko shouted, shoving open the door.

Selena swung her other sword around to stop the attack, but Malphas's other claw grabbed it out of her hand. His wing swooped up the first sword, and as her attention was drawn to it, his head reattached itself to the filleted body.

Nikko dove at it as it rose, bringing both swords down on Selena. She turned and stabbed the Hellkeeper in the heart with the switchblade. She screamed as the blades sliced into her back and shoulder, but the Hellkeeper screamed louder. Her hand was buried deep in its chest. Malphas's body struggled. Selena held fast.

"Tell me what I want to know, Malphas, and I will spare you."

"Apollyon knows your secret—if you destroy me, he will destroy you by destroying your dau—"

Selena ripped the nanorian from Malphas's chest. It beat hot and powerful in her hand. Already she felt the power of the five as the four stones around her neck warmed in welcome. Elation swelled. Two more hearts to collect.

Her gaze clashed with Johnny's astounded eyes. Tension poured off him in chaotic waves. Why had he helped her? Debilitating emotion she could not describe clogged her chest. She opened her mouth to ask him why, when he despised her, but she didn't. His answer didn't matter.

She had been aware of him the moment she detected his scent at the stairway. She had not wanted to take the nanorian from Malphas so early, she wanted information from him, but when he was about to expose her secret, she had no choice. She had come too far to care that Johnny looked at her now as if she had a raging case of herpes. Let him think the worst of her. It would keep him away, and his mind off their painful past.

She wiped the stone down her belly, leaving a bloody trail, and at the same time realized she was bleeding. Her back burned like hell. She pressed the bloody stone into one of the three empty settings in her necklace.

"Jesus, Selena, you're bleeding everywhere."

As if he cares. Ignoring Johnny, she knelt beside Vegas, not caring that her knees were soaked in his blood. She felt his carotid for a pulse. He was alive. Barely. She needed to get inside his head before he died. Not for Joran, but for Los Cuatro. Vegas's subconscious would retain whatever information Malphas had gathered while possessing him. As Apollyon's messenger, Malphas would know where that cask was.

She drew in a deep breath and looked up at Johnny. "I must do something. To do it, I need you to take a hike."

He sank down beside her, his gaze wary. "After that show, I'm not going anywhere, especially now that I know for certain you're in the hunt for that cask." He touched her bloody shoulder, and his voice lowered a decibel. "That's deep. You need to get to a doctor."

She sat back on her haunches and looked hard at him. He *needed* to go while Vegas was still alive. If she did not get in and out of Madeo before he drew his last breath, it would be hers as well. She had never before slipped completely into anyone's head. Leaving her body to enter another's left her vulnerable to possession. But she had no choice. The only way she was going to get the information was to leave her body and enter his.

"My business with Vegas is *my* business alone."

"Not if it involves national security." Johnny moved in closer. "Now tell me, what the hell just happened here?"

She moved back and stood up. "I can't explain right now. But trust me when I say, for the sake of national security, *I* need you to go, now!" She didn't even know if she *could* possess a body, but damn if she was going to do it in front of him.

"You have a hell of a lot of nerve asking for my trust. I'm not going anywhere."

"Damn you, Johnny! Vegas has information I need!"

"We want the same thing." His gaze dipped to her bloody, bare chest and he swallowed hard.

Despite the warmth in the room and her dire situation, her nipples pebbled. She shoved past him as a vampire and a mortal woman she instinctively knew was the vampire's lover came rushing through the same door Johnny had been hiding behind. They both looked at her in shock, whether from the blood or her bare chest she did not know and did not care.

She grabbed a sword with one hand and shoved it between her sarong and her back. She grabbed the other sword and pointed it at Johnny and his two friends. Without taking her eyes off them, she reached down and grabbed Vegas's arm with her free hand and dragged him into the open elevator.

Johnny moved forward, and the big vampire and the woman moved with him. Selena pointed the sword at them. "Come a step closer and I'll hack all three of you into chum."

All three of them rushed her. Selena speared the elevator door closed, lodging her blade into the paneled wall to keep it closed, and prayed she could get in and out of Vegas's head before the trio managed to open the doors or he died, whichever came first.

CHAPTER NINE

Selena called upon the stones around her neck to give her the power and wherewithal to vaporize into Vegas's head. She had never possessed anyone, never invaded anyone's dreams, never, as her succubi kin were fond of doing, had sex with a man while he slept. She had never had any desire to explore the daemon part of her. As far as Selena was concerned, she was mortal, albeit with a superior skill set.

Now she would see just how much of her father she had in her. She knelt beside the dying man and pressed her hands to his head. Closing her eyes, she regulated her breathing, called to the nanorians, and focused solely on transforming herself into vapor and then navigating what was sure to be a treacherous minefield of horror.

Her body lightened. Her breathing slowed and she felt weightless. Then she materialized inside a dark and terrible place. The lumbering but erratic beat of Vegas's heart mingled with screams, blood scents, and rage. The tumult tore at her senses with razor-sharp teeth. She pushed through it, stealthily maneuvering around in the Hell that was Armadeo Vegas's mind.

His troubled childhood in Cuba flashed before her. The beatings, the abandonment. His life flashed forward to his first kill. His sister's friend. She had laughed at him, so he'd grabbed a kitchen knife and stabbed her to death. He was nine years old. That was the beginning of a life of violent crime. Vegas liked blood sport. Selena cringed at the vision of a vampiress, who looked oddly familiar to her, going down on Vegas, blood dripping from his dick as she sucked him. When he staked her in the back, Selena gasped. *Jesus!* More screams. More death. Cartel kingpin Luis Fernandez asking Vegas if he had destroyed the bloodsucking bitch. Then Luis's laughter, as he promised Vegas eternal life for his loyalty.

From the depths of Vegas's mind, Hellkeeper Malphas's demonic voice reverberated around her. He had possessed Vegas so completely it was as if she were in the daemon's head. Through the daemon's eyes, she saw the arrogant Russian Noslov shaking his head. "My commodity is far more valuable than what you have offered. There will be an auction to the highest bidder!" he triumphantly crowed.

Malphas's rage erupted. "We had an agreement!" Ah, so the Russian had double-crossed Hell.

Vegas's heart stuttered. His life force struggled for survival. He slithered down the dark hole to Hell. Selena's instinct was to turn and flee to the light. If he died and she was still inside, she would be trapped and follow him to Hell. She hung on for a moment longer for the coveted information.

When is the auction? Where will it be held? Vegas's heart abruptly stopped. As if a vise clamped around her chest, she was paralyzed. Trapped! *No!*

She would not die a daemon! She would not follow Vegas to Hell! She had too much left in her life to do. Wrongs to right . . .

Vegas's heart struggled for another beat. It would be her only chance to escape, to survive.

Selena turned, the thick waves of death pulling her back. She could see the murky light showing her the way out. His heart fibrillated. She slogged through the trauma, the lies, the deception, the hatred. Her chest ached as if she had been underwater too long. She reached for the light just out of her reach. Flames scorched her hands, her face, her heart and soul. She was dying. Marisol's sweet little face so much like Johnny's swam before her.

Mama!

"Selena!"

She struggled to speak, to open her eyes, to tell him . . .

Nikko rushed to where Selena lay in the elevator. Sliding on his knees in Vegas's blood, he pulled Selena's half-naked body into his arms and shook her. His insides wrenched with unexpected fear. "Wake up, damn you!"

Her eyes fluttered open. She struggled to speak. Her hand lifted to his cheek. He lowered his head to her lips.

"I'm here, Selena," he whispered.

She grabbed his hair. "Johnny—the sun—"

"What about the sun?"

"It shines, Johnny, on the nuns. Remember?"

Her mumbled words made no sense. "Remember *what?*"

Her fingers loosened, then her hand fell to the floor. "Where it began . . . ," she breathed.

She closed her eyes, then lay still. He clutched her to

him, staring at her pale face. He didn't want her to die, damn it! He brushed her hair from her cheek. "Damn you, Selena! Don't do this to me!" But she didn't respond. He pressed his ear between her breasts. He could not feel the thud of her heartbeat. He refused to believe she was gone. It was a trick. A trick to slip away undetected. He shook her again. "I swear to God, Selena, if this is some kind of trick, I'll kill you myself!"

Cassidy knelt beside him and calmly felt for a pulse on her neck. After a long minute, she shook her head gravely. "She's gone, Nikko."

He couldn't move. The shock of Cassidy's words didn't register. Selena wasn't dead. She'd just opened her eyes. She'd spoken! She was warm. How could she be dead?

Her body hung limp in his arms. A maelstrom of emotions wracked Nikko. So much of him had wanted her dead, good riddance . . . but now—damn it! He wanted her alive! He refused to think about why, he just knew he did. He looked up at Cross, who stood quietly across the threshold.

"Do something!" he commanded.

The vampire shook his head.

Nikko looked at Cassidy. "He saved you, make him save Selena!"

Cassidy looked expectantly up at Cross. "You know I cannot," he stoically said to her silent plea.

Nikko looked back at Cross, as the body in his arms cooled. "*Will* not or *can*not?"

"Both."

Nikko glared at Cassidy, then back at Cross. "She knows where that cask is. She's the key to getting our hands on it."

"She's daemon, Cruz. I cannot help her," Cross solemnly said.

Daemon as in *demon*? Did Cross *literally* mean a daemon? "Daemon, human, vampire, I don't care what the hell she is. Save her!"

"Our laws forbid it. The bloods cannot mix."

"Maybe not your blood, but your laws don't govern me!"

"Nikko," Cassidy calmly said, "if Marcus could save her—"

"He won't! Tell *me* what to do," Nikko said menacingly, his gaze locked on Cassidy's. She knew what to do, and, damn it, she would show him.

She looked past him to Cross and let out a heavy sigh, but just the same she grabbed his arm and pushed his shirtsleeve up.

"Jax—" Cross warned.

"Cruz is right, Marcus, he doesn't live by your laws, so no harm, no foul, on your end. We need her alive." Cassidy looked at Nikko. "Bite the vein on your wrist. Open her mouth and give her your blood."

Cross leaned over them in full fang. "Mix the bloods and you have the potential for an out-of-control hybrid."

Nikko's fangs flashed. "I'll take my chances." The sharp sting of his teeth sinking into his own flesh didn't faze him. He yanked his mouth from the slow rush of blood. Cradling Selena's head, he pressed his wrist to her mouth.

She didn't respond.

"Take it, damn you!" Nikko yelled, shoving his wrist against her lips.

Frantically, he looked up at Cross. The vampire shook

his head and stepped toward him. Cross bent down, opened Selena's mouth, and squeezed Nikko's bloody wrist. The blood ran in a steady stream into her mouth. Nikko watched expectantly for her eyes to open.

A minute passed, then two.

Nothing.

Nikko shook her. "Damn it, Selena!"

She gagged. *Jesus.* She gagged again. Cross clamped his big hand around her head and forced more of Nikko's blood into her.

Selena's limbs twitched, and as if the saints had descended from the heavens and performed a miracle, Nikko felt the dull thud of her heart against his arm as it started up again.

Cross straightened and said, "I don't know what you'll be dealing with if and when she comes to, Cruz, but if your blood doesn't kill her, she's going to be pissed as hell when she comes out of it. In my world, daemons abhor vamps and we hate them more. It's your vamp blood that resurrected her, not your human blood. I'd get her somewhere where you can control her, then hurry the hell up and get the information we need before she unleashes on you."

Nikko moved his wrist away from Selena, but she grabbed it and bit. Voraciously, she drank from him, her teeth hurting, her grip unrelenting. Then, as suddenly as she had attacked him, she fell back, unconscious.

Nikko pulled his shirt off and clumsily put it on her. He was suddenly all thumbs. Cassidy helped him; then he hoisted Selena up into his arms. Her body was limp, her arms and legs dangling like noodles. He turned to Cross and Cassidy. "I'll take her back to my room at the hotel." He looked down at Vegas's body. "Can you two clean up?"

"Go, Cruz," Cassidy said. "We'll take care of this."

Nikko sat in an uncomfortable chair staring at the woman in his bed. She had not moved, save for the shallow rise and fall of her chest, since they had revived her. Revived her? Hell, what they had done was resurrect the dead! He shuddered. Had she done no less for him in Kyrgyzstan? And with vampire blood. The same way Cross had saved Cassidy's life. Nikko swiped his hand across his face. Shock and disbelief wrangled in his head. He felt faint. Sick to his stomach.

Watching Selena hack that . . . thing . . . to pieces, then cut out its heart, had still not sunk into his reality. Nikko had always considered himself an open-minded man. He believed in God, angels, and ghosts, to an extent. His suspension of disbelief had been challenged when Cassidy hooked up with a vampire. And despite the changes in him because of what Selena had injected him with, he was good with it. More than good. But what he'd witnessed come out of Vegas was flat-out unbelievable. What Selena had done to it defied his reality. Cross had called her a daemon. What the fuck was that? She was as human as he! For Christ's sake, he had impregnated her!

Nikko swiped his hand across his face again and stood. He paced the room, never once taking his eyes off the woman in his bed, his relief that she had lived warring with the fury at what she had so selfishly done.

He sucked in a deep breath and took a huge emotional step backward. He had tried to kill Selena in a fit of rage because she'd aborted his near-term daughter. She'd done the one thing he could never forgive her for. He didn't care that she had saved his life; she'd have done him a favor had she left him there to die. Until he'd opened his eyes on the side of that mountain road in Kyrgyzstan and seen her, he had not cared if he lived or died.

Seeing her tonight, touching her, had shaken him to his foundation. All of the forgotten emotions he had stuffed so far down into his soul had surfaced. Surfaced with every bit of the rage and heartbreak as on the day he'd first experienced them.

He dropped back into his chair beside the bed. What had she been trying to tell him as she lay at death's door? Remember the sun shines by the sea? No, the sun shines on the nuns? He shook his head, wracking his brain for the meaning. The only body of water he could think of was the Atlantic Ocean. They'd met on St. Michael's Island off the coast of Georgia. He had been an Atlanta PD sergeant in that life. He had been on extended R&R for a gunshot wound he'd sustained chasing a bad guy. Did she just want him to think of the good times? The hair rose on the back of his neck. *Remember where it began.* She *must* have meant St. Michael's. But why? For old times' sake?

Those memories, still so vivid, warmed his heart. But crashing right behind them was the knowledge of what she had done. The fury and heartache resurfaced full force. He stared at her blood-smeared chest. The blood on her hands.

Nikko went into the bathroom and grabbed some

towels, dampening one with warm water. Sitting down on the bed, he unbuttoned his shirt he had put her in and pulled it away from her chest. He averted his eyes from her breasts and slowly wiped the dried blood from her body. When he was done, he dried her, then buttoned the shirt back up. Save for the slow shallow rise and fall of her chest, she still had not moved.

For a long time Nikko stared at the soft flick of her pulse in her neck. The unusual necklace she wore moved with each beat of her heart. He looked more closely at it. The thing she'd ripped from that abomination's chest glowed softly in a setting. Two settings were empty. Were there two more to be had? He reached out a finger to the bloodstone; it pulsed with energy against his skin. Intuitively, he knew it was important to Selena. She'd risked her life for it. He turned the necklace around her neck so he could unclasp it, then pulled it free. He lifted it up against the lamplight for a closer look. Seven rustic settings, probably platinum by the weight of it, five filled with what looked like crimson stones the size of a quarter that hummed with vitality. Power. What kind of power he did not know, but he knew it was important. He slipped the heavy necklace into his trouser pocket and turned his attention back to the woman he loved to hate.

He traced a finger down her jugular. Her pulse jumped against his touch. Her skin was as soft as he remembered it. Warm. Human, damn it! But what if she wasn't? What if she was what Cross said she was? Was that how she had survived his attack? He had been livid. Out-of-his-mind crazy. He had strangled her. He had watched the color drain from her face, felt the life force leave her body.

"It's over, Johnny."

"What have you done?!" he'd screamed when he looked down at her flat belly, the same belly that, the week before, had been swollen with his child.

"I'm not ready to be a mother. I—I had an abortion."

His world had snapped in half at that precise second. What he did after, he had no control of. And though little Marisol's blood was on her hands, he'd lived with the guilt and self-loathing of murdering the woman he loved.

The body beneath his fingers shivered. She was coming to. He opened his eyes, and his own heart stuttered.

Deep onyx-colored eyes stared at him. Her body was still, her breathing barely detectable. Nikko's hand shook.

Her eyes flashed. She flung him off her with such force, he went hurtling backward into the wall. Nikko shook himself. It took a moment for him to comprehend what had just happened. She knew where the cask was, and she was going to make a break for it. His eyes narrowed. Over his dead body.

She stood on the bed, her fists raised at her sides, her chest heaving, her eyes flashing with fire. "Once killed, twice shy, Johnny boy."

So that was how she wanted to play it? Excitement revved through him. He smiled and lunged. She met him halfway. Their bodies crashed together and went tumbling back against the headboard, splintering it to kindling.

Selena twisted out of Johnny's grasp and heaved him off her. He grabbed her arm and flung her back onto the bed. She kicked his chest. The loud whoosh of his breath as it rushed from his lungs told her she had two, maybe three seconds before he regrouped. She grabbed the lamp from the nightstand, slammed it over his head, then leapt over him toward the window. It didn't matter if she was on the first floor or the fiftieth; it was the closest, most expedient exit. She was supercharged by the infusion of his blood, and she knew that, like a cat, she'd land on her feet.

He caught her by the ankle and flung her back onto the bed. The force of her landing broke the frame.

His big body covered hers. His fingers dug into her hair. His fangs flashed.

He laughed at her shock. "Third time's the charm." He sank his teeth into her throat. Selena arched against him and moaned. She hated herself for that. As she called upon the stones, she realized that her neck was bare.

Damn him! She kneed him in the balls. He grunted in pain, just enough that his bite loosened. It was all she needed. She head-butted him. He stared at her in shock, and she stifled a laugh. His look was priceless, despite her blood that glistened on his lips. "Fourth time is fatal." She head-butted him again and shoved him hard. But his grip held.

He forced her back into the mattress. His blue eyes burned bright as cobalt. His gaze swept her face, then lowered to her neck, then trailed lower to her exposed breasts. She recalled she had used her halter top to tourniquet Vegas's leg. The shirt she wore was Johnny's, she could smell his scent on it, but it had come undone when they'd crashed into the headboard.

He lowered his head and scraped his fangs along the rise of her breast. "Fifth time is final," he hoarsely said. Then bit her.

She screamed. She thrashed and clawed at his shoulders and back, drawing blood. His fangs sank deeper. Selena arched as her body tightened. She could not breathe. She grabbed his hair and pulled it. But his voracious grip on her was relentless. He grabbed her hands and shoved them over her head. He blocked her knee with his when she tried to gouge him in the groin again. When she tried a third time, he forced his hips and legs between her thighs, preventing any further attempts.

A moan escaped her throat. Selena squeezed her eyes shut, hating the daemon part of her that responded to the pressure of him between her legs. His body reacted immediately. His fingers dug into hers. She felt him swell. His tongue stroked her skin, soothing the sting of his bite, but he still drank from her.

She felt his body temperature rise along with hers. Without the power of the stones to fend him off, she was victim to his seductive strength. And there was something else. She felt different. Hungry for something she didn't understand. Empowered but in a different way from the nanorians. She could hear the rush of Johnny's blood as it pumped frantically through his body. She felt his turmoil. His desire to hurt her but also his carnal need for her.

His fangs slowly withdrew from her. He licked where he had bitten. Selena exhaled. Her relief was short-lived. He nipped at her aroused nipple. She gasped, afraid he would bite her, then moaned when he slowly licked it, making her ache for more. His fingers dug deeper into hers. He was fighting the same battle she fought.

"Johnny," she gasped, licking her dry lips. "Just get it over with."

He raised his head and looked at her. She caught her breath. Red tinged his beautiful blue eyes. His Michelangelo face had hardened in passion. Just as much for the kill as for the fuck.

"I despise what you did to our baby," he hoarsely said.

Selena's heart clenched with such unbearable pain she could not look at him. The anguish in his eyes, in his voice, tore her up. She would give anything, except his life or their daughter's, to be able to tell him the truth. But the truth would get him and Marisol killed.

Though he might never understand it, she had loved him enough to make him think the worst of her. Her heart pounded in her chest. She still loved him. That would never die. No matter what he did to her, she could take it.

"I'm sorry, Johnny," she whispered.

He bared his fangs. "What *are* you?" His arrogant gaze swept the length of her. She was practically naked— her chest bare, her belly exposed. The silk sarong twisted around her hips revealed her thighs and the fact she wore no panties. His nostrils flared as he inhaled her scent. Selena held her breath, afraid if she moved, she would provoke his passion to the point of no return. "What have you become," he sneered, "some kind of high-priced whore?"

His words were more painful than a sword in the

heart. But it was best for them both if he continued to think the worst of her.

"I do what I have to do to survive."

He clenched his jaw and shook his head. "You should be dead!" he ground out.

"Give me my necklace, and I will disappear from your life forever."

He threw his head back and laughed. "Over my dead body."

Selena cocked a brow. "That can be arranged."

He lowered his face to within inches of hers. "What were you doing in Kyrgyzstan? What did you inject me with? And what do you know about that cask?"

Selena knew she owed him some explanation, but that would only embed him deeper into her life. She needed him out of it! *Now.* But she was not leaving without the nanorians.

"If I divulge any of that information, it will get me killed."

"Oh, I can make it so when you leave this room, you won't be breathing."

"Try it."

Their gazes clashed and locked. Emotions played out in chaotic symmetry across Johnny's face. After what seemed like hours, he nodded. "Before I do," he said, his voice low and choked, "tell me where Marisol is buried."

His request stunned her. The true depth of his sorrow hit her at that moment. Her lie was vicious and cruel, but, damn her father! He'd gone after Johnny with a vengeance. Johnny had chalked it up to Atlanta's going to shit, but it was her father manipulating the criminal minds to go after Johnny. How else could she keep the man she loved from chasing after her and getting himself killed for the effort?

It took more power than a thousand nanorians not to tell Marisol's father that the girl was alive.

"She's in Georgia." And it was true. But she was a happy, healthy eight-year-old.

All of the fight went out of him. She felt it drain from him. He rolled off her and sat on the edge of the bed. He raked his fingers through his hair. Selena wanted to go to him, to take him in her arms and comfort him. But she didn't dare. Instead, she kept up the coldhearted bitch façade. "Where's my necklace?"

He turned so fast, she pushed back into the mattress. His eyes blazed red.

She had pushed too far.

CHAPTER TEN

W hat kind of coldhearted woman are you?" Johnny seethed. She watched his face harden to granite. "*What* are you?" Disgust laced his words, his tone, his facial features.

She blanched at his question, then gathered her pride protectively around her. Yes, she was coldhearted, but only because she had to be. For her own good. For Marisol's own good. And even for Johnny's own good.

She threw her hair over her shoulders and straightened her spine. "My father was a daemon who raped my human mother. So I guess that makes me a half-breed."

His eyes widened and his mouth dropped open. He moved off the bed fast, as if she were a pestilence. He walked to the large window and stared out over the restless Atlantic. His back was as rigid as a steel beam, his wide shoulders square, his feet planted firmly on the floor. "What is a daemon?"

Selena let out a long, exhausted breath, finding it oddly liberating that she could finally come clean with him. At least about what she was. "Everything you've heard and worse."

He turned slowly and faced her. Gone were the disgust and anger. Now he looked tortured. "Is that why you had the abortion?"

Selena held her breath. She hadn't expected him

to come to that conclusion so fast. To come so perilously close to discovering her secret. She hadn't aborted Marisol, but she'd lied about doing so because she was daemon. So in some way, she could tell the truth. Would it make him hate her less? Slowly, she nodded.

He swiped his hand across his face and shook his head. For a brief moment, understanding—maybe even compassion—swept his features before the anger resurfaced. "Why? Why didn't you tell me?"

She rose from the bed. "And what? Even if you believed me, you would have looked at me like you just did and told me to take a hike. Or do you expect me to believe you'd have wanted the baby, even knowing what I am? You've made your hatred of what I am, what I did to survive, clear. Even now you despise what I am. How would you have dealt with a child that wasn't all human?"

His jaw tightened. "It wasn't your call! That was a decision for me to make, Selena!"

"My father is the scourge of Hell!" she blurted out. "He has caused me nothing but pain and suffering all my life. He would have done the same to my child. He drove my mother to madness. She couldn't stand the pain. She killed herself. No way was I going to subject my child to that." Her voice lowered. "Or you." And it was true.

"It doesn't change the fact that you murdered my daughter!" he roared. He shook with passionate rage. He stalked closer. "If you knew all of this when you got pregnant, why did you wait so long, Selena?"

The blood drained from her face. The lies were eating her up. Selena inhaled slowly, held her breath, then exhaled. The moment of truth. Most of it. "I had hoped my father wouldn't find out, but he did. Then all of those close calls happened to you at work. He was trying to destroy everything I loved! I couldn't let that happen!"

"She was viable, damn you!"

Selena braced herself against his fury. His heartache. What would he do if he knew Marisol lived? Hate Selena more. She had never once questioned her motives, firmly convinced his hatred was worth it, but what she'd failed to consider was the pain he would live with every day. It was just as debilitating as what she lived with—or rather, what she lived without. Her daughter. She swallowed hard. No, it was worse. There was no anguish as terrible as the anguish he suffered.

"I'm sorry," she softly said.

He paced the room. She felt his turmoil—his hatred, his desire to hurt her, but also his need for her to live. Abruptly he stopped. With his hands clasped behind his back, he said, "Tell me what happened back at your club."

Selena tried to let go of the guilt, but it hung around her neck like a two-ton anchor, so she dragged it with her. It was her turn to go to the window and look out at the blackness of the night. Two hundred yards away, white-caps rolled onto the sands of Miami's renowned beaches. She hugged herself, suddenly feeling cold. Alone, and tired. How much should she tell Johnny? How much did his vampire friend know? Without breaking her stare, she said, "Vegas was possessed by a Hellkeeper by the name of Malphas, a very strong daemon, and a superior prick. I drew him out and killed him."

"Why?"

She spun around and faced him. "Because his death takes me one step closer to my father, and when I get there, I'm going to destroy him just like he destroyed my mother!" And just like he'd destroyed any chance of happiness with Johnny.

"Why did you cut out his heart?"

"Without it, he cannot regenerate."

He cocked a brow. "What else?"

She shrugged. "I couldn't leave it. In the wrong hands it can be deadly."

"In your hands?"

She smiled. "It *will* be deadly."

"After you killed Malphas, what did you do to Vegas?"

Selena walked past him, not wanting to go there.

He grabbed her arm, and while his grip wasn't brutish, it wasn't gentle either. Their gazes locked. "After you killed Malphas, what did you do to Vegas?"

"I possessed him."

Johnny let go of her arm and stepped back. "What does that mean?"

"It means I got inside his head. Had I wanted to, I could have driven him mad, made him do my bidding. Controlled him. Instead, I gathered information."

"What information?"

"Nothing that concerns you, Johnny."

He moved back into her personal space. "Since you shot me up with that concoction, everything about you concerns me."

She shook her head vigorously. "No, it doesn't. Forget the last four days. Forget I'm alive. Forget all of it, Johnny."

"Johnny is dead. My name is Nikko Cruz now."

Nikko Cruz? He would always be Johnny to her.

"I don't know why you came here, *Nikko,* but—" Selena's nose twitched, every sense on high alert.

Sulfur. And a lot of it.

"Do you smell that?" she asked, moving toward him.

"Sulfur."

"Daemons, Nikko, at least a legion of them. We need to get the hell out of here."

"What—"

She turned toward the window and shoved Nikko toward it. As he went flying through the glass, she leapt after him, grabbing him as they tumbled down several stories to the parking lot. She tried to turn him so that she took the brunt of the impact, but he maneuvered her so that he did. They hit hard. Shrill screeching came from the daemons circling the hotel as they hunted for her scent.

She grabbed his hand and took off through the parking lot toward the water. There she had a chance to keep them at bay.

"I need that necklace, Nikko," she said as they ran. "With it, we might have a chance." With it, she could fry ten legions with a wave of her hand.

"No deal."

Selena stopped short, breathing heavily, and glared at him. "I *need* the necklace."

"Call your own legion of daemons."

Her eyes widened. How the hell did he know she possessed that power?

"Call them."

"I cannot call upon them to battle their own kind."

"Then I guess it's just you and me."

"The necklace, Nikko!"

"Give me the answers I want, and I'll give it to you."

"The necklace is *mine*, you have no right taking it from me!"

"You took something from me that was far more valuable."

He would never forgive Selena for what she had done, regardless of why, and he'd be damned if he was going to hand over the necklace. He knew the minute after she took out the daemons, she would take off, then go to ground. As long as he controlled the necklace, he controlled her. "Then I guess we'll have to stand and deliver."

The shrieking whirl had caught up to them. He took a step back despite himself. To his surprise, she braced him. Stood just behind him, as if giving him strength.

"Face them, Johnny. Brace yourself, don't open your mouth or your eyes, and do not allow them into your thoughts or they will take possession of your mind. If that happens, you will wish you were dead."

She grabbed his hand and looked up at him. "When you get the chance, run like hell for the water. Daemons are terrified of water and won't follow you there."

Grudgingly, he admired her bravery. Nikko took the necklace from his pocket and wrapped it around her neck but held on to it, keeping possession. The minute it touched her skin, the stones flared. He closed his eyes and set his jaw. Together they turned and Hell was unleashed upon them.

Heat singed his skin. A percussion of energy pushed, shoved, and prodded for entry into his body. Wild, wicked screams bombarded his eardrums. He forced his mind to remember his childhood prayers. He chanted them in his head. The swirling forces screamed louder. The sulfur stench was stifling. Nikko fought the need to open his mouth and breathe deep, the pressure almost unbearable.

He felt Selena's body being pulled upward. Her fingers tightened around his. He reached out, grabbed her other hand, and pulled her against his chest. She nudged her head beneath his chin, pressing her lips to his chest.

The daemons ramped up their efforts. His prayers faltered. Instead, the image of his baby lying in a shallow grave erupted in his mind.

The maelstrom of the daemon attack ended as abruptly as it had begun. As if by magic, they disappeared into the night.

For long moments, Nikko stood silent and still, Selena pressed tightly against him. He slipped the necklace back into his pocket, wondering why she didn't grab it and run. When her arms relaxed and she pulled away from him, he opened his eyes and stared down into two dark ones. She looked away from him and started walking.

"Selena!" he called, and went after her. She started to run. He ran faster and caught up.

"Selena, stop!"

She whirled around and angrily faced him. "Give me my necklace, Nikko, then turn and run as far and as fast as you can."

"If you think you're protecting me, I don't need it."

"I just saved you from being torn to shreds by that swarm of daemons!" She took a step closer to him. "I know you're a big boy. And as long as you don't hang out with me, you can take care of yourself. I want you to stay the hell away from me! I have a business to run. I have a life to live, and I can't do that with you hanging around."

"I have business with you, Selena, and like it or not, you're going to cooperate."

"We have no business."

"What were you doing in Kyrgyzstan and what is Balderama to you?"

Selena shook her head. He was not going to leave her alone until she threw him a bone. Fine, she'd give Johnny—Nikko—just enough information to let him think she'd told him everything.

"I was in Kyrgyzstan collecting blood serums. I came across you dying on the roadside. I injected you with them because it was the only chance you had for survival. As I told you earlier, Señor Balderama was my mother's good friend. He has been a surrogate father to me in many ways."

"What kind of blood serums?"

"A little vampire—"

"More than a little—I feel like Dracula!"

"Okay, so a lot. And just so you don't go blab it to the world, it's illegal to extract blood from any immortal, and if I'm caught with the serums, the penalty is death." She held her hands out palms up. "Look, I know it's a lot, but you need to back the hell away. Forget all of it and go back to what you were doing."

He ran his fingers through his hair in a frustrated gesture. "Selena, in less than a week my entire world has been shaken up like a snow globe. I was on the verge of death and the woman I was sure I killed with my own hands shows up in the middle of a third-world country and injects me with something that turns me into Superman with a hard-on. Next thing I know, my ex, the one I thought I killed, is a half-daemon. Oh, and she fucking kills daemons for a living!"

He shook his head and glared at her. "And while I know you're feeding me some truth, you're keeping the majority of it from me."

"I don't owe you anything."

His rage flashed. "You owe me more than you can ever repay!"

"I deserve your hatred. But I'm not going to allow you to use it to manipulate me."

"I'll do more than manipulate you! You know about that cask, and you're going to share that information whether you want to or not."

"Or what? You'll kill me? *Again?*"

"Yes."

"Do you really think I care? I'm running on borrowed time as it is. Once word gets out that I'm the one destroying the Hellkeepers, my father will come after me, and if he doesn't get me first, then the Order will get me for the Rev."

Nikko pinched the bridge of his nose and slowly exhaled. "Rev? The Order?"

"Rev—it's a combination of blood serums that can save a dying vampire's life. It's like a dose of super-charged adrenaline. As far as the Order goes, ask your vampire friend."

"I'm asking you."

"I'm in enough trouble, I can't talk about it."

"Why did you save my life?"

She glared at him. "I owed you."

"At the risk of a death sentence?"

"Yes. Now we're even." She shrugged it off. "Besides, they'd have to catch me first, and if you haven't noticed, I'm pretty good with a sword."

"You're lying about Balderama. He wants the uranium, doesn't he?"

"I'm not doing this with you." She moved past him. When he grabbed her arm, she flung him off and turned on him. "Don't touch me again."

Nikko stood ramrod stiff and watched her walk away. As much as he wanted to hurt her, he wasn't going to beat the information out of her.

"If he is what he purports to be, we're on the same side, Selena," Nikko called after her.

"No, we're not," she called back, and kept walking. She crossed the boulevard and took off across the beach. When she waded into the water, then disappeared into the darkness, Nikko took off after her.

CHAPTER ELEVEN

Seldom did Selena run, but tonight she'd had enough. Infused with adrenaline and Johnny's blood, which was the equivalent of a shot of Rev, Selena swam to the *Black Widow,* moored just off the end of the Costa del Oro Marina, several hundred yards away. The ocean was calm, cold, and dark. A peaceful haven in her turbulent life. But with each stroke, her emotions churned as if in a blender. By the time she had the seventy-one-foot yacht in sight, Selena was more worked up than when she had run from Johnny.

Seconds later, she climbed up the aft ladder and stood soaking wet on the wide teakwood deck. Johnny's shredded shirt still clung to her. She ripped it off and threw it into the ocean. She pulled off what was left of her skirt and flung it in the water as well.

She sucked in a deep breath and exhaled.

She had to get the necklace back from Johnny. It held no power for him since she had not freely given it to him. She should have just grabbed it and run. The thought had occurred to her, but for some reason she did not want to take it, she wanted him to give it. But if he didn't come around quickly, she'd take it. Without it, she was a sitting duck. Without it, she had no chance of destroying her father. Without it, Marisol was in grave danger. And without it, Johnny would be vulnerable to her father's demonic machinations.

She pressed her hand across the biometric pad to the left of the sliding-glass doors. They silently slid open and she inhaled the familiar scents. Suntan lotion, the ocean, and . . . Closing her eyes, she inhaled deeper. Marisol. Several of her daughter's stuffed animals graced the boat. Selena and the *Black Widow* made sporadic trips north to St. Michael's Island and spent idyllic days sailing along the Intracoastal Waterway with the free-spirited eight-year-old.

Not a soul, not even Juju, knew of her refuge here aboard the *Black Widow*. The large motor yacht served several purposes, the primary one escape. The perfect antidaemon safe spot. Though she was half-daemon, Selena had never had an aversion to anything wet. It was the only place she felt remotely safe, so it was where she and Marisol spent the time they had together when they were not on St. Michael's.

She picked up the stuffed Minnie Mouse Johnny had bought for their daughter the day they'd learned the baby's gender. At the time, Selena had been naïve, thinking she could have a family and keep them safe. Then her father came to her in a dream demanding the child's life in return for her own and her lover's. When she refused, Johnny was attacked and hospitalized. When she still refused, that bastard had upped the ante.

She lifted the scuffed doll to her nose and inhaled. Marisol's fresh scent of sunshine and animal crackers infused her senses. Her fingers tightened and she hugged the doll to her chest. Powerful, protective emotion swelled within her. She could not imagine her life without the plucky little girl. She was everything good and right. If anyone so much as touched a hair on her baby's head, she would destroy them!

"Oh, Johnny, I'm so, so sorry." She *was* coldhearted. She would not have been nearly as restrained with Johnny as he had been with her. How could he stand the sight of her?

She sighed and set the doll down on the sofa. He couldn't.

As she walked toward the spiraling stairway to the master stateroom belowdecks, she caught a glimpse of herself in the mirror on the wall. She looked as if she had aged ten years. Her skin was dull, her eyes haunted. She flung her damp hair from her shoulders. She was all Marisol had. She would do what she must to keep Marisol's life a secret from Paymon; and once he was dead, now that Johnny knew Selena was alive, she would introduce Marisol to her father.

Selena's mood lightened. Johnny might try to kill her again, he might even succeed, but he would know his daughter. To that end, she would do whatever was necessary to destroy Paymon, even if it meant pushing Johnny further away from her.

Selena made her way down the stairway into the comfortable stateroom that took up almost half of the bottom deck. She felt more at home here than she did at her Star Island manse.

She turned on the shower and jumped in under the cold spray. For long minutes, she stood as the water warmed, allowing her mind to wrap around the only way she knew to get the necklace from Johnny. Pull the succubus card. She shuddered at how the idea made her feel. It was extreme, underhanded, and pure daemon, but she told herself he wouldn't know what had happened, only that he no longer possessed the necklace.

As she emerged glistening wet from the bathroom, she stopped short. Johnny sat on the edge of the bed staring straight at her. He'd removed his shirt, but his wet trousers were soaking the linen comforter.

Her body shivered. She felt her breasts plumpen and her nipples harden. His eyes locked on hers, then trailed downward.

"You don't take no for an answer, do you?" she softly asked.

He shook his head and stood. His eyes blazed with the faintest haze of red. Heat pulsed off him. He walked toward her. She didn't back away. She couldn't, not if she wanted the necklace.

"You can run, Selena, but you can't hide. Your blood courses through me. I can find you anywhere."

Selena's heart slammed wildly against her chest. He made no effort to hide his fangs. He stopped inches away, his eyes mesmerizing her. Her body flared with its own heat. She could blame her primitive reaction to him on her daemon side, but it would be a lie.

"Your boat is appropriately named. A *Black Widow* for a black widow." He traced a finger along her collarbone, then down between her breasts to her belly, and across the incision just above her pelvic bone. Her heartbeat stumbled. "What's this?"

"A scar." Her cesarean scar.

His eyes narrowed. "What kind of scar?"

"Appendix."

"Liar."

Selena swallowed hard and moved into him. His skin was warm, his muscles hard. His scent seductive. When her breasts brushed against his chest, they both hissed in a breath. His fingers dug into the curve of her hip. "John-Nikko," she breathed, running her hands up his defined pectorals, "I'm willing to meet you in the middle."

He smiled, his fangs glittering under the low light of the room. "I hold all the cards."

His warm breath caressed her cheek, signaling the sensitive nerve endings just below her steamy skin to a response. She snaked her fingers around his neck, then into his damp hair, and pulled his lips down to hers. "Maybe, but I have the ace in the hole."

She kissed him. He didn't resist, but he did not engage her either. Deepening her kiss, Selena licked his fangs. His body responded if his lips did not. He swelled against her belly. Still he did not engage her.

She opened her eyes and looked into his deep blue ones, then pulled slightly away. "Why are you fighting me?"

"Why are you trying to seduce me?"

"I want you."

"You want your necklace."

She couldn't help a small smile. She nodded, dropped her arms, and stepped away from him. She had her pride.

He tightened his grip on her hip and pulled her roughly against him. "Is it that easy for you? To pretend to want me, then step away?"

Selena shook her head. "No," she hoarsely said. "It's not."

He let her go and stepped back to the bed. "I want answers. I want them now."

Selena decided to give him what he wanted—most of it, anyway. "Let me get dressed and we'll talk." When he made no move to leave the stateroom, she cocked a brow and inclined her head toward the door.

"I'm not letting you out of my sight."

She threw her hands up into the air, then strode over to the closet and pulled out a wraparound deck dress of white jersey. It was casual and comfortable, and it accentuated her curves. As she tied a knot between her breasts, she looked over at him and noticed for the first time the deep stress lines around his mouth and eyes. He looked haggard. The Rev was wearing his body out.

"When was the last time you slept?"

"Before you shot me up."

Shaking her head, Selena sat down near him on the edge of the bed. Only once had she injected a human with the Rev, and she hadn't stuck around long enough to know if it had worked or how. Johnny was clearly suffering. She'd feel guilty only if it hadn't saved his life. "If you don't get some rest, you'll wear your body out. You might be Superman, but even he needed to sleep."

He shook his head. "Answers before sleep."

"What do you want to know?"

"Where is the uranium?"

"I honestly don't know."

Agitated, he stood up. "Tell me what you know about it. Who wants it and why were you in Kyrgyzstan?"

"I was in Kyrgyzstan to hijack the truck with the cask in it. I failed. Noslov has it now."

He looked at her as if she had grown a second head. "What does Los Cuatro want with enriched uranium?"

Selena wasn't surprised at the depth of his intel. "For safekeeping."

"I doubt it. What does Noslov want with it?"

"Why do *you* want it?"

"Same reason you do. Why does Noslov want it?"

"That wily Russian plans to auction it off to the highest bidder."

"Where and when?"

"I don't know, but I'll find out."

"How?"

She looked at the floor, then at Nikko. Yes, Nikko. She sighed. He was right, Johnny was dead. That part of her life was over. She had killed it. "I can get into his head."

"If you can get into his head, then you can control him?"

"In theory, I suppose. But I've never done it before. I don't know how." A small but effective lie.

"You did it to Vegas."

"I got into his head and had the unfortunate experience of observing his nightmare of a life as it flashed before his eyes. I didn't possess him."

"Four days ago Noslov was in Osh. With a phone call, I can have his current location. How close do you have to get to him to get into his head?"

"I need face-to-face access. It's easiest if the host is asleep." Selena bit her bottom lip. It was dangerous. She'd have to get an audience with Noslov, which wasn't the problem. He respected Los Cuatro's clout. But then she'd have to get him alone. Of course, there was the other way. The same way she was going to manipulate Nikko. If she told Nikko what she was capable of, he was smart enough to keep his mind *en garde* and keep her out. It was how she had managed to stay clear of her father all these years.

"Then you would be able to manipulate the date, location, and terms of the auction."

"Have you met Noslov?"

Nikko shook his head.

"I have, and he is a strong-willed man. The stronger a man's will, the more difficult it is to break him."

"You don't have to break him, just get the intel."

"And then what?"

"My people bid on it and take possession."

"Not so quick. *My* people want it. More specifically, my people want to keep it out of a certain Venezuelan dictator's hands. Those were his thugs riding shotgun."

"I work for a covert United States government agency. The cask will be safely stored on American soil."

"I work for an equally concerned and dedicated agency. We will make sure the cask is safely stored in a secure, undisclosed location."

"This isn't negotiable, Selena. We take control."

"Everything is negotiable. I say, to the highest bidder go the spoils."

He smiled. An almost genuine smile. What she wouldn't give to see the real thing. "You'll lose."

"Don't you know that the fatal flaw in the art of war is to underestimate your opponent?"

"Don't you know never to show up to a duel unarmed?"

Selena laughed, genuinely enjoying the verbal sparring. Johnny had always been quick-witted; he had won her over with his humor. Countless times he would have her laughing so hard, her cheeks ached for days.

His eyes narrowed as if he didn't find the humor where she did. "Me and mine play for keeps."

"And you think I don't? Have you forgotten so quickly what I did to Malphas? Before him, there were four just like him."

"We'll see." He strode to the doorway and said over his shoulder, "I'm going to help myself to your ship-to-shore." Then he disappeared.

Selena hurried to the nightstand and pulled a cell phone from the drawer, then rushed into the head and closed the door. Quickly she called *el patrón*.

"*Sí,*" his deep voice reverberated.

"*Señor,* I have confirmed that Noslov plans to auction the cask."

"*Yo sé.* I was just about to call you. The underground is abuzz with that info. He has set the auction for midnight Saturday. No other details."

Three days from now. "Damn it, I was hoping we could make him an offer he couldn't refuse."

"He's in Paris, at a safe house. Eleven rue de la Montmartre. There is a jet waiting for you at the airstrip. Get to him, and convince him to close the auction to just one bidder."

"His life or else?"

"No, a life far more precious to him. I have his two-year-old son. For each hour he refuses, I will send a body part."

"*Señor!*"

"The life of one child for the lives of thousands is a fair trade. See it done. And, Selena, a word of caution. This cask is big black-market news. Many are positioning themselves to get their hands on it. Many who are willing to lie, beg, steal, and kill for it. Trust no one."

"I will beware," she said.

She hung up just as Nikko opened the bathroom door. He grabbed her hand, trying to take the phone away. She turned and squeezed it so hard the LCD screen cracked.

"Damn you, Selena! Stop fighting me!"

"Stop interfering in my business!" She shoved past him into the bedroom and pointed to the door. "There's another stateroom down the hall. Get some sleep. We're going to need to be fresh tomorrow." But she was leaving tonight. *With* the necklace.

Nikko plopped down on the bed. "I told you, I'm not letting you out of my sight." He stretched out and patted the mattress beside him. "Lie down, and if you so much as move toward the door, you'll wish you hadn't."

She glared daggers at him. "You've turned into a bully."

"That's what happens when your life is pulled out from under you."

For almost an hour, Selena lay staring at a small spot on the ceiling. Nikko lay on his back with his hands behind his head staring at the same spot.

"I won't be able to get near Noslov without the necklace," she said, breaking the silence.

"You won't need the necklace. My people are moving in on him as we speak."

Selena gasped and turned to face him. "Why didn't you tell me?"

He turned to face her. "Why didn't *you* tell *me*?"

"Tell you what?"

He reached out, grabbed a hank of her hair, and drew her close to him. When their lips were but inches apart, he said, "Every third-world leader and terrorist group in the world knows what's about to go down. If your people aren't up on it, then you need to go to work for someone else."

"He's in Paris."

"He won't be for long."

"What leverage do your people have?"

"His life."

Selena smiled, though the thought of *el patrón*'s advantage sickened her. "Noslov doesn't care about his life. He won't give you what you want."

"We'll see."

She turned over and faced the wall, frowning into the darkness. She needed to get on that plane to Paris, track Noslov down, and convince him to take Los Cuatro's preemptive bid. But with Nikko's people getting in the way . . . Damn it! She had to get to Noslov first, the fate of thousands aside; she was not going to have the death of an innocent two-year-old on her hands.

She needed the necklace. She needed it now. She stilled her mind and concentrated on the man behind her. His blood coursed hot and potent through her veins. He had no idea that with the blood infusion, he had given her easy access to his emotions. It would make what she was about to do much easier.

Gently, she probed his thoughts, and recoiled. They were a chaotic swirl of anger, frustration, and passion. Each one focused squarely on her. Inhaling deeply, Selena collected her own chaotic emotions and settled down.

Sleep, she crooned. *Close your eyes and sleep.*

She felt him fight it. While his brain was wide-awake, his body was exhausted.

That's it, close your eyes. Think peaceful thoughts.

The rigid body behind her loosened. For what seemed endless hours, she calmly crooned to his subconscious, urging him to relax, to find sleep, to regenerate. Finally, deep, even breaths replaced the short, erratic ones.

Selena lay perfectly still, afraid if she moved, he would awake. She closed her eyes and imagined herself taking flight and slipping gently into his dreams. Then she was there.

He was aware of her. She smiled and touched his chest. His heart lurched against her palm. *Relax, it's only a dream. I can't hurt you.* I won't *hurt you. Just give me the necklace and I'll go.*

No.

Stubborn man. I give you my word I won't use it against you. Give it to me—

No.

You leave me no recourse, Nikko. She slipped out of her dress and slid her warm body against his. She hissed in a long, deep breath as her smooth skin slid against the hard planes of his body. His skin was fever hot. His body swelled, but as he had earlier, he resisted. *You want me, Nikko.* She pressed her lips to the pulsing vein in his neck and licked, then scraped her teeth along the thick artery. His muscles steeled, resistant.

No.

She pulled his pants from him; his cock sprang up hot and thick against her belly. *Your body does not lie, my love.* She moved over him, tracing her fingertips across his chest, around his hard nipples, then down his taut, defined belly. She followed the trail of dark downy hair that guided her to the root of him. His hips rose. *I've missed you so much,* she breathed against his lips. It wasn't a lie. He moaned and twisted away from her. She grasped his hips and slowly ran her hands down his thighs, then up, her fingertips grazing his warm balls, circling his thick root, tracing the pulsating vein that ran the length of his burgeoning shaft. His body tightened. He fisted the sheets. She lowered her lips to his.

He hissed in a long breath, his body straining to resist her. When she kissed him, her fingers wrapped around his cock. He groaned. Twisting his lips from hers, he reached up and grabbed the headboard, the action lifting his hips off the bed. He fought a colossal battle, one he would ultimately lose.

Selena was not unaffected. She might be invading his dreams, but it was as real to her as it was to him. She held the emotions that threatened to interfere under tight rein. She could not tell him she still loved him, how sorry she was, that she bled for him. She could not tell him that they had a beautiful, charming eight-year-old daughter who looked just like her papa. Instead, she focused on her carnal needs. There had been no one before Johnny, and no one after. Their brief but passionate encounter at the club had whetted her appetite for something more. Something deep. Something profound. Her body had been on slow simmer for him. Now it boiled.

Selena was kidding herself if she said she was seducing him solely for the necklace. He had left her panting for more of him when he walked away from her earlier tonight. Getting the necklace this way was simply an excuse to make love.

But first things first.

Where is the necklace?

He gritted his teeth, refusing to answer. She tightened her fingers around his shaft and began to slowly pump. His hips quaked against her. His body tightened. A slick sheen of perspiration dampened his skin. *Tell me to stop, and I will.*

Damn you! he cursed.

She laughed softly, enjoying his pain, but realized that even though it was a dream, she would not take from his body what his mind was not willing to give. She cupped his balls and gently massaged them. He groaned, and bucked against her hands. But that did not mean she could not push him to the edge. . . .

She nipped his bottom lip, then his chin, down his neck to his jugular. *I crave every part of you.* She scraped her teeth along the vital vein, then farther down to his chest, nipping a sensitive nipple, then sucking it. Her lips trailed down his belly, following the dark trail that led her to his groin. Nikko twisted, bucked, and thrust away from her. But he did not leave the bed. And in a dream, all things were possible. . . .

With just a little more persuasion, her body would convince his mind.

Selena pressed her lips to the sensitive spot between Nikko's hip and groin. In long, wet trails she licked around him, coming so close to the wide head of his cock, then dipping down to his root and balls. Nikko's body trembled. Just breathing on the sensitive areas made him squirm. Her fingertips caressed his tight thighs, his hips, and his washboard belly.

Her long hair trailed along his belly. He grabbed

a hank, but did not pull. Selena looked up at him, the thickness of his cock obscuring her view. She smiled and slid up his thighs, trailing her sultry sex along the length of his erection, then his belly.

His body tightened to steel. She straddled his belly, running her hands up his tense arms, to his hands grasping the headboard as if it were his life raft. She arched her back, thrusting her hips forward, lifting her swollen mons within inches of his face. Her musky sex scent filled the air between them.

Nikko's eyes flew open. He glared up at her, his fangs exposed, his face dangerously contorted.

Tell me to go and I will.

His glare did not waver.

She pressed her hips closer to him. He snarled; the ferocity of the sound sent shivers shooting straight to her womb. Selena closed her eyes, imaging his tongue and lips between her legs. . . .

Her body flinched and a long moan escaped her when he pressed his lips to the smooth rise of her mound. She sucked in her breath when he trailed the tips of his fangs across her skin to her clitoris. She held it, her entire body suspended in anticipation. She was so hot and so wet for him it embarrassed her.

She came apart when his lips parted her labia to get a better grip on her clit. His warm tongue swirled around her, teasing, sucking her enflamed flesh, making her hotter, wetter. Selena let go. She dug her fingers into her hair and arched her back, thrusting fully into his lips, wanting nothing more than to be devoured by him.

Only Nikko's lips and tongue touched her. His hands still grasped the headboard. He kept his hips still. She wanted him to break completely. But he remained in control. And though she'd held the power coming into his dream, now he wielded it.

Nikko.

He ignored her call; he would do what he chose, not what she demanded. His sinful lips sucked her nether lips; his tongue languorously lolled and rolled around her stiff clit, sending shock waves to the very ends of her. Selena grasped his hands on the headboard for support. Slowly, reverently, she rocked against him, her hips undulating in slow, sublime rhythm. Dear God, he felt good. When had he turned the tables on her? Deliberately he tormented her. She was so close to devastation, fighting the urge to let go and grind into his lips and demand he take her there.

She had to stop. She could not allow him the control. She—she squeezed her eyes shut as his lips slid along her seam to her clit. He gently suckled her into his mouth as his tongue caressed that so-sensitive place. "Ahhh," she exhaled. "That feels so good." Selena licked her dry lips, swallowing hard as she rode his torturous mouth in a slow, sensuous undulation.

His hands turned and grabbed hers, pulling her body taut. His legs pinned hers to the bed. Her body had betrayed her! She was trapped in his carnal snare. Selena struggled, pulling her hands, moving her legs, and dear God it would kill her to pull away from his salacious mouth, but she could not give him control. With every ounce of willpower she possessed, Selena pulled her hips away. He snarled, scraping his fangs along the inside of her thigh. Selena cried out in surprised pain. Her head snapped back and they locked stares.

Play with fire, you get burned, Selena.

She shook her head. Her long hair swirled around her shoulders. *I am the devil's daughter.* She sat back and grabbed his cock in her fist. His eyes narrowed but he did not move a muscle. He was hard. Thick. Warm. Slowly, she pumped him. His cock swelled in her hand. She stared at him, challenging him to resist her.

His eyes narrowed to slits; his jaw tightened and perspiration beaded his tanned skin. He was there, on the very edge of breaking.

We're going to burn together, Nikko Cruz.

Selena moved over his hips. When she rubbed the thick width of his cock along her slick opening, her body flinched as if she were being electrocuted. Nikko's body thrummed with energy beneath her. She squeezed her eyes shut, fighting for control. She could not hold out much longer. If he did not break first, then—she rocked her hips against him. She moaned, the friction so sweet. She was so slick and so hot for him that her body lured him into her. They gasped in unison when the wide head of his cock pressed into her. Selena squeezed her eyes tighter, fighting with every ounce of willpower she possessed not to go further. Her muscles quaked as she held herself from him. The urge to impale herself on him, to experience once again the sublimity of the thick heat of him filling her to overflowing, overwhelmed her.

Selena licked her lips and opened her eyes. Nikko's impassioned stare drilled into her. He hung as if suspended in the air, wanting what she wanted but still resisting. *Nikko,* she purred as she sat lower. She could not help herself. *Take me.*

She sat on him completely. The sensation of him

filling her to his balls, touching the end of her, was indescribably decadent. Her liquid inner muscles clasped him tightly in long-awaited welcome. And despite the welcome, he lay rigid and unbending.

It didn't matter, she told herself. She had what she wanted from him. He needn't do a thing. She knew what a junkie felt like getting that first fix after a long dry spell. The intensity of the first hit was unlike anything she had experienced. She wanted more. Savoring every inch of him, Selena moved her hips in a slow up-and-down undulation. Still he resisted. She closed her eyes, expelled a long breath, and allowed herself to experience the wonder of him on her terms. No battle of wills, no guilt, no ulterior motives, just—pleasure. It was beyond pleasure. Every nerve ending in her body lit up, as intensely as if a layer of her had been removed. Selena's breath hitched as the friction heated. Her skin slickened with perspiration. Her rhythm became urgent. Harder, faster, deeper. Her hips rose and fell to an age-old cadence. Hardening Nikko to steel.

Nikko, she moaned, arching her back as an intense wave built within her. Her knees clasped his hips, her fingers dug into his thighs. She—couldn't—breathe.

Then she felt it. He broke. His body shuddered hard; his hands dropped from the headboard, and his breath released in a wild, warm rush against her chest. In a fierce surge, he thrust high into her, nearly unseating her. Selena opened her eyes and screamed. In full fang, his eyes red, he rose up against her. He flung her onto her back and sank his cock deep into her pussy, his teeth into her neck, his fingers into her hair. *Dear Lord*— She arched high into him. Demanding more. He swiveled

his hips, grinding maddeningly into her as he raven-
ously sucked her blood.

It was wild, erotic, crazy, and death-defying. She
came in a violent rush of blistering sensation; the intensity of it threw her over the edge. She screamed again as
he slammed into her, clasping him tighter to her neck,
reveling in his ardent possession of her. As Nikko came
inside her, his mind opened up, and what Selena saw
astonished and terrified her.

CHAPTER TWELVE

Nikko came in a wild maelstrom of pent-up passion. As his body hurtled toward release, fury and unrequited hunger barreled through him, the latter so ravenous he knew if he gave in to it, it would kill him. He did not want to surrender to Selena's seduction. He fought it with every part of him, but in the end he was powerless to resist her call. The copper taste of blood coupled with the sultry sex scent of the woman beneath him was gasoline on his fire.

He had never been able to resist her. Even now, after what she had done to him—to his *child*—he craved her.

His soul cried foul, his brain demanded revenge, but a small, quiet part of him just wanted to be allowed to mourn. He had never mourned. Anger, hate, and revenge had filled his heart.

Yet now, even as he came inside of her, his heart mourned his daughter and the loss of the woman he had loved.

The woman beneath him.

Selena . . .

He felt her sorrow, her regret—her love. She *should* feel sorrow and regret. Love? She loved no one but herself.

But his instincts, coupled with his heightened senses, identified only truth. What did that mean?

Johnny.

Nikko squeezed his eyes closed. The rage in him quieted in time with their spent bodies. He withdrew his fangs from her neck and gently licked the wounds, then moved out of her. A compulsion he could not defy made him reach down to his trousers on the floor, pull the necklace out of the front pocket, and drop it onto her belly.

But the action came with a warning: *Do not use it against me.*

Never.

Nikko woke slowly. He swam in a deep pool, his vision hazy, his movements slow, but he rose to the light. As he surfaced, memories of the night before came crashing down around him. In fast-forward, he relived his reunion with Selena. How he had saved her. He remembered the daemon attack, swimming to her yacht, then—Jesus! He'd had one hell of a dream. They had fucked ferociously. He had—given her back her necklace. He sat up in the empty bed. Dream hell! She'd played him! And he knew she was long gone.

Quickly he dressed and ran up to the bridge to call in. As he passed through the salon, he stopped in his tracks. Under the cover of night, he had not seen the details of the interior, but now in the morning glare he saw everything—including the stuffed Minnie Mouse, sitting on a chair near the bridge door.

It was the same doll he'd bought for his unborn daughter.

Nikko's blood drained from his face. His heart slowed

to an erratic thud. A different kind of urgency filled him. One slow step at a time, he walked toward the doll. With a trembling hand, he reached out and touched it.

It was soft but worn, as if much loved by a child, as if a small hand had hugged and caressed it over the years. Emotions ruptured in his chest. A longing so powerful it hurt filled him. Had Selena kept it all these years? Did she regret what she had done? He brought the doll to his nose and inhaled. Gooseflesh erupted along his arms. The scent was not Selena's. The doll smelled of sunshine and animal crackers. A child's scent. Moist heat stung his eyes. Why was the doll here? Who had caressed it and infused it with its scent? Had Selena given it to another child? Or—Nikko's entire body shook with fear, hope, despair—to the one for whom it had been intended?

The sun shines on the nuns . . . where it began.

They'd begun on St. Michael's.

Nikko's heart shuddered to a halt. He'd thought Selena's words as she lay in the elevator were a dying woman's chaotic mumblings. Had finally understood why she—a daemon—would consider an island to be the safest place in the world. The safest place from other daemons.

But now, with the doll in his hands, with the desperate but real hope that perhaps the love he'd sensed in her *had* been truth—not just for him, but for their daughter—Nikko reevaluated her words.

Perhaps they hadn't been uttered for her benefit, but for his.

Perhaps they'd been a clue. If Selena thought she was dying, perhaps it was a clue meant to lead him to their daughter.

Was it possible?

Had she—? That scar on her belly. A cesarean scar?

He felt faint. His knees wavered. Nikko sat down.

Marisol, sunny sea. They were going to name their daughter Marisol. The sunny sea. Where she was conceived in love.

The sun shines on the nuns of St. Michael's.

Nikko inhaled deeply and slowly exhaled, fighting the excitement welling within him. He needed to rationally think this through. Selena's father. She'd said she meant to protect him from her father. Who else was she protecting? And what better place to hide a child from a daemon than on an island in the care of nuns?

When Selena thought she was dying, she had told him Marisol was alive and where to find her! *Holy Mother of God, his daughter was alive.*

He didn't know if he should laugh or cry. All this time, he'd thought Selena had destroyed his daughter, when all along she was alive. Just as Selena had lived. Why? Why had she kept him from his daughter? He had a right to know her. She had a right to know him. Renewed rage erupted. Selena had played God with his life and his daughter's life. She had no right, damn her!

He must go to St. Michael's to see for himself if he was delusional with grief, yearning, and plain old Rev-induced psychosis, or if Marisol was alive. But Selena's words about her father stopped him. Would he jeopardize Marisol's safety? It looked as if he and his ex were going to have a come-to-Jesus meeting in the near future. Because Nikko was not going to stay away from his daughter. Not when he'd already lost eight years with her.

He called Godfather.

"We've got a lock on Noslov in Paris," Godfather's voice boomed triumphantly.

Though it took every ounce of restraint he possessed, Nikko forced himself to focus on his mission and not St. Michael's Island. "Is he accessible?"

"He's got an armed detail surrounding him, as well as the perimeter buildings. Stone and Satch are on their way along with Cassidy and Cross. I have every reason to believe they will extract him."

"What makes you think he'll talk once we have him?"

"We aren't going to make him talk. Cassidy gave me the 411 on what your girl is capable of. She's going to get the information for us."

To hear Godfather speak so matter-of-factly about Selena's daemon powers was more than a little freaky. It was downright creepy to know she could get into people's heads and manipulate their thoughts and actions. Getting into Vegas's head had nearly killed her. Would getting into Noslov's push her to her limit again?

Was he willing to risk it? Her life for information they could easily get with a little L.O.S.T. coercion? A big part of him was not.

"Cruz, did you hear me?"

"I'm flattered you think I have that kind of control over her, which I don't, but it's a moot point. She's gone."

"Gone?"

"That stuff she injected me with ran me ragged. I crashed and burned last night. I woke up and she was gone. Your hunch was right about her connection to Balderama. She works for him. They got word that that asshole in Venezuela had struck a deal with Noslov for the cask. They went after it for safekeeping. We both failed. She's on her way to Noslov, and she's not going to share him if she gets to him first."

"Cruz, see that she does."

"You want me to stand by while she nabs him?"

"I want you to convince her we're all on the same side. Once we have the information we need, we'll maneuver the cask into our possession by whatever means necessary."

"Godfather, you don't know Selena—"

"No, but you do. Do whatever you must to get the information from her. I'll alert our hangar at Miami International to have the jet ready. You're going to have to fly it yourself, I'm fresh out of pilots. Now, get on it pronto. Word on the street is that deposits are being made on that cask. It's become the hottest commodity to hit the black market since opium."

Godfather hung up.

Nikko let out a long breath. He was torn between chartering a seaplane and flying up to St. Michael's to see for himself if his suspicions were true, and the call of duty. In the end, duty trumped. Only because *if* Marisol was alive, she was safe. For the moment, at least. Besides, Selena Guerrero had a lot of explaining to do.

Dusk gently blanketed Paris. Selena hopped off the slick black Ducati Streetfighter she'd ridden in on, rocked it back on the kickstand, then pulled off her helmet. She shook her long hair as she covertly surveyed the activity on the street. She stood in the heart of Montmartre, the Sacré-Coeur looming just beyond the buildings surrounding her, its great white dome reflecting the setting sun. Just down the street on the same side as where she stood, a dozen armed men unsuccessfully attempted to blend in with the barren winter landscape. Noslov was in the building they milled in front of. She didn't have to look up to know that at least a half dozen snipers patrolled the rooftops adjoining the building. Noslov had the misconception he was protected. Maybe against most threats, including Nikko's team, but Noslov's highly trained mercs were no match for the power she would unleash on them.

Selena smiled, anxious for the encounter. She'd always had a bit of an adrenaline junkie in her, but after Johnny—well, having realized what she must do to survive, she lived for this kind of stuff.

Farther down the street, she noticed two men who were doing a much better job of looking to be part of the landscape. One was disguised as a starving artist slowly lugging his canvas-laden bike up the hill, while another had set up shop as a street vendor selling secondhand frames.

Her nose twitched. The vampire from her club and his consort were near. She was impressed. Whatever agency Johnny, er, Nikko worked for certainly knew its trade. The woman was undetectable, and the vampire? Her gaze rose toward the rooftop directly across the street from the building Noslov was holed up in. The vampire's blood scent was strong, but so was the decay of the guards he had taken out.

She wasn't worried about the humans, but the

vampire was formidable. She'd keep an eye out for him. Nikko was formidable, too. The Rev had upped his strength, his senses, his attitude—his libido. A warm flush washed across her cheeks. Last night was, damn, it was crazy sexy. What had started as a simple push to get him to return her necklace had turned into a—well, it was crazy. And she had no regrets. They both had gotten something out of the deal. Her bonus, the necklace.

Selena pushed the heated moments of last night deep into her memory banks for later. Her focus now was 100 percent on extracting Noslov.

Her sharp gaze swept the perimeter again, this time for a sign of Nikko. He would show up soon enough. She could have told him not to waste the time and jet fuel. She had no doubt in her mind who would walk away with Noslov. Selena turned and strode away from the building she had been standing against, turning at the next street corner and then down the alley running parallel to the street behind the buildings. The sun's receding rays had long since disappeared.

The thud of two feet landing on the cobblestones behind her alerted her to company. His blood scent revealed his identity.

"This is none of your business, vampire," she softly said.

"You are very much my business, slayer."

She nodded and turned slowly to face him. Nikko's accomplice from Lost Souls. Her nose twitched. A young vampire, but a deadly one. Arrogant, too. As she lay dying in Vegas's body, she'd heard him refuse Nikko's pleas for her life. "Have you told Rurik my identity?"

"I will—eventually."

"Let me guess, you'll snitch after *you* get what you want from me?"

"He is my king, I am his enforcer. Regardless of what I *get* from you, I will enforce the rules of the Order."

Selena quirked her lips. "Yeah, the king thing. I hear you, but I happen to be in possession of some information your king would sell his soulless self for."

The vampire's blue eyes reddened. "You have broken cardinal rules, rules that if ignored would set off a chain reaction of violence among the Others. War and death would follow. You must be punished."

The stones around her neck warmed as she silently called to them for strength. She could take the vampire. The power of the nanorians, combined with the Rev-infused vampire blood coursing through her veins, gave her superior power. "You realize I possess the power to destroy you where you stand." She took a step toward him. "In fact, I can destroy ten of you."

"You may be able to destroy me, but you will not stand a chance against Rurik."

Selena smiled seductively. She cranked up the phero-mones and slowly sauntered toward him. "Your consort is watching. What do you think she'll do when she sees you kiss me?"

"She will understand you have used your daemon powers to seduce me."

Selena threw her head back and laughed. "You disap-point me, vampire. I thought you had more fight in you than that."

He moved with blinding speed. The air whooshed

from Selena's lungs as he slammed her hard against the stone wall of the building behind her. The nanorians flared, as did her reaction. She hurled him from her. He went flying across the alley, but slowed his momentum midway, then rose high into the air and, like a missile, dove at her.

Selena shoved her hands, palms open, straight at him. The force of her power sent him sprawling back into the brick and mortar of the building behind him with a sickening crunch. She knew it would only stun him. She strode toward him as he shook his head and staggered to standing. "Believe me when I tell you this: If Rurik and your kind are to survive, he must leave me alone. *I* am the key to your survival."

She turned and started toward the fire ladder.

The vampire dropped in front of her. "How are you, a rogue half-breed, key to my survival?"

"Only *I* have the power and the knowledge to destroy the piece of crap who schemes to take control of the Order by destroying the very thing you need to survive."

His deadly eyes narrowed. "What are you saying?"

"Blood. Your kind needs blood to survive. And your blood source is . . . ?" She raised her eyebrows. "Use that vampire superbrain of yours to figure it out." She pushed past him.

He grabbed her upper arm and spun her around to face him. "Are you saying there is a plot to destroy humanity?"

She yanked her arm from his brutal grip and turned toward the building Noslov was housed in. "You're just going to have to trust me on this one, big guy." She looked over her shoulder at him. "Now, do me a favor and keep your friends off my back until I get in; then it's every man and woman for themselves."

She knew he would not stop her. Too much of what she had imparted was feasible, and though she was a rogue slayer, there was some honor among the thieves that they were. She grabbed hold of the fire ladder and hoisted herself up to the closest rooftop. She ducked just as two armed men on the building next door turned.

As stealthy as a shadow, she crouched, making her way toward them. In just the few moments she had been on the rooftop, darkness had completely settled over Paris. Selena picked up a piece of debris from the roof and tossed it over the closest man's head. He moved toward the noise, while the other hurried to his side to investigate. She leapt into the air and came down on both of them. In two quick moves, she snapped their necks. She divested them of their weapons, slinging one AK over each shoulder. She wouldn't need them, but they would make anyone she encountered think twice before coming after her.

Selena moved with shadow stealth to the next rooftop. Three floors down and directly below her, she heard Noslov speaking in Arabic, outlining the terms of the auction. *Jesus.* With Muslim dictatorships falling like dead trees all over the Middle East and North Africa, any number of deposed dictators might consider using a dirty bomb as leverage to regain power.

A new urgency took hold of her. Easily, she took out the three guards on the rooftop. She jumped to the next rooftop and dealt with the two there. With the rooftops clear, she would be able to easily access Noslov. Just as she was ready to climb down the back side of the building, the radios her victims wore erupted with chatter. Russian voices alerted them that the front of the building had been breached.

Johnny's covert US government agency friends. Had to be. Those two men out front, plus the vampire and his consort. And Johnny. She could smell him. They had more opposition to get through than she did. She had to hurry if she was going to get to Noslov first and extract him—alive.

Like a lizard, she climbed down the rough stone wall, then launched herself gymnast-style through the only window to the room where Noslov sat behind an enormous desk frantically typing on his laptop. Selena landed on her feet as glass shattered around her.

Noslov stood, slamming the lid shut on the computer.

"Step back or I'll shoot you into a piroshki."

He raised his hands and put them behind his head. "I will pay you triple what you are being paid," he calmly offered.

Selena stepped forward and grabbed his laptop, then yanked its power source from the wall. As she stuffed it down the back of her jacket, she said, "Tell me where the cask is, and you have a deal."

"Vat cask do you speak of?"

"Shut up, Noslov." Selena snatched the Russian's cell phone off his desk and slipped it into her jacket pocket. "Come around the desk slowly. That's it." As he rounded the corner, he flung the dagger he had hidden behind him at her. Selena caught it in midair by the tip, instantly she hurled it back at him. It sliced off half of his left ear and stuck into the wall behind him.

He screamed, grabbing the bloody stump.

"Don't fuck with me."

She grabbed him by the collar of his shirt as he bolted for the door.

It crashed open from the hallway, and the two dudes and the vampire's consort from outside burst in, catching Noslov between them.

Blood streaming down the side of his face, Noslov shouted out in Russian for reinforcements. Knowing his calls were futile, he slammed his heels hard on the wood floor, and two blades popped out of the toes of his leather shoes. In a tight roundhouse kick, he nailed one of the men in the shin. As he came down, Selena lit up the wall behind the intruders with the two AKs, forcing the operatives out of the room. The scent of new blood sprang into the air. Someone had caught a round. She wasn't going to stay and ask whom and say sorry. Not her problem, they should not have challenged her. She grabbed Noslov by the scruff of the neck and hauled him backward toward the window.

Nikko stood at the base of the Sacré-Coeur. Selena's sultry scent overrode every other scent in the City of Light. He sensed her excitement. Other familiar smells infiltrated his senses. Cassidy and Cross. Stone and Satch. And blood. Satriano's blood. His lips curled back from his fangs and he took off. As he rounded the street corner to the opening of the alley, he saw Selena climbing down a fire ladder with a struggling Noslov dangling from her right hand. She coldcocked him, then slung him over her shoulder. She hit the alley, running straight toward Nikko, and stopped in her tracks when she saw him.

By the nonchalant look on her face, she wasn't surprised to see him. But he had to admit, he was surprised to see her decked out in smooth black leather from head to toe with the Russian slung over her shoulder. She reminded him of a sleek black she-panther trotting off with her prey. Part of him respected the hell out of her, part of him wanted to fuck her on the spot, and part of him was furious she had gotten to Noslov first. Where the hell was his team?

Nikko smiled. "I told you, you can run, but you can't hide."

"Back off, Cruz."

"How can I when you shot one of my men?"

"He'll survive."

He let her move past him, but only because Cross and Cassidy were in position. She crossed the street, ignoring the gaping bystanders. She was quite a sight, dressed in black leather, black boots, and two crisscrossed AKs, the double-dealing Russian hanging over her shoulder like a fox stole.

Nikko watched Stone and Satch come up behind her on the left side of the street, Cross and Cassidy on the right side. Looked as if Satriano would survive after all.

Nikko grinned. Now they had her. Nikko strode parallel to her, admiring the sure strut of her stride. "You can run, Selena . . . ," he taunted, moving in on her as his team tightened the noose.

"Back off, Cruz, or you'll wish you had," she said as she trotted down the middle of the street, ignoring the pedestrians and rubbernecking motorists.

Nikko continued to shadow her while his team moved in closer behind her. He looked ahead to the opening of the alley to her right. Lightning quick, Nikko rushed her, forcing her to take that route. As Nikko cornered the building giving chase, she decked him. He went flying backward into Stone and Satch. Instantly he was up and after her. This time, fury propelled him. She leapt over the iron gate at the end of the alley. Nikko flew after her. He tackled her on the other side, this time not caring if she hit hard. Their bodies went sprawling. She was on her feet in the blink of an eye, with Noslov's moaning body slung back over her shoulder. She leveled an AK at Nikko's heart.

"Another step and you're done." Her tone was as firm as her stance. Not a ripple in it.

"We both know you won't pull the trigger."

"You underestimated me eight years ago, and see what it got you? Are you willing to do so again?"

Nikko smiled. She was all smoke and mirrors. "I'm willing." He laughed at her stunned expression. "I'm calling your bluff, Selena. And know you're going to pay for it."

The sounds of thudding feet behind him alerted Nikko to his backup. Not that any of them, even Cross, would have much effect on Selena. She was super-charged, and in a throwdown, she'd probably kick the crap out of all of them. But he wasn't going to give her the opportunity to try.

"We had a deal," she said, waving the automatic at him. "I won, now back off."

"Our deal didn't specify a time limit. Give me Noslov and I'll let you walk away."

Selena threw her head back and laughed. "You force my hand, Nikko." She readjusted the Russian on her back and brought the second AK to bear on a target behind him. "Your friends or Noslov?"

Nikko growled. She'd do it, too, just to prove she could.

She smiled wider and began to walk slowly backward. "I have a parting gift for you, Nikko Cruz and friends." She reached behind her and pulled a laptop from the back of her jacket, and tossed it to Nikko, who reflexively caught it. "I'm sure your covert government agency will find lots of goodies in there. I might even share the auction details with you once I have them."

She kept the AK aimed behind him and with her other hand grabbed hold of the wrought-iron fence behind her. "I suspect it's going to be one of those black-tie affairs. Brush up on your Arabic, and bring your checkbook. I overheard Noslov say the bidding will be silent, but beginning at half a billion."

Nikko watched her climb the high fence with the ease of a kid on a jungle gym. Then she disappeared into the night.

"Go after her!" Stone said, running past him to the sixteen-foot fence.

Nikko shook his head. "Letting her go will not only get us into the auction, but with the information stored here"—he held up the laptop—"at the very least we might learn who the other players are."

Satch shook his head and said, "You actually trust her?"

Nikko turned to look at Cassidy, who oddly didn't glare at him with the same accusation that Satch and

Stone did. Cross remained his usual stoic self. Nikko let out a long breath and nodded. If anyone had asked him that question twenty-four hours ago, he would unequivocally have said, *Hell, no.* Now? Now he simply did.

"I know all her dirty little secrets. She'll come through." He looked at the widening bloodstain on Satch's shoulder. "We need to get you to a doc, then get the hell out of this town."

CHAPTER THIRTEEN

The thrum of the jet engines did not quell Noslov's moaning. He had been out cold for almost the entire return flight to Miami. His ear had finally stopped bleeding, not that Selena cared.

She would have cut his head off if she didn't need him. She had contemplated just diving into his thoughts to get the information, but even though it was just the two of them and the pilot, she didn't like the vulnerability she'd experienced when leaving her physical body. It left her wide open to possession, and if that happened, she'd be stuck in Noslov's body.

No thank you. She'd get the info the good old-fashioned way.

Selena kicked his foot. "Wake up, Vlad," she hissed. His head lolled back and forth, his moans louder. She knew the instant he became cognizant of his reality. "Try anything and I'll throw your ass out the door."

His pale-lashed lids fluttered open, and he gave her an arctic glare.

Ah, there was the Vladimir Noslov she loved to hate. Selena sat forward in the seat directly across from him. She flipped open her cell phone and pressed a button. "Papa, Papa!" a little boy's voice cried. She shoved the screen in Noslov's face, showing his son in the company of a big, ugly man. "Little Yuri in the care of my associate an hour ago." She watched the blood drain from Noslov's face.

"The cask for your son."

She caught the flinch in his eyes, the tightening of his lips before he relaxed and looked lazily at her. "I don't have a son or this cask you speak of."

Selena sat back in the leather seat and crossed her legs and arms. "Do I have *dumb ass* stamped on my fore-head?" She hit the play button again. Little Yuri's cries for his father raised the hair on the back of her neck. If she thought for one minute the child would actually be harmed, she would have insisted *el patrón* find another way.

Vlad didn't flinch this time. He was either a cold-hearted bastard or a skilled operator playing a high-stakes game of poker with his son's life. She hoped for his son's sake, he was the latter.

"My instructions are to inform you that, for each hour you refuse me, the man who has possession of your son will chop off a body part until there is nothing left of the boy. Should you still refuse, I am to do the same to you." Selena slowly withdrew one of her long swords from the sheath strapped to her back. Vlad paled a few shades when she pressed the razor-sharp edge to his intact ear. "I can begin with you, if you prefer."

He glared at her but didn't flinch.

"No woman will want you for yourself, comrade," she continued. "You're a rooster, Vlad. The guy who struts his stuff for the ladies. And I have to admit, if I were attracted to handsome, blond terrorists, I'd do you. But—I'm not. So when I get done with you, even all of your money won't be able to entice a woman into your bed." When he didn't blink, Selena turned up the heat. "I think I will instruct my boss to begin with little Yuri's eyes. One at a time."

The only sign he was thinking about it was the sheen of perspiration glossing his pale forehead. Selena flipped open her phone and began to text while the video of little Yuri crying for his papa streamed.

"Stop!" Vlad screamed, pressing his hands to his ears, then screamed louder when he touched the bloody stump that used to be his left ear.

"Same deal. I won't offer it again."

He winced, looking at the coagulated blood on his hand, then up at her. His glacier-cold eyes glittered viciously. "The auction has been set. I cannot cancel it."

"For every hour you refuse . . ." She pressed the video stream again.

His eyes narrowed to slits. His heart rate skyrocketed and he inhaled deeply, trying valiantly to hide his quickened breathing from her. He shifted in the leather seat and flatly said, "Millions in deposits have been made just for an invitation."

"Eyes first."

His heart stopped, then restarted. "The money has been paid," he said. "I cannot undo what has been set in motion."

"In the States, we call it a refund."

Desperation strained the deep lines in his face. "If I refund the deposits, there will be no rock my family could hide under."

"At least your son will be alive for a while longer. I'm sure you could find a way to protect him."

In an uncharacteristic move, the Russian dropped

his head into his hands and shook his head. Desperate pain washed off him in waves. And something else. Hopelessness on the heels of defeat. He'd given up! The prick had given up on his child? Had she pushed too hard? In his mind, he could do nothing to save his son. And now her leverage was gone.

Damn it!

Selena sat back and contemplated Noslov's dilemma. In his mind, his son was dead regardless of his choice. Give him a third choice then.

"I think, Vlad, my friend, you may have overlooked a few invitations."

His head snapped back. "What do you imply?"

"You need to make room for one more seat at the table." Selena almost said two seats—but all she'd promised Nikko was the info, not an invite.

"For whom?"

"A very powerful man, the same man who currently has your son. The man who will guarantee Yuri's safe return so long as his needs are met." If the Russian called her bluff, she would have no choice but to risk possession and get the information the daemon way. Something she did not want to do. Holding firm to her resolve to tighten the vise, she leaned into him and softly said, "Tick . . . Tock . . ."

She watched the wheels turn in Noslov's brain. First resistance, followed by frantic reasons it would not work, then how he could make it work. Finally, acceptance. "I will add this man, but just as the others did, he must make a fifty-million-dollar deposit in gold to a designated Singapore account."

"I don't see that as a problem." She had not discussed

money with *el patrón,* but $50 million seemed like a deal in light of the risk of losing the cask to anyone else, most especially Apollyon. Selena smiled and leaned closer to the wary Russian and softly said, "Now, sit back and relax, because I'm going to make you an offer you can't refuse, comrade."

The desperate Russian nodded vigorously.

An hour later, the jet touched down in Miami. Selena didn't take any chances with Noslov. She knocked him out, bound and blindfolded him, and stuffed him into the waiting car; driving to the dock, she hauled him in the small motorboat to her island house. She ushered him to the same hospitality suite that had hosted the Venezuelan truck driver.

She roused Noslov with a whiff of smelling salts she kept on hand for exactly that purpose. When he came to, she yanked the duct tape off his mouth and unbound his feet and hands. "I'll give you something for the pain when we're done here."

Her offer earned her a harsh glare.

She handed him a throwaway cell phone and a fresh laptop. "As agreed, you will contact all of the invitees with the change of time and venue, and my personal guarantee of security. My private airstrip on Ilusion Island will be provided, along with a private yacht for each attendee. They are welcome to bring their own crews and to run security sweeps to their hearts' content. Once on board, each will motor to a designated secure dock in Miami and be transported from there to Lost

Souls. Once again, for their peace of mind, they are welcome to procure their own rides, or one will be provided for each attendee and his entourage. My club is world-renowned for its discretion. Each attendee is welcome to bring a security detail, limited to four, to the front doors of the club. However, only the actual bidder will be permitted into the inner sanctum of the auction. No exceptions." Noslov's color began to rise. He didn't like being told what to do and certainly not by a woman. She handed him his cell phone to pull numbers from and a throwaway to enter them into. Once he had the numbers transferred, she took his personal cell and pointed to the throwaway. "Now, make the calls. You have three minutes."

He hesitated. Selena fisted her hands to keep from slapping the arrogant Russian. She was so close; if he hesitated now, she didn't like her alternatives. "Any questions?"

"If they refuse?"

"Then they're SOL and out their deposits. The terms are not negotiable. I'm sure if you explain as succinctly as I just have, they will understand."

As Noslov looked down at the phone, Selena put her hand over his and looked hard at him. "I suggest you instruct each person willing to cough up the national debt for that cask to show up in person. That way, if there is an issue, he will have complete authority to make whatever decision necessary, because there will be no communication allowed once the auction convenes."

"There will be no issue. To the highest bidder goes the spoils."

Selena smiled slowly. "Comrade, here in America,

anything is possible, and all things probable. Hope for the best, expect the worst. No agents, only the real deal or no deal." She released his hand and stood back. "Now, make the calls."

As he made the calls, Selena thought ahead. Half a billion dollars was an exorbitant amount of money. How would Los Cuatro procure that amount in three days' time? Or would they have to? Selena secretly smiled. Knowing *el patrón,* he had already thought his way out of this dilemma. Roberto Balderama was a strategic mastermind. His patience and attention to detail had served him well. Thank God he was on the side of justice. His brain in enemy hands would be a terrible thing.

"Each of the invitees has agreed to the new terms," Noslov said, visibly relieved.

Selena smiled and snatched the cell phone out of his hand. "I had no doubt, Vlad. Enriched uranium doesn't fall off trees. I'm sure there are a few among the invitees who have sold their souls to the devil to get their hands on it." And that was a fact.

Once she had Noslov settled, Selena closed and locked the heavy metal door behind her. She let out a long, exhausted breath. Three days. In three days, the cask would be in Los Cuatro's hands. In three days, she could resume her hunt for the sixth and seventh nanorians. Then she would call out her sire and destroy him. For the first time since she'd made the fateful decision to break all ties with Johnny and hide their daughter, Selena felt a flicker of hope that maybe, once Paymon was a pile of ashes, she might have the semblance of a normal life.

With Johnny.

Her entire body warmed as she fantasized about the three of them happily running hand in hand along the beach, a happy, *normal* family. It was wishful thinking. Nothing could repair the damage she'd done, the emotional chasm too wide to be healed. But one thing Selena was determined to mend: Marisol would know her father. Selena would move heaven and Hell to see them reunited. Hah, she would have to move heaven and Hell. If she survived Paymon, and the Order's strict justice, she'd have to survive Johnny's wrath when he learned his daughter was alive and well. If she did not survive? At least Johnny and Marisol would be reunited. Upon her return from Kyrgyzstan, she'd drawn up a will explaining everything in detail as well as leaving all of her worldly possessions to her daughter. The minute she had the document notarized, she had felt an insane sense of relief. She wished she could say the same for how she felt now. An urgency she had never before experienced gripped her.

Selena pushed off the door and hurried up to her sprawling bedroom. She stripped and jumped into the shower, the totality of what she had to do pushing her through her emotional quagmire. She must be honed, focused, and prepared for the auction. Thinking of all the woulda coulda shouldas would not help her now. As she wrapped a light linen towel around her, she padded into her dressing room.

"I don't like to be ignored," Joran's deep voice said from behind her.

Jesus! How had he sneaked up behind her? She was too preoccupied, that's how. If at any time in her life she needed to be *en garde,* it was now. Joran was intuitive,

highly intelligent, and damn strong. He was also her eyes
and ears into the daemon world. She needed him now
more than ever. Selena collected herself. The stress of the
last few days was beginning to wear on her. Though the
stones provided power, her metabolism had processed
the Rev part of Nikko's blood. She was, quite simply,
exhausted.

Slowly she turned with a forced smile as she glanced
out the open window. The sun had just begun its descent
over the western horizon. "You're up a little early."

"Assassinating Vegas was not part of our deal."

She shrugged and moved past him. "He kind of left
me no choice." She stepped into the vast dressing room
and motioned for him to sit down on a nearby silk divan.

"I did not come here to watch you pick out shoes,
Selena." His voice had lowered dangerously.

"No?" She smiled over her shoulder at him. Padding
behind a dressing screen, she walked into one of the
three closets in the large room and searched for something to wear. She would have to change again and head
to the club, but for now she wanted to be comfortable.

"You wound me to the quick, Selena," Joran called to
her.

"What did I do now?" she asked, sorting through one
outfit after another.

"You bear another's mark."

She peeked around the side of the screen and winked.
"I took a walk on the wild side." She returned to the
closet.

"I would have given you everything."

Selena laughed. "Until you were bored!" She grabbed
a gold silk caftan and slipped it over her head. When

she came out of the dressing room tying the silken cord around her waist, Joran rose and propped himself against the arched doorway, "You asked me to get information from Vegas, but you never said *not* to eliminate the lousy bastard," she pointed out.

"His death has created some difficulty for me."

"His death nearly killed me. I offer no apologies for his demise." She slipped on a pair of matching sandals. "So stop whining about your troubles. Do you want the information or not?"

He stood silent for a long time, then nodded.

"Vegas's boss, Luis Fernandez, is, er, *was* in bed with Malphas. I took care of that little problem, thank you very much for that. But you have bigger worries. Luis has bought more than a few daemons by promising them fresh souls. He's amped up the human trafficking in Dade, Broward, and Palm Beach Counties. And he's leaving a bread trail straight to your door."

The vampire nodded. He'd been feeling a lot of heat lately.

"He has all three DAs in his pocket."

"Impossible! They are mine!"

Selena smiled. Vampire or human, a man's ego was a fragile thing. "Remember in *Godfather II* when Michael asked the Nevada senator for a favor and the senator turned around and demanded an exorbitant payoff from Michael just for the hell of it? And Michael told him to take a hike?"

Joran shook his head.

"Are you kidding me? You haven't seen *The Godfather*?" Selena asked in disbelief. Who hadn't seen *The Godfather*? "Well, anyway, Michael, the godfather, needs the senator's backing to ensure his purchase of a casino in Vegas. The greedy senator refuses. So Mikey's brother, who just so happens to run a whorehouse off the Strip, has a plan. He slips the senator a Mickey and sets him up to take the fall for killing a prostitute. Of course, it's documented. So now the senator is beholden to Michael for fear of being exposed. Luis has done the same thing to the DAs. Every one of them. They're kicking down cases, cases connected to Luis and his thugs, that would normally be charged." Selena dropped into a chair and watched the arrogant vampire fume. "Well played, I say."

Joran growled and began to pace the thick Aubusson carpet.

"One other thing I discovered while I was in that cesspool of a brain." She had debated telling Joran about the death of the female vampire, but figured she owed him the bonus.

"What?"

"Do you know of a vampiress, midtwenties, dark hair, green eyes, a pretty woman who disappeared within, say, the last five years?"

She would never have believed it, but Joran Cadiz's cheeks blanched white. "What did you see?"

"Vegas staked her." She kept the details of what the vampiress was doing at the time of her death out of the mix. Somehow, Selena knew it would upset Joran more.

"My—sister," he hoarsely said. He ran his fingers through his long hair. "I knew she had been killed. I felt it the night it happened, but I didn't know where or how." He turned glowing eyes on Selena. "She was wild and unpredictable."

"Your *sister*? Blood sister or vampire sister?"

"Blood sister."

"How the hell, Joran? Did you turn her?"

He strode past her and stood at the window, peering at the sinking sun. "She was twenty-three and dying. I had been turned years before. She begged me to turn her. I was never able to refuse Antonia. I wish I had."

"How old are you?"

He turned fiery eyes on her. "Nearly nine hundred years old. I was thirty-four when Rurik turned me. Something I will never forgive him for."

"Ah, now I get your contempt for the Order and its rules."

"The Order serves its purpose, it just doesn't happen to be mine."

"Does Rurik look the other way when it comes to your Miami game because he made you?"

Joran laughed a deep, genuine laugh. Selena was stunned. She didn't think he had it in him.

"It was I who, as a human, introduced the almighty king of vampires to his consort. He repaid me by making me like him."

"What's so bad about it? You have everything."

"Except the woman I loved. By turning me, he took that away from me!"

Selena felt the first inkling of compassion for this man. Love had nearly destroyed the very thing precious to her. "Love is overrated, Joran. Our kind are better off without that complication."

He stepped closer to her, so that only inches separated them, and cupped her chin with his hand. "I have never loved since then. I have no desire to lose my heart again. Yet"—he rubbed his thumb across her bottom lip—"I enjoy all the pleasures a woman can offer a man."

Selena smiled and grasped his hand, pushing it away from her, then rose from her chair. "I'm sure the ladies enjoy all the pleasures you offer them."

His dark pupils dilated. "Who broke your heart, Selena?"

Such a loaded question, and one she had no intention of answering. "I guess you should know that it was Luis who ordered the hit. He knew Antonia was a vampire. He promised Vegas eternal life for his loyalty."

The information had its desired effect. Joran hissed in a sharp breath and turned red eyes on her. "Then that makes what we have to do that much sweeter."

"*We* implies you and me." She shook her head and stepped farther away from him. "I'm out."

He smiled, showing his fangs. "You're not out until I say you're out."

CHAPTER FOURTEEN

"D o we have to go through this again, Joran?" Selena said sternly. "I'm my own boss. I have my own agenda at the moment. I don't have time to be your weapon of mass destruction."

"Perhaps we can help each other on a more personal basis?"

"No way."

"You do not trust me?"

"I trust myself and only myself. You of all people know that's the only way to survive in our world."

"Survival in our world becomes more complicated every day. To thrive, strategic alliances must be formed." He bowed as if she were the queen of the Order. "I am at your disposal, Selena. Use me."

Selena pretended to contemplate his offer. "Until you get what you want from me." It was not a question.

"We have always been frank with each other. I offer you my services, in whatever capacity you require. In return, I ask for yours."

"I work alone."

His eyes flared red.

"You don't need me to get to Luis."

"I need you to get into his head. I want to know why he thinks he has the power to grant immortality. I want to know every person on his payroll, every politician he's blackmailing. I cannot get that detailed information without you."

"I'm not the only one capable of what you ask."

"You are the only one *I* trust."

"You trust me because you know you hold a sword over my head with the Rev."

"You underestimate my respect for you. As far as I can trust, I trust you. And not because of any leverage."

"Damn you, Joran! I can't. Not now." She strode past him. "Maybe never."

Picking up on the desperation in her voice, he dropped down in front of her. "Other than Paymon, who threatens you?" He touched the mark on her neck. "Your vampire lover?"

Selena smacked his hand away, shaking her head. Could she tell him about Apollyon's plot to take over the Order? She could, but *should* she? No, he would interfere and want to take over. The groundwork had been laid; if all went according to plan, no one, mortal or immortal, would be the wiser about what could have happened. "I—look, there are things happening I cannot discuss. Things that if leaked could threaten our existence."

"Do I look like the *National Enquirer*?"

Selena smiled. "No, never. Everything at the moment is under control. If it goes to crap, I'll call you." And she would. She had a newfound respect and a grudging trust for the ancient vampire. If she needed him, he would come.

He stood silent for several moments, contemplating, she was sure, whether to force his issues and extract her cooperation or find another way to get what he wanted. "If, as you say, our very existence could be compromised, how do you expect me to take that information? Stand idly by and hope the world does not come to an end?"

She nodded. That was exactly what she expected. "You said it yourself—you trust me."

"Yes, but you are not infallible. You are one, I am many."

"I'm more than one, Joran."

"Ah, yes, Los Cuatro." Her head snapped back in shock. He smiled that suave vampire smile of his. "Do you think I'm so blind as not to know of your involvement with that clandestine organization?" His smile turned wicked. "It is my job to know those I do business with." He moved closer. "And who my associates do business with."

"Los Cuatro is a noble organization. It has never interfered with what I do for you."

"Be careful where you place your loyalties, Selena."

She blanched at such an outrageous statement. "Do you question Los Cuatro's intentions?"

He shrugged. "All is not as it seems. Trust no one."

Her skin shivered. Those were the same words *el patrón* had said to her. But she didn't need the warnings of others. Trust was not a commodity she dealt lightly. She lived life on the edge, always on guard, always sleeping with one eye open. She had to—for Marisol's sake.

"I'll take that to heart the next time you ask me to trust you."

His smile deepened; then his face became that of a serious man with bad news. "Your father is drumming up souls along the Georgia coast with a vengeance, Selena. He's searching for information. Specific information about a woman named Selena. Would you happen to know what information he seeks?"

The blood drained from her cheeks. Drumming up souls was one thing, but probing for specific information regarding her was another. Given that St. Michael's was off the Georgia coast, it was no coincidence. Did he suspect Marisol was alive? Was that how Malphas knew her secret? "Why didn't you tell me this sooner?"

He shrugged nonchalantly. "We are speaking of trust. Consider it a gift from me, with no strings—this time."

"I need you to go, Joran. I have things to do." She moved past him toward the hallway and abruptly stopped. A pissed-off Nikko Cruz stood at the threshold in full fang; his red eyes blazed with preternatural passion. Her blood pressure shot up another fifty points.

"Your lover . . . ?" Joran lazily asked from behind her.

Selena sucked in a huge breath, counted slowly to ten, then exhaled. "Joran, take a hike."

"I'm only a thought away," he whispered against her ear, then was gone.

Selena looked up into two furious eyes. Rage radiated off him in harsh, biting surges. "Are you jealous?" The need to taunt him was strong. The need to push him away was stronger.

"Don't flatter yourself," he snarled. But he walked past her into her bedroom, sniffing the air as if he would find proof she and Joran were lovers.

"You really have a hard time controlling the vampire in you, don't you?"

He strode into her bathroom. "I'm working on it."

Selena didn't follow him. She needed to get to Marisol and move her. But to where? She'd thought her daughter would be safe on the island with the nuns in their little retirement convent. But with Paymon sniffing so close, he might ferret out someone who knew his granddaughter lived and where to find her. Paymon was a powerful Prince of Hell, he could easily possess someone and go to the island—but was he strong enough to withstand the power of consecrated ground? No. No daemon could, except perhaps Apollyon, and even he could not defeat the souls of the nuns, or the soul of Saint Germaine, whose bones were embedded in the altar of the small sanctuary. Marisol would be safe—*if* she was installed inside the sanctuary until this entire mess was cleaned up.

"Selena!" Nikko said loudly in front of her.

She shook her head and blinked, only now realizing he had been talking to her. "What?"

"Noslov. I want him."

"He's not here."

"I can smell him on your clothes in the bathroom."

"His whereabouts is irrelevant. I gave you the laptop and have the information you wanted. The auction will commence this Saturday at midnight at Lost Souls."

"That's all well and good, but I need a seat at the table."

She looked up at him, her eyes unfocused. All she could think of was getting to Marisol. "Fine, I'll arrange it. Now, I need to go." She brushed past him into her dressing room. In her peripheral vision, she saw he followed, but she didn't care. She pulled off the caftan and dressed in jeans, a light-blue cashmere sweater, and a pair of soft leather mules, then grabbed a jean jacket.

"Where are you going?" he softly asked, touching her arm. His tone caught her off guard.

"I need to take care of something. I'll be back tomorrow." She moved past him, but his hand tightened around her arm. "Damn it, I don't have time for your Neanderthal antics!"

"Let me help."

A powerful rush of emotion erupted in her heart. Selena caught back a sob, so tempted to let go of the tidal wave of emotion she had been holding back since the day she'd lied to Johnny. She put her head down, not wanting him to see the hot sting of tears in her eyes. She desperately wanted his help. But she could not ask for it. Johnny needed to stay under Paymon's radar, because if anything happened to her, Marisol would need her father. "You can't help me." He let go of her arm and she rushed past him, calling for Juju.

She motioned for the woman to follow her outside, where she whispered her instructions as she hurried toward the dock, then hopped into the Chris-Craft and sped for the private airstrip she had just hours before left.

Two hours later, Selena stood at the edge of the small courtyard in front of St. Michael the Archangel church and convent. It had been almost five months since she had been here. How she longed to hold her baby, to give her Eskimo kisses, to hear her laughter and watch her smile in wonder at butterflies. This was the longest she had ever stayed away. She had no choice. If they were to have a normal future, securing it now was the only way to make it happen . One day, when her daughter was old enough, Selena would explain what she was to Marisol, just as her own mother had.

She inhaled the cool winter air. Marisol's scent was fresh. Vibrant. Alive. But for how long?

A renewed sense of panic welled inside Selena. She could not take Marisol from here. In her gut, Selena knew this was the safest place for her. But what was she supposed to do? Tell the nuns and Father Ken that daemons lurked and to keep Marisol inside the sanctuary?

She drew in a deep breath and exhaled. Maybe that was exactly what she needed to do.

The side door to the little stone convent opened. She stepped back into the shroud of trees lining the side of the courtyard. A little girl's laughter filtered through the air, followed by the most precious sight in Selena's life. Her daughter. She ran giggling from Sister Agnes, who softly clucked her displeasure behind her.

"Marisol," the ancient nun called, "it's time for your studies."

"I want to play!" the girl chortled as Father Ken emerged from the church. The chubby Filipino priest smiled at her, shaking his head.

"Marisol, listen to Sister," he said as she skipped past him and blew him a kiss.

Selena's heart tightened. Marisol was such a char-ismatic child. It didn't matter whom she met, she had them eating out of her hand with just one dimpled smile. Selena wanted nothing more than to sweep her daughter into her arms, but she did not move. Her spine tingled with awareness. She was not the only person watching Marisol.

Selena closed her eyes and deeply inhaled. God help her, her lies were over.

And suddenly, despite everything, all she felt was relief. She exhaled.

"Why didn't you tell me?" Nikko softly asked from behind her.

Selena opened her eyes and struggled not to break down in tears. Without turning around, she said, "Because my father would have killed you both."

She felt it then, his fury. His restraint. "You had no right, Selena!" he ground out. "No right, damn you!" He grabbed her shoulders and spun her around, shaking her. "I loved you, damn it!" He shook her again. Harder. "With every cell in my body, I loved you! I would have died for you, for our daughter! But you never gave me, *us,* a chance!" His fingers bit into her skin. "I swear by all that is holy, Selena, if you get between me and that little girl again, I *will* kill you!" He pushed her from him, his eyes red, angry, and—Selena swallowed hard—regretful. Regret stamped every inch of his face.

"Johnny, what I did, I did because I loved you both."

"You have a hell of a way of showing it." He strode past her toward the courtyard.

"No! Don't!" she said, grabbing his arm.

He turned furious eyes back on her, flinging her hand from him. "You lied to me! You were prepared to let me go to prison for your death and kept my daughter from me for eight years! How dare you tell me no!"

"John—Nikko, listen to me. She's safe here. If you go to her, if you—" Selena's body trembled violently. "Until my father is dead, she's vulnerable. *You're* vulnerable. I could not bear to lose either one of you."

"You lost me eight years ago," he bit off. But he didn't proceed. He swiped his hand across his chin and stared hotly at her. "Why are you here?"

"Joran told me my father has been soul-searching in the area and asking questions. I'm afraid he may know Marisol is alive. I had to come to make sure she was safe."

He turned and looked at the little girl who was happily being pushed on a swing by Sister Agnes. "Did you tell her about me?"

Selena wanted to take him into her arms and hold him. But she resisted. It was her life. Forever yearning for the love she could never have. "Yes."

As she said the word, Marisol looked up across the courtyard and caught Selena's gaze.

"Mama!" she cried, jumped like a champion off the low swing, and ran toward her.

"Baby," Selena whispered, and ran past Nikko to meet her halfway. Selena's heart was so full of love, joy, and fear, she could not breathe. The sweet little girl launched herself into Selena's arms and hugged her with all the might of an ecstatic eight-year-old.

"Mama, Mama!"

Nikko stood frozen to the earth. A maelstrom of emotions heaved in his chest with such ferocity he could barely draw a breath. Marisol was *alive,* and not more than twenty feet from him. He could not take his eyes off the beautiful little girl who looked so much like her mother but had his deep blue eyes. Her laughter was like magic; her sweet scent of sunshine and animal crackers would forever be burned into his memory. His daughter.

Moist heat stung his eyes. He tried to swallow but could not. When Selena turned with the smiling girl in her arms and looked at Nikko, his legs trembled.

Marisol was alive.

He took a step toward them, then another and another, until he found himself reaching out for her. Selena moved into him, handing him the small, squirming body. The moment he touched her, the moisture in his eyes spilled over, blurring his vision. When the small arms wrapped around his neck and she pressed her cheek to his, his heart exploded with emotion.

"Marisol," he breathed, hugging her to him.

She hugged him as tightly. "Daddy," she said as if they had known each other all their lives.

It all came crashing down around him, his love, longing, and fury at his daughter's mother for keeping such a precious gift from him. As those emotions clogged his chest, another one emerged: fear. Fear of losing this precious child of his.

He opened his eyes and glared hard at Selena, who stood silently crying beside them. His arms tightened.

"Oww!" Marisol cried, squirming in his arms.

Nikko loosened his hold and kissed the top of her head. "My apologies, Marisol, I am just so happy to meet you." He swung her around on his hip as if he had been doing it for years. "We have a lot of catching up to do. And Mama and I have to have a very long talk."

Marisol pulled back and smiled at him, her dimples captivating him. "Are we going to live together now?"

"We have a lot to work out, but I promise you this

much, sweetheart, you and Daddy will be spending a lot of time together."

"With Mama." It wasn't a question. The little girl had a mind of her own at eight. It shouldn't have surprised him. She was as willful as her mother.

Sister Agnes approached, staring at Nikko warily. "It's okay, Sister," Selena said, "this is John—Nikko, Marisol's father."

Sister Agnes nodded and extended her arms to Marisol. Nikko resisted, and Marisol grunted and turned away from the nun, quite content where she was. Nikko smiled and whispered in her ear, "That's my girl."

The padre reemerged from the church and gave Nikko the same unsettled look as the nun. "Father Ken, this is Nikko, Marisol's father."

The padre looked at Selena, then Marisol, then Nikko. He smiled and extended his hand. "It is a pleasure to finally meet you. Selena and Marisol speak of you often." Nikko shook the priest's hand, but looked at Selena. She just shrugged. In that moment, he noticed the stress lines on her face. She was pale and looked as if she had dropped weight in the last few days.

"I want to go to the fair," Marisol announced.

"That is up to your parents," Sister Agnes said.

"That's not a good idea," Selena said.

"Can we go?" Marisol sweetly asked, hugging Nikko tighter as she pressed her face to his and smiled. "Please."

"We'll see," he said, smiling, and realizing at that moment he would never deny his daughter a thing. In that instant, he also realized with crystal clarity why Selena had done what she'd done. Not that he agreed with her methods, not that he would have done the same. But he understood the fierce need to protect his child. And the woman he had loved. He would kill for them then. He would kill for them now.

Hours later, Marisol slept soundly in her bed next to Sister Agnes's. Nikko knelt down beside her and smoothed a damp curl from her cheek. "Sweet dreams, angel," he softly said. "Daddy loves you." He kissed her on the cheek and inhaled her sweet scent again, grateful for the last few hours. They had been a whirlwind of emotions and catching up. His overwhelming love for his daughter and his need to savor every second with her had put his anger at her mother on hold. But now . . . As he rose, his gaze locked with Selena's as she stood quietly at the doorway. Leaving the room quietly, shutting the door behind him, he said, "Tell me everything, Selena, and don't leave out one part."

CHAPTER FIFTEEN

An elderly nun led Selena and Nikko to a small guest room down the hall from where their daughter slept. The stuffy space had a narrow bed pushed against the wall in a corner, a nightstand with a lamp, and a coatrack.

Selena sank down on the edge of the bed.

If she could, she would curl up and sleep for a decade. But so much more had to be done before she could close her eyes and sleep with no fear of the future.

Her eyes burned from a river of tears. Watching Marisol and Nikko together for the past few hours had been an emotional avalanche. Her heart ached with so much bittersweet pain she doubted she would ever recover.

"Start with your mother and father and go forward," Nikko softly said.

Selena took a deep breath and nodded. She owed him answers and more. "When my mother was just a teenager, my father, Paymon, a daemon—a Prince of Hell—took a fancy to her. He invaded her dreams night after night. In those dreams, he seduced her. When she resisted him, he raped her. He returned repeatedly. Sometime later, she gave birth to me in a church. I was immediately baptized. That's why, unlike other daemons, I can withstand being on consecrated ground.

Any other daemon would burst into flames. I believe, too, it is why I am immune to the fear of water." Selena smiled bitterly. "I remember when I was little and taking my first Holy Communion, I was sure the priest's finger would catch fire when he placed the host on my tongue. Unfortunately for you, that didn't happen."

She thought she saw Nikko's gaze flicker for an instant, but other than that, his expression remained hard.

"Paymon was charming, suave, too handsome for words. My mother hated him but could not resist him. He never left her alone for long. In his own way, he was as possessed by her as she by him. When she became pregnant a second time by him, she began to lose her grip on sanity. She'd mumble how she'd gotten lucky with me . . . always with an added *So far.* . . . But she was worried. What were the chances she'd bear two children by the devil that wouldn't turn out to be pure evil? When she couldn't take it any longer, she jumped from her apartment window. I later learned I would have had a sister. I was eighteen when they died." Against Selena's will, her voice cracked.

"I'm sorry," Nikko softly said.

Selena shook her head. "Don't be. She was finally out of her misery. And my sister was better off never having to live with the curse of her parentage."

"Unlike you?" Nikko asked softly.

Selena ignored his question. "I swore that day I'd hunt the bastard down and kill him. And so I shall."

A prolonged silence dragged by and she saw Nikko clench his fists. Probably to keep himself from strangling the abomination in front of him.

"What did he do when your mother killed herself?"

Selena flinched when he finally spoke, his voice tight. Controlled. "He came after me. But I was stronger-willed than my mother. And smarter. My mother taught me how to shut off my mind when I slept, how to mentally protect myself and keep predators like my father out. I forced him from my thoughts, and he couldn't find me. Then I took off." She smiled. "And I met you."

"Is that why you were here? Hiding from your father?"

"Yes, my mother told me to always stay close to consecrated ground. She also told me of daemons' aversion to water. What better place to be than on an island named after a mighty archangel? It's why I chose to hide Marisol here. Paymon never found me here. He won't find her."

"If this island afforded you so much protection, why did you leave it to come with me to Atlanta?"

She turned her gaze away. "You know why."

"Because you loved me?" he queried softly.

She nodded. "With all my heart. I couldn't bear the thought of not being with you." She looked back at him. "We were so damn good together. I loved how you loved me. How you made me laugh. Made me feel normal. You never judged me, you just let me be me. I loved you first for that." She looked down at her hands, then back at his intense stare.

"I would have followed you to the ends of the earth. I had had no contact for almost three years with anything remotely daemon, I thought I was free of him. But I was wrong. When I got pregnant, it was as if I'd sent up a flare. He found me in a dream and demanded Marisol's soul for yours and mine. I refused. I thought our love was strong enough to beat him."

"Your faith didn't last very long."

"Things started to happen to you."

Nikko shook his head. "Nothing happened to me."

"Yes, it did! Remember the night you worked that undercover sting? What happened, Johnny? You were shot! My father orchestrated that! He came to me and taunted me with what he had done! And while you were in the hospital, they gave you the wrong medication and it nearly killed you. Do you think that was an accident? And then—"

She choked on her emotions. "I started bleeding." She dropped her head into her hands. "It was his doing. He would have killed you just like he killed my mother! I couldn't bear the thought, so I did what I had to do." She looked up at him through damp eyes. "I went to the doctor and had Marisol early. By cesarean section. No one knew. I immediately brought her here to St. Michael's, and then I came to you. I—I had to do something you would never forgive me for. I thought if I pushed you away, my father would leave you alone. So I lied to you about Marisol, and you turned on me!" Bitterness sprang up within her. And anger. "What if what I told you had been the truth, that I was afraid of being a mother? That I didn't love you? That gave you the right to attack me? You tried to kill me, for God's sake, and almost did! I'm a little pissed off about that, Nikko!"

She raked her fingers through her long hair, wincing at the pull of the tangles. She shook off the pain and looked hard at him and collected herself. "But I forgave you a long time ago. You're alive, Marisol is safe. It was what I wanted above everything else."

Nikko sat down beside her, though he didn't touch her. For a long, uneven moment, he stared at her. His face gave nothing away. No anger, no hate, no understanding, and certainly no love. "Tell me about Balderama."

She couldn't blame him for playing it cool. "Los Cuatro was the one thing in my mother's life that she had control of. It gave her a profound sense of purpose. Señor Balderama was always there to pick up the pieces after my father did his damage. He was like a father to me in many ways. It was he who found me unconscious on the floor after you attempted to kill me. It was he who made my past go away so that I could start over."

"You would have let me rot in prison." His eyes flared red, his fangs just noticeable. Yet she was not afraid. This Nikko she could handle; it was the quiet one she feared.

"You're wrong. I would have come forward. At the time, I didn't know how to do it and not alert my father. And whether you believe me or not, at the time you were safer in jail than out on the streets. As I was getting my bearings, I heard you had escaped, and then after Señor exhausted all of his connections searching for you and came up empty, I thought you were dead or had left the country. I had no idea what had happened to you—I still don't. I just know I was shocked to see you on that mountainside in Kyrgyzstan. I also knew there was no way I was going to let you die there."

"What do you do for Balderama?"

"Mostly reconnaissance, sometimes cleanup."

"Assassinations?"

"I think of it as exterminating vermin."

"Just because *he* says they're vermin?"

"Since I also consider cartel leaders vermin, then yes. But I'm not blind. I know who is who and what is what.

The people love it when I disperse the dearly departed's cash and coin in the village streets."

"You're a regular Robin Hood," he remarked cynically.

"More like a black widow who shares."

"Why does he want the cask?"

"I told you, for the same reasons as you."

"And you believe that?"

"Why shouldn't I?"

"Why not let us do all the heavy lifting? You know it will be safely stored on US soil where no third party can touch it. Where does your Señor plan to store it? Some remote island? With what—a security system that can be breached by a few dozen mercs?"

Everything he said made sense. Why not move aside and allow the United States to do exactly what Nikko suggested?

He seized on Selena's hesitation. "Ah, so you agree?"

"In theory, but how do I know you work for the US government? Señor will want proof."

"I have never lied to you, Selena. But if it will make you feel better, I'll be happy to have the president vouch for me."

"The president of the United States?"

Nikko nodded. "The president of the United States."

She sat back in the corner, using the wall for support, and contemplated what he'd said. "If the president of the United States can vouch for you, it makes perfect sense to stand back, especially since we know that louse Chávez had an inside track to the cask. It was his men you heard speaking Spanish out there. He had a deal with Noslov. . . ."

"And?"

She exhaled loudly. "Apparently there were others who made him a better offer."

"Who else?"

Selena swallowed hard. The moment of truth. How did she tell him the devil had a hand in this? "The daemon king, Apollyon, wants to threaten the Order with it."

"The Order?"

"The group that controls all immortals. The daemons think if they threaten humanity with a dirty bomb, Rurik will hand over control of the Order to Apollyon."

"For what purpose?"

"The daemons are tired of being told what they can and can't do. The truce among the factions is tenuous at best. I don't understand it all, but I do know since the treaty was signed several decades ago, there has been relative peace."

"Why haven't you gone to this Order with this information?"

She sat forward. "Because I've been killing daemons, a huge no-no, *and* extracting blood from more than a few not-so-willing vampires and other immortals, another huge no-no."

"The Rev?"

"Yes. I, um, do it in exchange for information on my father and, more important, the locations of Hellkeepers."

"To get the stones."

"Which give me the power I'll need to end my father's existence."

Nikko shook his head and looked at her with such an odd expression she didn't know what to make of it.

"What?"

"You. Marisol. This entire scenario amazes me in a mixed-up, terrifying way. I don't know how to process it all."

"Don't try, just go with it. Otherwise you'll drive yourself crazy."

"All this time I have hated you with such a vengeance all I wanted to do was kill you again. For eight years I thought you and Marisol were dead. I have walked this earth a hollow, broken man. Now everything is different. I don't know what to feel anymore."

Compassion and the need to soothe away this man's pain took hold of Selena. Tentatively, she reached out a hand to him. He stared at it, not moving a muscle. When he didn't respond, she slid her hand over his and softly said, "I hope one day you can forgive me."

His clear, blue eyes looked deep into her soul. "I don't know if that's possible."

CHAPTER SIXTEEN

Selena and Nikko had fallen into an exhausted sleep on opposite sides of the narrow bed. Somehow, sometime in the night, they met in the middle. His arms had wrapped around her. Her head had tucked under his chin. He hadn't consciously woken until her body began to twitch and tremble restlessly in his arms.

He knew so little about her, how she'd lived the past eight years, yet he knew so much, too.

How she'd made a safe life for Marisol. And the emotional toll it had taken on her. Her tireless efforts to hunt down and kill Hellkeepers so that she could destroy the thing that threatened their daughter's life. How she'd lived with the lie she'd created, and the guilt she must bear because of it. Never knowing if her child really was safe, but having no choice but to make it all work.

And now she was reliving the nightmare that had become her life.

Maybe his life, too?

Selena's trembling body quieted in his arms. He sat back against the wall, bringing her with him, and wondered where it would end.

He'd missed eight years of his daughter's life. His lifestyle was not conducive to any type of family life. No L.O.S.T. operative had a family. Cassidy was the only one in a relationship. It was allowed only because Cross knew so much and was an asset. How was Nikko supposed to juggle his work and his daughter? Whom could he trust other than Selena to care for Marisol when he could not? He'd be damned if he'd be one of those absentee fathers; Nikko would be a part of his daughter's life. He'd give anything to get the last eight years back. But they were gone. So was any chance of normalcy.

And what about Selena?

He didn't want to feel anything for her, not even the hatred that had consumed him for so long. He accepted why she'd done what she had done, but he did not, could not, forgive her for the pain he had endured. Not only the tragedy of losing a child, but also the self-loathing and self-hatred that came from thinking he had actually killed the woman he loved in a fit of anger. It had molded him into the hard-as-nails, cold-as-ice L.O.S.T. operative Nikko Cruz. There was no going back.

It was who he was now. Who he would always be. Johnny Cicone had died the day he thought he killed Selena Guerrero.

Selena cried out again. "Hurry, Johnny!"

That she said his name snapped something inside him, and everything he'd just been thinking about Selena suddenly didn't matter. His daughter was alive! Her mother was alive! He was alive. It was enough. For now.

"It's just a dream, Lena. You're safe," he shushed, smoothing the damp hair from her cheek. Like those of a fearful child, her fingers dug into his skin, holding on for dear life. Nikko drew in a shaky breath. More of his hardened heart crumbled when her eyes blinked open, the haze of sleep giving way to a horrified awareness.

"He got her, Johnny, he got Marisol," she sobbed. "I couldn't save her." Her heartbreaking sobs tore at him.

No wonder she'd been so agitated. Whatever he could fault her for, her love for their daughter was indisputable. "Marisol is asleep in the next room with Sister Agnes. She's safe."

The body in his arms stilled. Long moments passed. Then . . .

He felt a slight tremor. It was followed by a much stronger one. Then the body in his arms was wracked with crying. Selena's hands fisted his shirt as she buried her face in the crook of his neck. Her warm tears soaked his chest, her body pressed tightly against his. He felt each of her sobs as if they were his own. And in so many ways they were. He had suffered eight years ago what she suffered now.

He'd had no one to console him, to tell him he would be okay, that it was all a terrible nightmare. His life had fallen apart that day. He had not wanted to go on. Had it not been for Godfather's extracting him before he reached the prison and forcing him back into reality, he would have been another prison death statistic.

He'd cursed God for the second chance.

Nikko tightened his arms around Selena, drawing her closer to him. He didn't know what to say, how to ease her heartache. How could he, when he was as damaged? He did what he would do if it were Marisol coming to him with a broken heart. He held her, comforted her, and told her it would be okay.

He kissed the top of her head as he gently rocked her, soothing her with words that soothed himself.

"Johnny," she hoarsely said, pulling away just enough

to look up at him. He steeled himself. The torment in her dark eyes was almost more than he could bear. "I'm so sorry." She pressed her lips to the base of his throat, the contact eliciting a much different but just as profound response from him. She kissed him again. "So sorry." When she looked up at him again, her swollen eyes widened.

He could imagine what he looked like. The man in him had responded, but so had the vampire. His blood coursed hotly through him. His arms tightened around her, his legs tensed beneath her bottom. Her proximity was making his head spin.

He lowered his lips to hers, brushing against the soft skin. The taste of her salty tears moved him in a most unexpected way. Admiration for her strength, courage, and determination to protect their child as well as him under the most terrifying of circumstances suddenly struck him. She was a fighter, a mama bear protecting her young and her mate, sacrificing her happiness to preserve their lives. All of the pieces fell neatly into place, then. Life's tragedies happened for a reason. Sometimes the reasons were not clear until the painful wounds were nothing but scars. Reminders but no longer painful.

Digging his fingers into her hair, he cupped her head in his palms and brought her lips to his. "Lena, don't cry for me."

"I can't help it. I would do anything to take back the pain and suffering I've caused you."

"If you did that, then we wouldn't be here." He kissed her. A long, slow, soulful kiss. He savored it. He savored the softness of her lips. The way her tongue swirled languorously around his. Her scent, her touch, her tears, and her surrender. He savored it the way a condemned man savored his last meal.

Her fists loosened as the tension in her body lessened. Nikko squeezed his eyes shut as an intense wave of passion swept through him. God help him, but he still wanted her. Had never stopped wanting her. Despite all the pain, that had never changed.

And if he took her, what about after? They were two different people now, their only commonality their daughter. Loosening his hold, Nikko tore his lips from hers.

What had happened at the club had been an act of revenge. Her seduction of him on her yacht had been a dream. He gently pushed her away and sat up on the edge of the bed.

"Johnny," she breathed. "Don't."

Raking his fingers through his hair, he looked at her. What he saw tore him up. She was as ravaged as he. "Selena, nothing is the same. Johnny is dead. I'm Nikko Cruz now." He inhaled deeply, then slowly exhaled. "There is no room in my life for you."

Her body flinched as if he had gut-punched her. Her eyes glittered with fresh tears. She nodded, and the action sent them rushing in a steady stream down her cheeks. He reached out a fingertip to catch one. It pooled warm and wet on his skin.

"What about Marisol?" she asked.

"When this is all over, I'll find a way to make it work."

She captured his hand and pressed it to her cheek. "We *are* different people today, Nikko, but we're also the same." She kissed his damp fingertips. "I've been to Hell and back for you. I'll do it again if I have to, but I'm not going to let you walk out on me."

He stared at her.

"Give me, give *us,* a second chance." She sat up on her knees and cupped his face in her hands. "After everything we have been through, we owe it to ourselves and to our daughter to try."

He continued to stare at her. He wanted her body with a vengeance, but her heart terrified him. She would never settle for just a piece of him; she would want it all. He could not give her all. Even if he could find a way to trust her again, he was a L.O.S.T. operative. He could not walk away from who he was, what he did. Not even—for her.

"I can't."

She rose up and pressed her lips to his. Her arms slipped around his neck, her breasts pressing intimately against his chest. "Can't or won't?" She opened her lips against his, and her tongue slipped along his bottom lip, then swirled upward and around his fangs.

"Both," he roughly said.

She smiled sadly and nodded. Her arms tightened around his neck. She kissed him. "Then make love to me one last time."

His body tightened. His fingers itched to touch her. Her lips trailed from his mouth to his chin, then to his throat. When she dragged her teeth along his jugular, he hissed. Her hands slid down his shoulders to his biceps, then to his rigid forearms. She wrapped his arms around her waist. She surged against him, digging her fingers into his hair and her teeth into his flesh.

Nikko snapped. The need for her was too powerful

to resist. Hell, he didn't want to resist. He dug his fingers into her back and turned her over, pressing her into the mattress. "No promises, Selena."

"No promises," she echoed.

Selena closed her eyes and gave herself up completely. Every barrier crashed to the ground, exposing her vulnerable core to the man above her.

His big hands swept up from her hips to her breasts, cupping them painfully as if he still resisted what they both wanted. She felt his turmoil, his frustration, and his overpowering need for her body. It matched hers for his.

The hot sting of tears surprised her. It shouldn't have. She had cried more in Nikko's arms tonight than she had in her previous lifetime. Emotionally, she was raw. She was so tired of running, of the lies, of being afraid. Seeing Johnny and Marisol together today had been so right.

He pulled the sweater over her head, turned her on her side facing away from him, and yanked off her jeans. His big, warm hands rested on her ankles, his fingers lightly caressing her skin. Selena didn't move, afraid if she did, he would change his mind. She bit her bottom lip when his fingers traced along the curve of her calf. "You're still so soft," he whispered against her skin. Gooseflesh erupted across her chest, stiffening her nipples. His lips followed his fingers' trail. He kissed the back of her knee, then traced along her thigh to the curve of her hip. He nibbled the thong strap of her panties before his hand slid along the dip of her waist. She closed her eyes and savored his touch. He was a considerate lover, never taking what he was not willing to give.

He dug one hand into her thick hair, pulling her head back against him, exposing her neck and chest. With his free hand, he swept his fingers across the tips of her bra. Selena hissed in a sharp breath. She was wound tight, her body desperately needing to uncoil and be taken.

"I've never touched another woman the way I touch you," he said against the swell of her breast. He unhooked the front clasp of her bra.

Selena could barely breathe. "I've never touched another man the way I touch you."

She felt the hitch in his breath. Her declaration had taken him by surprise, given the way she dressed and conducted herself in Lost Souls.

His warm lips nudged a tight nipple. Selena closed her eyes and exhaled. His tongue slid across it, the sublimity of the oh-so-simple, yet oh-so-erotic caress pushing her again to the verge of tears. There was no one else on this earth for her. No one could make her feel the way Nikko made her feel. He'd always loved her fully until she begged him to stop.

"Jesus, Selena," he breathed against her. "You make me forget everything." He pressed her back into the mattress; his hands cupped her breasts, and his mouth voraciously suckled a nipple.

Selena gasped, arching into him. The deep pull of his lips lit a fire in her womb. He pressed his body tightly against hers, his hips undulating in rhythm to his lips. She slid her fingers into his thick hair, digging her nails into his scalp, arching deeper into him.

"Nikko," she moaned. "Don't ever stop."

Tearing his lips from her, his hot gaze caught hers and held it. He was a magnificent sight. His blue eyes blazed with furious passion. His nostrils flared; his swollen lips parted, the barest hint of his fangs beneath. He grasped her chin and brought her lips to his. Then she was lost.

They strained against each other. Hip to hip, chest to chest, lips to lips. Hands grasping, stroking, caressing. Wanting desperately to make up for the lost years. Nikko tore her panties from her, and yanked off his shirt and jeans. Their gazes caught and held. Selena held her breath. Her entire body burned with primordial fire. Eight long years she'd dreamt of this night. Eight long years she'd imagined being in this man's arms again. For eight long years she'd yearned for his love. In a push-up position, he moved over her, his intense gaze not wavering from hers. Selena reached up and wrapped her arms around his neck. As she pulled him to her, he slid hotly inside her.

She caught her breath, but could not catch the fresh tears from leaking. Dear God and all that was holy, the sensation of Nikko filling her was a testament to the sublime. And worth every day of the eight-year wait.

Selena arched, drawing him deeper into her; her heart thumped wildly against her rib cage and her body melted as he filled her completely.

Nikko sucked in a deep breath and threw his head back. When he dropped his head, his intense blue eyes locked on her. Her liquid muscles clamped around his cock. Nikko moaned, moving against her. Caught up in sensual awe of him, Selena watched the play of expressions on his face. His jaw clenched, his nostrils flared, his eyes flashed.

"Selena," he breathed, gathering her into his arms. Desperately she clung to him. His hips thrust, hers answered. His lips found her lips. Hers responded. Merged as one, their bodies undulated to an ancient, primordial beat. Slowly, madly, deeply.

"Nikko," Selena rasped. "Closer." He pulled her up into his lap, wrapping her legs around his waist. Grasping his shoulders, Selena rose up, arching her back. His fingers slid down her slick back to her bottom. Grasping her cheeks, he pulled her into him, and held her as he rotated his pelvis up into hers.

The tension in her body drew tighter. Digging her nails into his back for better leverage, Selena ground her hips down on him. Her breasts bobbed against his chest. The feel of his slick skin against her sensitive nipples drove her mad.

He nipped a hardened peak, then ran his fangs along the top swell of her breast. Shaking her long hair from her neck, Selena threw her head back, exposing the soft skin of her neck. "Take all of me, Nikko."

He swelled past capacity inside her. His fingers dug into her skin, his thrusts deepened. Anticipation sizzled inside her as he sank his fangs into her neck. The orgasm that erupted deep inside her womb blindsided her a millisecond later.

"Ahh, Nikko—" she cried out as intense tidal waves of pleasure slammed through her. Raw, erotic sensations overloaded her nervous system. Her body trembled, barely able to process the barrage of sensual stimuli. .

His big hands steadied her thrumming body. Selena's eyes rolled back into her head, and amazingly, she did something she had never done before: she let go. Of everything. Completely. The fear, the worry, the heart-ache. The guilt. For this one moment in time, she was simply a woman who laid bare her heart and soul to her lover.

Nikko came crashing right behind her. His body cleaved to her, wracking her senseless with the intensity of his orgasm. He grasped her tighter to him, their sweat-slicked bodies sliding against each other. As if they had been dropped to earth by an invisible hand, Selena and Nikko hit the bed, their arms and legs entwined, their hearts racing together.

For almost an hour they lay awake as they had fallen, no words spoken. Only the quiet sounds of their breaths and the dull thud of their heartbeats disturbed the silence.

As the sun rose, Selena broke the silence. "I won't be going back to Miami with you," she said, stroking one of his nipples until it hardened.

He grabbed her hand, staying it. "Why not?"

She looked into his hooded eyes. "I have a date with two Hellkeepers."

"Where are they?"

"I don't know, but I don't have the time to waste look-ing for them, so I'm going to conjure them."

"Conjure?"

"Yes." She grinned, sliding her hand down the hard contours of his belly to his groin. "Just like I'm going to conjure that lovely cock of yours again."

Nikko rolled over onto her. She laughed as she stroked his velvet cock. It flared, thickening in her hand. "See? Think it. Feel it. Voilà."

He hissed in a breath. "Selena—"

Her smile deepened as her fingers tightened around his burgeoning shaft. "You're going to miss me when I'm gone." His eyes flared red. She spread her thighs, catching the wide head of him in the slick opening of her pussy. She tipped her hips up and pushed, pulling him into her waiting warmth. He groaned, thrusting into her. Selena closed her eyes, releasing the air from her lungs. "Nikko," she moaned. "You feel so good."

He lowered his lips to hers and smiled against her. "So do you."

Selena wrapped her arms around his neck, and for the second time that night, she let go.

"Mama?" Marisol's little voice said from outside their door.

"Marisol?" Selena gasped.

"Oh, shit!" Nikko said, falling off the bed; jumping up, he yanked on his pants. Selena hastily pulled her clothes on and hurried to the door. She opened it to find the sleepy little girl rubbing her eyes.

"Mama, are you hurt?" the little girl asked, looking past Selena to Nikko, who stood barefoot and barechested in his jeans looking as if he had been caught redhanded breaking into Fort Knox.

When Nikko chuckled, Selena shot him a hard glare. "No, baby. I was, uh, I had a bad dream and Daddy came in to see if I was okay."

Marisol looked up at her father and scrunched her little brows, then looked back at her mother. Selena stood sheepishly looking at her bare feet. "Give Daddy a kiss, and I'll tuck you back into bed."

"Can you sleep with me?"

Selena let out a long, shaky breath, not used to the

new dynamics. Marisol had been her life for eight years. Her reason for being. Her reason for getting up each morning. She guarded her time with the girl fiercely. But it was hard to leave the secure comfort of Nikko's arms. He made her feel safe the way she had always made Marisol feel safe. "Of course, I can." She looked up at Nikko, asking him with her eyes to understand. The expression on his face stopped her cold, a litany of emotions from happiness to heartbreak and everything in between. If she did not know better, she'd say he looked as if he were about to cry.

He reached down, picked Marisol up, hugged her, then kissed her on the cheek. "Protect Mama from her nightmares."

Marisol hugged him and nodded. "I will."

CHAPTER SEVENTEEN

Saying good-bye to his daughter a few hours later was harder than Nikko had imagined it would be. She clung to him, then her mother, wailing the entire time he and Selena walked away. He hated leaving her, but promised her, and pinkie-swore as she insisted, that he would be back for her soon and she could come stay with him for a while. Marisol calmed some but wanted to know why they had to leave.

"Mama and I have a very important job to do, so that we can come back and be happy."

"But I'm happy now!" Marisol insisted.

Nikko hoisted her up into his arms and hugged her again. "We'll be even more happy." He kissed her on the nose. "I promise."

Selena scowled when he told Marisol she could visit him, but he shrugged it off. He would take some time off and spend it with Marisol. The thought of caring for and getting to know the precocious eight-year-old was more terrifying than staring down the barrel of an AK. Dealing with her mother was another scary thought. His heart, his head, and his willful libido were at war. He admitted he loved her. Had never stopped. But long ago he had encapsulated his heart. What was there was locked away. To open it would expose his raw innards, leave him vulnerable. She had nearly destroyed him.

What she'd done and what had happened afterward was so deeply burned into him, it was as much a part of him as his heart, or his arms and legs. Even if he wanted to, he could not just surgically remove it and get over it. He did not trust Selena. But that didn't hamper his desire for her. On that front, his human and vampire impulses were in complete accord.

On the ferry back to the mainland, Selena seemed to have gone off into her own world. Each time Nikko looked her way, she was staring at some far-off spot on the horizon. Finally, she turned to him and said, "Don't you dare break your promise to Marisol."

"I won't." Sensing her turmoil, Nikko reached over and squeezed her hand. She pulled it away and stared past him. He shook his head and squinted at the morning sun, realizing he was becoming light-sensitive. He was also becoming stronger, and his ability to control his vampire impulses was slowly coming around. Ignoring the burn, Nikko looked out over the rough, gray Atlantic. His guts churned along with the cold ocean waters.

Last night with Selena had shaken his resolve. Their emotional parting with their daughter this morning had shaken him more. He had responsibilities not only to L.O.S.T. but to his daughter. And, if he was honest with himself, to Selena as well. He looked at Selena's proud profile. She sat rigidly beside him, the ocean spray moistening her flushed cheeks. His belly did a slow roll. She was beautiful. Passionate. And damn if she couldn't fight better than half the men he knew. She was his for the taking, and yet, since leaving their room with Marisol earlier that morning, she'd acted as if last night had never happened.

They didn't speak another word as the ferry chugged along the six-mile waterway separating St. Michael's Island from the mainland. Selena was in a deep, contemplative mood. No doubt thinking of all the ways she could cut his balls off. After his rejection, he didn't blame her. But she had to understand they led two entirely different lives than they had eight years ago. And even if they didn't, he could not get past the eight years of emotional hell she'd put him through.

Nikko was tired of trying to sort out emotions. He was a man of action. "Selena, we need to talk about Saturday night."

The ferry nudged the pier with a smooth bump. The passengers around them stood. Nikko glanced at Selena, who had not moved a muscle. "Set your emotions aside for the moment and give me your undivided attention."

She nodded without looking at him, then stood. Great, moody Selena had arrived.

Nikko blew out a long breath and followed her toward the gangplank to the bustling pier. He stopped at the rail and looked suspiciously at the crowd. Beside him, Selena did the same thing. For so early in the morning, a substantial line had already formed for the return ferry to St. Michael's. Nikko didn't like it one bit. If he could find a way to shut down the steady stream of visitors, he would.

"Is all of this activity normal?" Nikko asked.

"It gets worse in the warmer months."

"I don't like being so far from Marisol."

Selena looked at Nikko, and this time she squeezed his hand. "Welcome to my world."

As they disembarked, Nikko abruptly stopped and sniffed the air. Sulfur. He looked down at Selena. The color had drained from her cheeks. "A Hellkeeper," she whispered.

"Why is it here?"

As her dark eyes scoured the people coming and going around them, Nikko narrowed his eyes and, like a photographer, took a mental snapshot of each person in view. "My loving father has been poking around down here for information. He may have found what he was looking for."

"Your father is *here*?" Nikko grabbed her arm and started back up the gangplank. "We need to get to Marisol."

Selena shook off his hand. "Not so fast," she said, surveying the people in line. "We have twenty minutes before the ferry begins boarding."

"Tell me what to look for."

"Daddy dearest isn't here. He won't show until the grand finale. He sent a Hellkeeper to do his dirty work for him. Find a soul to possess, get to the island, then report back to dear ol' Dad." She started walking along the crowd waiting to board the *Georgia Peach*. "Or maybe"—she sniffed the air—"his lackey has already found a host, and he or she is waiting in line."

Nikko scanned the thickening line. Every person looked normal. "I thought you said daemons didn't like water."

"They don't, but the more powerful ones can tolerate it in a host body."

Anxiety hyped up Nikko, whereas Selena seemed to have become calmer. Maybe this was old hat to her, but it was not to him. "We're not leaving here until we track that thing down and kill it."

Selena smiled slyly and looked up at his determined face. He had no clue what he had just volunteered for. "We?"

"Yes, *we*. I'm in this all the way with you, Selena. I love that little girl back there with every cell in my body. I'll die for her, *and* I'll kill for her."

Nikko grabbed her hand and pulled her along to a small café across the street, then barreled past the caffeine-starved patrons lined up three deep to the restrooms in the back.

"What are you doing?" she demanded.

"Loading you up."

He pushed open the door to the ladies' room. A woman stood at the sink washing her hands. She looked up at him, shrieked, then ran past them out to the café. Nikko slammed the door shut, wedging the trash can beneath the doorknob.

"Was that really necessary?" Selena asked, wondering what the Hell he was up to.

He turned fiery eyes on her and shoved up his shirt-sleeve. He bit his wrist and held it out to her. "I know you think you're all badass with that necklace, but I want you to take my blood. Selena, it's still raging with Rev. It will give you more power. And if we get separated and you need me, I can hear you." His eyes softened. "And if I need you, you will be able to find me."

Stunned, she could only stare at him. Drink his blood? She barely remembered his saving her life with his blood before. That had been an act of desperation on his part to collect information. But now? Despite her aversion to drinking his blood, emotion clogged her throat. What he offered was born out of concern. Selena swallowed hard. She could do this.

Slowly she reached out and took his arm. Those annoying tears threatened again. Why, she didn't know. What he suggested made perfect sense. With his blood, she'd be stronger to kill the Hellkeeper and destroy the immediate threat to Marisol. There was no hidden meaning behind it. Though she wished there were. She pressed her lips to his wrist. The warmth of his blood was oddly comforting. She closed her eyes and took what he offered. The minute it entered her own bloodstream, she felt the kick. She grasped his wrist tighter to her lips and drank.

When she'd had enough, she stepped back and wiped her lips with the back of her hand. She looked down at the smear of his blood on her skin. Her heart pumped wildly. They were bound by more than their daughter. She looked up at his edged face. "Thank you."

He nodded, then took her hand, kicked the trash can out of the way, and strode with her in tow through the suddenly silent café.

As they stepped outside, they stopped. Like the hunters they were, they lifted their noses to the breeze and caught the scent.

"Let's go hunting," Nikko softly said.

"I have my swords, but you need at least one knife. There's a bait shop at the end of the pier. Stay here and make sure that bastard doesn't board the ferry. I'm going knife shopping."

"I'll go. You stay and cut him from the herd."

He strode past her, the shop in sight seventy-five yards down the pier.

Selena anxiously paced the loading area to the ferry. Dozens of tourists stood in line to board. The sulfur scent intensified. Casually she strode along the chatty throng, her senses on high alert.

A young couple conversed with an animated elderly woman and her husband. A single woman smiled at the toddler grasping her hand. A large blond family chattered away in what she was pretty sure was Swedish.

Then there was the suit. Silent, staring straight ahead, trying hard to mind his own business and appear non-threatening. Even without the stench, he stuck out like a sore thumb. Selena stopped beside him and admired the blue sky. Casually she looked over at the man, who could not have been any more nondescript if he had been a brown grocery bag. Short brown hair, brown eyes, ordinary face, and medium build. Only his tailored suit set him apart, with everyone else wearing casual tourist attire. "I'm thinking of going to the island," she said to him. "Is it worth my time?"

He didn't so much as blink in acknowledgment. He just looked ahead. The line began to move; he moved with it. The sulfurous smell swirled around her like a noxious gas. "I asked you a question, mister." He continued to ignore her. "Ya know, ignoring me isn't a smart move." She needed to get him alone, but that was going to be difficult with so many people surrounding him.

She grabbed his hand and pulled him out of the line. The contact opened his mind to her. Selena hissed in a breath. He turned cold, predatory eyes on her. Scenes from his mind flashed before her: black-hooded priests surrounding a bloody altar, the screams of innocents. The deep drone of demonic chants pounded ruthlessly in his mind.

Dear God. The host was a disciple of Paymon's! Her

father was a benevolent master to those who served him faithfully. This man would be among his most trusted to be sent on such a sensitive mission. His power combined with that of the Hellkeeper inside him would test her mettle as it had never before been tested. If she failed? She refused to think of what would happen to Marisol and Nikko.

She had to ensure that this man did not board. "How can you leave me and the kids for a fourteen-year-old?" Selena shrieked, kicking him in the shin.

He grunted but made no move to defend himself. If he thought ignoring her would make her give up, he was wrong.

The crowd around them stepped back, visibly shocked. The man glared at her. "We need to talk about this, Bob. *Please,* can we speak in private?"

When he shook his head, the old lady in front of him whacked him in the back with her suitcase-size purse. "You should be ashamed of yourself! A fourteen-year-old girl!"

Selena sniffed back fake tears. "And she's pregnant."

The old lady kicked him. The female half of the couple beside her smacked him on the shoulder with her umbrella. "Pig!"

"Please, Bob," Selena pleaded. "*Talk* to me!"

He turned and strode past her just as Nikko jogged toward her. She inclined her head toward the man, who was moving faster now in the opposite direction. He took off, and they went after him.

He was fast, but they were faster. Nikko tossed a serrated gutting knife to Selena as their prey turned down an alley. She caught it as Nikko leapt into the air after the daemon, tackling him into a Dumpster. The daemon turned on Nikko, his eyes blazing.

"Don't look at him!" Selena screamed as she skidded to a stop beside them. She grabbed the struggling host up by his short hair and pressed the blade to his throat.

"Come out now, Hellkeeper, or die with this soul."

"You would not slay an innocent," a rough female voice hissed.

Lamia. Selena's heart rate kicked up several notches. Not only a Hellkeeper, but a half-vampire Hellkeeper. Lamia was so powerful even the devil could not kill her. One bite from her was fatal.

"There is nothing innocent about your host! He worships Paymon!" Selena struck quickly, slitting the devil worshipper's jugular.

He screamed, writhing, clawing, teeth bared, snapping at the air. Selena looked up to Nikko. "Hold him down until he bleeds out, then stand back. One bite from Lamia and she'll own you."

Selena pulled her swords from the sheath at her back and crouched next to the dying host, waiting for the serpent daemon to vaporize. And waiting. The body subsided, obviously void of life, but still nothing happened. The hackles on Selena's neck rose. Something was terribly wrong. "Get out of here, Nikko," Selena whispered.

"I'm not going anywhere."

Her breathing shallowed. Lamia was alive, her stench still fresh. And if she was strong enough to survive in a dead host, she was strong enough to— Selena looked across the bloody body to Nikko. He watched her intently, waiting for her to direct him. *Please, for Marisol, go,* she mouthed.

He shook his head, his eyes riveted on her. *I'm not leaving you.*

His words rattled her heart. He had no idea what they were up against, but he was standing by her. Maybe, together . . . Selena nodded, knowing what she must do. With Nikko close, maybe she could pull it off. But it would leave her physical body exposed and vulnerable to possession. If the daemon would not come to her, then she would go to it. The idea of fighting for her life in a dead body terrified her, but she had no choice.

"Nikko, I have to go in there." She pointed to the host's body, then looked back at him. "I need you to protect my body. Don't allow anyone near it. No vapor, no animal. Nothing."

"How can you go in there? He's dead. You'll die, too!"

"If Lamia can survive in there, so can I. And besides, I have more to live for than she does." Selena rubbed the stones and did something she rarely did. She made the sign of the cross. "Pray, Nikko, pray like you've never prayed before."

And so would she. Closing her eyes, Selena grasped each sword and called on the stones for strength. They lit up around her neck, their energy building, infusing her shoulders, her arms down to her hands, and finally the swords. As they vibrated with power, she raised her arms to the heavens, and for the first time in her life Selena called to the Blessed Mother for help. As one mother to another. For the life of her child, she begged for assistance. As her lips moved in silent prayer, the air around her swirled, lifting her hair, brushing warmly against her skin. She shivered, not in fear but in awe of a presence so powerful and loving, it overwhelmed her. And then it was gone.

She opened her eyes to Nikko's intense blue ones. "I'm going in, Nikko. If that bitch comes out, grab my body and run. Do not allow any energy but mine near it!"

Then she was gone.

Demonic laughter filled the dank, dark cavern of the host's postmortem mind. Selena was not intimidated. She felt strong. Stronger than she had ever felt. Her swords thrummed with power. The infusion of Nikko's blood coupled with the five nanorians blazing with energy around her neck powered her to step deeper into the serpent's lair. Long, burning hisses swirled around her; the lash of a forked tongue pricked her ankle.

"Show yourself, Lamia!" Selena turned in slow circles, her swords raised, every sense on red alert. The vast, gray wasteland of the host offered few places to hide. It looked like a postapocalyptic desert. Lamia's toxic vapor swirled tauntingly around her. "Coward!" Selena challenged.

"It'sssssss you who are the coward, daughter of Paymon," Lamia hissed.

"I am here!"

"You cower from your destiny."

"My destiny is on earth, not in Hell with the likes of you."

"That is unfortunate for you, but," she cackled, "fortunate for me. Give me the necklace and I will spare your life and that of your lover."

The strength of the five could not be taken, only freely given. "Over my dead body!"

"It will be my pleasure."

The daemoness materialized in the form of half-woman, half-serpent. The naked female part of her rested on the thick, shiny coils of a constrictor. Long, fiery hair sparked around her pale face and exaggerated fangs. In each clawlike hand, she wielded a blazing saber.

"You cannot defeat me, slayer. My power is too strong."

"No power is unconquerable, Lamia. Not even yours."

Lamia's coils tightened, raising her upward so that she towered over Selena. In a lightning-quick strike of her tail, Lamia caught hold of Selena's left foot and yanked her forward and off-balance. Selena hacked off the tail, freeing herself, and was back on her feet. She ducked as the bloody stump tried to pound her into salt. She rolled out and away from it, then backtracked and lunged at the stump, slicing off a large chunk of it. Furious, Lamia struck out with a fireball from one of her sabers. It hit Selena in the chest, sending her airborne. She cut the fire from her, slowing the velocity of the attack, leaping higher into the air so that she came down upon Lamia's back. Selena dug her heels deep into the daemon's back, eliciting shrieks of rage. The fiery sabers slashed around her. Selena counterthrust and parried, hacking the fiery hair from the daemon's head. Lamia rose up, twisted, then slammed Selena into the ground. Like a cobra, Lamia puffed up, her fangs extended, and spat her venom at Selena. Selena closed her eyes and rolled out, but not before the venom sprayed along her back, burning into her flesh.

Selena hissed in pain, but pushed through it. Nikko's blood would repair the damage. Selena shot straight up into the daemon's chest and pierced her with the right sword, then dodged Lamia's fiery sword as it swung beneath her feet. Like a corkscrew, Selena shot straight for Lamia's heart. The daemon knocked Selena's right sword from her hand, but Selena held steady and drilled her left sword into Lamia's chest on the other side of the first cut. Four more cuts, and she'd have cast the pentagram; then she would go in for the kill.

"You have met your match, Lamia," Selena taunted, bolting up again and dodging the fiery serpent's sabers.

Lamia hissed and spat her venom. The spray caught Selena in the face, the acid burning her eyes, blinding her.

"Durendel!" Selena called to the sword Lamia had knocked away. It cleaved to her hand. "Be my eyes!" It heated in her hand and, as if she directed it, lunged and sliced another cut for the pentagram. Lamia screamed, spewing her venom. It rained down on Selena. "Repel!" she called to the nanorians. They flared with so much heat they scorched her skin. Lamia's shrieks of pain were music to Selena's ears.

"Don't like to taste your own vile medicine, Lamia?" Selena pressed forward, the powerful nanorians infusing her body with surging power. Lamia cackled as the sound of escaping gas alerted Selena. Lamia was escaping the host! *Nikko! Prepare yourself! She's coming!* she called to him in her mind. *And don't be a damn hero!*

Selena hurled herself from the vacant dead host and tumbled back into her own body. Her vision still impaired, Selena knew the swords would guide her, and the nanorians would power her.

She sprang up and blindly reached for Nikko but caught only air.

Demonic laughter reverberated around her head. "I hold your lover in my hands! The necklace for his life!"

"Don't do it, Selena!" Nikko shouted. "I've got this bitch!"

Lamia's shrieks of pain reverberated in Selena's head. Her swords flew out of her hands. Lamia's screams intensified, the smell of sulfur so strong Selena could barely breathe. Fire flashed around her, singeing her skin, as the grunting of struggling bodies and the copper scent of blood filled her senses.

"You picked the wrong bitch today, vampire," Lamia screeched at Nikko.

The sound of steel piercing flesh and bones shivered through Selena. The warm spray of blood across her face, immediately followed by the sound of a dying heart, terrified her.

"Nikko!" she screamed. "Nikko!" she screamed again when he didn't answer. *Not him, please. Not Nikko!*

"You fucking bitch!" Selena screamed, rushing forward.

A large hand caught hers and pressed something hard, warm, and wet into it. "That bitch's heart," Nikko said in Selena's ear.

"Oh, my God!" she breathed. Her knees gave way and Selena sank to the ground as wave after chaotic wave of relief crashed into her. Tears burned her sightless eyes, and her chest tightened so hard she was sure she was having a heart attack. Strong arms wrapped around her. Lips pressed to her forehead.

"We did it, Selena," Nikko whispered, gently rocking her.

She touched the face she could not see, her shaky

hands tracing over his lips, his cheeks, his nose, his eyes. "You're alive!" she cried.

His body stiffened; then he gently brushed a thumb over her eyelids. "Your eyes, Selena?"

"Lamia's venom."

He growled. "You can't see?"

"Not at the moment." Maybe never again.

"The heart, Selena," he said, opening her hand. He took it from her and pressed it into the sixth setting of her necklace. "Will that help?"

She brushed her fingertips across the warm, sticky stone lying against her skin. It flared with warmth and power. The other five vibrated in welcome. With her own natural power, combined with the staggering power of all seven stones and Nikko's blood, not a single immortal save for the devil himself or Rurik would be able to challenge her and win.

With Lamia dead, one heart remained.

It was hers for the taking. But she needed to hurry. Her father was closing in.

"Nikko," she whispered, grabbing his shoulders. "We need to go before Paymon realizes he has lost a valued disciple and another of his Hellkeepers."

"I'm not leaving without Marisol," Nikko said, helping her up.

Selena's stomach dropped to her feet. Moving Marisol now would be signing her death warrant.

CHAPTER EIGHTEEN

S he's safe where she is!" Selena shouted.

"Paymon knows where she is!"

"No, he doesn't. Lamia never made it to the island to confirm it. You have to believe me when I tell you, for now she's protected in the sanctuary with Father Ken."

"She'll be safe with us both."

Selena dug her nails into Nikko's arms. "Nikko, she *must* stay on the island. Please, trust me on this."

Tension steeled his body. "That bitch daemon was on her way to nab her! She *isn't* safe." He lowered his head to Selena's and lowered his voice. "Trust in me that I can protect her, Selena. The people I work with can protect her."

Vehemently Selena shook her head. He didn't understand. "Lamia would not have been able to set foot on consecrated ground without alerting the priest. Father Ken and Sister Agnes understand Marisol is not to leave the grounds." Selena grabbed Nikko's hands. "Paymon is playing a high-stakes game of truth or dare. He only suspects I'm in the area. He doesn't know about Marisol. He thinks she's dead. I don't know how Lamia knew to come here or even suspect I had a daughter! But I can bet you Paymon doesn't; if he did, he would have made a move a longtime ago. When I collect the seventh stone, I'm going to call him out, and it will end!" Selena felt Nikko's resolve stiffen when his muscles continued to tighten. "Can you protect her from being possessed by even a mundane daemon?"

"If you teach me, yes."

"I *can't* teach you. Unless you are daemon, it cannot be taught. Can you fight a legion of daemons?"

"As you taught me, I can resist them."

"Even in a panic room constructed of lead, if they wanted Marisol, they could swarm in and rip her from your arms. And if they can get that close, they can destroy her mind." Selena reached up to his face and cupped it between her hands. "Nikko, she's on an island, in a Catholic church in the presence of a renowned exorcist and a woman married to Jesus Christ in mind, body, and soul. There is no other place in our world safer. Please. Let's get out of here before Paymon tracks down his dead bitch and her sidekick."

Finally, Nikko's muscles loosened. "I don't like this, Selena, but I trust you to know what's best for Marisol."

"Thank you."

They had been airborne on the L.O.S.T. jet for almost an hour. Worry wore on Nikko's mind. Selena's sight had not improved, and she had become uncharacteristically quiet. She sat staring out the window at the sky she could still not see. Trying to draw her into conversation had been futile. She had erected a wall around her. And damn if he could get through it.

The stubborn set of her jaw, her tight lips, and her continued silence had him feeling completely helpless. He didn't know what to do. *If* there was anything that could be done.

He moved into the seat next to her and touched her fist, unprying her stiff fingers. She tensed. "Selena," he softly said, "tell me what to do."

She turned to him, her face rigid. "When this is over, I don't want to see you again." She laughed bitterly. "*If* I can actually see again, I don't want any contact with you. I want your word you'll respect that."

He stiffened as the bottom dropped out of his gut. "What the—"

"My attorney will handle the visitation details for you with Marisol."

She turned back to stare out the window. Nikko sagged in his seat.

He knew what was bugging her. And he couldn't blame her.

He'd told her there was no room in his life for her. Was this her revenge? He'd meant it when he said it and still believed it—but not the way she thought. Didn't she know there would always be a place for her in his life, just not the house with the white picket fence?

Nikko shook his head, moving across the aisle from her. Women! He had never been able to figure them out. He stared out his own window, welcoming the burn of the sun. His vampire habits were becoming more ingrained—his desire for blood, not food. His strength was still peaking. He'd handled Lamia. And while he was still learning to control his impulsiveness, half the time he didn't want to. Especially when it came to Selena. He looked over at her relaxed body. *She drops that grenade on me and she's relaxed?*

He looked back out the window, squinting, his fingers drumming the armrests. Unable to remain still, he stood and, with his hands locked behind his back, scowling at Selena, began to pace the aisle from the cockpit to the aft bedroom/meeting room.

Each time he looked at her, she remained unmoving. His frustration mounted. "Damn it, Selena!" he shouted. "Millions of lives are at stake, and you choose now to play head games with me." It gave him a small amount of satisfaction to see some color rise in her cheeks. "It nearly killed me to keep that fucking daemon out of your body! And now you shut down?" He crouched down beside her seat and touched her knees. "We're a team. You need me. You can't just walk away from that."

"I don't need you. But rest assured, I have no plans to walk away from what we have to do."

He grasped her knees. She flinched. Damn it, he didn't mean to— He rubbed where his fingers had probably bruised. "Then why did you say what you just said?"

She turned from the window and looked at him. "How did you kill Lamia?"

Hell if he knew, he just had. "I'm a trained observer, Selena. I watched every move you made carving up Malphas. I simply repeated it."

"How did you keep her from entering my body while I was still in the host?"

Should he tell her how it had scared ten years off his life when he thought that daemon bitch had killed her and left her to rot in the dead body? "I saw the vapor trail coming out of the host's mouth and made a beeline straight for you. I started hacking away at it. The daemon manifested in pieces. I grabbed her torso and started cutting, but she got hold of me with one of the arms still attached to it."

"She said she had you."

"She did, but I had her more." He touched beside her eyes. "Will you see again?"

Selena turned her head away. "I don't know."

Not letting her pull away from him again, Nikko moved into the seat beside her. "What does what I did to Lamia have to do with anything?"

She sighed and sat back in her seat. "No mortal knows the extraction procedure. No mortal has ever killed a Hellkeeper before you."

"You forget, you shot me up with some powerful vampire blood, not to mention I have enough of your blood circulating inside to give me a few of your dae-mon moves."

"You always were strong and smart, Nikko. You're much stronger now, and learning about my world. It's Marisol's world too. You could hold your own against most immortals." She swallowed hard and squeezed her eyes closed.

"What is it, Selena?"

She was silent for a moment. "If something happens to me, Nikko"—she inhaled deeply—"take my necklace and my swords, and—harvest my heart the same way you har-vested Lamia's. Set into the necklace, it will give you the power to destroy my father."

His heart stopped. His jaw fell open. He shook his head, stunned.

She grabbed his hands. "Promise me you'll do it!"

"I can't make that promise, Selena."

"You will do it! It's the only way to kill Paymon and give our daughter a normal life."

Nikko squeezed his eyes shut. His guts churned as if they had been tossed into a blender on PUREE. He couldn't do it. Nor could he allow her to give up. "Your sudden lack of spirit disappoints me, Selena," he taunted.

"I don't lack spirit, Nikko. I am just a realist. I'm blind, in case you haven't noticed. I don't know when or if my sight will return. I only say what I say to you so that you are prepared in the event something happens to me." Her body trembled, and despite her show of bravado, a single tear tracked down her cheek. "I'm not invincible, Nikko. Paymon has the power of ten Lamias."

Nikko leaned in, wanting simply to comfort, but he could not resist kissing the tear away. "Lamia was a piece of cake."

He felt Selena crack a smile. He smiled back and kissed her cheek again. Then her nose. Her chin. Her bottom lip. He inhaled her familiar sultry scent, glad she did not stink like the other daemons. His fingers slipped into her hair and he pulled her lips against his. Heat flared inside him with just these chaste kisses. God, he wanted her again. But he could not go there. He would want her again, and again. She was a drug he was addicted to and had to kick if he was going to live on his own terms. His life wasn't set up for a full-time family. He was a full-time L.O.S.T. operative. The best he could offer Selena was a part-time-lover position.

Selena shook her head, pulling his hands from her. "Don't make this harder than it has to be."

He rose and moved back into his seat. He felt like a

yo-yo when it came to his feelings for Selena. One minute he could not keep his hands off her, the next he was telling her there was no future for them, then he turned around and comforted her.

He raked his fingers through his hair and dropped his head into his hands. Each time he told himself there was no room for her, he found himself wanting more of her. He shook off the longing and shifted to safer ground. "I'm going to text my handler and see if he'll okay a conference call among the three of us. We have a lot of details to hammer out before the auction."

Selena nodded and turned back to the window.

Nikko sent the text and was immediately given the go-ahead. He picked up the remote on the table across from him and hit a button. The flat screen on the bulkhead flashed on. Nikko hit a few keys on the laptop beneath it, and immediately a blue screen flashed. While they would not be able to see Godfather, for obvious reasons, he would be able to see them.

"Do you copy, Mr. Black?" Nikko asked.

"I copy," Godfather's computer-regenerated voice answered.

"I have Selena de la Roja here with me. She has agreed to act on our behalf—"

"Whoa, slow down, cowboy," Selena said, sitting up and looking toward the screen. "I agreed to not make waves. Don't volunteer me for something I have no clue about the details of." She turned toward Nikko. "And I have not run any of this past Señor Balderama."

"And you won't," Godfather stated.

"I don't work for you, sir," Selena said to the screen.

"Alerting your handler will serve no purpose, Miss de

la Roja. The American government will take it over from here, with your much-appreciated help."

Selena stood and moved out from between the seats, stumbling as she turned too early. Nikko reached out and steadied her. She flung him off.

"Are you impaired?" Godfather asked her.

"At the moment, I can't see."

"Is the condition permanent?" he asked matter-of-factly.

Selena shook her head. "I don't know. But regardless, you cannot ask me to in effect double-cross the man I trust like a father. His intentions are the same as yours. Why not work together?"

"We are, he just won't know it."

Selena shook her head and felt for a seat. Finding one to her right, she sat. "I don't roll that way, Mr. Black."

"Selena," Nikko said, "it's not that big of a deal. Balderama will make his bid, lose, and think the world is going to shit, and you can tell him after the fact that the cask was picked up by the US government."

She looked up to Nikko with her blind eyes. His heart broke for her. "If it's not that big of a deal, then allow Los Cuatro to take possession of the cask and store it."

"Negative," Godfather said. "With US possession, there will never be doubt of its nonuse."

"Are you insinuating Los Cuatro has nefarious intentions?"

"I'm not insinuating anything, I'm stating a fact: in US possession, the cask will be safely stored and left untouched."

"So you're saying the US would never use nukes for any reason?"

"Not at all, but not *that* nuke." Godfather paused, and

Nikko knew he was working hard to remain patient with the defiant Latina. "Miss de la Roja, we're taking possession of it with or without your cooperation."

"Well, that's going to be pretty damn hard, since the auction is happening at my club with my security. If the venue is changed again, no one will show up, and you can kiss ID'ing the players at the table *and* getting your hands on that cask *adios*."

"Cruz tells me you have the power to get into heads and extract information. Let's make this easy. Get the location of the cask from Noslov and we bypass the auction."

"And keep Los Cuatro out of the mix?"

"Yes."

She shook her head. "No deal. Besides . . . Noslov doesn't have the cask or knowledge of its whereabouts. He's merely the agent."

"And you believe that?" Nikko asked.

"It's the truth." She gazed toward the screen. "For the sake of argument, let's say you know the location. You botched the job once—how do you expect me or Los Cuatro to trust you'll succeed a second time?"

Nikko cringed. Damn her, that was a smack in Godfather's face as well as Nikko's.

Unbelievably, Godfather chuckled. "I can see why Cruz fell for you. A woman who stands firmly on her principle and is loyal to the marrow. Come to work for me, and there will be no reason to feel as if you've betrayed your cause."

Nikko's head snapped back in shock. What the—?

"*Lo siento*, Señor Negro, I already have a job."

"Then keep what you have, but forgo the info sharing with Balderama."

"I'll consider it," Selena said.

Selena was dug in. The only way to get her to cross the line was to compromise.

"A small compromise then, Miss de la Roja."

"I'm listening."

"Take a meeting with Señor Balderama with Cruz in attendance"—Selena opened her mouth to protest—"solely in the capacity of an ambassador of sorts, to vouch for the integrity and seriousness of the United States government's interest in the cask."

"What if he refuses to cooperate?"

"Then it will be up to you both to convince him we are on the same side and that it would be most detrimental to his organization should he refuse."

"That, Mr. Black, sounds ominously like a threat."

"It was meant to."

Selena sat back and crossed her arms.

"She agrees," Nikko said, looking at the screen.

"I can see that," Godfather said drolly. "Check in when you hit the ground, Cruz, and coordinate with your team. We have a lot to go over."

"Roger that," Nikko said, then clicked the connection off. He touched Selena's shoulder. "Thank you."

"Señor is not going to like this one bit, and because I am the bearer of doom he will no longer trust me."

"I don't understand why it should be so difficult for him to understand we're on the same side, and it's in his best interest to let us do the heavy lifting. What does he have to lose?"

"Señor has worked tirelessly for the entire Latino world. I expect he will think the cask will be safest with him, since he knows his true motivations are noble. His elaborate security measures will ensure the cask stays out of the wrong hands. And he's going to be furious that I broke the strict code of never allowing a stranger into our inner sanctum." She sighed. "When he learns I have spoken about the cask to you, he'll be enraged. Now I'll have to come completely clean about Kyrgyzstan to prove to him I didn't just trust you because I'm a reckless woman."

"What weren't you honest about?"

"I omitted information. You specifically. Because I got hung up staying with you after I injected you, the cask got away from me. Had I gone right after it, I would not be sitting here talking to you right now."

The realization that Selena had not only risked her life to save his but put her mission aside to make sure he survived the Rev rattled his resolve a little bit more. "Does he know about your father?"

Selena closed her eyes. "No. He thinks I don't know who my father is."

"Does he know about Marisol?"

"No."

A monumental wave of relief washed through Nikko. He did not know why he felt that way, but he was damn glad Selena had the wherewithal to keep her paternal parentage and their daughter secret from the world.

"Will you tell him?"

"I have no reason to. Even if I did, I wouldn't. The

fewer possessable minds with that knowledge, the safer Marisol stays."

Good.

"I want to hook you up with a camera Saturday night, Selena. For obvious reasons, we're going to want images of each participant to run facial scans and ID them."

"I can do that. I had planned on getting DNA and fingerprint samples, too."

"Those guys won't touch a thing. Hell, they'll probably come disguised."

"The cloth on all the seats in the room where we'll be conducting the auction are specially treated to absorb the slightest traces of moisture. I'm going to turn the heat up in there. When their asses begin to sweat, we'll get all the DNA we need."

"Well played, Selena," he said, impressed. "Sounds like you've done this before."

She smiled wickedly. "I have. It's how I've stayed in business all these years."

Nikko contemplated her last comment and wondered how much of that business included the vampire in her bedroom. Nikko wrestled with his ego, but it lost to his jealous bone, and he blurted the question that he had been burning to ask. "Who was the vampire in your bedroom, and what does he mean to you?" Nikko almost bit his tongue for the last part of the question. He sounded like a jealous boyfriend.

Selena's smile faded. But her eyes sparkled mischievously. That jealous bone of his was about to snap. "Joran Cadiz. Undisputed lord of the Miami underworld."

"Are the two of you—" His pride kept him from making a complete fool of himself.

"Romantically involved?" Selena finished for him.

His cheeks flushed, and he was glad she could not see him.

She turned her face up to him, her expression open and sincere. "Have you not heard anything I've said to you since you barged back into my life?"

"You've said a lot, my brain is on overload."

She leaned forward but did not touch him. "I'm going to spell it out for you, Nikko Cruz. I was a virgin when you and I met. You were the first, and though I look like a sleek, high-priced call girl, it's an act. You are the only man I have been intimate with."

"That's not true," he said, biting his tongue.

Selena sat back and crossed her arms over her chest. "You mean that little show with Vegas at the club?"

"Yeah," Nikko roughly said, not liking the way his rage simmered as he replayed the scene in his mind's eye.

Selena shrugged. "It was nothing." She crossed her legs and gazed out the window.

"He had his hands all over you! That was not *nothing*." Nikko checked his rage.

She turned toward him and demanded, "How many women have *you* slept with in the last eight years?"

"That's different!" he blurted, realizing he sounded like a monumental dick. "I didn't mean it like that."

"How many?"

"I don't know."

"You don't know because you lost count, or you don't know because you forgot?"

Nikko sat back in his seat. "I get your point, Selena." Didn't mean he liked it.

Selena shook her head. "Does it really matter? We've made our choices, Nikko, now let's stop acting like jealous teenagers and act like the adults we are and accept the consequences."

With no comeback worthy of the truth, Nikko sat angrily staring at her. He was torn up inside. Torn between self-preservation and the woman he loved. Between confronting Paymon right now and his duty to his country and the millions of lives he was sworn to protect. Between L.O.S.T. and a normal life as a normal family man. He wanted it all. But that was impossible.

Selena set her jaw, silently cursing Lamia for blinding her, her father for existing, and her weak-ass heart when it came to Nikko Cruz. She had yet to recover from the trauma of thinking she had lost him to Lamia's fatal fangs. The split second she realized he was alive, she'd known she could not live through that trauma again. She had jumped off the emotional roller coaster that had become her life. Nikko had been frank when he told her there was no room in his life for her, and she'd set out to prove that *she* was his life! But after Lamia, the fear of losing him shook her to her foundation.

She'd rather have no contact than live through his death. She'd nearly lost it on that mountainside in Kyrgyzstan when she'd seen him blown to hell, and this morning, after knowing him again, being with him, seeing him with Marisol? She had died a torturous death in her heart and soul, thinking Lamia had him and he would be lost to her forever. She had lived the last eight years without him, knowing he thought the worst of her; she could live out her life alone knowing he'd lived to know the truth.

Because once she extracted her father's heart, she would be all-powerful, and no one, not even Rurik, would dare challenge her. Selena vowed her life would be so simple and uncomplicated then, she'd be able to bore paint off a wall. She was done hiding behind lies. Always looking over her shoulder, sleeping with one eye open. Pretending to be someone she was not.

She wanted normal, and, damn it, she would have it, even if it meant living without the one and only man she would ever love. Selena sighed, finding solace in her future. Marisol would know her father on his schedule, which Selena would never stand in the way of. And the little girl would blossom, and Selena could watch her embrace the world without worry she'd be snatched away by Paymon.

CHAPTER NINETEEN

As they disembarked from the jet, Nikko took Selena's hand to guide her down the jetway. She tolerated it only because she did not want to face-plant into the tarmac.

"Last step," he said.

When she touched solid ground, Selena let out a long breath. She was just beginning to see shadowy outlines. What she needed was a shot of Rev to boost her immune system. As soon as she got home, she would telepathically call Joran and hope he'd wake and come to her. She should have thought of it sooner.

"I'll take you home," Nikko said.

She didn't argue. Once there, though, she'd insist he leave.

As they drove to the marina where her motorboat was docked, Nikko asked, "Do you really think Father Ken and Sister Agnes believed us this morning when we told them about the daemons?"

"I told you, Father Ken has done numerous exorcisms. Sister Agnes has been with Marisol from the beginning; she'd die for that little girl. They understand and thankfully don't judge."

"How do we find the last Hellkeeper?"

Annoyance swept through her. "I told you, I'm going to conjure him."

"How do you go about that?"

This time she hesitated. He already thought she was a freak. She might as well embrace it. "The usual way, blood sacrifice."

"*What?*"

She shook her head, smiling tiredly. "I'm pulling your leg. I'll dangle the necklace in front of Vetis."

"Vetis?"

"Yep, tempter of the holy. I would have expected Daddy dearest to send Vetis, not Lamia, to the island."

"What do you mean, 'tempter of the holy'? Doesn't that mean the priest and nun will be susceptible to its possession?"

As if she hadn't already thought of that. "Not likely. That said, Vetis is the only daemon who can tolerate standing on consecrated ground for a prolonged period of time, as well as possessing the ability to tempt those of the cloth with less than stellar faith to open their weak minds to him. If I thought for one minute Vetis knew of Marisol's existence, I might have taken you up on your offer, but she's safe. Father Ken and Sister Agnes are faithful and strong. She's in good hands."

"So when do you plan on dangling the necklace? And what the hell does that mean anyway? What's going to make Vetis come for it when you call?"

"Nikko, c'mon. You know the power it holds. No one knows I possess it, but the entire underworld is abuzz with the news of the Hellkeepers' deaths and the disappearance of their hearts."

"The sooner the better, Selena. I want Paymon dead."

"Right after the auction."

"Right after the auction, we're going after the cask."

"*You're* going, I'm not."

"You're not going hunting without me!"

She shrugged and turned toward him. "Then I guess you're going to have to make a choice." Would he choose her?

"Damn it. What about your sight, Selena? You can't go daemon hunting blind."

His words sank her heart. He was going after the cask, not hunting with her as he had originally vowed. Her spine stiffened, as did her resolve.

"I'll have my sight back by then."

"How can you be sure?"

She shrugged again. "I just know. Now, would you stop asking me all these questions? You're giving me a headache."

The rest of the drive to the dock was silent, as was the motorboat ride to her house. Nikko helped her out of the small craft and into the house. Juju buzzed anxiously around Selena like a bee on a fresh bloom. Selena swatted her away after introducing Nikko as a friend who'd helped her home. "He's leaving. I'm getting a shower."

"Selena," Nikko called.

She just waved her hand over her head in a dismissive gesture and slowly felt her way toward her bedroom. Once there, she sank onto her bed and expelled a long, tenuous breath.

Holy Hell, when had her life become a three-ring circus? She felt like the plate juggler. Only her plates were lives! Two lives that were critical to her survival.

She rubbed the heels of her palms into her eyes, cursing Lamia for the hundredth time. The bitch! Selena had a hundred things to do, things that required her vision.

She turned toward the window, knowing it was too early for the vampire to be awake but desperate to rouse him. "Joran, if you can hear me, I need you now!"

Selena flung off her clothes and carefully walked naked into the large bathroom. She felt around the smooth, cool marble for the fixtures, then started the shower. Not bothering to wait for the water to warm, she stepped in.

"I thought you said you and Cadiz weren't lovers?" Nikko sneered from the doorway.

"I asked you to leave!" she snapped, tired of his ignoring her wishes. How the Hell had he sneaked up on her? Even without her vision—ah, yes. Of course. She had not detected his scent because it was all over her.

"I heard you call to him," Nikko said, so close to her she felt his passion hard against her belly.

While she was exhausted and supremely pissed off at Nikko at the moment, the lusty daemon in her warmed to his arousal. "So?" she challenged.

Like a funnel cloud, she could feel his passion swirl around her. "*So? That's your defense?*" His voice was low, controlled, furious.

Nikko's jealousy was heady. Part of her didn't know what to make of it. The other part couldn't help the spark of hope that ignited inside her. Foolish, that. "Nikko, get out of my shower."

His warm breath caressed her cheek when he defiantly said, "Not until you tell me why you called for him and not me."

She stiffened at that. She wasn't an emotional yo-yo he could play with at his whim. He said one thing and his actions said another. But he'd made it crystal clear there was no room in his life for her, and, damn it, she wasn't going to force the issue. Not after this morning. Not *ever*.

"Did you really just ask me that?" She flung him away from her and unleashed her version of Hell on him. "You come into *my* club and practically rape me, threaten me in order to get information, steal my necklace, and follow me to my yacht, then to Paris, then to St. Michael's, all the while telling me how much you hate me. Then when you see our daughter, you think it's okay to make love to me and *then tell me there is no room in your life for me*?" She shoved him hard against the shower wall. "And *now* you barge in here, with a hard-on no less, and ask me why I called out to another man? Are you fucking kidding me? I don't owe you any explanations. Maybe I did once but not now!"

She pointed to what she hoped was the shower entrance. "Get out of here, Nikko, before I really unleash on you."

Her entire body shook with rage. With one hand still pressed against his chest, she felt him exhale. Then she felt the rush of air his body disturbed as he exited the shower. For long minutes, she stood in the middle of the enclosure, shaking violently as angry tears streamed down her cheeks. "Damn you, Nikko Cruz! Damn you for coming into my life and screwing it up!"

Twenty minutes later, Selena had calmed enough to clean up, dry off, and slip into a cotton baby-doll romper. "Juju!" she called.

"I'm here," the woman said from close by.

"Is he gone?"

"Yes. I don't know what you said to him, but I have never seen a man so furious as that one."

"He deserves it." Selena felt for the edge of her bed and sat down. "How's our Russian guest?"

"First tell me, what happened to you?"

Too tired to play a game of verbal cat and mouse with her friend, Selena said, "I was attacked and my attacker threw some kind of liquid at me. I can't see. It's only temporary." She hoped.

She heard Juju pull down the linens and fluff the pillows. "*El patrón* was looking for you last night. He seemed irritated when I told him you had left without word of when you would return."

El patrón. Mr. Black's arrogant words came back to her. As well as her agreement to take Nikko along for clarification. That part she would sidestep. *El patrón* was the last person she wanted to see right now. Though she dreaded the conversation with him, it needed to transpire. He was a reasonable man, and should he agree, an enormous weight would be lifted from her shoulders, not the least part of which would be feeling as if she had somehow betrayed her mentor. Selena nodded. "I'll call him."

"Our guest is fine. I stitched him up and gave him the sedatives. I also measured him as you requested for a suit. The tailor promised to have it delivered first thing in the morning."

"Did he have anything to say?" If Noslov knew what was good for him, he would have kept his mouth shut.

"Only that you were an abomination of a female." Juju smirked.

"Yeah, and he's the cat's meow." Selena slipped between the cool, smooth sheets and yawned. "Amy took care of everything at the club?"

"Yep, she said it was as dead as a graveyard last night."

"Good." Selena yawned again, the fatigue drugging. "I'm just going to take a nap before I get ready for work." If Juju responded, Selena didn't hear her because she was already asleep.

She dreamed of daemons, arrogant vampires, and dead babies. Of flying priests and fanged nuns. She tossed and turned, flinging the sheets from her feverish body. Nikko called to her from the end of a long tunnel. She called back to him until her throat was raw, but he did not hear her. He turned and walked away.

"I'm here! Don't leave me!" she screamed, running down the tunnel after him.

Flames lashed out around her, scorching her limbs, melting them into wax puddles, stopping her progress as her father's demonic laughter reverberated around her. "Where is your lover now, Daughter?"

A firm hand stroked her limbs in a slow, soothing rhythm. A deep voice calmed her racing heart. Her arms rested at her sides, her legs quieted.

Joran?

"You called, I came."

"Thank you," she whispered.

He leaned over her, his warm breath brushing across her chest, singeing her sultry skin. "I brought you something, Selena," he purred, his lips hovering just above hers.

Fog shrouded her mind. Warm breath fanned her lips. Her nipples tightened and she moaned. "Nikko?" He'd come back for her? Just as her hope flared, her reality came crashing down around her. No, Nikko had turned his back on her. Just when she needed him most, he'd walked away. He could go to Hell.

"Ah, *coqueta,* I am not your lover, though I would happily take his place."

Joran.

Yes, it is me. He dragged his fangs across her lower lip, across her chin, then down her throat. Selena gasped and arched, wanting it to be Nikko. Instead, she felt the sharp prick of a needle in her thigh.

The rush was instantaneous. Her blood shimmered like perfectly cut diamonds beneath the sun, infusing her with healing properties and strength from the marrow out. Every part of her body tingled. From her fingers to her toes and everything in between. Selena arched, gasping as the rush of the Rev hit her between the thighs. *Jesus.* Her eyes flashed open. She could see!

An arrogant smile twisted Joran's handsome lips. He cocked a dark brow, daring her to follow through on her body's sudden, intense need for a man.

"Jesus, Joran, that's some potent stuff."

"My personal supply."

Her body thrummed with sexual energy. Selena closed her eyes and exhaled as she wrestled with the intense throb along her aching breasts and womb. Keeping it under control was going to be a distraction she could ill afford. Until her body processed the Rev, the potent urges would persist, strumming her nerve endings, a constant stimulation. She opened her eyes and stared at the tricky vampire. God help her, it was going to be an interesting night.

"Why didn't you take advantage of my daemon lust while I slept?"

He had the aplomb to look wounded. "I am not a

knave, Selena. I will gladly share your bed, but not when you are incoherent and think I'm another man."

"Shut up."

"It's true," he sniffed.

Selena grinned, enjoying this side of the deadly prince of the underworld she would never have guessed existed. "Why, Joran, I'm impressed. Who knew you even knew the meaning of the word *honor*."

He moved to the edge of the bed, straightening his tailored Versace jacket. "Hardly a notion I entertain on a regular basis."

Selena laughed, her affection for the vampire growing by the minute. "One day, Joran, you just might make someone a good husband."

"Never!"

And she would never be wife to Nikko. They were a sorry pair, she and Joran. Selena sat up and looked out the big window, her mood having turned with thoughts of Nikko. Dusk had settled into night. She slid off the bed. "I need to go to the club."

His vampire eyes burned brightly. "Would you like some company?"

"Yes, as a matter of fact, I would." She strode toward her dressing room and said over her shoulder, "But be warned, the way I'm feeling, I might get us into trouble."

"I live for trouble," he roughly said.

Yes, she knew that, despite his recent amicable gestures, Joran Cadiz was a cold-blooded killer his immortal peers feared. And that he never acted without planning his next three steps.

The instant Selena walked into her office, the terrible, familiar scent of Paymon hit her.

"You've had a visitor," Joran said from behind her.

Selena whirled and faced him.

He put his hands up defensively. His eyes narrowed dangerously. "Do *not* go there."

"How did he find me then?"

Joran sniffed the air and cocked a brow. "Ask your *precioso*."

"Nikko would never—"

"The other one. Your almighty *patrón*."

Selena's brow crinkled as she sniffed deeper into the room. It was there, the rich scent of Señor's special cigar tobacco. Why had he been here when she was not? Because Señor here, with Paymon, made no sense. Except in the case of betrayal, which made even less sense. "Juju said he was looking for me last night. He must have come by to speak with me sometime in the last twenty-four hours." *El patrón* was the least of her worries. What of Paymon?

Paymon's awareness of her current location was a giant-size wrench thrown into the master plan she had set in motion eight years ago! *Damn it!* She was not yet prepared to take him on! She needed that last stone to solidify her strength. Even then, it might not be enough. She had always known that. She had been willing to take the risk. But lately . . . She harshly exhaled and forced herself to be honest. Lately she'd begun to hope for assistance from Nikko to destroy the root of all her problems. Wanting a man to ride in to save her was never a good idea.

Nope, she was going to have to take care of her father on her own. Whether she was ready or not.

The stones around her neck warmed. Absently she stroked them. Her cell phone rang, startling her.

She looked at the number and her adrenaline spiked.

Again, a flash of doubt made her hesitate before she connected. "*Buenas noches, Señor,*" Selena said.

"*Cazadora,* I have been looking for you. We have much to discuss," *el patrón* said.

Selena looked up at Joran and asked, "I just walked into my office to call you. Were you here . . . ?"

When her voice trailed off, he replied, "*Sí,* Señora Amy was kind enough to show me into your office last night as I tried unsuccessfully on your business lines to reach you."

The tightness in her chest relaxed. "I was—kind of out of it."

"You are feeling better tonight?"

"Much. Would you care to meet me here so that we may have our discussion?" A discussion she was suddenly dreading. Damn Nikko and his Mr. Black!

"I am just making my way up." *El patrón* hung up.

Nervous energy sparked along her spine. "He's on his way up. Joran, can you disappear for a while?"

"Use me, abuse me, then dispose of me. You women are all the same." He nodded. "I will be downstairs selecting my entertainment for the evening."

"Leave some for the other guys."

The fury that threatened to eat him up continued to gather steam. Nikko had literally run a marathon since he stormed out of Selena's house. Instead of its dissipating off the quagmire of emotions, his anxiety level continued to rise. Now he paced a noticeable path in the Spanish tile of the secured house Godfather had procured for the team. Cassidy, Cross, Stone, and Satch kept clear of him.

"Cross, this stuff is eating me up. I can barely sleep. I'm fucking Superman twenty-four/seven. I don't know if I'm coming or going and I can't keep my hands off Selena! Is there some kind of antidote?" Nikko asked the reticent vampire.

"You can't blame all of what you're experiencing on the Rev, Cruz. Some of it is just you."

Nikko looked down at the vampire. "I don't follow."

"Your enhanced senses, strength, and to an extent your libido, you can blame on the Rev, but your emotional state? That's all you, man."

"But I'm not like this!"

"You were when you first came to the compound," Stone said from his seat next to Cross. "You were a powder keg of pissed-off. Controlling that temper of yours was what held you back. Once you got a leash on it, you were good to go, but now? You've regressed, Cruz. All the way back to Johnny Cicone. You've strayed off course, and you've become a detriment to the team. Anyone wanna guess why?"

Nikko opened his mouth to defend himself, but Stone

was right. Selena had fucked with his head all over again. And he'd allowed himself to get sucked in by her. But how could he not? She was the mother of his daughter. *His daughter.*

"Nikko," Cassidy softly said, "I feel your pain. Been there, done that. But you need to find a way to process your past so that you can live in your present."

Nikko sank into an empty chair and looked around the room. "My daughter is alive."

"What?" his team asked in collective shock.

Nikko dropped his head into his hands and rubbed his eyes. "I saw her yesterday. She's amazing and beautiful."

"You have a kid?" Satch asked, slapping him on the back. "Congrats, man!"

"What the Hell kind of woman lies about having murdered your child?!" Cassidy demanded. "What a monumental bitch!" She began to pace the track Nikko had worn in the tile. "I'll kill her for you, and make no mistake, when I'm done with her, she won't rise a third time."

Nikko rubbed the heels of his hands into his eyes. "It's damn complicated."

"Why don't you fill us in, Cruz," Godfather said from the flat screen on the wall behind them.

CHAPTER TWENTY

With all that is obviously at stake, Selena, I find it disconcerting that you would just take off without warning. In the future, inform me of your destinations."

Selena blinked. What was it with the men in her life thinking they owned her? She let it slide with Señor. And not because he was who he was and she was fearful of offending him. *Only* because she did not want him on the defensive when she told him that what he thought was going to happen tomorrow night, wasn't.

"My apologies, sir, but I have good reason, which I shall explain to you now." She indicated the chair in front of her desk, while she pulled up the one from the corner and sat down to face him. "You recall when I returned empty-handed from Kyrgyzstan; I told you there was another faction waiting to hijack the cask? The one that was shot to hell?"

He steepled his index fingers and nodded. "*Sí.*"

"There was a survivor. He saw me, tracked me to Lost Souls, and showed up here a few days ago, demanding I pony up what information I had regarding Noslov and the cask."

"Of course you declined."

She took a deep breath and slowly exhaled. "I did. But, this man, I know him. He knows me from Georgia, and he works for the US government. They want the cask for the same reasons we do and are insisting that we step aside at the auction and allow them to do what they need to do."

The only clue to Señor's reception of this new development was the slow rise of blood in his cheeks. "Are you so naïve, Selena, as to trust this man? Do you have any idea of the value of that cask? And the destruction it could wreak in the wrong hands?"

She blinked, taken aback by his insinuation. "I am well aware of the importance of the uranium, sir, *and* its deadly potential. I am also one hundred percent certain that this operative is on the level. I have explained our position on this—"

Incredulous, he demanded, "You have discussed Los Cuatro's business with an outsider? Do you forget our cause?"

Selena raised her chin a notch, though she felt like dropping it. Disappointing this man who was like a father to her had never been easy. She had never compromised the cause of Latino human rights. She'd fought tirelessly over the years to see village children clothed, fed, and educated. She'd braved the jungles to take medical supplies to obscure mountain clinics. She'd fought their battles for them. She had bled for them. Lost Souls was not only a front to lure daemons but a profitable business that sponsored many children and their families in Central and South America. To even insinuate she had set aside the cause for her own purposes was insulting. "I do not forget the cause. It is because of my love for the cause that I broke protocol."

"You never break protocol!" he hissed, leaning forward. "*Never*, under any circumstances, discuss our business with *anyone* outside of Los Cuatro!"

"Señor, please. He did most of the talking about Los Cuatro. My only contribution was that you would not be agreeable to their terms."

"In that you were correct. What do they know?"

"Who you are, your connections, your mission statement. All superficial information. I can assure you, I did not enlighten them on any level."

"You enlightened them on many levels. That you have knowledge of me, that you work with me—but more important, or should I say damning, by not denying our interest in the uranium, you confirmed it, which is an automatic red flag not only to the US government but to Interpol! With our interest exposed, we will be recast from benevolent crusader for Latino human rights to a Watchdog-list organization trolling for nuclear weapons!" He stood so suddenly, he knocked the chair over.

Never had she seen his temper so openly displayed. Until that moment, she had not realized the full scope of the damage she had caused the organization she believed in. "I trust him not to allow this information to go any further than where it is," Selena defended herself.

Señor adjusted his cuff links, set the chair upright, and sat back down. On the surface, he appeared to have composed himself. Her heightened senses read a different story. His heart pumped blood double time. A thin sheen of perspiration glossed his face. The scent of his pungent anger made her eyes water. He looked directly at her. "Does this *operative* know of your past and what I did for you?"

"He knows of my past. He has not indicated he knows of our personal connection."

"Who is this man?"

Selena hesitated a millisecond before she answered. "His name is Nikko Cruz."

Señor's eyes flickered. "And what agency does he work for?"

"I don't know, but I do know his handler's name is Mr. Black. He was uncompromising, Señor, but genuine in his intent."

"So, this Mr. Cruz from your past shows up at the base of the Tian Shan in Kyrgyzstan to hijack a stolen cask of enriched uranium but fails, then approaches you in Miami and tells you that he works for a covert government agency headed by a man named Mr. Black, who insists they want the uranium cask so that *they* can, for the greater good of mankind, store it safely on US soil. Is that correct?"

When he put it like that, she felt like a fool. But she stood by her belief that Nikko was on the up-and-up. "Yes."

Señor stood, this time slowly, placed his hands behind his back, and looked sternly down at her. "You are my top agent. Shrewd, deadly, exact. Your unintentional outing of Los Cuatro aside, do you know how gullible this preposterous story makes you appear, Selena? Have you learned nothing in the last eight years?"

"Trust no one." As she said the words, she asked herself how she could trust a man who had no room in his life for her. A man for whom she had sacrificed all and who threw it back in her face. A man, she grudgingly admitted, who was not perfect, but a man who loved his daughter. Would die for her, and kill for her. In that, at least, she trusted him.

"This man is playing upon your emotions to get what he wants from you. In this case, the cask."

Selena shook her head. *No.*

"What lies has he told you to gain your trust?" Señor's eyes narrowed. "Did he seduce the information from you?" Heat rose in her cheeks. "Ah, I see that he did. You are a beautiful, lonely woman, Selena. Ripe for romance, and the pillow talk that follows."

She was not a complete fool. She knew from the very beginning Nikko had wanted one thing from her: the cask. He'd told her so. But when she'd resisted, she saw now, he had resorted to down and dirty tactics. Using their attraction and their past to get what he wanted. And with her eyes wide open, she'd been sucked in by him.

Her heart swelled with emotion all over again. She was gullible and naïve because, despite his manipulations, she loved him. And despite his lies, she knew somewhere in his angry, double-dealing heart he still had feelings for her. But not enough to make a life with her. It would be easy to double-cross him, but ultimately that would hurt Marisol, and she would not do that to the only good thing in her life. The girl deserved her father in her life, even the small part he would carve out for her. And because of Marisol and Selena's belief in Nikko's motives for the cask, despite how he'd manipulated her for the information, Selena would stand by her agreement to help him.

"Trust no one, yet you expose us to the world and are willing to hand over deadly enriched uranium to this man because he beguiled you?"

She could admit that. "Perhaps, but that doesn't

negate the fact that I believe his intentions are as noble as ours. And if he and his people are willing to shell out the cash and do the heavy lifting to get the damn thing, why not let them? Doing so takes Los Cuatro off the international cops' radar."

"Because, unlike you, I do not know this man or his handler or their *intentions*. What I am certain of are mine! My intentions will not be compromised for any reason, under any circumstances. As for your thinking our not bidding for the cask will change anything, you are a fool. The die has been cast—we cannot retract the fact that we are or were in the market for the makings of a nuclear bomb!"

He shook his head. "We have nothing to lose now. The players are in place, the strategies set, and the moneys collected. On behalf of Los Cuatro, I will make the securing bid, and then we will take possession of the cask." He pulled a cigar from his inside jacket pocket, snipped the end off with his custom cutter, and lit it. The aromatic smoke filled the air. He took a deep puff and looked at her as he exhaled. "There will be no more discussion on the matter."

Selena nodded. The conversation was what she'd thought it would be. "One word of caution from Mr. Black, should you refuse to step aside." He turned a sharp glare on her that sent shivers down her spine. "He said to tell you that should you refuse his offer, your operations here in the States will be compromised."

He took another puff of the cigar, tilted his head back, and smiled as he exhaled. "As the Americans are fond of saying, tell him for me, Selena, to bring it on."

For the first time since she had been introduced to

the consummate gentleman and world leader, Selena doubted *el patrón*'s judgment and his motives. Why not ask for proof that Nikko's agency was legit and leave it at that? She did not understand Señor's reasoning. "I'll relay the message."

He turned full on her. "My disappointment in your poor judgment knows no bounds, Selena. After all we have been through, to come to this."

Selena had always been respectful, never questioning Señor's reasons. She understood that sometimes the means to the end were not pretty, but necessary. It was her mantra when it came to daemon hunting and her relationship with Joran; but for Señor to question her intelligence, in effect calling her *estúpida,* pushed her to the edge. "Come to what? An impasse? Am I expected to follow blindly? To not think for myself? Not to think what would be better for Los Cuatro? I feel the same could be said of you and your judgment call on this. You are the supreme leader, mentor, benefactor, and oh-so-wise and benevolent head of Los Cuatro. What you are being now is stubborn and shortsighted, refusing for reasons beyond me to see the bigger picture. Why deplete Los Cuatro's accounts and go to the time, trouble, and added expense and most likely loss of life to secure the cask when the American government will do it for us?"

"*Trust* is the issue."

"Then speak to Cruz and Mr. Black yourself. I would venture to say the remaining three of the four who make up Los Cuatro's quorum would have a different opinion once they understood the gravity of this situation."

"Do you challenge me?" he demanded, his cheeks shaking with his anger.

"I challenge you to look at this proposition with different eyes. We have until midnight tomorrow night to gather intel on Mr. Cruz and his handler, Mr. Black. I suggest we get on it, and, sir, with all due respect, if they prove to be legit, which I am sure they are, then I say we stand back."

He squashed out the aromatic cigar on her custom Parnian desk. His handsome features morphed into something violent and ugly. Selena leaned back, unsure of his next move. "I will not be dictated to. There will be *no* deviations from the original plan." He schooled his features back to normal as he strode to the door and opened it. He turned and said, "I love you as if you were my daughter, Selena. Do not give me a reason to feel otherwise."

Then he was gone. Stunned by Señor's radical change in personality, Selena sat silent for long minutes in her office, trying to come to terms with how she felt. Gradually she realized that she didn't give a rat's ass whether Nikko got the cask or Señor. Either one would do right by it, so why jockey for position? What she cared about was getting her hands on Vetis's heart, then going after her father. Because what mattered was her endgame. Once Paymon was ashes in the wind, she was taking Marisol and starting over. No more Miami, no more Los Cuatro, no more immortals. She was going to be Betty Crocker and Donna Reed rolled into one. She had enough money stashed to live comfortably for ten lifetimes.

Let Nikko and his Mr. Black fight with Señor over the cask. Regardless of who ended up with it, it would be safely stored.

Nikko told his team everything, most of which they already knew. His past with Selena, his present, her reason for collecting the nanorians, and whom her final showdown would be with. He laid it all out on the table, except how he felt about Selena. He could not articulate that even to himself. As he told her story, his admiration and respect grew. She was an amazing woman who had done amazing things, and all of it for the love of her child—and him.

He swiped his hand across his face and looked at the stone-cold-sober faces of his team. They had remained silent the entire hour it took him to tell the tale.

"When all is said and done, Cruz, what do you want?" Godfather asked.

"My family." The words escaped before Nikko thought about them. He sat up and looked Godfather straight in the eye and said with more conviction, "I want my family." When put to task, there had been no hesitation in his heart. He wanted his family, and that included Selena.

"That is not possible," Cross said. "The Order will exact punishment for the Rev."

"Only if they find out about it. After what I just told you, don't you think your Order would be grateful to Selena for outing that daemon Apollo?"

"Apollyon," Cross corrected. "There is also the assassination of her own kind to consider. The terms of the truce are specific: we cannot kill our own kind."

"You killed Lazarus and your mother, both vampires," Cassidy said. "*And* were pardoned. Why would it be different for Selena? Sounds to me like she should get a medal, not executed."

"I do not make the rules, I only enforce them," Cross said, looking none too happy with Cassidy for taking a stand opposite his.

"Okay, kids, let's get back to why we're here. That cask," Godfather refereed.

"Mr. Black," Cross said, looking at the screen. "This news of Apollyon's plans to take over the Order must be immediately delivered to Rurik. I need to go—"

"A minute first, Cross," Godfather said.

The vampire nodded.

"I can't take any chances that your people will mess up the acquisition of the cask for us. I want your word there will be no interference on your side."

"The Order does not involve itself with mortal business."

"But what if that mortal business threatens immortal business?" Nikko asked.

"The Order will not cross the line into mortal business."

"Not even when immortals make humans their business?" Nikko pushed.

"The immortal is dealt with, not the human."

Cross's ominous prediction about Selena's future churned in Nikko's gut. He looked at Cassidy, who stared at him, unblinking. When she had needed them to save Cross from the vampire Lazarus, they had only watched as Cross lay dying. Not, Nikko justified, because they didn't want to help, but because they didn't know how to help or if any action would have sucked the team into a peril they had no way of escaping. It had been an incredible revelation that immortals walked among them. Not acting had been prudent then; this situation was different.

"Go do what you have to do, Cross," Godfather said.

Cross nodded.

"Wait!" Nikko said, standing up. "Give me some time, Cross, before you out Selena."

"It's out of my hands."

"No, it isn't," Cassidy said, coming to Nikko's defense. "Once we have possession of the cask, the threat by Apollyon will be moot."

"Do not meddle in matters that do not concern you, Jax," Cross growled.

"The mental and psychic well-being of my team concerns me. Put Rurik on alert, but keep Selena's name out of it."

"I will not lie."

"You don't have to lie, Marcus, just don't tell him everything." She approached the angry vampire and took his hand. "Rurik showed compassion when you exposed Lazarus. Who is to say when this is over he won't show the same to Selena?"

"Because it will reveal weakness. The only reason Apollyon has the balls to do what he's doing now is because Rurik showed weakness by allowing me to live!"

"I will not surrender Selena to you or any other immortal entity," Nikko stated.

"It will be done if the Order demands it," Cross said, and strode from the house.

A heavy pall hung over the room. Nikko's fists opened and closed. He was a righteous man. A passionate man. A man who understood that sometimes rules had to be broken for the greater good of the whole. Selena would not pay with her life for outing the daemon king's world-domination plot.

"We have work to do," Godfather curtly said from the screen. Nikko looked up to find Godfather's arctic gaze on him. He knew what was coming next. "Cruz, I understand your predicament, I also sympathize with it. However, there is a greater cause here than all of us combined. We can do this with you or without you. I prefer with you. It's your call."

Emotions churned within Cruz. Godfather was asking him to use Selena to land the cask, then to stand by while the Order meted out its punishment. He would not do it.

CHAPTER TWENTY-ONE

Nikko sat stone-faced as ideas, emotions, and resolutions careened through his head. In less than a week, his world had been turned upside down and inside out. He had been forced to come to terms with the ghosts that had haunted him. Who he was—*what* he was—had been challenged, stripped bare, and rebuilt. Johnny Cicone and Nikko Cruz had melded, becoming a stronger, better version of both men, wanting the same world, the one that came with an eight-year-old girl and her mother. No, not wanting—*needing* that world, those people.

The fear of losing them both after just finding them hovered on the perimeter of his mind.

Nikko didn't do things half-assed. He loved and hated hard. Played and worked hard. But what was he to do now? He was loyal and couldn't let his team down. But he also loved, more deeply than he'd ever thought possible, and he couldn't let his daughter or her mother down.

Resolved, he turned to Godfather. "I'll use Selena to get the damn cask, but once we have a lock on it, I want something in return."

"Doing your job comes with conditions?" Godfather demanded, his voice barely contained.

"I am a L.O.S.T. operative. I will remain a L.O.S.T. operative, but I'm not a fucking cyborg!" He turned to his teammates, who regarded him closely. He should not reveal his weakness—he never did—but this time he had no choice. "None of us are. We're human, with human emotions, human needs. My daughter needs her mother alive." Nikko sucked in a deep breath, then cursed. "I need her mother alive. And I need L.O.S.T.'s help to save Selena from the wrath of the Order."

"How do you propose we achieve that?" Godfather asked.

"I'm putting money on a daemon, courtesy of Apollyon, possessing one of the bidders at the auction tomorrow night. Selena's powers are so honed, she'll be able to sniff it out the minute it steps into the club. She will then eliminate it, thus foiling any chance the daemons have of getting their dirty hands on the cask. Once the auction has commenced and the deal goes down, dispatch a team to go after the cask, and another team, made up of myself, Selena, and, I hope"—Nikko looked at Cassidy, then back to Godfather—"Cassidy and Cross to go after the last Hellkeeper. We'll collect the seventh stone, and then eliminate her father." Nikko held his breath for a long moment, then said what had just come to him: "I will convince Selena to give Rurik the necklace. A trade. Her life for the power of the necklace."

"Why would he do that?" Stone asked.

"Its power is untold," Nikko answered. "You have no idea what can be achieved by the one who possesses it. It would be the equivalent to a prison for the daemons, and I'm going to assume that so long as Rurik holds on to it, he will be supreme commander, his position unchallengeable."

"If she does not agree to hand it over?" Cassidy asked.

Nikko raked his hand through his hair. "Then I will."

"And get your ass kicked in the process," Stone said.

"She'll get over it," Nikko shot back. Better than her being dead. Better than Marisol not having a mother and Nikko having to live without the woman he loved.

"Team?" Godfather asked the group.

"I'm in," Cassidy said. She looked at Stone and Satch.

"Count me in," Stone said.

Satch stood and clasped Nikko's shoulder. "I'm all yours, buddy."

Nikko's fists opened and closed. He nodded, not trusting his voice.

"I'll head the extraction team," Godfather flatly said.

Nikko's head snapped back. Every eye in the room stared at the screen. "Are you serious?" Nikko asked, not believing what he had just heard. Godfather was the maestro; rarely did he go out into the field.

"As a heart attack." Godfather smiled a rare smile. "Once you all stop gaping, I'd like to get back to the matter at hand."

Four jaws collectively snapped shut.

"Thank you," Godfather said with his game face back on. "Now, a most interesting development has come to light."

"Please tell me it involves humans," Cassidy said, sitting forward in her chair. "Those immortals are a pain in the ass."

"Tell me about it," Nikko said, but smiled thinking of his half-immortal. He could not love her more if she were all human.

"For now, it does," Godfather said, tapping the touch pad in front of him. Balderama's face flashed up on the screen. "From the moment we learned Los Cuatro was in the hunt for the makings of a nuke bomb, I knew it was not for philanthropic purposes. So, I contacted Interpol and Scotland Yard and asked them to snoop around for intel on Balderama. They came back with little usable info. But something told me to keep digging. My next call was to an old friend in Tel Aviv. No one watches nuclear traffic more closely than the Israelis, Mossad specifically. Lo and behold, Balderama popped up on their radar a year ago while they were surveilling Manuel Arias, one of Venezuela's old elite. Manny and friends want their pre-Chávez capitalistic life back. They have been hard-core buying arms and mercs. Mossad took a closer look at Balderama. A little more digging revealed that Balderama had been part of Chávez's MBR-200 movement in the eighties. After the failed coup, Balderama and Chávez had a major falling out. Chávez was imprisoned, while Balderama mysteriously was not. He flew the coop to his mother's people in Cuba, where he was welcomed by Castro. Once he regrouped, he set off for Miami, where he began his quiet grassroots project Los Cuatro."

"So Los Cuatro is not the benevolent Robin of Locksley stealing from the rich and giving to the poor. Los Cuatro is King John disguised as Robin Hood, stealing from all but his most influential nobles and then lining his own pocket?" Stone summarized.

"Yes," Godfather said.

"Balderama is working right beneath Chávez's nose to—what? Launch a financial coup?" Nikko asked, shaking his head. Selena was going to be furious. And hurt. He felt for her. But he could not change what Balderama was.

"Right again, but with power. Nuclear power."

"How?"

"I don't know. But he's positioning for a strike, a strike he can only make with a dirty bomb."

"Massad knows our interests in Venezuela—why are we just now hearing about this?" Stone asked, pissed off.

"You need to understand something about the Mossad. They are highly functional, highly capable, and rarely require outside help once they lock onto something or someone. Plus, according to my contact, they have been recently compromised."

"I guess they've been trusting the wrong people," Satch said.

"Why did this contact tell you, then?" Cassidy asked.

Godfather hesitated, then said, "Back in my heyday, I was on an extraction team with several Sayeret Matkal operatives. As you all know, the bonds forged under extreme duress are lifelong and impossible to break. My contact trusts me. I trust each of you. What I'm going to tell you next cannot, under any circumstances, leave this room."

The team nodded in unison.

"My contact will have a plant at the auction table tomorrow night. They want the cask, and like us, they want to ID each bidder." Godfather looked pointedly at Nikko. "They are well acquainted with Lost Souls. And Selena de la Roja."

Nikko's heart leapt against his rib cage. His reaction must have shown.

"Relax. It's all good," Godfather continued. "She's one smooth operator and has impressed some very important people in some very high-level positions. As an aside, my contact told me once the cask is secured, his people will be heavily recruiting Selena."

Nikko shook his head and stood, looking for something to punch. He grabbed a pillow from the sofa and hurled it across the room. No fucking way. Even if the Sayeret Matkal was the Israeli equivalent of L.O.S.T. "Once the cask is secured and her father dust in the wind, Selena is going to be recruited by a much more formidable force than the Sayeret Matkal. The position being offered is full-time mother and wife," Nikko flatly said.

Cassidy coughed. "Yeah, right."

"Here's what's going to go down tomorrow night," Godfather said. "Selena will play hostess to Noslov's master of ceremonies. With the spyware we're installing in each of the laptops being used to make the bids, we'll be able to track the bids through keystrokes. Cruz, as our representative, you will be alerted via Selena, whom we will alert and who will be wearing an earpiece, when all the bids are in as well as their amounts. You will enter an amount one dollar higher than the highest bid. Once it's confirmed you are the highest bidder, the money will appear to be transferred, and the instructions will be given for delivery. My team will take it from there, and you and your team are free to go with Selena and do what you have to do."

"What's the backup plan if something goes haywire and we don't make the highest bid?" Nikko asked.

"Then your girl will have to get in the head of the person who wins. We need the location of that cask."

Nikko didn't like it. "It puts Selena at grave risk to do what you're asking. It's her call, not mine."

"I'm aware of that. Cross gave us a Daemon 101

course while you were gone. We will do everything humanly possible to protect her."

"And if Selena balks at any of this?"

"Then you will convince her."

"I have to tell her about Balderama."

Godfather nodded. "Do that as soon as possible. I don't want her to have that conversation with him as we discussed. It's imperative Balderama goes into the auction thinking he's in the clear. If he suspects Selena has spoken to anyone about his intentions, she may be in danger."

Nikko stood. "I'm outta here."

As Selena stepped out of her office into the ante-room, she had the unnerving feeling she was being watched. Her nostrils twitched at the acrid smell of sulfur, so strong her eyes watered. Simultaneously, the soft rustle of dry wings vibrated around her. Her head snapped up and she caught her breath. Dozens—no, at least one hundred—power daemons hung like bats from the high domed ceiling, their iridescent gray bodies still, their red eyes closed. Higher in rank and power than the soldiers that had attacked her and Nikko on the beach, these daemons were masters at emotional manipulation. And they usually preceded a more powerful daemon. Vetis? Or had her father decided to pay her a visit?

The stones warmed around her neck. The floor beneath her feet shook. Above her, two hundred wings began to vibrate, creating a rush of air strong enough to push her several feet backward.

Selena stood her ground as the wings began to beat furiously. Red eyes flared open, followed by shrill screeching. They fed on human fear; it was how daemons were able to access human dreams and thoughts. Dropping en masse from the ceiling, they furiously dove at her. Their sharp teeth and claws tore at her hair and clothing. Their mad tempers slashed at her mind and heart, viciously digging to fashion even the tiniest of openings. Once in, they would drive her mad.

Selena flung her arms into the air with her hands open, fingers extended. "Begone!" she commanded. The instant she opened her mouth, a daemon flew in. She spat it out. Closing her eyes and lips, she turned in a tight circle, like an ice-skater doing a two-footed spin, propelling herself until she was a human funnel cloud. The velocity of her maneuver flung the daemons from her.

Outraged shrieks reverberated around her. Then eerie silence.

"Selena!"

Nikko? What the hell was he doing here? He was going to get himself killed! They would devour him! Selena slowed her spin, and as her vision cleared, her heart fell to her feet. The swarm of daemons covered Nikko like ants on a dead bug.

"Close off your mind!" she screamed as she pulled her swords from their sheath on the wall. She hacked her way to Nikko. Part of the swarm turned back on her. The necklace flared around her neck. As if they were butter, Selena hacked through the daemons as the other half continued to tear at Nikko.

He was ripping them in half and throwing them against the wall.

"Nikko!" she called to him as she tossed him one of her swords. He caught it and turned his fury back on the avenging daemons.

Selena and Nikko backed up to one another, and as one, they destroyed every daemon that came within sword range. As suddenly as the swarm had attacked, they vaporized and disappeared.

Breathing heavily, Nikko turned to Selena. "What the hell were those?"

Heart thumping wildly against her ears, Selena put her finger to her lips and listened. Silence. She scanned the ceiling and the open elevator car. Empty. She lowered her sword and motioned for Nikko to follow her into her office. She shut the door behind them. Exhaling, Selena laid her sword on her desk and turned to Nikko. Her adrenaline spiked, and her body warmed at the sight of him. His shirt had been ripped off, and his slacks, though still intact, were not fit for public appearance. His lean muscles glistened with blood; his wide chest moved up and down as he came down from the rush. His blue eyes sparkled with excitement. "Are you okay?" she asked, touching a long gouge in his forearm, then running her hands all over his body to check for damage.

He grabbed her hand and pulled her toward him. "Yeah," he roughly said. He ran his fingertips along her eyelids. "Your sight. It's back."

"As good as ever." She smiled.

His fingertips traced down her neck to her shoulders and lower. Her skin warmed. Everywhere.

She looked down at the shredded emerald silk that ten minutes ago had been a chic little dress. The flimsy fabric was literally hanging together by a thread. The bloody scrapes covering her were, however, healing before her eyes. "I'm fine." She hoisted up the sagging fabric, covering the high swell of her breasts, and pulled away from him to a safe distance. Being touched by Nikko, she reminded herself, was no longer an option.

"What the hell just happened?"

Selena sat against the edge of her desk, in the exact spot where Nikko had ravished her several nights before. She imagined him clearing the desktop and roughly taking her. Pushing her to places she had never gone. She barely stifled a moan and readjusted her bottom on the edge of the desk to ease the building pressure between her thighs. She looked up at him. With his arms crossed over his chest, Nikko watched her closely, his eyes so deep blue they looked black. His nostrils flared dangerously. He could smell her desire for him.

Subtly, she swallowed and shook her head, warning him off. He didn't appear intimidated, just narrowed his eyes and took a step toward her. "That was a test," she said quickly, her voice low and husky.

"What kind of test?"

Selena shifted against the desk again, unable this time to bite back her moan as the movement launched a jolt of pleasure straight into her swollen sex.

"A test to—to measure my strength."

"Did you pass?" he asked, stalking closer.

"Yeah." Selena's chest rose and fell in short, shallow breaths. She licked her dry lips and shook her head. "Don't."

He stopped a foot away from her. He reached a finger out and hooked it around the lone thread holding the bodice together. He plucked it. It snapped. In a slow, sensuous slide, the silk slipped down her breasts to her waist. Selena gasped as Nikko's warm breath swept across her turgid nipples.

She arched, biting her bottom lip and drawing blood. "Oh, Selena, that isn't fair," he crooned as he stepped between her trembling thighs. He slid an arm around her waist and pulled her against his bare chest. The contact was electrifying. He dropped his lips to her throat and kissed her pulsing jugular. "I want you so badly right now," he whispered. "I can't stand it."

Selena closed her eyes. He had no idea what bad really was. Her body was on fire. Only he could make the ache go away. But—"Nikko, please. Don't."

"Don't, because you don't want this?"

"Don't, because it will make saying good-bye harder."

He pressed his lips behind her ear. Gooseflesh erupted along her entire body. "Why say good-bye at all?"

"Don't mess with me."

"I'm not messing with you." He took her chin in his hand and tilted her head up. "Open your eyes."

She didn't want to. She didn't want to see the desire in his eyes. She didn't want to want him. She didn't want to give in to his seduction. She didn't want to love him and let him go. Not again. She was strong in so many ways except this one. She shook her head.

"I'm sorry for being a monumental ass the last time we saw each other." He kissed the tip of her nose. "And all of the times before that." He kissed her chin. "I'm sorry for trying to kill you. I thank God I failed." Selena's heart slammed against her chest. "Can you ever forgive me for that?"

Selena opened her mouth to say she'd forgiven him

a long time ago, but she was afraid the overwhelming emotion surging inside her would prevent her from uttering a sound. So she nodded.

Warm lips pressed against hers. Her fingers tightened around the edge of the desk. His lips pressed hers open and his tongue slid across hers. Her eyes flew open. Dark blue eyes sparkled with a secret. He smiled against her lips, then pulled slightly away. He cupped her face between his big hands. "All of my apologies aside, I came here to tell you, I love you, Selena. I do not want a day to go by that I don't wake up beside you. I know you're scared, but I want to you to be brave and take the leap of faith with me."

CHAPTER TWENTY-TWO

Selena's heart stopped for several harrowing beats. *He loves me? He wants to share his life with me?*

How could he, when he did not trust or forgive her?

How could she accept being loved by him, sharing her life with him, when just the thought of losing him paralyzed her?

Hot tears stung her eyes. She shook her head and pushed him away. She was a coward. "I. Can't."

He let go of her and stood back. Her heart cried out for him and she had to bite her lip to stop the sound from coming out. Her soul was only half without his.

He regarded her steadily. "Can't or won't?"

She exhaled a shaky breath. "You don't trust me. How can we build on that?"

The muscles in his jaw tightened. "I trust you to be honest with me. I trust your instincts. I trust your love for our daughter, and I trust your love for me. What else is there to trust?"

"But you don't forgive me. And because you haven't forgiven me, a part of you despises me. I can't stand the idea that you'll lie awake at night and think of me that way."

"I don't despise you, Selena. I despise what you did. Forgiveness works both ways. How can you expect me to forgive when you can't forgive yourself?"

She shook her head as more tears swelled, blurring her vision. "I was wrong not to trust you."

"You were afraid. Desperate. Desperate people do desperate things." He raked his fingers through his hair. "And who knows, maybe you made the right call. Marisol is safe; you're stronger, smarter, and so am I. Together we have the power to do what is necessary to live in peace."

Everything he said made sense. She did need to forgive herself. Marisol was alive and thriving. But . . . She looked at him through her tears. "I'm a coward, Nikko. I can't bear the thought of losing you again."

"Do you think the thought of loving you doesn't terrify me?" He shoved his hands into his torn pockets, as if to keep from touching her. "I don't know if I'm going to always be like this, part vampire, or if we'll be on the run from the Order for the rest of our lives. I don't know what tomorrow will bring, Selena, but whatever comes, I want you beside me when it does."

Selena shook her head. Dear God, she wanted what he wanted, but—"You make it sound so romantic, but there is more at stake here than love."

His blue eyes widened at her denial. "What is more important than love? Is living alone and miserable because you were too afraid to fight for your family what you really want?"

"I want guarantees!"

"Selena! Nothing in life is guaranteed. It's a crapshoot." He touched her cheek. "But the odds are stacked in our favor if we're together." He sank his fingers into her hair. "We're each other's second half. I can't live with the most vital part of myself missing." He lowered his lips to hers. "My heart cannot bear losing you again, Selena."

And hers could not bear losing him for one more minute. But—how did she tell Superman that Superwoman was afraid? She tried to say it, to admit to him aloud that she was afraid, terrified to be more exact, but the words caught in her throat.

"Selena," he breathed. "You are the bravest woman I know."

Tears stung her eyes. She shook her head.

"Part of being brave is admitting you're afraid," he softly said against her lips.

Her body trembled. Her heart raced, and she could scarcely draw a breath. Panic gripped her as the urge to bolt became unbearable. His deep blue eyes held hers hostage, refusing to let her run.

His long fingers stroked her cheek. His breath warmed her. "Don't run out on me. On us. Not now when we've found each other again."

She closed her eyes and made the leap. "Nikko," she whispered, barely audible against his lips. "I'm so afraid."

"I will protect you," he whispered back.

He had her then. Though in her heart, he had never lost her.

His lips captured hers in a deep, soulful kiss. Her arms wrapped around his neck, drawing him closer to her heart. Love filled her. Happy, delirious, terrified tears ran down her cheeks.

Never in her wildest dreams had she imagined she would be in Nikko's arms like this again. Never had she imagined that she could love this man more deeply than she had all those years ago. But she did. The depth of her love was all-consuming, terrifying, and emancipating. Like the Rev, it infused her with strength, vitality, and energy. With Nikko by her side, there would be nothing they could not accomplish.

They had so much to do before they could have that life. But first, she would savor this small chunk of time with him. "Nikko," she breathed, tearing her lips from his. "We need to clean up. We need to talk. About the auction—"

"Shh, there's time for that later." His arms tightened around her. He would not let her go. She would not let him. She slid off the edge of the desk and pulled his head down to her lips. Drawing him with her, she stepped around her desk and pressed a button on the wall. A hidden door slid open. She pulled him in and pressed another button on the interior wall. The door slid shut behind them. He picked her up, strode to the large bed, and laid her down, their lips still locked. Ripping away her tattered clothes and then his own, he gathered her tightly in his arms, pushing her thighs apart. He was hot and thick against her. She shivered in fear, anticipation, and a craving for him so potent her stomach did slow desirous rolls.

"Open your eyes, Selena."

As she did, he reverently slid into her. Every nerve ending in her vaginal walls ignited in response to his hard, hot entry. She was so tight, so sensitive, so aware of him, she could feel every contour from the wide head of his cock, to the large pulsing vein that ran the length of him, to the imprint of his balls against her swollen nether lips.

Electrified, she stared in stunned silence at his wonder-filled eyes.

Love changed everything.

"Tell me we don't belong together," he said.

"We belong together." There had never been any doubt, just the cold hand of fear, but even that had thawed.

Selena arched and moaned at the pure sublimity of him. He filled her completely. Her breath hissed when he pressed the head of his penis to the sensitive spot deep inside her.

He smiled tenderly and smoothed stray strands of hair from her face. "I never want you to stop wanting that."

"For as long as I can breathe."

His lips swept hers, taking away what little breath she had. As his hips moved excruciatingly slowly, his kiss deepened, his tongue swirling in slow, languorous strokes against hers. He drew almost completely out of her, then thrust so deeply into her, he took her last breath away. Her liquid muscles wrestled to draw him deeper, constricting, stroking, reluctant to let him go.

Each time he withdrew, her body cried out for succor. Each time he sank so deep inside her she could feel his heartbeat against hers, she wept with pleasure.

Nikko ran his hands up her arms, extending them over her head, entwining his fingers through hers. She was stretched taut, her body arched, straining against his. But he took his time. His thrusts deep, long, and languorous. Her need for him hard, urgent, demanding. Impatient, she fought for a faster pace. Patiently, he unwound her.

"Nikko," she gasped, tearing her lips from his. "Stop

torturing me." She was right there, just on the verge of a complete meltdown, but he held her back.

His slow, deep thrusts drove her mad. Her body thrashed, her nails clenching his hands. She could scarcely breathe. Every inch of her screamed for release. She stiffened and pressed her hips to his, holding herself against him. He swirled his hips, grinding against her.

Shock waves rocked through her. She struggled against his hands, wanting to pull his hips tighter against her, but he held her at bay. "Nikko," she begged. "Please!"

His lips silenced her pleas as he maintained his slow, torturous pace. He drove her mad with desire. Mad with need, mad with desperation. Her body slickened with sweat. Her womb pulsed with her unreleased orgasm. He was driving her insane.

His tongue swirled around her swollen lips, down her neck, and along her jugular. She felt the scrape of his fangs. From her hard nipples down to her aching pussy, her body shivered with anticipation, wanting his bite. Craving it. His thrusts increased in tempo. Her breathing faltered. Her muscles liquefied. His fangs sank deep into her neck, and Selena came undone. Her body snapped like a downed electrical wire during a thunderstorm, sparking, catching everything around her on fire.

Frantically, she twisted and thrust beneath him. Her entire body shuddered and quaked as one intense wave of sensation slammed into another. Impaled by Nikko's fangs and with his cock buried so deeply inside her, their hearts stuttered to a haunting halt—her liquid muscles constricted around him like a fist. In tight, deep draws, they milked him. In a hard, feral rush, he came inside her. Only then did their hearts resume beating—this time, as one.

Nikko crashed back to earth, shattering on impact. Every part of his body throbbed in the aftermath of their torrid lovemaking. Still hard inside her, he wanted more. If he could, he'd shut them away from the world forever and never release her.

He licked the puncture wounds on her neck and slowly withdrew from her slick body. He smiled to himself, reveling in the vampire. She lay sprawled on the rumpled sheets, her eyes closed, her lips parted, her breathing hard. Blood and sweat smeared her chest and chin, and her hair was a wild mass of soft tangles around her head, spilling off the pillow to the bed. His gaze traveled down her slender neck to the necklace she always wore. The stones were quiet now. His gaze swept lower to her chest. Her lush, dewy breasts trembled as shock waves still swept through her. The chocolate-colored nipples hard, still stimulated. He resisted them, too entranced by her dark, sultry beauty. Her skin was light caramel, smooth, soft, and just as appetizing. His gaze slid down her taut belly to the horizontal scar just above her pubic bone. Emotion squeezed his heart. He would give his right arm to have been present at Marisol's birth. He smiled to himself and leaned down to kiss the scar.

He'd be there for the next one.

Selena moaned. Her hips flinched, and her fingers dug into his hair. Her thighs parted, filling his nostrils with the essence of floral and spice. As his cock thickened, he kissed the small patch of damp curls, inhaling her alluring sex scent deeply into his brain. He'd never forgotten her scent. It was burned into him. She was unique and wild, wantonly so.

He slid his tongue across her hard clitoris. His thumbs parted her slick, swollen lips. Her hips rose, and her nails dug into his scalp. His cock ached. He was addicted. "Selena," he breathed against her sweltering pussy, "do you want more?"

"Yesss."

He suckled her clit, flicking it gently with his tongue. Her body surged against him.

When he sank a finger into her, she screamed and pulled his hair.

When he tapped her sweet spot, she shivered.

When he bit the tender flesh on the inside of her thigh so close to her sweltering sex, she launched.

He couldn't help it. He was ravenous for all of her. Her blood infused him with her vitality. He would always carry this sacred part of her within him. Each time he took from her, he craved more. And each time he asked, she freely gave.

Even in his lust-induced frenzy for her blood, he was careful not to take too much. Her pussy tightened around his finger and clenched as it spasmed, her body rolling as one wave of sensation after another crashed through her.

Carefully, he withdrew his fangs from her vein. Her thighs tightened, holding him inside her. He felt another wave cresting. He rose to his knees and pulled her legs around his waist. Her hot, creamy lips slid down his shaft until once again they were connected. Selena shook her damp hair from her shoulders and pushed him back into the mattress so that she straddled him. Eyes wide open, she moaned loudly as he thrust up into her.

She smiled wickedly at him. In long, sensuous undulations as if she were riding a bronco in slow motion, she rode him. She pushed his arms over his head, entwined her fingers through his, and ground so agonizingly slowly against him, he could not bear it.

"Nikko," she breathed, throwing her head back. "Payback is a bitch." Her lush tits teased his lips. He captured a nipple and suckled her hard. She strained against him, grinding on his aching cock so fervently he lost all control. He broke free of her hands and clasped her ass, holding her immobile as he thrust into her. She leaned down and licked the indentation between his pecs. He swelled inside her as her teeth grazed the skin above his heart.

She grabbed his hand and wrapped his fingers around several of the stones on her necklace. They flared with heat. Nikko's body stiffened to rigid. Her tongue slid around a flat nipple and sucked. Her hand tightened around his holding the stones. Nikko's skin burned as the slick, hot friction of his sliding in and out of her intensified. He grabbed the headboard with his free hand. His hips rose and fell furiously. When her teeth grazed along his chest, he came in a violent, primal rush.

"Lena," he groaned as his body jerked in and out of hers. Selena's body twisted and shook. Her fingers dug into his shoulders and chest as she moaned and gyrated against him. His orgasm shifted into a more intense gear. He released the stones and rolled her over and rammed into her as she clung to his chest.

Her muscles milked him, her lips clung to him, his orgasm hit the stratosphere, and in a wild spiral he released deep inside her. Long moments later, with no parachute, he plummeted back to earth. It was chaotic, violent, and remarkable. Though he did not understand what had just happened, Nikko knew the beginnings of a profound, indestructible bond had been forged.

Selena pushed back the mass of hair in her face and turned to face him. Reaching out to him, she stroked his jawline. "Nikko," she said, her voice hoarse.

"Hmmm," he said, kissing her fingertips.

"I don't think I can walk."

He laughed and rose above her. She smiled up into his eyes. "You look like a complete glutton."

He kissed a nipple. Her body trembled. "Guilty." He kissed her nipple again, then drew her against him.

"We need to talk."

Selena rolled her eyes. "No more relationship stuff."

"A different relationship." His eyes grew serious. "Balderama is a problem. You can't talk to him."

"But I already did."

CHAPTER TWENTY-THREE

H e wasn't happy when I told him about you," Selena said.

Nikko's eyes closed. "Shit. You've already spoken to him about the auction?"

She nodded slowly, not understanding his reaction. "He was angry. Didn't trust you. Didn't trust me when it came to you. Why?"

"You're not going to like this, love, but Balderama is as dirty as the day is long."

"No." She shook her head in instinctive denial. "That can't be . . ." She trusted Señor. Perhaps Nikko's information was inaccurate. But—Señor had acted so out of character earlier. Could there be some truth to what Nikko said? With so much at stake, she would not assume anything. "Tell me everything."

When he did, her heart didn't want to believe any of it. But her instincts told her every bit of it was true. Not just because she trusted Nikko and his intel above all others, but because when Señor had snapped that driver's neck, she'd seen a side of him she never had before. And then kidnapping little Yuri Noslov— She gasped. "Nikko! He has Noslov's son. If Señor doesn't walk away with the cask, he'll kill the boy."

Nikko sat up. "Do you know where he is?"

Selena slid from the bed and pressed the button

opening the door to her office. She grabbed her cell phone off her desk and ran back into the room. She scrolled through her videos and found the one of little Yuri. Nikko had her play and replay it, slowing each frame. Then she saw it, in the corner, the shadow of a brass-and-Spanish-tile outlet cover. "That outlet cover, Señor has them throughout his hacienda."

"Where is it?"

"In the heart of Little Havana."

"Balderama isn't going to return the boy alive."

Selena nodded. "I just realized that. I feel terrible for my part in this. I need to fix this, Nikko. We have until the auction to get to him."

Nikko rummaged through his shredded slacks and pulled his cell phone out. "We can safely extract him."

Selena slid her hand over his and squeezed. "That place is swarming with guards. I have a better idea. One you aren't going to like."

Nikko's eyes glittered with understanding. "Not that vampire?"

"I trust Joran. Plus he has a soft spot for kids. He can get in and out before anyone knows the boy is gone."

Nikko's fist tightened around the cell phone. Selena rose up and kissed his tight lips. "Be careful there, cowboy, you're going to crush that." Selena smiled when he didn't respond to her. "Are you jealous, Nikko?"

"I don't trust any man or vampire who wants what I have."

She laughed. "Don't be so caveman. Joran has been downstairs most of the evening waiting for me to come down and join him, and is probably more than a little miffed I've kept him waiting all this time."

Nikko pulled her to him and his erection speared up between them. Selena laughed again. When he frowned, she laughed harder and cupped his face between her hands. "I'm not laughing at you, Nikko, I swear. I just—you don't have to mark me to prove I am yours. Joran knows it."

"He wants you."

"And a thousand women want you. You don't see me pissing all over you, do you?" She pushed him away and bounced off the bed. "I'm getting a quick shower, then calling Joran, but before I do, I'll have Amy run down to Versace and pick up something for you to wear."

Nikko growled, told her what size he wore, then watched her like a petulant child who had had his favorite toy taken away.

As she hung up the phone, she looked over her shoulder at him. "Are you going to sit there and pout like a little boy or are you going to come scrub my back?"

She ran into the bathroom when Nikko sprang off the bed; he was behind her before she could turn the water on. As it sprayed, she shrieked. It was damn cold. Nikko grinned and pulled her into the circle of his arms. He kissed her and shoved her, sputtering and fighting, under the cold spray. It was the hottest coldest shower she'd ever taken, and unfortunately over too soon.

After she had dried off, Selena slipped a robe on and called Joran the traditional way, on the phone. Using her regular method would appear too intimate for Nikko. She didn't want to rattle the green monster any more than she had to.

"Selena, I was just about to come up there. What the hell is going on? This place is crawling with daemons."

"I had a few visitors earlier. Sounds like they brought friends. Listen, something important has come up. I need you up here now. I'll leave my office door unlocked, just come in."

"I'm on my way."

Selena looked at Nikko, who had not moved from the doorway to the bathroom. She swallowed hard. He had wrapped a towel around his waist, which did little to hide the line of his cock or the defined muscles of his thighs. His dark hair was damp from the shower, his skin dewy, accenting his lean muscles and every dip and valley of his hard body. She could barely believe that she was his. Forever. Finally.

"The club is chock-full of daemons tonight," she said, tightening the slender belt of her white silk-and-linen-blend robe. "Joran is on his way up, I'm meeting him in my office. I'll be right back."

"Not like that, you aren't," Nikko flatly said. "And not without me."

Selena let out a long, patient breath. She looked down at the robe. It clung delicately to her sultry skin. Her nipples were clearly outlined, as was the curve of her hips. "Fine, Nikko." She stalked past him and changed into a flowing caftan she wore when she spent the night at the club.

She shook her head and punched the button to the door, then slid into her office. Joran stood out on the balcony. When she heard Nikko step in behind her, Selena was about to tell him to grow a set. One look at his face told her something was wrong.

"Juju," he said, handing her the phone.

"What the hell?" Juju never called her at the club. *Never.* She took the phone. "What's wrong?"

"Mr. Noslov is gone."

Selena's belly did a slow, nauseated roll. She glanced up at Nikko. "Juju, are you sure?"

"Yes. I went down to give him dinner. His room was empty. I looked everywhere. He isn't here!"

"Okay, I'll be right there." Selena slapped the phone shut. "Noslov is gone," she said to Nikko.

His features tightened. "Who knew you had him?"

"Señor, and—" Selena looked at Joran, who stood casually at the doorway giving Nikko the stink eye. "Joran?"

He raised an aristocratic brow and adjusted his cuff links. "I knew you had someone down there, but not who. Who is Noslov and why is he important?"

"That's classified information," Nikko said.

Selena's desk phone buzzed. "That's Amy." She picked up the phone. "Bring them up and leave them on my office-door handle." She hung up and looked at Joran. "We need your help. You are familiar with Señor Balderama's hacienda in Little Havana?"

"Intimately."

"He's holding a two-year-old boy hostage somewhere in there. We need him extracted. Quietly and alive. Tonight. Now."

"So now I'm your retriever?"

Selena stepped toward the arrogant vampire. "I don't have time to play games, Joran. You were right about Señor. And he's worse than even you thought. He is going to kill that little boy if his father, who has escaped from me, does not deliver some very important cargo to him within the next twenty-four hours. Please, do this for me."

When Joran did not acknowledge her request, Selena folded her arms over her chest. "What do you want, Joran?" Because he never did anything for free.

"Your discretion."

"That's a given," she said, insulted that he would question her integrity.

He nodded. "Then of course I will assist. Is there anything else on the list?"

"Yes, have your vamps put their sonar ears to the ground and listen. Ask for any and all information about Señor and this man Noslov. If you hear anything, contact me."

Joran looked past her to Nikko, who had not moved. "Should I call you the regular way or on your cell?" Thankfully, Nikko didn't take the bait.

"I don't care. I just want the info and that little boy safe."

"What do you propose I do with the child when I have him?"

Selena looked at Nikko. Where would he be safest? "Bring him here," Nikko said. "I know of a safe house."

Joran bowed. "One word of caution, Selena?"

"What?"

"The daemons have been rather chatty down there, and your name keeps coming up in the same sentence as Rurik's. I don't need to tell you that—"

"Worry about your own ass, vampire," Nikko said. "I'll worry about Selena's."

Joran's eyes burned red on the edges.

Selena tensed. Nikko was strong, but Joran was an ancient with the most powerful blood in vampiredom. Rurik. It would be no contest.

"Your petty jealousy is misplaced, human. My interest in Selena is not reciprocated the way you think."

"It doesn't have to be."

Joran cocked a brow and looked at Selena. She nodded and took Nikko's hand. Joran smiled at Nikko. "Bravo. You have tamed the sleeping tiger." Joran bowed again to Selena. "I will do as you have asked of me, Selena. It is what loyal friends do for loyal friends, is it not?"

His meaning was not lost on her. Selena would not out Joran and his Rev enterprise. "Of course."

They fought the entire way to her Star Island mansion. Nikko hammered her about Joran. But Selena would not incriminate him. Joran was a lot of things, but he had always come through for her. She would not rat him out about the Rev or any intimate details of his life or business. There was no point.

"Joran is far from a model citizen, Nikko. He breaks the law ten times a day. But he's never forced me to do anything I didn't want to for my own gain. Leave it at that."

"You're not going to tell me?"

"Tell you what? That he has half of southern Florida's politicians in his pocket? That he fixes races, runs whores, and schemes criminals out of their blood money? Do you want me to tell you more or is that enough?"

"He would turn on you if it meant saving his own skin."

"Maybe, maybe not. And speaking of my skin, the

Order is coming after me. Do you know what that means?"

"You have something they want, Selena, something they will barter for." His gaze dropped to her throat.

Relinquish her stones after what they'd cost her? She grabbed her necklace. "Never!"

"I know how important the necklace is to you, but after we take care of your father, why not consider the trade? It may be our only chance."

"We're going to keep that cask out of Apollyon's hands, and I'm going to wipe out the last Hellkeeper and my father, the king of daemons' BFF. If that doesn't satisfy that bastard of a vampire, he can go to Hell, because I will fight him."

"Selena, that's your anger talking. Just think about it, okay?"

"Sure." But she had already thought about it. The answer was the same. With the power of the necklace, she could fight and win. Without it, she was powerless.

As the Chris-Craft docked, Selena raised her nose to the air. It was heavy with moisture, tension, and the stench of decay. The hair on the back of her neck rose. "Do you smell it?"

Nikko's lips tightened. His eyes flared red and his fangs flashed. "Death."

CHAPTER TWENTY-FOUR

Selena ran toward her house, Nikko right beside her. A man she did not recognize lay sprawled on the granite patio. His eyes were wide open, and even in death the terror in them was palpable. She had seen the look many times. A discarded host.

Selena moved past him to the open back door. She stopped and listened. An eerie silence hung like a death pall around them. The cloying copper scent of blood was strong. The pungent scent of sulfur was stronger.

"Careful, Nikko, we're not alone," Selena whispered.

The stones flared around her neck with wicked heat. Carefully, Selena stepped across the threshold and into a warm, sticky substance. Blood.

She moved farther into the kitchen and stopped short. Juju lay just beyond the center island, her neck sliced to her spine. Her face bore the same terrified expression as the stranger's on the patio.

Instinctively, Selena moved toward her friend, but abruptly stopped. There was nothing she or any other person, mortal or otherwise, could do for her now. Selena shelved her sorrow to a place she would deal with later. Her fury, however, she allowed to gather steam.

She looked toward the doorway leading to the large Florida room off the dining room. Inclining her head toward it, to tell Nikko to follow her, Selena drew her swords and stealthily made her way through it.

Abruptly, she stopped. Balderama's scent, though faint, whiffed in the heavy air. Her heart pounded furiously against her rib cage. Was it a remnant from before, or had he come for Noslov? Her skin flinched. If he had, then he no longer trusted her, and if he no longer trusted her, the cask could end up in dangerous hands.

Selena turned and handed Nikko one of her swords.

"I smell daemon," he breathed, shadowing her.

A Hellkeeper—and one with the power to cross water, albeit in a host.

Vetis.

Trepidation ran neck and neck with excitement. Vetis was the Keeper of the Seventh Hell; only the princes and the king were more powerful. Both his power and the seventh stone were within her grasp!

Here, in her home, waiting for her.

Every sense alert, Selena moved down the short hall and into the Florida room. She cleared it, then moved to the dining room. Clear. As she approached the living room, two heartbeats reverberated around her. One the erratic staccato of a terrified human. The other the arrogant thud of a Hellkeeper.

Her eyes adjusted to the dim light. Her own heart stuttered a beat as her gaze lifted toward the ceiling. Bound and gagged, hanging from the chandelier, his eyes wide with fear, was Noslov. His eyes widened further as he spotted her and Nikko and . . . something behind them?

"Behind you!" Selena called to Nikko as she catapulted into the room. As she turned in midair, the daemon hurled Nikko straight at her. Nikko's body slammed into her, the impact sending them both careening through the floor-to-ceiling window overlooking the waterway.

They hit the concrete retaining wall, busting through it, then tumbled down the slope into the water.

Selena turned over, pushing Nikko behind her. The stones flared as she rose and faced Vetis.

He was a ghoulish sight. His distorted human face and muscled body were overblown and chunky, like a villainous superhero's. His deformed fist pointed a glowing, spiked devil sword at her chest. The short, sharp horns protruding from his forehead flared red hot.

Lightning quick, the daemon reached past her and plucked Nikko from the water. "Give me the necklace," Vetis hissed, hovering above her, careful not to touch the water. His spiked sword dug into Nikko's neck. Blood dripped in slow, thick rivulets onto Nikko's shirt.

"Release him, and I may consider it," Selena bargained.

Vetis hissed in fury, "I will not bargain with you!" He flung Nikko back into the water and brought his sword down on hers, forcing her to spin. He grabbed her by the throat and yanked her up against his chest, her arms dangling. Hissing his sulfur breath against her ear, he jabbed the sharp, serrated tip of his sword into her neck.

The copper scent of her blood, mingled with Nikko's, wafted around her nostrils. Her vision blurred as violent rage consumed her.

Selena twisted and with her empty left hand grabbed the blade of Vetis's sword. As she did, she swung her own sword up behind her and into his back. The daemon screeched in rage. But he did not release her. Her hand was cut nearly in half from grabbing his sword, but she dug her own sword deeper into his body like a shish kebab. He screamed in rage and flung her away from him.

With all the fires of Hell burning in his eyes, Vetis contorted his body, realigning it until it was once again whole. Selena looked past him to Nikko, who slowly moved up the slippery embankment. *Thank God.*

In that split second, Vetis struck again. His sword sliced into her shoulder with such excruciating heat, she cried out. He ran her through, pinning her to the ground. He was strong, stronger than any other daemon she had faced. But she could beat him. If she was patient. His human form gave him a distinct advantage over the others with their animal forms. Her left hand was nearly severed in half and no use to her. But it would regenerate. If she lived. He kicked her sword from her right hand; snatching it up, he turned it on her.

"The necklace."

Selena tried to rise. For her efforts, he impaled her other shoulder with her own sword. *Son of a bitch!*

Selena lay staked to the ground, and for the first time in her quest for the stones, she doubted her skills. Fervently, she called to the stones for power. They flared hotter in answer, so hot the scent of her burning flesh assailed her nostrils.

Selena lifted one shoulder high enough so she could grab her sword, and yanked it free from her shoulder. She used her feet to kick up off the ground, and the velocity of her move pulled the daemon sword from the ground. She grabbed it with her damaged hand barely able to wield it. She had no such difficulty with her good right hand. As Vetis had done to her, Selena turned the daemon's own sword on him.

"You underestimated my power, Vetis."

Nikko rose up behind the daemon and ran him through from behind, the blade slicing at an angle near his heart. The daemon screamed in rage. He grabbed the sword protruding from his chest and pulled it through. And once again he was armed.

"As you underestimated mine." He propelled backward, slammed Nikko into the ground, then grabbed him up by his shirt and flung him toward the house. Nikko's body flew like a missile toward the stucco, but he used his power to slow his velocity, barely touching the wall. Red eyes glaring, fangs bared, Nikko turned on the daemon.

"As you underestimated mine," Nikko taunted, hovering just above the ground.

Nikko moved in behind Vetis. The daemon's eyes burned an unholy crimson.

Selena stalked from the front. She struck, slicing another angled cut into his chest on the opposite side of the wound Nikko had inflicted. She yanked the sword back and struck a third time. Half of the pentagram was cast.

Vetis shrieked in rage, grabbing his chest with one hand, thrusting his sword with the other.

Selena pushed him back toward the water. Nikko lunged at the daemon, hitting him hard in the chest. As they tumbled to the ground, Selena struck again, this time from behind, slicing another angled cut around the daemon's heart.

Four!

He shot up into the air, furious flames contrailing behind him.

"You have no host to aid your retreat, Vetis," Selena said, standing stalwart beneath where he hovered. "And no legions to carry you." She smiled and beckoned him with her sword. "Come, take your chances with me, my lord. I will carry you home."

Vetis belched great balls of fire at her. Easily, Selena deflected them. "Is that all you have left, Keeper of the Seventh Hell? Surely you can dig deeper than that."

"The daemon kingdom is afire with word of your father's quest for your daughter. Unite with me and together we will slay him."

"Why unite with you when I can kill him myself?"

"Only with the seventh stone do you have a chance, slayer."

She smiled. "I'd say my chances are pretty good." She cocked her head sideways. "Yours, on the other hand, not so good."

"If you defy our king, he will not rest until you and all your loved ones burn in his private Hell!"

"Your king will have to answer to the Order first!"

"As will you! Unite with me, and we can have it all!"

"That you bargain with me now, Vetis, tells me you are weak. I give you a choice: fall upon your sword or I will cut your heart out myself."

"I can save your daughter!"

Selena calmed the storm in her heart.

"She is in no danger," Nikko said, stepping closer. His eyes met Selena's, urging her to remain calm.

Vetis hissed his putrid sulfur breath. "No mortal is

safe from Paymon. His disciples are ruthless and determined. They will find her if they have not already. He will demand the stones for her life."

"With the seventh stone, I will kill him."

Vetis screeched and flew past her in through the shattered window. Noslov's muffled screams followed.

"He took possession of Noslov!" Nikko said, running for the house.

Just as they entered, Noslov dropped to the floor. He turned his icy eyes on them both.

Selena didn't hesitate. She tossed her sword to Nikko and leapt into Noslov's head.

As she did, Vetis leapt past her and—

Nikko!

It happened so fast Nikko could not get to Selena's body before Vetis took possession of it. The daemon didn't leave his physical body behind as Selena did when she took possession of a body. These Hellkeepers completely vaporized, making it more difficult to gain the advantage.

The daemon who now controlled Selena's body laughed and pirouetted around Nikko, stroking the necklace. Terror he had never experienced before shook violently inside Nikko. He would not raise a sword against her. But if he did not—

"Come to me, vampire," Vetis hissed, the words coming from Selena's lips. "Come to me now and I will kill you quickly."

Noslov slammed into Selena, sending her body

careening into the carved alabaster mantel. She lay stunned. Nikko rushed to her, but Noslov shoved him away.

"Do not touch the host," Noslov warned. He grabbed Selena's sword and raised it above her. Nikko kicked it from his hand. Noslov turned and hissed, "Let me kill him!"

Nikko stared at Noslov, stunned. He spoke with Selena's voice. The daemon was in Selena's body, she in Noslov's. But if she killed her own body, would her soul wither and die with it?

Selena's body grabbed the sword from where it had fallen, but Noslov kicked it from her hand. Nikko tackled her body and, not knowing any other way to keep the daemon from fighting back, sank his fangs into her neck.

The daemon screamed and struggled. Noslov's body crumpled to the floor beside him, and Nikko watched Selena's vapor swirl around her head, then dive into her open mouth.

Nikko released her body and waited, praying it would be Vetis who emerged next. He had both swords in his hands ready to carve the final two cuts for the pentagram.

"I know your secrets!" Vetis's voice screeched from Selena's mouth. "I am the tempter of the holy. I will corrupt the priest and take the child for my disciple!"

"The Hell you will!" Selena shouted from deep within her.

Vetis's agonizing screams reverberated.

"I cast you from me, by all that is holy, I cast you from me!" Selena's righteous voice chanted.

Vetis screeched. Small wisps of vapor puffed from Selena's mouth.

"Begone from me, daemon!" she commanded. A long, thick orange vapor rushed from her parted lips. Although Selena had rejoined with her earthly body, it lay motionless on the floor.

The vapor began to solidify. Nikko impaled the torso on each side of the heart so that the six angles of the pentagram were cast. Vetis screeched, thrusting against the swords, grabbing them and trying to pull them from his body. Nikko stood over him, pushing all of his body weight into the hilts, holding the blades secure.

"Selena!" Nikko urgently called.

Her body slowly roused beside him. He looked down into her dazed eyes. "Now, Selena."

She shook her head and sat up, then focused on the writhing Hellkeeper. She crawled over on her hands and knees and looked up at Nikko.

He smiled, and at that moment he felt more love and pride for her than he ever thought he could. "It's all yours, baby. You earned it."

Selena turned back to the Hellkeeper. His skin was flaming, his hair sizzling, his horns flaring. "I'll see you in Hell, Vetis," she whispered, then thrust her hand into his chest. He screamed, trying to gouge her with his fiery horns. Selena slapped his head back and pulled her hand free of his chest, the bloody nanorian beating in her hand.

She looked up at Nikko in wonder. He dropped the swords and pulled her into his arms. "Your quest is nearly complete, Selena."

He took the stone and pressed it firmly into the

necklace's last setting, then splayed his hand over her thundering heart. He lowered his lips to hers and deeply kissed her.

Something amazing happened. Each stone hummed one after the other until all seven of them united into one loud sustained hum. Red, gold, and orange sparks shot from each stone, fusing into a spectacular rainbow of color; the hot pricks bounced off Selena's skin. Nikko could feel the power vibrating between them and into Selena. Wave after shocking wave built until, in a deafening crescendo, it zapped her with a sharp electrical bolt, the infusion illuminating her skin a shimmering gold and silver.

Wide-eyed, she stared at Nikko. He stared at her in equal awe. "The powers of the seven have fused as one, creating a superpower," Selena breathed. Gingerly she fingered the warm stones. They glowed beneath her touch. "My father does not stand a chance."

"I'll tell you where the cask is," Noslov's terrified voice said from behind them.

Startled, Nikko and Selena turned to face him; they'd forgotten he was there.

"You said you had no knowledge of its whereabouts?"

"I lied."

Selena rose and strode toward him. "You lied to me when your son's life was at stake?"

"I am an expert liar, but after what I just witnessed, I'm going to become a priest. So long as you save my son, the cask is yours."

CHAPTER TWENTY-FIVE

"Was there anyone else with the daemon?" Selena asked the pale, trembling Noslov.

He looked down at the pile of ashes on the floor. "My God!"

Selena snapped her fingers under his nose. "Was he alone?"

"Yes."

"What did he say to you?"

Noslov shivered and covered his mouth as if he was going to vomit. His body convulsed, then he turned and retched. When he was done, he looked up at Selena and Nikko, and wiped his mouth with his sleeve.

"He was alone when he came to my room. He took me outside and waited for Juju to go downstairs and then call you. He told me how he was going to kill her and how upset you would be. He—then he told me what he was going to do to you and then to me." Noslov's body was wracked with shudders. "He slit her throat. Then he hung me from the chandelier and waited."

Selena's heart broke for her friend. She collected her emotions. Juju was avenged, but she knew Vetis had not come here on his own initiative. She smelled her father's hand in this. "Nothing about who sent him?"

"No." Noslov's body began to convulse again. He turned and dry-heaved for several minutes.

Nikko took Selena's hand. "I'll take care of Juju, and the body out back. Then we need to get Noslov to my team and figure out what we're going to do."

Selena nodded but said, "Other than you and Juju, the only other person who knew Noslov was here is Balderama. I want him."

"So do I."

Selena yanked Noslov up by his arm and said, "Let's get you cleaned up. Then we're out of here."

Even though it was the middle of the night, Selena called the convent. The sleepy sister who answered the phone assured her all was quiet. Selena insisted she check on Marisol. The minutes dragged by like hours while the nun checked on her.

"She is fast asleep," she reported to Selena at last.

"Thank you," Selena breathed, her voice cracking with emotion. With a relief she could not express, she hung up.

Nikko hugged her and said, "We'll get through this, Selena. I promise." She swallowed hard, wanting to believe him.

Using the same landline, since their cell phones had been destroyed in the water, Nikki called his team with the news that Noslov did in fact know the location of the cask.

A half hour later, Selena, Nikko, Noslov, and the sheet-wrapped body of the stranger, who had no ID and whom Noslov swore he didn't recognize, motored back to Miami. As they approached the dock, two blacked-out Suburbans were idling at the end of the pier. "My team," Nikko said.

The body was loaded into the back of one of the

Suburbans. Nikko, Selena, and Noslov piled into the other one. The woman, Cassidy, was behind the wheel, and one of the men from Paris in the passenger seat. Nikko didn't make a formal introduction and Selena didn't ask for one. She got that they needed to maintain anonymity, especially in front of Noslov. The man turned and handed Nikko a blindfold. "For our Russian friend."

Once the blindfold was secured, they drove off. Twenty minutes later, they pulled into a driveway and then into a cavernous garage. The doors came down behind them. Noslov was unloaded and taken inside. Selena didn't give the sprawling hacienda much notice. She wanted to get down to business. As they walked into a small viewing room, a large flat screen flashed blue.

"I need to make a call," Selena said to Nikko.

He looked at her like *Who the hell do you have to call at this hour?*

"Joran."

He scowled. "Excuse us for a minute," he said, steering her from the room and into the great room. He handed her a landline.

Selena dialed the number. On the fifth ring, Joran answered, "Cadiz."

"It's me. Do you have the package?"

"Barely, and you owe me big-time."

Selena gave Nikko the thumbs-up, but he'd heard and was nodding. She let out a long, relieved breath. If anything had happened to that little boy, she would never have forgiven herself. "Hold on to it until I call you back."

"I don't know what to do with a crying two-year-old!"

"Entertain him. And, Joran? Thank you." She hung up

to his loud grousing. "We've got our leverage," she said to Nikko.

Noslov was left in the media room while Nikko's people assembled in the great room. Introductions were quickly made. Selena smiled at Satriano as she shook his hand.

"How's the shoulder?"

His dark eyes narrowed but his lips twitched. "No worse for the wear."

"I'm sorry about that."

He shrugged it off. "It happens."

The flat screen in the room blipped on. They all turned to face it.

Once again, the screen was blue, but this time Mr. Black's voice was not computer-regenerated. It was deep, authoritative, and knowledgeable. "De la Roja, I understand Cruz has brought you up to speed on Balderama?"

"Yes, sir." She noted Mr. Black no longer used formalities but spoke to her as if she were one of the team. She liked that.

"Bring us up to speed on your end."

"Noslov has been in my care since Paris. On the flight to the States, he convinced me he was only the agent for the cask and did not have actual knowledge of its location. Since I was holding his son's welfare over his head, via Balderama's instructions, I believed him. As you know, he was lying, but having the boy, I had leverage to manipulate the auction to Los Cuatro's benefit. I convinced him that it would be in his son's best interests to give the nod to Balderama at the auction, regardless of his bid. I also convinced him it would be in his best interest to have the auction at Lost Souls. I guaranteed the safety of the bidders through the use of my private island, Ilusion, as the entry point into Miami."

"How many have purchased a seat?" Mr. Black asked.

"Six including Nikko."

"And the boy?"

"A business associate owed me a favor and picked him up earlier this evening." Selena paused, then added, "From Balderama's Little Havana residence."

"Does Balderama know the boy is no longer his bargaining chip, and if so, does he know you had a hand in the kidnapping?"

"I don't know the answer to the first question, but even if it's yes, he would have no reason to suspect I had a hand in it. However, after I had a discussion with him earlier this evening regarding our conversation yesterday, I believe he has lost some confidence in me."

"I take it he didn't want to make the compromise."

"No. He was adamant. I understand his trust issues. But he would not even entertain the thought of vetting Nikko."

"You understand now why he was so rigid?"

"Yes," she said, feeling greatly saddened and more than a little foolish that the man she'd believed to be a great philanthropist and friend was nothing more than a thug. And she had been his handmaiden.

"With a few tweaks, I want the auction to commence as planned. To accomplish that, we'll need you to keep up the pretense of loyal compadre and play along with Balderama. We have much to gain by allowing the players to assemble later tonight. In one fell swoop we can nab a handful of the highest-ranking terrorists in the world."

"That will mean the end to my club."

"A small price to pay when you consider the cache of criminals we'll be taking off the world market."

Selena looked at Nikko, who regarded her quietly. It didn't matter anyway. Because after the auction, she was going after Paymon. If she survived that, she would not need the club. She'd have Marisol and Nikko.

"Okay."

"I understand you could use our help in a little matter concerning your father? We're happy to lend a hand."

Selena's head snapped back and she looked at Nikko, who nodded. The others in the room nodded in agreement. Other than Nikko, these people didn't know her from Adam, and they were willing to put their lives on the line for her? She didn't know what to think. How to take it. All she felt was humbled.

"Cruz didn't tell you we would be available in whatever capacity you require after the auction?"

Selena looked at Nikko.

Nikko's cheeks reddened. He cleared his throat. "I, uh, we were busy and I didn't get a chance."

Cassidy snorted. "I bet you were busy."

Selena grinned, enjoying Nikko's discomfort. Little by little, she was glimpsing the man she'd fallen in love with in the amazing man he'd become. "I would accept any help you could spare."

"Let's get Noslov in here, and once we can confirm the location of the cask, we'll discuss the details of the auction."

A few minutes later, Nikko brought the Russian in and sat him down. The blindfold remained. "Comrade Noslov, my name is Mr. Black. I work for the United

States government. It is my understanding you have knowledge of the location of a hijacked cask of reprocessed enriched uranium. Is that true?"

"Yes."

"I would like you to give me the location. Specifically, the coordinates."

Noslov's body tensed. "The cask is on an abandoned barge in the Aral Sea. For the exact coordinates, I want my son, alive, in my arms, tonight."

"If I give you what you ask for, I have another request of you."

"Request or demand?" the Russian sneered.

"Perhaps a little of both."

"Vlad, Yuri is safe. I just spoke to the man, a friend of mine, who has him," Selena reassured him.

"I want him here!" Noslov shouted, emotion straining his voice. He was about to crack. They needed him focused.

Selena looked at the blue screen, then touched Noslov's knee. He flinched. "We want the man who kidnapped little Yuri. The man who would have cut him up and delivered him piece by piece to your wife. We need your help to get him."

"The same man you work for?" Noslov accused. "Why should I trust you now?"

Selena exhaled. Why indeed. "I believed I was part of a righteous cause, comrade. I know now the man I trusted and followed blindly used me for his own personal agenda, not that of the greater good. With your help, we can put him out of business. Permanently."

"What do you want?"

"We want the auction to go ahead as planned tonight," Mr. Black said.

"Why?" Noslov said, shaking his head, wanting none of it.

"Because Balderama has reserved a seat at the auction. We want him and every other terrorist who sits down at that table."

The Russian paled, perspiration beading on his forehead. "If I refuse?"

"Then I would have to insist," Mr. Black said.

Noslov deflated in the chair.

"I will guarantee the safety of your family, comrade," Mr. Black said. "A new life anywhere in the world you choose."

Noslov nodded, then straightened. He faced the blue screen. "I will do it. But only if I hold my son in my arms first."

Selena smiled. "I can have him here within the hour."

"Then arrange it, but not here," Mr. Black said.

Nikko led Noslov back to the media room. When Nikko returned, they got down to business.

It was simple. The auction would go down as it had originally been planned. Upon arrival, each bidder would be led into the same specially rigged conference room. A room that once they entered they could not exit. They would be given instructions. As they made their bids and the monies transferred into a US government account, Nikko's team would move in and, bada-bing-bada-boom, the terrorists would be taken into custody.

"De la Roja, you need to touch base with Balderama and let him know you're still with him on this. Don't say you're having second thoughts about Cruz. Perhaps apologize for even suggesting Los Cuatro deviate from the plan. We cannot have him back out of this now. He's too dangerous to let slip through our fingers."

"I don't have any reason to contact him," Selena stated. "If I call to reassure him, he'll know something's up. I think we should allow him to proceed as he would normally. My only concern is the kidnapping of Yuri. He may suspect I had something to do with it."

"You're going to have to convince him you didn't."

Selena nodded. It wasn't as if she had much of a choice.

"There's a Hilton a few miles from here. There's a keycard to room 3071 in the middle desk drawer in the next room. Take Noslov there to meet his son," Mr. Black instructed. "When you return, get some sleep. You're going to need it. We'll reconvene at twelve hundred hours."

Selena made the call to Joran. He was not amused.

The sun would be up in a few hours. They didn't have much time.

Less than an hour later, Selena stood silently by while father and son reunited. Joran was not in attendance, which royally pissed her off. Instead he had sent his bulldog, Ramos. Selena made the decision to take Yuri back to the hacienda. He would be safe there and could spend more time with his father. Nikko agreed.

It was heartbreaking to watch Yuri cling to his father and Noslov assure him he was safe. No one understood better than Selena the heartache a parent felt at such a moment. She looked up at Nikko, who watched her watch father and son. He reached for her hand and squeezed it. He brought it to his lips and kissed her. "We'll be with Marisol soon," he softly said.

On their way back to the house, Noslov, still blind-folded, held little Yuri curled in his lap and gave them the coordinates. Nikko called them in to Mr. Black, along with the news they were bringing the boy back with them.

Hours later, once everyone was settled, Nikko led Selena to the bedroom and bathroom assigned to him. He had not slept one night in the big bed, but was looking forward to sharing it with Selena. He turned on the shower-heads in the shower and pulled her in, clothes and all. He did not undress her. Instead, he wrapped his arms around her and just held her. He knew she was hurting over losing her friend. He knew she missed Marisol, and he knew she was emotionally exhausted. He felt the same way. Part of him could not wait for the next few days to come and go, but a part of him feared one or both of them would not survive Paymon. Even with the stones, and he and Selena working together, Vetis had proven formidable. Paymon would be a completely different animal.

Nikko smoothed back the hair plastered to her face and forehead and smiled down at her. His heart swelled with love. She was fearless, fierce, loving, and—his hands slid down the small of her back to the top swell of her righteous ass—sexy as hell.

His body tightened. He wanted to make love to her, but he did not want to push. He grinned as he felt the devil between his legs rear against her belly. That part of him had no sensitivity to her fragile emotions.

Droplets of water dotted her long lashes like tiny, sparkling diamonds. A mischievous smile twitched along her full, pouty lips. She pressed closer into him and ran her hands down his back to his ass. "We're over-dressed," she said, lifting up on her toes to kiss him.

"Selena," he said against her lips. "You don't have to."

Her eyes flashed. Pushing him back against the tile, she pulled her clothes from her body. Nikko's cock lengthened. He would never get his fill of her magnificent body. Her skin was alabaster smooth with just a hint of cinnamon for spice. Long, lean, and curvy in all the right places, she could be the Playmate of the Month or Time's Woman of the Year.

He pulled his torn shirt off, then peeled his soaked trousers off, kicking them to the side. The best part about Selena's body was, it was all his. He'd kill any man or woman who tried to take it from him.

Three feet separated them. Neither one moved; they just stared at each other in anticipation. Nikko was literally salivating. He reached out to her. She reached out to him. Their fingers entwined. Slowly, Nikko pulled her into his arms. His lips lowered to hers. In a slow, sanguine kiss, he took her lips captive.

CHAPTER TWENTY-SIX

The stones around Selena's neck flared against Nikko's chest. He reached up and traced his fingers across them. Pulling his lips from hers, he asked, "What do they want?"

She wrapped her hand around his so that his hand held them. They pulsed with warmth. He looked at her in wonder. She smiled. "They are eager for a fight."

He felt the powerful thud of her heart against his palm. Her skin there flared with the same heat as the stones. "Is your heart like these?"

"In a sense, yes. While not a true nanorian, our hearts heat with the power of a Prince of Hell. Singularly, Paymon's heart has the power to control any nanorian, but not the combined power of all of them. One day, Marisol will understand the power she holds."

"I won't stand a chance," Nikko teased.

Selena grinned a flirty grin. His heart melted. "As if you ever had a chance."

He shook his head and pushed her up against the tile. "You had me at hello, baby."

Selena's eyes darkened. She reached up behind her neck and unclasped the necklace.

"What are you doing?" he said, afraid she would be vulnerable to attack.

"So long as I possess the necklace, their power is mine to command." She pulled him closer and wrapped it around his neck, then hers, and fastened it. It flared. "Now, shut up and make love to me."

His blood blazed with such intensity it burned. His cock stiffened to the consistency of steel. He pushed her legs apart and, with no preamble, filled her to his root. Selena closed her eyes, pressing her head back against the wall, bringing him with her. "I love that," she moaned.

Nikko swelled more, if that was possible. Lightning bolts of desire shot through him. "God, Selena," he hoarsely groaned, his rod throbbing inside her. Her liquid muscles clamped around him. He could feel every part of her. Slick, tight, demanding. Pulling him deeper. The intensity of the feelings nearly brought him to his knees. He pushed higher into her and she responded by arching into him. He pulled back, her muscles reluctant to release him. The erotic drag inside her pushed him to the edge. He thrust back into her. Every part of him sparked with fire, every cell of him pulsed, raw, aching. He thrust again. And again. The wild sensual whirlwind of bonding with his woman, the mother of his child, the woman he loved so intensely, caused a mist of heat to sting his eyes.

She hung on to him, meeting his fervor with equal fervor. He came in a high, searing explosion of lightning strikes. Her body imprinted every inch of him. Her cries of passion stormed through him, pushing him higher, so high he became dizzy with sensation. Her body voraciously accepted his heavy burst of seed, milking him for more.

Still inside her, Nikko carried her to the bed and laid her down on it. He wanted more. Could never get enough. He ground into her. Selena writhed beneath him, her nails digging into his back, her rushed cries for more fueling his insatiable need. He came again.

Their bodies slick with sweat, their hearts pounded against each other's while the stones flared red-hot, searing into their skins.

Nikko collapsed on top of her, his chest heaving so furiously he could not breathe. Selena roused herself to unclasp the necklace so that he could move. He did not go far. He rolled onto his back and pulled her into his arms.

His head spun. His nerve endings pulsed. His limbs felt as if they were filled with lead. Sliding her fingers into his hair, Selena slid against his slick body and kissed him. Her lips were tender, loving, grateful. She pulled back and smiled at him. He brushed the waves of damp hair from her face and his heart stumbled. Her dark eyes radiated love, and his eyes stung with tears for a second time. "What did I do to deserve you?" he whispered.

"Hmm, just luck, I guess." She kissed him again. "I love you, Nikko Cruz."

"I love you, Selena de la Roja."

Selena awoke to soft kisses traveling down her back. She smiled and moaned.

"Good morning, sunshine," Nikko said against her right butt cheek.

A sharp knock on the door jerked them both out of their lazy haze. "You two need to get out here," Cassidy urgently said.

Two minutes later, Selena and Nikko emerged dressed and hurried toward the great room.

"A Joran is on the phone for you," Cassidy said, looking at Selena, hitting the speaker button.

Nervous tension skittered along Selena's back. It was day-light. Joran calling now could bring nothing but bad news.

"What's wrong, Joran?" she asked, looking at Nikko and the assembled team.

"Paymon asked me to give you a message." Joran's voice sounded forced.

Selena gasped and looked at Nikko, who had paled a few shades.

"He came to you?"

There was a long pause. "He wants the necklace. He said if it is not delivered to the convent on St. Michael's by this time tomorrow, he will take your sunshine away."

Nikko caught Selena in his arms as she crumpled to the floor.

"Selena?" Joran said, his voice unsteady. "He told me he will take her apart inch by inch if you so much as think about defying him."

"I—did he say anything else?"

"No, but—fuck it all to Hell. He—he's going to kill me if I—"

"What?" Selena cried. *Tell me.*"

"He's possessed Balderama. Get that piece of shit and you'll get Pay—"

The line went dead. "Joran!" she screamed, coming to her feet. "Joran!" Silence. Selena looked up at Nikko and the team in shock. "I think Paymon just killed Joran!"

"We'll do a reverse on the number," Cassidy said, "and get a location on him. I'm calling Marcus."

Nikko took Selena's shaking body into his arms. "Listen to me, Selena. For now, Marisol is safe. The nun confirmed it."

Selena shook her head. "We have to go to her now!"

He took her face into his hands and forced her to look at him. "Listen to me! He hasn't done anything yet. And he won't, not if we get him first."

"But he's—" Selena shot to her feet. "Paymon has possessed Balderama to get the cask! He'll be at the auction tonight!"

"And we'll get them both."

"You're damn right we will!" She grabbed the phone. "I need to call Father Ken and make sure Marisol is all right."

Father Ken answered the phone on the first ring, his voice strained.

"Father, it's Selena."

"I was told to expect your call," the affable priest said flatly.

Her heart stopped. It was all she could do to ask the next question. Who'd told him? Paymon. "Tell me, is Marisol safe?"

"She is unharmed."

"Is there someone there?"

"Not at the moment."

Selena grabbed Nikko's hand and squeezed so hard she thought she would break his fingers. "Listen to me. Keep her in the sanctuary, on the altar. Douse her with holy water and pray like you have never prayed before. And, Father? Do not let her out of your sight for one minute. I'm going to make everything right. Okay?"

"I will do all that I can."

"Keep Marisol safe!"

The line disconnected.

Selena inhaled deeply, then looked at the assembled team. "When I'm done with Daddy dearest, he's going to wish he never had a daughter."

CHAPTER TWENTY-SEVEN

The stage was set.

Selena stood at the third-floor railing looking down onto the empty dance floor. Lost Souls was shut down to host the event of all events: the final showdown between the Prince of Hell and his daughter.

Low lights glowed behind the bar and along the perimeter of the dance floor, giving the illusion of anonymity to those who entered. The tables stood empty, the chairs stacked on top, the low leather ottomans pushed against the wall. The place looked lost. Vacant. A shell of a once vibrant life. A dead host. And so it would remain. She would not open the doors again. Not as Lost Souls. When she walked out of this club later tonight, this chapter of her life would be closed. Forever.

The stones around her throat vibrated powerfully. She smiled and fingered the empty setting she had fashioned just an hour earlier. It was larger than the others, a worthy seat for the crown jewel of all nanorians. Paymon's black heart.

Selena glided down the winding stairway, her hand sliding lightly along the metal railing down to the ground floor. Power and confidence infused her. Tonight she was untouchable.

The place was wired for sound and video. Outside, a three-block radius was crawling with undercover operatives. All of Nikko's team were wired with ear-pieces, as was Selena. In a room somewhere close by, Mr. Black was dialed in via video and audio feeds.

Not only was Paymon going down tonight, but so were the five unfortunate bidders who were no doubt salivating in anticipation. Enriched uranium, the king of mass destruction, was within reach—for a price.

Selena smiled and nodded to Nikko's team, lined up in front of the bar. Cassidy looked hot in the black-and-red Lost Souls cocktail uniform. Satch, Stone, and the vampire Cross, who'd showed at the last minute, looked every bit her security detail. Her gaze drifted past them to the double brass doors and the man dressed in a slick black-on-black suit who stood sentry at the entrance. Nikko. Her heart fluttered and her belly softly tumbled. It was game on, winner take all.

I love you.

He turned his cobalt-blue eyes on her and smiled. *I love you.*

Selena inhaled deeply and nodded.

The first limousine would arrive shortly. Then in twenty-minute intervals, the others would arrive, with Balderama coming in last. He had insisted on it. It served her purposes beautifully. As each bidder arrived, he would be escorted to a specially equipped confer-ence room on the second floor, where Noslov would entertain them until they were all assembled, and then? At exactly midnight, the action would appear to com-mence, and, *poof,* their lives would forever be changed. Good riddance!

Selena smiled inwardly. All except Señor. For him she had a very special surprise in her kill room.

"Team?" Mr. Black's voice reverberated through the small device in her ear.

A collective "I copy" followed.

"De la Roja, do you copy?" Mr. Black asked.

"Yes," she softly said, realizing that despite her confidence, she was nervous.

"Limo one is approaching," Mr. Black announced. "The occupant has been photo ID'd as Amir bin Asheed. Founder of the small but terrible and very organized Egyptian Militia. They were responsible for the bombing last month in Cairo after their candidate lost the election for president. They vow to continue to bomb Egypt until sharia law is established. I suspect they hope to achieve that by detonating a dirty bomb."

Selena inhaled and ran her hands down her skirt, then slowly exhaled. She was literally dressed to kill. Her outfit was created precisely for this type of event. To the unsuspecting eye, she looked like a cross between a dominatrix and a genie. She wore thigh-high leather boots beneath a long, hip-hugging carwash skirt made of diaphanous black material, clasped to her by a wide, supple, studded-leather belt that doubled as sheaths for two short daggers that lay horizontally across her belly, easily accessible. The bikini-style top was of the same diaphanous material but provocatively twisted with the same black studded leather as her belt. Her midriff was bare except for the twinkle of a bloodred ruby belly-button stud. She wore assorted razor-sharp, metal-bangle bracelets on each arm halfway up to her elbows. They were easily released and launchable to slice and dice. Her hair was pulled back into a high knot atop her head, then fell freely down her back. Proudly, arrogantly, deliberately, she showed the necklace off to its every advantage. After Nikko and Marisol, it was her most precious possession. One she would defend with her life.

She fingered the extra setting again, anxious to fill it.

Preceded and followed in by a security detail, the Egyptian entered with little fanfare. Selena strode toward the front door as Nikko ushered him inside. She smiled graciously at the nondescript man and greeted him in his language. He looked surprised, but quickly collected himself.

"I'm afraid, sir, your detail must remain outside," Selena firmly said, looking directly at Asheed.

He motioned away the four sphinx-size goons surrounding him. Nikko showed them the door.

"Follow me, please." She led the Egyptian to the elevator, and once the doors closed behind them, she said, "Mr. Noslov will be your host as we await the others." The doors opened and she escorted him to a doorway at the end of the hall. She opened it to a pacing Noslov, who immediately morphed into cool, calm, and collected.

"Velcome," he said, extending his hand. The Egyptian cautiously entered the room, eyeing every corner. With the black slate conference table, the six black leather seats, a laptop sitting before each one, and the loaded beverage cart, the room was simple and nonthreatening.

Just as Selena had the Egyptian settled, Mr. Black piped up in her earpiece, "Our next guest has arrived."

As Selena hurried down to the entrance, Mr. Black filled them in. "From what we have managed to gather, this chap is Mohammad Abdul Rahim, founder of the Al Rahim Trust, or ART. Since UBL's demise, Rahim's

organization has swelled with former al-Qaeda members. He's based in Karachi, but this Pakistani rebel has
his sights on Kashmir. His plan? To create then rule a
self-sustaining terrorist country. He's well funded by
way of heroin. He is the largest peddler of the drug in
Pakistan."

Selena was met with a derogatory once-over by the lone
Pakistani. He was dressed in a formal *shalwar kameez*. His
choice of clothing surprised her. She would have thought
he would not want to bring attention to himself and would
have, like the Egyptian, donned Western clothing. She
smiled graciously at the arrogant prick. He would not be so
high-and-mighty when the clock struck twelve.

As Selena showed him into the conference room, he
abruptly stopped at the threshold and chipped off some-
thing to Noslov in Urdu. Noslov smirked and looked at
Selena, then shot back in the same language, to which
Rahim responded by flinging his hand dismissively at
Selena, then sitting down with his back to her.

"Rahim just told Noslov he was insulted by your
attire," Mr. Black chuckled. "Noslov told him to suck
a goat dick, to which Rahim said he wouldn't touch
Noslov's mother if she were the last goat on earth."

Selena backed out of the room and shut the door. "He
can go back to his own damn country if he doesn't like
the way Western women dress."

"Hurry up, de la Roja, the next limo just pulled up,"
Mr. Black said.

"That was a short twenty minutes!"

"We just hit the jackpot," Mr. Black said, the excitement in his voice palpable. "Our next guest is none
other than Abdul ali Rashid. Cousin and confidant of

Muhammad Atef, the brains behind al-Qaeda. I'm going to guess al-Qaeda is in the market for enriched uranium for a little payback. Once he's inside, do not allow him to leave."

Selena greeted the terrorist as she had those who preceded him and led him into the conference room. Rahim stood and started in on Rashid. Selena closed the door on Noslov's elevated voice trying to placate them.

Next up was a Somali general, followed by an ousted Malaysian prince.

Once all the men were comfortably seated around the wide conference table, Selena shut the door to the room and turned to face them.

"Gentlemen," Selena began, "if I may have your attention, I have a few ground rules to go over before I turn the auction over to Mr. Noslov. If any of you need to use the facilities, please do so now. Once we begin, there will be no coming or going until all bids are locked in and verified." She looked around the room; no one moved. "I'll take it then that you are all ready to proceed." She looked at Noslov, who stood quietly but alert in the corner. "You may open your laptops and boot them up. A number will appear in the upper-right-hand portion of your screen. Enter that number seven times in succession with no spaces. The next screen will instruct you how to verify your account. Once that is done, a blank box will pop up. That is the box, when you are told to do so, in which you will enter your bid, calculated in US dollars. Whole numbers only. No dollar signs, no commas, and no decimal for cents. You will have only one chance to submit it, so make sure before you do, it is your final offer."

She looked at Noslov and nodded, then nodded at the group of men. "Mr. Noslov will take it from here. Good luck, gentlemen."

Selena exited the room and shut the door firmly behind her. She smiled at Cassidy and Stone, who were waiting in the hallway. "They're all yours."

"Balderama's limo just pulled up," Mr. Black said. "We'll wait until you have secured him before we move in on the conference room."

"Copy," Selena said. The last thing they wanted was to call attention to the sting and have Balderama take off. No way was Daddy getting out of Lost Souls alive.

As she hurried down to greet Señor, Selena's nerves began to unravel. *Not now!* If ever she needed to remain composed and focused, it was now. She was a seasoned warrior, an assassin! She had enough power and backup to stage a successful coup. She needed to calm down. As she did when she needed strength, her fingers caressed the warm stones around her neck. They flared in understanding. And just like that, her heartbeat slowed to a regular rhythm.

Manufacturing a welcoming smile, she made her way to Los Cuatro's figurehead as Nikko ushered him into the quiet club.

"Señor," she warmly said, taking his hand. The faint stench of sulfur swirled around him. "I am so glad to see you made it safely." He eyed her coldly. She pretended not to notice. She dropped her voice and said, "I'm very nervous. We are so close to our goal, but—" She pulled him along out of earshot of Nikko and away from the door. "Noslov has been acting strange."

Señor's brows rose high into his forehead. "Strange, how?"

Selena lowered her voice conspiratorially. "Like he has something up his sleeve. I can't put my finger on it. But I've had him under my thumb since I spoke with you yesterday."

"Why did you not alert me?"

Selena squeezed his hand and released it. "After our discussion yesterday, I didn't want to cause you more worry."

"Speaking of our discussion, have you had second thoughts?"

"Regarding Mr. Cruz and his handler?"

He nodded.

Selena chose her next words carefully. "No, but I should have recognized it was not my call to make. *You* have the vision of the bigger picture. I only have snapshots. My apologies for questioning you." She inclined her head in contrition, though it grated on her every nerve to do so. While she knew Paymon lurked behind Balderama's odd-colored eyes, she doubted he had full possession of the man. A human host as strong-willed and downright evil as most daemons, such as Balderama, would be difficult to completely possess.

So Selena played on her relationship with Balderama, hoping to reach him and his mind and perhaps restore some trust. Then. Strike.

Balderama took her hand into his and smiled. "I have something for you, Selena. A small token to show my appreciation for all you have done for our cause and all you will continue to do."

Her heart leapt in her chest. "That is not necessary, Señor. My reward is in the final result."

A malevolent smile twisted his lips. He opened her hand palm up and placed something in it. "Indeed. To final results."

Selena looked down at a bloodstained signet ring. Her stomach roiled in recognition. Heat stung her eyes. Dear God, it was Joran's ring.

CHAPTER TWENTY-EIGHT

For all that was dear to her, Selena maintained her composure. She cocked her head, forced a small smile, and looked questioningly at Balderama. "A new ring?"

His malicious smile broadened. "As you know, not just *any* ring."

She held it up in the dim lighting. Dried blood distorted the design and engraving, but she knew without a doubt it was Joran's. She had never seen him without it. Guilt riddled her composure. He was dead because of her.

"It's beautiful. It should clean up nicely." She lowered the ring and slipped it on her right thumb. "Thank you." She had never been this close to her father, never wanted to destroy him more. It took every ounce of self-control Selena possessed to appear calm, indifferent, and focused. She wanted to sink her daggers into his chest and cut his black heart out. She wanted him to pay for her mother's death, for what he'd forced Selena to do, how he forced her live. But Selena remained outwardly calm. Their showdown was inevitable; it would be here, tonight, and she would triumph.

Frustrated rage flashed across Balderama's face. Quickly he concealed it. "I'm glad you like it. I have something else for you, but you will have to wait until after the auction for that surprise." He extended his arm. "Shall we?"

Selena summoned a smile. He was the one in for the bigger surprise. Forcing herself, she took his arm and walked to the back elevator. Instead of selecting the button for the second floor, where she had taken all of the others, Selena hit the third-floor button. As the elevator doors opened to her kill room, she turned to Balderama and asked, "You are familiar with this room?"

His eyes sparkled with excitement. "Intimately."

Selena stepped onto the smooth gray marble. In her mind, she could see Balderama's blood pooling around him after she slit his throat, and her father's vacant daemon body beside him, a gaping hole in his chest where his heart used to be.

"We've got a problem down here," Cross said in her earpiece.

"Go ahead," Mr. Black answered.

"We've just been surrounded by a bunch of daemons."

"You're going to have to handle that, Cross," Nikko said. "I'm on my way up to Selena."

Selena kept her cool.

Balderama's eyes gleamed preternaturally.

He knew. The devil inside him knew.

Selena did not waste a heartbeat. She struck. Grabbing her daggers from their sheaths at her waist, she scissor-slit Balderama's throat from his Adam's apple out. Warm blood spurted in a high arch across the room, splattering her chest and arms. Blood filled Balderama's mouth, stifling his screams. Grasping his filleted neck, he dropped to his knees, his eyes wide in shock. She planted her right foot on his chest and kicked him to the floor. He landed on his back, gasping for air, groping his jugular. "Selena—" he gurgled. "Help, me—"

Selena reached behind her and grabbed her swords from their sheath on the wall. She pointed them at Balderama's heart, digging the tips into skin and muscle. "You lied to me," Selena hissed. "You lied to the cause! I killed innocent people for you! Your death will serve me twice. Once for your terrible crimes." She shoved the swords into his heart. "And twice to draw my dear old dad out!" She shoved the blades deeper until they struck the marble floor beneath him.

His body contorted once before it went still. His eyes glazed, his mouth gaped. His final breath was at hand.

Withdrawing the swords, Selena crouched beside Balderama's dying body and leaned toward his ear. "Come out, Daddy dearest, come out so I can cut your black heart out."

Two daemon hands reached out from Balderama's gaping mouth and grabbed Selena. She blocked her descent into Balderama by crossing her swords, but Paymon was stronger.

"Selena!" Nikko shouted from behind her. He grasped her around the waist and pulled. Selena shoved her swords into Balderama for leverage, then kicked away from him and broke free. As she moved backward, she sliced Paymon's outstretched hands from his arms. A furious roar erupted from Balderama's body. His chest and torso wildly undulated as if his body were snake infested. His eyes bulged out of his head, and a thin orange vapor trail hissed from his mouth and nostrils.

The shuddering stopped, and then, like a scene from the movie *Alien*, Balderama's chest and gut split open. Paymon emerged in all his raging daemon glory.

Nikko clasped her hand, uniting their strengths.

"You defy Hell, you will burn in it!" Paymon roared in his daemon form, which was disturbingly humanlike. Paymon was handsome, glaringly so. Like Michelangelo's *David*, his dark, beautiful features were finely sculpted by an expert hand. Selena remembered the first time she had seen him as a young girl and thought he was an angel sent from heaven. Her mother had schooled her well to avoid him.

Selena raised her swords, then pointed them at his heart. "If I go down in flames, you're going with me!"

Paymon slapped the swords away as easily as if they were gnats. He pointed his bloody stump arms toward his hands on the floor. They lifted and reattached themselves.

Paymon smiled grotesquely at her. "I am impressed by your power and cunning, Daughter. When will you realize your place is beside me in Hell?"

"You raped my mother, then drove her to suicide. You tried to harm my daughter while she was in my womb! You tried to kill the man I loved! How can my place be beside you?"

"I loved your mother!" he roared. He pointed a daemon finger at Balderama's dead body. "*He* pushed her from that window! *He* drove her mad with his lies and deceit!"

No! Señor would never—Selena's face blanched white in shock. Señor—would.

"You are shocked?" Paymon laughed. "You are as blind as your mother was. Your precious Señor used her to get close to me! He wanted to control the power of Hell through her devotion to him! I would never permit that!" Paymon held out his hands to Selena. "Come with me now, Daughter. With the necklace and the cask, our power will be untold."

Selena shook her head. It changed nothing! He was crazy to think she would go with him, under any circumstances!

"Only I can protect you and your daughter from the wrath of the Order! Without me, you will die by their hand!"

Selena shook her head. "You are wrong on both counts, Father." She raised her swords and brought them together as one, pointing at his heart. "After all of the heartache you have caused me and the people I love, how could you think I would ever go with you!"

Paymon's body flared furiously. "You choose the human over eternal life with your father?"

"I made that choice long ago," Selena defiantly said.

"Then you leave me no choice." In a move so fast it was only a blip of a blur, Paymon plucked Nikko from where he stood behind Selena and slammed him against the wall. His body hit with a sickening thud. Twirling her swords out of the way, Selena shoved the air in front of her, and slammed her father against the wall he had just thrown Nikko into. She held him there as she moved toward her beloved. As she approached, she heard the dull thud of Nikko's heartbeat.

Selena looked into her father's furious yellow eyes. "You're not messing with a scared girl anymore." The stones flared powerfully around her neck. She shoved hard, forcing his body into the wall. "Not only do I possess the power of the stones"—she turned her hands clockwise; his body turned with them—"but my own heart beats with the strength of my father and the love of my mother!" She shoved him so hard he pushed three feet into the solid concrete wall.

Paymon roared, his stench unbearable, his power a chaotic swirl of disturbance around her.

"You are so not worthy of my time," Selena said, going for the kill. Swords at the ready, she approached the hole in the wall. She thrust a sword tip into his calf. He kicked her in the chest with his other foot, knocking her to the ground.

She leapt up, but he was all around her, his velocity tearing at her hair, her clothing, her swords. Selena stood her ground, and battled back, her swords a furious flurry of destruction. She hacked his limbs from his body, went for his head.

Limbless and raging, Paymon's torso slammed toward her. She leapt high into the air and, somersaulting as she came down, like a picador to a raging bull, she drove one of her swords through his chest. That *really* pissed him off. He screamed furiously, turned, and, with his long daemon teeth, pulled the sword through his chest. Selena thrust her dagger into his head from behind. The tip of the blade protruded on the other side out of his right eye. Raging, Paymon twisted his limbless body and head-butt her, flinging her off him. She slowed her velocity and like a funnel cloud whirled high into the air. The red-hot glow of the stones filled the anteroom.

Paymon grabbed Nikko with his teeth. Crashing through the door, he flew with him down the stairway and out onto the catwalk circling the second floor. Selena flew after him but abruptly halted in midair.

A grotesque specter floated in the air before her, Nikko's limp body dangling from Paymon's regenerated hand in the middle of the club two stories high. In Paymon's other hand, a fiery sword.

"Your lover for the stones," Paymon taunted, pointing the tip of his devil sword at her neck.

The stones flared white-hot. Though the heart stones had once belonged to Hellkeepers, they recognized Selena as their mistress now. They were in tune with her thoughts, knowing her next move before she did. She launched at the daemon prince. Paymon laughed and flung Nikko across the room.

Selena dove after him. But amazingly, Nikko halted his descent with his own power, halfway down. Their gazes raked each other for damage. *Nikko?*

I'm okay, he said, shaking his head. He looked up at Paymon, who hovered above them. Selena followed his glare.

I'll take him from behind, you go for his chest, Selena said as she shot up into the air behind Paymon. Selena banked away as Paymon twisted around going after her. Anticipating his move, she stopped short, then drove her sword into his back, slicing him wide open.

Paymon screeched hideously, hovering between the first and second floors. His yellow eyes burned molten red now. His teeth had elongated, saliva dripping onto his chest. Selena shuddered to think such a disgusting creature was her father. But father he was, and there was at least one part of him she was grateful for.

"You forget my power, Paymon!" Selena said, perched

atop the large chandelier that hung from the three-story-high ceiling. "My heart may be half-human, but the dae-mon half holds the power of a dark prince!" She dove again and skewered him in the gut. Yellow blood oozed from him.

Selena corkscrewed in the air away from him; Nikko launched up and stabbed him with Selena's dagger. Paymon roared, spewing yellow fluid from his mouth.

Nikko stabbed him again. Paymon flung him away, but Nikko slowed himself before hitting any walls. Her focus on Nikko, Selena moved around Paymon for a better vantage point. Nikko turned and slammed into the daemon, pushing him toward the railing, but Paymon was too quick. He whirled and slammed Selena into the second-floor railing instead. The velocity of the hit loosening the sword from her hand.

The instant she hit, Selena felt it: the harsh burn of the metal spindle through her heart. The stones around her neck flared in protest, infusing her with power. Yet she dared not move, afraid she would sever her damaged heart in half, and with that, she would die. Her world went dark for a moment before it was light again. She dropped her swords.

Nikko. Help me.

Selena!

Paymon's demonic laughter reverberated around her. "The princess warrior is not immortal after all!"

Paymon rose above her, holding Nikko by the neck. Nikko's eyes widened when he saw how she lay still and broken on the metal spindle where Paymon had flung her.

"The necklace, Daughter! Give it to me!" Paymon raged.

Nikko, she gasped spitting up blood. *My heart, it's broken.*

Selena— He reached out to her face.

"The necklace for your lover!" Paymon roared.

"Go back to Hell, you motherfucker!" Nikko shouted, and sank his fangs into Paymon's forearm. The daemon screeched and furiously shook him.

"Come to me, Father," Selena called in a weak voice, "and I will give you the necklace."

"No!" Nikko shouted.

Let him come to me, Nikko.

Subduing Nikko with the fiery sword to his neck, Paymon came to her.

"Closer," Selena enticed, stroking the white-hot stones.

Paymon's red eyes glowed as he approached. When he stopped, Selena swallowed hard. She needed him closer.

"They call for you, Father. They recognize their place is with you, a true prince, not me, a half-breed."

Paymon reached a hand out for the necklace. "Give it to me."

Selena made a show of trying to move her hands, pretending she had no strength left. "My hands are numbing. I cannot unclasp the hook, help me," she hoarsely said.

Holding Nikko out to his side, Paymon lowered himself closer to her. His sulfurous breath rasped fast and furious in the air with his excitement. *Do not forsake me now,* Selena called to the stones. They flared so hot her skin sizzled.

Paymon's eyes flared with flames, mesmerized by the fiery spectacle around her neck. "They are ravenous for their true master!" he cried, reaching out a hand for them.

"Yes," Selena said as she turned her head to the side, exposing her neck. "Come closer and take them."

Paymon leaned down until his face was only inches from hers. Selena's right hand slid beneath her hip; her fingers tightened around the hilt of the second dagger hidden there.

"Father?" Selena gasped. He dragged his blazing eyes from the stones and locked stares with her. "Would you use your power to save me?"

His lips thinned into a nasty smile. "You had your chance, Daughter. But do not despair, little Marisol will reap what you have so thoughtfully sown."

"Where she is, no daemon would dare to go."

"With the necklace, I will be king! I will have the power to go anyplace in heaven or Hell or on earth!" Paymon moved closer and touched the necklace, his fingers curling around the front stones. They sparked in protest. "Release them to me, Daughter, and I give you my word, no harm will come to Marisol."

Selena inhaled a deep breath, the pain of her injury intensifying. "I would release the stones to you, Father—but—"

Selena exhaled, and stabbed the dagger deep into his chest. Paymon cursed, twisting away from her hand. With her other hand, Selena grabbed the closest metal spindle, yanked it free, and plunged it like a stake into his chest on the opposite side.

Paymon screamed the fury of ten thousand daemons. Selena shoved the dagger deeper into his chest. So deep, the knuckles of her fist scraped against his beating heart.

Releasing the dagger hilt, Selena turned her hand and reached for the heart.

The shrieks of a thousand daemons reverberated around them, each one dying as their master's heartbeat slowed. Selena pushed deeper into Paymon's chest, all the way to his heart. Her fingers opened and she grasped it! With the force of a lightning bolt, its power infused her. A loud roar filled her ears. A scream tore from her lips. Her body jerked and convulsed. Molten hot, the energy filled her veins, her organs, her muscles. Every cell, every molecule. Down to her soul, her body exploded with it.

With her free hand, Selena grabbed the metal spindle sticking out of her chest and yanked it. She screamed as it passed through her damaged heart. But in its wake, the power of the black nanorian healed her.

"Selena!" Nikko yelled from beside her, looking up. "We've got a bigger problem than Paymon!"

Selena followed his gaze. The chandelier hanging from the high ceiling had begun to shake and sway, thousands of fine crystals shattering, dropping to the floor like raindrops.

"Daemons! Thousands of them!" Selena pulled her hand from Paymon's chest, and placed his black heart in the platinum setting. When it clicked into place, she squeezed the prongs tightly around it. The necklace lit up like a circle of fire.

A cacophony of screeching swirled outside the building. "What's going on?" Nikko demanded.

Selena stood. With her arms straight out, she pushed him back against the wall.

"Apollyon has come to collect his henchman's body."

"Holy Hell!"

Selena looked over at Nikko's anxious face and smiled. Slowly, she traced a finger along his bottom lip, then leaned in and kissed him. He pulled her hard against his chest. "Selena, God knows I love you. But we kind of have a crisis going on here!"

She threw her head back and laughed. Her heart swelled a thousand times over. She had never loved him more than at that moment. She looked up at him and smiled. "Apollyon is going to wish he'd left well enough alone."

Hot air swirled wildly around them. Led by the heavy chandelier, the ceiling came crashing down. It hit the dance floor below with a thunderous roar. Thousands of daemons poured in through the ragged opening. Selena leapt to the top rung of the railing and flung her arms forward, palms out. The swarm consolidated and smashed into the opposite wall, destroying the railing, rooms, and the wall itself. In a wide arch Selena pushed her hands up, and with the force of the air she disturbed the broken swarm flew out the hole through which they had just descended.

"Show yourself, Apollyon!" she challenged.

"Selena!" Nikko called out. She turned, but he wasn't there.

"Looking for this?" a deep voice roared from behind her.

Slowly, Selena turned and faced the King of Hell himself. She bit off a cry and checked her impulse to reach Nikko. His skewered bloody body hung from the Daemon of Death's burning lance. If Nikko was dead, she could not help him; if he lived, she could only help him by destroying the devil who had him. Either way, Apollyon would pay!

Selena calmed her racing heart to listen for life sounds. Faint though it was, Nikko's heart still beat. It was enough.

Selena raised herself up to eye level with Apollyon. His spiky black hair sparked with fire. His red eyes drilled her with laser intensity, but she was too powerful now to be scorched by them. His thin black lips pulled back, exposing bright white teeth. His pasty skin covered a muscled humanlike body. He was naked save for the swarm of locusts encompassing his legs and groin.

"Paymon tried that trick." Selena looked down at her father's rapidly decaying body. "You can see how well that worked."

Apollyon hurled his javelin with Nikko on it straight at her. Selena caught the sharp tip with one hand, pulled Nikko off with the other, then turned and hurled it back at the King of Daemons, all in the space of half a blink.

Carefully she laid Nikko on the floor. "Let's get this over with, Appy."

Selena lunged, shoving her hands in front of her, wildly disturbing the air. Apollyon shoved back with tidal-wave force, sending her careening backward. Selena caught herself before she hit the wall.

Apollyon flew around her so fast he was just a blur, and she could not get a shot at him. The force of his movement created a funnel cloud in which she was trapped. And coming fast and furious at her, he pummeled her with sulfuric fireballs.

Selena dodged them instinctively, so quickly her eyes blurred. Sulfurous smoke clogged her lungs. Heat seared her chest when a fireball hit her with the impact of a meteor. The necklace flared. Selena shook off the hit and changed tactics. She spun just like Apollyon, but in the opposite direction. In seconds, her velocity matched his. Seconds later, she broke free of his gyroscope hold.

Selena dove toward the dance floor and grabbed her swords where they had fallen. As she launched upward, Apollyon dove down at her. They crashed onto the floor in a furious fiery clash, he with his burning lance, she with her mighty swords.

"You are more worthy than I anticipated, slayer," Apollyon said, moving counterclockwise around her. He lunged.

Selena somersaulted out of the way of his burning lance. "You aren't," she said, and launched a sword at his chest. It struck dead center. The necklace lit up.

Apollyon stood rooted to the floor, staring at her with such a shocked look that she laughed. She grabbed the hilt of her sword before he could get his grubby hands on it. As she extracted it, she ran him through with her other sword.

She pushed it all the way through his chest to the hilt. It brought her face-to-face with him. "You're lame, Appy. It's why all you pricks resort to cheating to win." She pulled slightly back, put her foot on his chest, and, as she had done to Balderama, kicked him backward off her sword.

He didn't go down. Indeed, her attack had only pissed him off more. He spewed a terrible litany of curses.

"You have awoken Hell with your destruction and thievery, slayer! You will pay with your life and the lives of those you have fought so valiantly to protect!" He raised his hands above his head. "Even your power is not enough to stop my plague of locusts! They will descend upon you and every person you love. Inch by inch, they will devour you!"

Apollyon raised his arms higher and called for his plague. The sound of millions of dry wings fighting for airspace filled the room.

Selena! Nikko called to her. *We need to get the hell out of here!*

Can you move?

Yes.

Drop down here. Now!

"You are wrong, King of Daemons! I have the power!" As the last word was spoken, Nikko dropped down behind her.

Watch my back, she said.

His back to hers, Nikko wrapped his right arm backward around her waist, holding her tightly against him. His trust in her fortified her. Any fear she felt, she locked away. She would live happily ever after with Nikko and their daughter. She was hell-bent on it. Selena tilted her head back and raised her hands to the sky. "I dare you to attack!" she challenged the devil.

Noise boomed around her. The wings furiously vibrating above created a vacuum so powerful it lifted Selena and Nikko off the floor. She pushed against it, her building power formidable. Nikko pulled them back to the floor. And then the locusts descended, swirling thickly around them. So close the tips of their brittle wings scraped against their skin, but not close enough to do damage.

Selena pushed back harder. To prove her power

over Apollyon, she would have to disperse the entire plague!

Harder! she demanded of the flaring necklace. The stones swelled. The black one in the middle burned viciously into her neck. She cried out, the pain more intense than any she had ever experienced. "You must obey me, Father! You cannot win!"

The black stone flared again, this time infusing its heat into the two stones on either side of it. Those in turn infused the ones beyond them until all of the stones had swelled to twice their size.

Hands still outstretched, her palms open and forward, Selena took a step forward. "Begone!" she commanded the locusts.

Apollyon's furious screeches penetrated the cacophony of sound. Selena smiled confidently, and took another step forward. "Now! Before I burn your wings from your body!"

The brittle sound rose to the sky and then—was gone. A deep, eerie silence followed in its wake. Cautiously, Selena scanned the destroyed club for Apollyon. His sulfurous scent was gone; his once-burning lance lay smoldering in the rubble.

"We did it!" Selena cried. Turning, she flung her arms around Nikko's neck. "We did it! Paymon is dead! Apollyon beaten! We can go home, Nikko!" His arms wrapped around her waist. He pulled her into his chest and his lips lowered to hers.

"Who then would pay for your misdeeds, slayer?" a deep voice asked from the double brass doors behind them.

Selena's skin frosted as every hair on her body stood straight up.

Rurik, Nikko said.

Selena stepped back from Nikko and lifted her gaze to his. His deep blue eyes screamed his love for her. For their daughter. But past that, she recognized his fear. It matched her own. *I will kill him if he tries to separate us,* Selena said.

"You do not possess the power to slay me, daemon," Rurik said, reading her thought.

Selena bristled and turned toward the vampire king. She caught her breath, speechless. The tall, half-naked king of vampires and all-powerful leader of the Order was an awe-inspiring sight. He strode into the middle of the dance floor as if he walked on air. His long, dark hair waved behind him. Deep, dark eyes flared red. His muscled chest was bare except for a dark tribal tattoo that began on the right side of his chest and twisted up and around his neck. With each stride, long, lean muscles bunched and gathered beneath his low-slung jeans.

You can stop looking now! Nikko said.

I've never seen him before. . . .

You don't have to stare.

Selena smiled at the absurdity of their quips when she stared death in the eye.

"Would you like to find out if I have the power, vampire?" Selena taunted the king.

Rurik gazed at the damage to the club. It was totaled, from the ceiling to the dance floor. When his penetrating gaze returned to Selena, she stiffened. "I don't need to *find* out. I know," he said. His dark eyes flared. "As do you."

He *might* be able to best her, but she'd make him earn it.

"You are aware of our laws, yet you broke them. Repeatedly. What made you think you were above our laws?"

Selena shrugged. "I guess the human part of me thought I'd get away with it."

"That is the trouble with humans—they think too much."

"We might think too much," Nikko said, stepping past Selena, "but it was Selena who learned of Apollyon's plot to overthrow the Order. And it was Selena who waylaid that plot. Apollyon was going to use a cask of enriched uranium to begin polluting humans, with the goal of wiping out humanity—and ultimately, the Order. That has to count for something."

Rurik looked pointedly at Nikko. "What of you? You are human but smell like a vampire. How is that?" His tone was rhetorical.

"You know about the Rev," Selena said. She stepped up beside Nikko. "What do you want in exchange for you walking out the front door and Nikko and I out the back?"

"For starters, who produces the Rev?"

"I don't know." And she said that honestly. She *assumed* Joran did, but she had never witnessed him doing it and he had never admitted to it.

Rurik smiled a deadly smile. "Let us not play a game of semantics, slayer. Answer my question."

"I said, I don't know."

Tell him, Nikko said.

No.

Rurik snapped his fingers. Three dozen black-leather-clad vampires materialized out of thin air and formed a half circle behind him. "We can do this the easy way, or the hard way. Which way matters only to you," Rurik drawled.

Tell him, damn it! Nikko hissed.

"If I gave up the name you ask for, my word would be worthless. If I gave you the name you ask for, I would betray a dear friend, a friend who not only saved my ass a few times"—Selena looked at Nikko and took his hand—"but saved the man I love. I will not repay those gifts by ratting that person out."

"Then prepare for your execution." Rurik stepped back as his henchmen moved past him.

"No!" Nikko said, stepping forward. "You cannot do this! You owe Selena for foiling Apollyon's plan. Because of her, he doesn't have the cask and never will! He is the one you should execute, not her!"

Rurik raised his hand, staying his hit squad. "Apollyon has been dealt with."

Selena's blood chilled for the second time since Rurik's arrival. The vampire king smiled that wicked smile of his again and said, "Are you so arrogant that you thought it was *your* power that drove away the daemon king?"

"It *was* my power!" The necklace flared in agreement.

Rurik nodded. "I will admit you made my job easier." He took a step closer to Selena. "I will also admit I respect your loyalty. But I do not respect your deeds. You are guilty of numerous immortal homicides, and also guilty of countless serum extractions."

He waved the hit squad forward.

In full fang, Nikko pushed Selena behind him. "I will not allow you to destroy her!"

Rurik's eyes blazed red. "Because you are human is

the only reason you are still alive after challenging me. Now, step aside or die with her."

Selena pushed Nikko behind her, shielding him from the angry vampire. "Touch him and I will bring Hell down on every vampire in this world and the next!" Nikko tried to push her behind him, but she was stronger.

Rurik raised his hand, holding off his death squad. "Stay," he said as if commanding a dog. "This one I will see to myself."

"A compromise!" Selena shouted stepping toward Rurik. She swallowed hard and touched the stones around her neck. As they always did, they warmed. They were her talismans. For so long they had meant so much. They were her power, her leverage. If she gave them up, she gave up her power, and without power, she could not protect her family. But if she was dead, it wouldn't matter. They would all die.

Selena knew when to fold. She had hoped it would not come to this, but without Nikko and Marisol, the necklace meant nothing. She unhooked the necklace from around her neck and dangled it in front of the vampire king.

"The necklace, if you walk away and forget you ever saw me or Nikko. The necklace for your word we will be left alone by all immortals."

Rurik looked uninterested, but she heard the acceleration of his vampire heart. "What makes you think I want the necklace or would even consider saving the life of a rogue slayer? Your crimes are not pardonable. Each one alone is punishable by death."

Nikko growled and stepped up beside Selena. "The necklace holds the power of seven Hellkeepers and a damn Prince of Hell! With it, you could keep the devil himself along with every fucking daemon in Hell jailed." Nikko looked at Selena, then back to Rurik. "The necklace for her life, or I swear by all that is unholy, when she gives it to me, I'll make the same deal with the devil!"

"I do not respond to threats," Rurik seethed. His gaze slid to the necklace dangling from Selena's hand.

"Decide now, Rurik! Her life for the necklace. Yes or no!" Nikko raged.

For the first time in a long time, Selena felt powerless. Rurik's death squad would suck her dry in less than a minute. If she fought them, Rurik would do the deed himself. He was too powerful to stop. She would die trying, and Nikko would die trying to protect her.

Marisol needed one of them alive.

Nikko, promise me you will not try to save me. Marisol needs you.

You will not die.

Promise me!

I give you my word we will both be alive and with our daughter before the sun sets tonight.

"You are a fool, Selena," a deep, familiar voice said from behind her.

Selena whirled around, and stared. "Joran!"

The disheveled vampire smiled crookedly at her, and despite the blood-soaked clothes, he didn't look half bad. "I am not worth your life." He looked disdainfully at the king of vampires. "Long time no see, cousin."

"I should have known it was you behind the Rev," Rurik said, shaking his head. "Only you would be so bold to defy me in such a way."

Joran shrugged. "Someone had to shake things up." He looked at Selena, then back to the vampire king. "Take the necklace and let her go."

"You are hardly in a place to give me orders," Rurik said.

"For every immortal life Selena has taken, I have saved three vampires. It is because of her skill set that I was able to save lives. Take the necklace and let her go, Rurik. It is not only in her best interest, but in the best interest of the Order. And if you don't kill me in the next few minutes, I'll explain why."

Selena stepped to Rurik. She took his right hand and pulled his arm up. Her eyes caught and held his simmering red ones. Turning his hand palm up, she pushed open his hand and pressed the necklace into it. "For my life, Nikko's life, my daughter's life, and Joran's life, I freely give you this necklace. It holds the hearts of all seven Hellkeepers and the black stone heart of Paymon, Prince of Hell." She curled his long fingers around her hand and the necklace. "Do you accept?"

Rurik held her gaze for several long moments. Selena's heart slammed against her chest with each beat. His lips quirked as his eyes settled back into their natural color of deep aqua. His fingers tightened around hers. "I accept."

Selena let out a long, ragged breath.

She thought her heart stopped beating; her stomach certainly was doing somersaults and back flips. Her knees shook so hard she could barely stand. Nikko's arms wrapped around her waist. Slowly he turned her around. Tears blurred her vision.

"We're free, Selena, we're free!" he said before he kissed her.

Reverently she returned his kiss. He picked her up and spun her around and around and around until, too dizzy to stand, they fell laughing to the floor.

"Nikko!" she said, kissing his eyes, his nose, his chin, his cheeks. "I love you, I love you, I love you!"

He pulled her up into his arms. His deep blue eyes danced happily. "I'm never going to let you out of my sight."

She wrapped her arms around his neck and smiled. "As if I'd let you!"

They turned around to an empty club. Rurik, Joran, and the death squad had vanished. The front door burst open as Nikko's team poured in.

They stopped as one and looked around at the rubble, then up to the huge hole in the ceiling.

"What the Hell happened here?" Cassidy asked.

"*Hell* is what happened!" Nikko laughed.

Cross came in behind them and looked stoically around. "Rurik was here?"

"He was here, all right. I sent him packing though," Selena said, trying to keep a straight face.

The always serious Cross cocked a brow. "You gave him the necklace?"

"I did."

"What happened to the daemon? And what the hell came through the ceiling?" Satch asked.

Nikko threw his arm around Selena's shoulders and drew her close. "Where the hell were you guys when we needed you?"

Stone shook his head. "Where were *we*? We were damn busy! You're never going to believe what happened once we got those assholes outside."

Nikko looked down at Selena with a knowing look. "Oh, after tonight, I'd believe just about anything."

EPILOGUE

St. Michael's Island, eight months later

The autumn sun hung low over the ocean, casting a warm glow across the silvery Atlantic. The gulls cried above the gentle waves as they ambled ashore. Nikko's hand rested on his wife's swollen belly, while his rosy-cheeked daughter buried his feet in the sand.

"What are you thinking," Selena asked, sliding her hand over his.

Entwining his fingers with hers, Nikko smiled and looked at her radiant face. The sun had nothing to do with her beauty. As she had when she'd carried Marisol, Selena glowed with health carrying his son.

He brought her hand to his lips and kissed it. "I was thinking how lucky I am to have a second chance."

"We're both fortunate for our second chances," she softly said. She leaned into him and brushed her lips across his. His free hand cupped the back of her head, pulling her more intimately against him, deepening the kiss. He would never get enough of her. Since that fateful day almost a year ago when she'd found him dying on that mountainside in Kyrgyzstan, there was not a second that passed when she was not in his thoughts. He could die at one hundred, and would still want one more kiss, one more caress, one more chance to say, "I love you."

They were meant to be. And would always be. There was not a force in heaven, in Hell, or on earth that had the power to tear them apart. Not now. Not tomorrow. Not ever.

"Daddy, look!" Marisol shouted with all the enthusiasm of a nine-year-old. Nikko smiled against Selena's lips and turned to his daughter. Her blue eyes, so much like his, sparkled with excitement. A crab dangled from her hand by one of its back legs.

"Marisol!" Selena gasped, leaning forward. "That's a crab—put it down before it pinches you."

Marisol's little face scrunched up as she realized the potential danger. She shrugged and said, "I'm not afraid of a *crab*." She held it up higher for a better look.

Nikko chuckled. "You are your mother's daughter."

"His mommy is probably worried about him," Selena said. "Why don't you let him go?"

In true nine-year-old fashion, Marisol turned and tossed it toward the ocean, then proceeded to pile more sand on her father's feet.

Nikko sat back in his chair and replaced his hand on Selena's belly, but kept his eyes on his daughter. They were far enough from the waves not to be overly concerned, but his daughter had a mind of her own. She was a constant buzz of activity, and if he took his eyes off her for one minute, she would find something to get into. "I told Cassidy we wanted her and Cross to be godparents to John Marcus," he said.

"And?"

He smiled as Marisol globbed a bucketful of sand on her mother's foot. "She tried to act all badass, like it was no big deal, but she couldn't say yes fast enough."

Selena smiled. "I'm glad." She glanced at him. "When do you leave?"

"Monday, but only for two days, and then no travel for a few months." He rubbed her belly. "I'm not going to miss my son's debut." The baby moved, as if to say, "Damn straight, you won't!" Nikko grinned, pressing his hand more firmly against Selena's belly. The baby moved vigorously again. He kissed her belly and then looked up into his wife's liquid eyes. They filled with tears. She did that a lot lately.

"Happy tears," she told him.

Each minute away from his wife and daughter was torture.

Still an intricate part of L.O.S.T., Nikko had flip-flopped from fieldwork to support. He flew in for briefings once a month but worked primarily from his home office here on the island. He had the best of both worlds.

He would not trade places with anyone, human or not. He was content. Selena was happy, and Marisol was their sunshine.

They were left alone, his family in no danger. His body had finally purged the Rev from his system. He was glad about that. Mostly. While he missed the perks of the stuff, he was more comfortable in his all-human skin.

His fingers caressed Selena's taut belly. He ached for her. He hadn't wanted to press her in her condition. . . . He kissed a trail across the high mound of her belly, stopping at the base of the deep valley between her full breasts.

"Nikko," Selena said, holding his gaze. "I want to go home, take a shower, eat dinner, put Marisol to bed, then get naked with you."

"You're reading my mind." He stood up so fast he knocked his chair over.

"Daddy!" Marisol scolded. "You broke my castle."

"I'll build you another one, sweetheart, a better one. But right now, we need to go home and eat dinner."

He took Selena's hand in his right and his daughter's in his left, and as the sun set on the western side of the island, Nikko walked with the two women in his life he could not live without.

Desire a little something different?

Look for these thrilling series by today's hottest new paranormal writers!

The Naked Werewolf series from Molly Harper

The *Daughters of the Glen* series from Melissa Mayhue